"This book . . . is like a finely grained, well-sea
from the white oak core of American literature in the 20th century. It burns long and clean and gives us an abundance of light and warmth."— ROBERT ELY, *Montgomery Advertiser*

"You'll stay up late turning the pages of this suspenseful and inspiring tale . . . rich in period-piece details. Bone-chilling scenes of cruelty . . . serve as the background for characters who allow their hearts to shine out from the darkness." — SENA JETER NASLUND, author of *Ahab's Wife; or, the Star-Gazer*

"Miller builds the story of a man characterized by his hard work, dignity, pride, and determination. In him we see the struggles of the poor and dispossessed. We behold not only the dreamer, but also the triumph of love." — NATASHA TRETHEWAY, poet and author of *Domestic Work*

". . . reminds us of what we can't lose: the language of our people, the details of our land, the spiritual lust we crave—all of which Miller brings together in this masterful first novel." — VICKI COVINGTON, author of *Gathering Home*

"Solidly grounded in the Southern rural scene . . . a compelling tale which addresses questions of identity and the struggle of good with evil. A story vividly told and, from first to last, rewarding to read." — HELEN NORRIS, author of *The Christmas Wife*

"What a story! Fantastic! It is reminiscent of *Gone with the Wind* . . . It is one of those sagas that will keep the reader reading and when the words of the story are complete, the memories of the very real characters remain on the reader's mind. . . . This is one author whose name will be on the top of readers' lists for a long time! Bravo!" — Southern Scribe

"Charlotte Miller . . . sketches a scene and then returns to it with a fuller brush and yet again with even more descriptive detail until the canvas looks like that of an old master, full and ripe with color, complete to the most minute item, with every nuance of setting and action captured." — PEYTON BOBO, *The West Alabama Gazette*

And when they saw him afar off, even before he came near unto them, they conspired against him to slay him. And they said one to another, Behold, this dreamer cometh. Come now therefore, and let us slay him, and cast him into some pit, and we will say, Some evil beast hath devoured him: and we shall see what will become of his dreams.

*Genesis 37: 18-20 (KJV)*

# BEHOLD, THIS DREAMER

CHARLOTTE MILLER

To Cynthia,
May life be as beautiful as your dream.
Best wishes,
Charlotte Miller

NewSouth Books
MONTGOMERY

NewSouth Books
P.O. Box 1588
Montgomery, AL 36102

This book is a work of fiction. Names, characters, places, and incidents are either products of the author's imagination or are used fictitiously. Any resemblance to actual events or locales or persons, living or dead, is entirely coincidental.



ISBN 1-58838-061-0 (paper)

This book was first published in hardcover in October 2000 by NewSouth Books, with the following classification:

Library of Congress Cataloging-in-Publication Data
Miller, Charlotte, 1959–
Behold, This Dreamer / Charlotte Miller.
p. cm.
ISBN 1-58838-027-0 (cloth)
1. Racially mixed people—Fiction.
2. Distilling, Illicit—Fiction. 3. Cherokee Indians—Fiction.
4. Land tenure—Fiction. 5. Rural Poor—Fiction.
6. Alabama—Fiction. 7. Georgia—Fiction.
I. Title.
PS3563.I+B+
00-061310

Second Softcover Printing
Design by Randall Williams
Printed in the United States of America
by Phoenix Color Corporation

*To Justin*

# Contents

# PART ONE

# I

THERE WAS AS MUCH PRIDE within Janson Sanders as there was in any man in Eason County, though few people saw in him any reason for pride. Pride had no place in patched overalls and calloused hands, in a remade shirt and sunburned skin, or in the mixed blood that showed so clearly in his face and his coloring.

He walked beside his father that gray Saturday morning in late November of 1924, the short, brick-paved downtown section of Main Street in Pine seeming to him choked with traffic and noise such as he was little accustomed to. Black and gawky Model T Fords rattled by, Chevrolets of varying colors, a Packard, an expensive-looking Stutz blatting its horn to get out into traffic—they were all dust covered, red from the Alabama clay, for this was the only paved stretch of road in all of Eason County, other than the short, brick-paved strip of Central Street just in front of the county courthouse in Wylie.

People pushed past Janson and his father on the narrow sidewalk as they made their way from the wagon lot at the far edge of downtown, men in blue serge suits and starched collars, young dandies wearing plus fours and pullover sweaters, Janson meeting the eyes of each who passed with his father's Irish pride and his mother's Cherokee dignity, though his own overalls were faded and patched, and the shirt he wore had once belonged to another man. He knew that many people in the County looked down on him for the Cherokee heritage that showed so clearly in his face and his coloring, in the prominent, high cheekbones and the black, straight hair, but there was no shame in him for the man he was, or the past he was a part of. He was proud, as both his parents were proud, and he had been raised to know there was no man alive any better, or any less, than he—and he met the eyes of each who passed with pride and dignity, and with the independence born of his blood.

His father was talking as they walked along, about the recent town ordinance that restricted horse and mule drawn wagons from Main Street any farther down than the wagon lot at the far edge of downtown, past Abernathy's Feed and Seed and the dry goods store, and about the ugly Model T's and the Chevrolets that crowded the roads enough already without restricting the short strip of downtown for their use alone. Janson listened, though he had heard the same comments many times before, not only from his father, but also from many of the neighboring farmers and churchfolk, and he started to say something in agreement, for he considered motor cars a luxury that he could see little need or use for—but a car horn sounded and drew his attention instead, and he looked toward the traffic to see a girl in a dark cloche hat crossing the narrow street toward them, the girl running slightly to avoid a Packard whose driver honked irritably for the second time as he had to slow for her.

The short skirt of the navy-blue dress she wore covered her knees by only a bare few inches, and, as she stepped up onto the sidewalk out of the way of the motor car, Janson fancied he saw for a moment the top of a rolled stocking, and perhaps even a bit of exposed kneecap below the hem of the skirt—he looked away quickly, and then back again; after all, he was almost seventeen and a half now, and not unwise to the ways of the world, having become a man the year before at the hands of a girl from a neighboring farm, a girl who had known much more than any girl her age ought to have known.

The girl in the cloche hat smiled appreciatively at the look in his eyes as she walked past—as bold as a flapper, he told himself, though he was not really certain how bold a flapper might be, for he had never been close to one in all his life. He found it difficult to even imagine a girl as bold and daring and promiscuous as he had heard city flappers to be, girls drinking liquor and smoking cigarettes, dancing and carrying on. The girl had face paint on, rouge and lipstick and face powder, and her hair was bobbed short beneath the cloche hat, curling in at her cheeks in the style some of the town girls had taken to wearing in the past several years, such girls actually visiting barber shops to have their hair cut just as men did.

He glanced around at her as she walked by, admiring the slender calves encased in silk stockings, the dark seams so straight in back below the short skirt, though he knew she was the sort of girl his mother would say was no lady, for he well knew that ladies did not wear face paint and powder, or bob their hair, or roll their stockings down to their knees.

"Janson, boy—" he heard his father say, a note of reprove in his voice, and he started to turn back to go on about the business that had brought them here into town today, so they could go back home to the land and to the barn roof waiting for repair, to the fall garden that needed hoeing, and the bow basket he had been working on earlier, as well as the scrap cotton still left in the fields waiting to be picked and sold for the money they would have Christmas on this year.

And then he saw the car.

It drove by slowly, the old man staring out through the open side at Janson's father. Janson watched as it slowed even further still, and, after a moment, made a wide U-shaped turn at the far end of Main Street, the other cars there seeming to stop or move out of its way, one driver of a Buick honking his horn loudly before seeming to recognize the car, the driver, and the passenger, then falling silent and inching over to make way for the black, 1915 Cadillac touring car, as did everyone else. They knew that car; everyone in the County knew that car, for, though it was nine years old now, there was not another like it in all of Eason County—and it belonged to Walter Eason.

The car went by, and then pulled over just ahead, in the only empty space among the Model T's and the Buicks and the Chevrolets, blocking the way to a fire plug as it came to a stop and waited there. After a moment, the old man got out and walked up onto the sidewalk to stand waiting for them, his manner as unyielding as the black suit he wore, and the white shirt with its starched and detachable collar.

Walter Eason remained silent as they approached him, his eyes never once seeming to leave the face of the tall man with the graying reddish-brown hair who walked at Janson's side, his own face never changing—just the cold, gray eyes moving at last as they flicked for one moment to Janson, and then back again.

"Mornin', Mr. Eason," Henry Sanders said as they neared him, nodding his head in greeting, but not tipping or removing the battered old hat he wore, as many men would have done in the presence of the powerful old man. Henry Sanders tipped his hat to no man, as his son well knew.

"Good morning, Henry—young man—" The gray eyes moved to Janson again, and Janson nodded. Walter Eason stared at him for a moment longer, and then turned back to his father. "Doing some shopping, Henry? We don't see you and the boy in town too often."

"My wife's birthday's comin' up," Henry Sanders answered, explaining no further, and the old man nodded.

"It's good to see you doing your business in Pine; it's good for all our County people when they do their business here in Eason County," he said, and Janson knew what was coming, as he had known from the moment the car had first begun to slow, and then had come back to stop before them, hearing the words only a moment later; "I hear you sold your cotton out of the County this year, Henry, over in Mason, to Taylors—"

There was a moment's silence, so quickly gone Janson was unsure as to whether it had been or not. "Yes, sir, I reckon' I did." There was no tone of apology in Henry Sanders' voice, and none of subservience—he owed Walter Eason nothing, and they both knew that. It had been his crop, grown on his land, with his own seed, and he had sold it where it had brought him the most dollars, though no other of the County farmers sold out of Eason County, though few ever had.

"County farmers usually sell in Eason County," Walter Eason said. "Most men find it pays to do their business at home." There was no threat to the old man's words, just the clear message—Eason County farmers sell in Eason County. There was no room left for compromise.

"Cotton's bringin' a better price over in Mason, an' they're payin' a premium for long staple—I got a mortgage t' pay on my place; I got t' sell where I can get th' most money."

"Money isn't everything, Henry," Walter Eason said quietly, staring at Janson's father.

For a moment Henry Sanders did not speak. "No sir, it sure ain't," he said at last, his words quiet.

Janson stood watching the two men, but neither spoke for what seemed to him to be a very long time as they stood staring at each other. Then he found Walter Eason's gaze on him again.

"The boy takes after his mother, doesn't he?" Eason remarked after a moment, as if no conversation had gone on between the two men as just had. There was appraisal in the look directed on Janson, a summing up he did not altogether like, and he returned the cold stare without looking away, lifting his chin slightly as he met the old man's eyes.

"Yeah, he looks a lot like his ma—" Henry Sanders's hand came to rest on his son's shoulder, just as it had done so many times in the past, though Janson was fully grown now and as tall almost as any man in the Sanders family. Janson could hear the pride in his father's voice, the affection inherent in the words, and he looked up at this man who had given him life more than seventeen years before, seeing in him the pride and dignity and determination of a man who wore faded overalls and a patched and remade shirt—then he looked back to Walter Eason, and he found the old man's gaze now directed at his father as well, something in the gray eyes Janson could not understand.

But his attention was suddenly drawn away, toward the black Cadillac, and the husky young man who had gotten out from behind the wheel of the vehicle. Buddy Eason, the old man's only grandson, stood now beside the car. He was perhaps a year younger than Janson's seventeen and a half years, but broader of build, with a square jaw set into an angry and defiant line below slicked-back, wavy brown hair. Buddy Eason was a bad sort, with a quick temper that could be both violent and unpredictable by what Janson had heard in the years of growing up in the County, though he himself had been lucky enough to have had few dealings with Buddy Eason in that time.

But Buddy Eason was staring at him now, staring at him with a look that became only angrier as Janson returned the stare, Janson lifting his chin and returning the gaze without once looking away. Buddy shifted with almost restless motion, then again, his hands tightening into fists at his sides, his eyes not leaving Janson's face until he heard his name spoken, and then Henry Sanders's reply.

"You know my grandson, Buddy, don't you?"

"Yeah, how're you doin', son?" Henry Sanders asked, and Buddy Eason's eyes shifted quickly to him, eyes that were suddenly furious, filled with rage it seemed only because he had been spoken to as he had, had been addressed as "son," and not as "Mr. Buddy" or "Mr. Eason" as Janson knew most of the County folk would have addressed him. Then Buddy's dark gray eyes moved back to Janson, and Janson realized suddenly this younger man was waiting now for him to speak, waiting for him to ask after his health, to call him "Mr. Buddy" with the respect Buddy believed himself due as an Eason.

Janson Sanders remained silent and returned his stare.

"I'm sure you'll come to realize before ginning time next year that it's best for a man to do his business at home, Henry," Walter Eason was saying, as if they had never once left the subject. Janson brought his eyes back to the old man, finding no doubt written there on the almost unlined face. "We'll see you at the gin next year," he said, and then started to turn away.

"Next year's a long way off, Mr. Eason," Henry Sanders said, and the old man turned back for a moment to stare at him. There was something in Walter Eason's eyes that seemed to understand what was being told him, something that for the first time seemed to know the sort of man it was who stood there on the sidewalk before him that day. After a moment, he nodded his head, and said quietly:

"We'll see, Henry. We'll see . . ." He turned and started again toward the black touring car, stepping down off the sidewalk without ever once looking back.

HENRY SANDERS was a man who owed his livelihood to no other man. It had been a decision he had made, a choice taken in long years past before memory could even serve him. He had come into life over fifty-six years before there in Eason County on sharecropped land his parents had worked for more years than they could count, only the third generation removed from an Ireland of tenanted farms, famine, and starvation. He could remember no time in his life when he had not wanted land that was his own, a home no one could ever take from him, and a crop he would not lose half of each year for use of mules and plow and sometimes pitiful earth. Together with his wife, Nell, he had seen that dream a reality, had made it so, with work and sweat and doing without. Their son had been the first Sanders ever born to his own earth, the first Sanders ever to come into life not owing the land he lived on to another man. They had seen to that.

But as the early months of 1924 had come, it had seemed they might be close to losing the land they had worked so hard to have. Eason County existed in cotton, as did most of Alabama and much of the South. Cotton had brought them through slave times and civil war, through carpetbaggers and Reconstruction, and to a South that now stood in mills and villages and company towns. Cotton had helped Henry to buy the land—but now in 1924 Henry could no longer look at a field of cotton without feeling worry. The going price per pound of lint had not been good since the year after the armistice to end the World War had been signed in 1918, and even the sharp rise in price in '23 had been little felt by the farmers in Eason County. The Easons, as always, seemed to be paying a few cents less per pound of cotton than were any of the cotton merchants buying in the surrounding counties—but Eason County farmers did not sell out of Eason County. They sold their cotton to Walter Eason, as their fathers had done, and their fathers before them, all the way back to the hard years following the war with the North that had ended almost sixty years before. They owed their allegiance to Walter Eason, as fathers and grandfathers long dead had owed allegiance to Walter's father—few men in the small towns and countryside of Eason County could not credit their livelihoods to Walter Eason, either to the cotton mill, ginning operation, or overall factory; the many sharecropped and tenanted farms he owned; or the businesses he operated from the busy, brick-paved downtown sections of Main Street in Pine, or Central Street up in the County seat of Wylie. And even fewer still could come to doubt his power, or his word. Eason County was his county, and the people his people—few men had dared to go up against Walter Eason in Eason County. It was well known those few had quite often lived to regret their courage.

But Henry Sanders had owed Walter Eason nothing. No man had given him the red land he and his son worked behind mule and plow, the crop they sweated and prayed over. And no one would take it from them now. There was a mortgage to pay on the farm, the credit run at the store, a wife and seventeen-year-old son to see through the winter months ahead. To sell at Eason prices this year would have meant losing the land, losing what he had worked so long to have, losing what he had worked so long to give his son—if Henry Sanders owed anything, he owed his son the pride of walking his own earth; the dream of owning land, and a crop that was all his own; of never being a man worked and owned and sweated into old age by a man such as Walter Eason. And that was a debt Henry Sanders was willing to pay, a debt that had come from generations long past, and dreams that would never die, dreams that were as much a part of his son Janson as life or breath or pride would ever be.

Janson had been reared on those dreams, but, as that cold winter of 1924-25 passed, and the spring months of plowing the red earth and planting the cotton, he knew those dreams were no less in danger than they had been the year before. Cotton prices were falling, and production was up. Many farmers were no longer even getting enough per pound of lint to cover the costs of growing their crops. There would be no more choice this year than there had been the last; the cotton would have to be sold out of the County if they were to hold onto the land.

The fields were lush and green by the time the hot summer weeks of laying by came in 1925, the long, curving rows thick with green cotton plants, leaving little to be done there now but wait. Soon enough the bolls would burst open and the back-breaking work of picking the cotton would begin—until then there were only chores to be done at the house, the garden to tend, the barn to sweep out, or work that could be done for a neighboring farmer at a day's small wage. Janson soon became restless, bored in those days, unaccustomed to having time on his hands with little or no work that had to be done.

He visited with his kin, walked the green fields just as his pa did, and courted several of the girls from church, but there never seemed enough to do in the days to help make the time pass. He cleared land with his Uncle Wayne and his gran'pa, and wove baskets for sale from white oak splits he prepared himself—bow baskets, egg baskets, cotton baskets; and bottomed chairs for hire—but still laying by that year seemed to pass more slowly than had any other he could ever remember. He knew that soon enough the green fields would turn white with cotton, and that the long hours of dragging a pick sack behind him down the never-ending rows would begin—and also would begin the trouble with Walter Eason, for, sometime between now and the time the cotton was sold in the fall, something would have to happen, something aimed toward preventing them from selling the crop out of the County. Something—one farmer's rebellion might bring two, two might bring three, until the system that had been in operation in the County since the hard years following the War Between the States might finally come to an end. And Walter Eason could never allow that.

So far there had been few incidents, things for which there was no explanation, but things behind which Janson could see clear meaning—windows broken out at the front of the house, sending shards of broken glass into the old sofa and braided rugs there; several of his pa's hunting dogs shot through the head and left; a brush fire set near the front of the house. Warnings alone—but the real struggle lay ahead in the fall when the time came again for them to sell out of Eason County. And that was still months away.

On a hot Saturday morning toward the end of laying by that year, Janson started the eight-mile walk toward town, unable to find anything more useful to put his mind or his hands to. It was a warm morning, the hot July sun already baking down on his shoulders through his faded workshirt and the crossed galluses of his overalls as he turned off North Ridge Road and onto the road toward Pine. There would be a long walk ahead of him, and a hot one, but it was a walk he had made many times in the past, and in weather even hotter than the weather of this day. Besides, it was likely someone would stop to offer him a ride before he had gone too far a distance, some passing farmer or one of the churchfolk, for someone almost always did.

There was a little money in his pocket from hired work he had done the day before, and, after several hours debate with himself over the waste, he had decided to treat himself to a phosphate at the soda fountain in the drugstore, and then to some time spent watching girls pass along the street. He would have liked to have gone to the picture show as well, to see the moving picture people he heard so much talk about: Clara Bow, whose photograph he had seen once on the front of a moving picture magazine in the drugstore, Tom Mix, Charlie Chaplin, John Barrymore, Theda Bara; but he knew he would not go. He had been to a movie show only once in his life, on a day he had told his parents he was going elsewhere, only to go to the picture show in town instead. When his mother had found out, his pa had taken him out behind the smokehouse—but Janson had not gotten a whipping that day, or ever again since. His pa had told him he was a man now, and that it was time he learn to choose right from wrong on his own—Janson had never again gone to see a picture show after that, though he still could not see why it was supposed to be wrong, even if the preacher did say it was; any more than he could see why it was supposed to be wrong for a man to curse, if the occasion warranted it; or to drink corn liquor, even if Prohibition had made liquor illegal since five years back; or to dally with a girl who was not a lady, so long as he did not have a wife at home to take care of the things any man needed.

He was thinking on that subject as he walked toward town that morning, of a wife, and of how nice it would be if there were a girl in his bed at night. He was a man now, eighteen years old, with the needs of any man. He knew plenty of nice girls—and a man only married a nice girl—plenty of girls who were pretty, with nice figures and long hair, girls who had been raised to be ladies, who would not let any man see their bare knees until they were married, and then only in the privacy of a bedroom with the door closed behind them, and then maybe only if he was very lucky and all the lamps were blown out. His pa had said ladies did not know much about the sort of things that happened between men and women, and that a man had to be understanding with the girl he married, for ladies were delicate in such matters—there were good girls and there were bad girls, and a man only married a good girl. He was not really supposed to have fun with a bad girl before then, or ever—Janson knew plenty of good girls, and a few bad ones, but he had not found one he could really think of himself being married to.

There was the sound of a motor car coming along the road behind him, headed in the direction of Pine, but Janson paid little attention to it as it drew near. It seemed to have an expensive sound to it, unlike the rattly Model T Fords and the Chevrolets that most people who could afford cars drove, sounding nothing like the sort of car that would stop to give someone like him a ride, someone in patched overalls, and with feet dirty from the walk over the red clay roads—but the car did stop, slowing and then coming to a halt beside him, the door opening after a moment, and a female voice calling out: "Hey, honey, you want a lift or not?" as he continued to walk on.

Janson stopped and turned back, staring with surprise as he saw the car, and then the driver.

Lecia Mae Eason, the oldest of Walter Eason's two granddaughters, sat staring at him from behind the wheel of the black Cadillac touring car, one eyebrow raised in question. She was perhaps at least a few years older than his eighteen years, with a well-known reputation in the County for being "fast," as Janson's mother would have called her—and in that moment she looked to Janson as he thought a "fast" woman would look. Her brown hair was bobbed short in the current style, her face painted with lipstick, powder, and rouge. She was not exactly pretty, with the same square jaw and self-possessed attitude that her brother, Buddy Eason, often wore, but she was pleasant enough to look at, and she seemed almost to have an air of sexuality about her that

Janson fancied he could sense even over the distance.

Her eyes seemed to move over him for a moment through the windshield of the Cadillac, her eyebrow raising again, this time in irritation. "Well?"

"Ma'am," he asked, unsure.

"You want a lift or not?" she asked, her voice rising with impatience.

He never knew later why it was he said yes—or perhaps he did, finding himself seated beside her in the touring car as it headed on toward Pine. He looked around the interior of the Cadillac with curiosity, never once in his life having thought to be inside such a fancy machine—then the girl took his attention away, or the woman, he told himself, for she looked perhaps even a few years older now that he was sitting beside her. She kept glancing at him, and he tried not to stare at her too openly, for her knees were actually visible below the edge of her skirt, her silk stockings rolled right down to them, and, even as he tried not to stare, he knew she noticed, and that she did not seem to mind.

"You like this car?" she asked a moment later, after having secured his name and where it was he was headed.

"Yeah, it's nice."

"It's ten years old now, you know. It's not mine; it belongs to the Old Man, my grandfather, but I had to borrow it for the day. Had a new Packard myself, that is until I got a bit blotto and ran it into a tree a few weeks back—"

Janson stared at her for a moment, but did not respond, not knowing what to say. He had never before met a woman who drank, much less one who admitted to having done so.

After a moment, she reached and took up a paper sack from the seat between them, pulling down on the top of it with a thumb to reveal the shiny cap of a hip flask. "You want a drink, honey?" she asked, holding the flask out toward him.

"No, ma'am—" he said, staring at her openly now. He had tried corn liquor several times in his life, as had any other young man his age in the County, but had never really acquired a taste for it—besides, she was a woman, even if she was not a lady, and a man never drank in front of a woman, not even a woman who herself might drink.

"You sure?" she asked, bracing the flask between her exposed knees and unscrewing the cap. She tilted it up for a moment, the car almost going off the road as she swallowed a mouthful and then offered it to him again. "It's good gin, smuggled in off a rumrunner, not any of this bathtub swill—"

"Yes, ma'am, I'm sure—"

"Stop calling me ma'am," she snapped. "I'm not any older than you are—" It was a lie, and they both knew it. "My name's Lecia Mae—"

He looked at her for a moment, surprised at her words, reminding himself again who she was. "Yes, ma'am—I mean, Lecia Mae."

"Good—" She smiled, glancing at him again. After a moment she asked: "How old are you, anyway?"

"I'm eighteen."

"Eighteen—" she said, but said nothing more.

Silence fell between them for a time, and she seemed again to appraise him with a side-long glance. He felt that look, and he wondered again if she was thinking the same thing he was thinking—if women, even "fast" women, thought such things.

"You in any particular hurry to get anywhere?" she asked after a moment.

"No, ma'am, not really."

"Good—" she said, and glanced his way again. He felt the gray eyes moving over him, and he understood. "Good—"

When they reached Pine, she skirted the town, going out through the edge of the mill village, passing through quiet dirt streets that were lined with row upon row of identical, white two-family houses. She drove too fast, paying little attention to the few other cars that were on the road, or even to the children playing near the edges of yards, then she doubled back toward Main Street, going back toward downtown. Janson watched her, a nervousness growing in the pit of his stomach, at the way she was driving, and at more—he was anxious, wondering how much experience she had actually had, for he had never been with anyone like her before in his life. This afternoon, he well knew, would be far different from the times in the hayloft with Lois Dewey. Far different.

She stopped the touring car on Main Street before a large, white two-story house that sat up on a hill not far from the brick-paved section of downtown. She stared out the open side of the car for a moment at the big house on the rise, and at the shining, new green four-door Cadillac that sat in the circular drive before it.

"Dammit—" she swore under her breath, and Janson stared at her for a moment with open surprise, for he had never before heard any woman curse in all his life. "We'll have to go out back to the coach house. Daddy's home, and the Old Man'll be with him—"

Before he could speak, she pulled the car into the drive and on around toward the rear of the house, causing Janson to flinch inwardly at the risk they were taking so close to her father's home, and to her grandfather. But his unease was quickly replaced by curiosity as he stared past her and out her side of the car toward the big house with its many windows, then at the large kitchen standing separate and apart at the back of the house, connected only by a bricked footpath, and at last at the flower garden with the small, white-painted gazebo at its center. She drove the Cadillac up to a large brick building sitting at a distance beyond the house, the two open archways in its center opening onto a wide hall, and windows above to rooms in a second floor. She pulled the car in through one of the archways and over an oilspot on the bricked floor, parking it beside a new-looking roadster that had been pulled beneath the second archway; then she shut the motor off.

Janson looked around the white walls of the large open space, hearing the car's engine tick as it began to cool. Lecia Mae took up the hip flask and drank again, then retrieved her lipstick and a small mirror from the handbag at her side, freshening the makeup she wore as she talked absently of things Janson paid little attention to. His eyes came to rest on the narrow flight of stairs that rose from the rear of the hall to the floor above—surely they would go up there, to some room, maybe even to a bed, before they did it, he told himself, feeling the openness of the archways behind him, the presence of the large house beyond.

She was watching him when he brought his eyes back to her.

"You, nervous, honey?" she asked, absently patting her bob with one hand. "Ain't you ever done it before? You'd relax, you know, if you took a drink—"

But her hand went to his knee, then slid up along the inside of his thigh, and he knew there was nothing that would help him to relax—and he also knew it would happen right here, right where someone could walk in and catch them; and he found that he really did not care anymore.

Her hands were moving over him in ways that he knew should have shocked him, her mouth coming easily to his, tasting of the liquor, her tongue moving over his own. He was aware of the open archways behind them, her father's house beyond, but for some reason none of that mattered.

There was a sudden, prickly sensation along the back of his neck, an uneasy feeling in the pit of his stomach, and he tried to take his mouth from hers to look toward the archways, but she would not release him, tightening her hand on him, making him moan instead as he pressed her back against the seat of the touring car—it was safe, he told himself. She would not have brought him here if it was not safe. It was—

"You goddamn—" The car door was suddenly yanked open behind him, and he was hauled off the girl and out of the car, then turned and slammed hard back against its side, the impact driving the breath from his body as he found himself staring into the face of Buddy Eason—the younger man's face was red with rage as he stared from Janson to his sister, his body shaking as he forced almost unintelligible words through tightly gritted teeth. "You goddamn red-nigger trash with my sister—you goddamn—"

Before Janson knew it was coming, a hard fist to his stomach doubled him over, knocking the breath from his body again, making him gag and choke and fight for air, then a second sent him stumbling backwards, bloodying his nose and sending him reeling back into the open doorway of the touring car. Lecia Mae shoved him away, sliding to his side of the car, yelling something toward her brother, words Janson finally understood, and he looked back at her quickly, seeing the sudden excitement in her eyes at the diversion before her—and Janson realized with a sudden and complete anger that a diversion was all he had been as well, a moment's diversion for a damned rich girl. She had never wanted him, or even the pleasure, but only the diversion. Only the—

He hauled himself to his feet from where he lay half against the side of the Cadillac, his eyes on Buddy Eason—he might be whipped by an angry brother under such circumstances, but there was no way he would allow the hell to be beaten out of him just to entertain a bunch of rich folks. There was no way—

He began to fight back as Buddy started toward him again, landing a hard blow to Buddy's jaw that made his knuckles ache, and then another to his midsection that sent the younger man reeling backwards against the red roadster parked nearby—Buddy suddenly seemed to go into a rage, his entire body shaking, the blood rushing to his face to darken it even further, not at what he had found Janson and his sister doing, but simply because Janson was fighting him, was fighting him and whipping him. Buddy screamed and came at Janson again, one hand going to his pocket, then coming up quickly—there was one brief second, a glint of light off metal, and then the hand began to descend—

Janson blocked a sweeping arch of the knife with his free hand, the hard impact of the blow making his arm ache all the way to the shoulder. Buddy stepped away, keeping the knife between them, the cold, gray eyes searching for an opening. Janson watched him, wary, cautious, leaping away as Buddy lunged again, the knife missing him by only a bare few inches, then again, as Lecia Mae urged Buddy on, her legs now out the door of the car and crossed, her skirt now seeming to be hiked well above her thighs.

Buddy lunged at him again, the knife blade slicing into Janson's hand as he tried to fend it away—for a moment, there was no blood; then it came, running down over his wrist as a burning pain filled his palm. Buddy slashed at him again, missing his cheek by only a bare few inches, then again, and Janson twisted away, stumbling, almost falling, catching himself, starting to turn—then the cold impact of the knife blade hit him, the shock of the metal driving up to the hilt through his right shoulder. For a moment, there was nothing; then a wash of pain swept through him, turning him sick and making the coach house twist about him. His bowels felt suddenly weak, his face cold from the shock, the smells around him intensified—the oily smell of the cars, the odor of gasoline, of Buddy's sweat, the decidedly sexual scent of the girl. Vomit rose to his throat as he grasped the knife handle in his left hand, a cry finally escaping him as the blade cleared his flesh—he held it in one bloody hand, staring down at it; at the red on its blade, soaking into the knife handle, covering his hand, soaking through his shirt sleeve—blood, his own blood.

A sudden, blind anger engulfed him. His senses were dazed, his mind unclear, making it impossible for him to control the sudden, violent rage that swept through him. He lunged at Buddy, throwing the full force of his weight against the husky younger man, sending him reeling backwards onto the brick flooring—suddenly Janson was kneeling over him, the knife held to Buddy's throat in one bloody hand. Janson stared down into the younger man's eyes, shaking with rage, watching the gray eyes widen with fear and self-concern. Perspiration beaded on Buddy's upper lip as he began to tremble—there was the sudden strong smell of urine, and Janson realized with disgust that the man's bladder had voided itself. In that moment, he wanted nothing more than to kill Buddy Eason. Nothing more than to—

He slowly forced himself to his feet, weaving slightly as a wave of light-headedness hit him. Pain throbbed through his right shoulder, a sick feeling in the back of his throat—but he tossed the knife away, and then stood staring down at Buddy Eason where the man lay on the brick floor at his feet, seeing Buddy begin to shake with rage, with fury that Janson had fought and whipped him, and even that he had let him live. Then he turned his eyes toward Lecia Mae where she sat in the open doorway of the touring car, her words stilled now, her eyes never once leaving his face, her hands not attempting to pull down her skirt—he stared at her for a moment longer, then turned and walked away, through the open archways of the coach house and out into the clean summer air, one hand pressed to his bleeding right shoulder.

For a long time he could hear Buddy Eason's voice yelling after him as he walked away, the same words, over and over again. "I'm gonna kill you, you red-Injun' nigger! One day, somehow, I'm gonna kill you!"

But Janson Sanders never once looked back.

HE NEVER knew exactly how he got home that day, just that someone stopped and picked him up, gave him a ride—how he swore to himself over and over on that trip home that he would never go into town again, never trust another fancied-up modern woman, never risk losing his life for—

His mind was muddled by the time he reached home. There were confused thoughts about the land, about his home, about fields green with plants, white with cotton—then one last clear image as he stumbled from the car, his mother seeing him, dropping the clean wash she had been hanging on the line, running toward him as he stumbled and fell. Then there was only darkness.

THE HOUSE was quiet those hours later as Nell Sanders sat by the side of the old rope bed in the back bedroom of her home, the softness of her son's breathing the only sound to be heard in the quiet around her. Dawn would not be long in coming, but sleep was still very far away—she had been sitting here for hours now, throughout the night, just watching as Janson slept, listening to the sound of his breathing, as she had done on so many nights when he had been little more than a baby. Henry sat on the bare wood floor at her feet, much the same as he had done over thirty years before when they had been young together and courting, his hand holding hers, resting on the arm of the rocker, his eyes on their son as well—there had been no sleep that night for either of them, only worry, concern, and prayer, for Janson was their only son, the only child they had given life to, and he had been so badly hurt.

When Janson had arrived home those hours earlier, had gotten out of the car, his face paling beneath the sunburn, the blood soaking his shirt and hands, his steps staggering, Nell had thought her heart would stop within her. She could remember running toward him, catching him somehow as he fell, though she was small and slight and the top of her head did not even reach his shoulders—she knew she must have screamed for Henry, for he had been suddenly there, taking the boy up in his arms and carrying him toward the house, laying him on the old rope bed in the back bedroom, then running out again a moment later, through the pine woods and toward his parents' home, for they had been unable to stop the bleeding, no matter what they had done.

It had seemed an eternity later when Henry had returned to the house with his mother, an eternity in which Nell had thought she would see her son bleed to death there on that old bed, an eternity in which she watched blood soak into the clean petticoat she pressed to the wound, and into the sheet and linens on the bed, an eternity in which she prayed for sight of her husband and her mother-in-law. Deborah Sanders had not even spoken a word as she had come into the house and to the bed of her grandson, but her presence alone had helped to calm Nell's fears, for Nell had seen her stop blood so many times before, had seen her draw fire, and cure thrush.

Henry's mother slept in the next room even now, near in case she should be needed through the night. She said Janson would be all right, that he would live, and that his shoulder would heal, but still there could be no sleep that night for Henry or for Nell. Janson was their only child, and he was all that mattered to either of them, other than each other.

Nell sat now, staring at her son's worn and calloused hands, a farmer's hands, where they lay at rest on the pieced quilt, remembering the tiny fingers and toes she had counted and touched those eighteen years before when her body had still hurt even too much to move. She looked at his face, seeing Henry there as well as herself, even with the green eyes now closed in sleep—how they had wanted a child, children; but there had been over thirteen years of wanting and prayer before this one had come. So many nights they had held each other and prayed, wanting to give each other a large family, sons and daughters to share the years ahead, but for so long there had been only the two of them, and they had been happy in each other alone—and then this miracle had come, a child, a son, and their world had been complete. They had the land; they had each other, and they had a son—what more could any man or woman want.

She looked at Henry now, watched him, though his eyes never once left the sleeping young man on the bed, noticing again the white that now liberally streaked the reddish-brown hair she had known for so many years. He would soon be fifty-seven, and she was now already forty-six, but his face seemed just as handsome now, just as loved, as it had on that first day she had ever met him, and she loved him even more—could that really have been almost thirty-two years before. Thirty-two years, over two-thirds of her life, and it seemed now as if it had been only a day.

She had not even been fifteen then, newly come to Alabama with her father because of a job he had been promised in Eason County. Until then she had spent her entire life on the Qualla Boundary reservation of the Cherokee people in North Carolina, very sheltered, over-protected, and greatly loved by a father who had been widowed at her birth. It was only the second time she had ever been away from home, the first having been the few months she had spent at the boarding school on the reservation, the few months that were still marked in her mind by having had her mouth washed out with soap for speaking her native Cherokee and not English—and then her father had died as well, in an accident within days of coming to Eason County, leaving her alone in a place of strangers, where there was not one other person with a face or heritage as her own.

She had been living with a farm family there in Eason County, tending their children, earning the money she would need to return home—and learning the meaning of cruelty for the first time in her less than fifteen years, hearing words she had never thought would be said to her, words spoken by the decent, good folk of the County, people who knew nothing of her, or of the people she had come from, words said simply because her skin was darker, and her heritage different from their own. Many of the people in the church the family attended had been kind to her, accepting her into their homes, looking after her until she could go home again to grandparents and an aunt who would take her in—and it had been at that church that she had met Henry.

He had been staring at her, staring at her long and hard until she could feel it and turned to look at him—but he did not look away, as did so many of the people who stared at her only because they had never seen a person of Cherokee heritage before. He only continued to stare, making her both nervous and at the same time happy, for she had never been stared at by a man so handsome before, so tall, or so good looking.

As soon as church was over, she had wondered who she might ask to find out who he was, and if it were even proper to make such an inquiry—but he had walked up to her before she could do anything, finding her waiting on the church steps for the Parker family, whose children she was tending. He had apologized for staring, had told her his name, and had asked her own. She had thought he might ask to call on her before he walked away that day, thinking that might have been why he had been staring, but had been disappointed as he had tipped his hat to her, and then had left her standing there.

That disappointment had been short-lived. He had shown up at the Parker house the next day with a load of fire wood he said he owed them, and had come almost every day the following week on one pretext or another before he had at last asked to call on her. It was less than a month later that he asked her to marry him, pacing back and forth in the red dirt of the side yard of the Parker's sharecropped home, telling her his dreams and his plans for red land that already seemed such a part of him, though it was not yet his own. "I ain't gonna be a sharecropper all my life, Miss Nell. I'm gonna have my own land—th' old Stilwell place; you know it. It's good land, and it could make us a good livin'; that is, if you'd be my wife—"

They were married a week later, on the day after her fifteenth birthday, in the little church where they had met, returning to his parents' home that night where they would live until they could set up housekeeping on their own. There had been long years of hard work ahead of them, a decision they had made to have the land, no matter the cost it might bring to them. There had been a year of sharecropping for old Mr. Aiken, with half a crop lost for use of the land, the other half lost to the store bill; and then years in the mill village, in half a rented house, and long twelve-hour shifts in the mill for Henry—but at last they had the money, enough for them to get started on, and a mortgage for the rest. They had moved into the house Henry had dreamed of for so long, to the rolling red hills and the crop that no one could take from them, the land that was their own—and she had known Henry was at last home. Together they had worked the fields, planting or hoeing or picking the cotton, happy together in this place that had become part of them both.

For so many years there were no babies, and, as the years had passed, they had almost given up hope, though they often still prayed at night as they held each other, each wanting a child, but both knowing that, even then, they could be no happier. Then the miracle had happened, and she had been almost too happy to believe it could be true, and then another month had passed, with no blood as she had always known—Nell had taken the little money she had saved and had gone to see a doctor before telling Henry, not wanting to give him false hope until she knew for certain, for they had been waiting for so long.

After a horrid examination that had left her blushing and wanting to go home, the doctor had told her she was with child—at last, she was with child. She and Henry were to have a baby.

Henry had been in the fields when she had gone to tell him, and somehow that had seemed fitting, for she knew that nothing meant life and birth and continuance more to him than did the land—she was going to have his baby, she told him, their child. He had held her for a long time, not speaking, and, when she had looked up at him, he had been crying. And she had understood.

It had been a difficult pregnancy, a long labor, and a difficult birth. Henry had been banished from the house almost from the moment her pains had begun, told to wait on the porch with his father and his brother, Wayne, while his mother and a granny woman from the church tended Nell. It was his child, he had told them, his wife, and he had a right to be there; but they would have none of it, not even allowing him past the front door, telling him that a birthing was no place for a man to be, that he should find something to do in the fields to make himself useful until the time came when he could see his wife again, and his child.

It had seemed to Nell that the labor would go on forever, the pains continuing into the evening and late into the night, until it seemed to her the child would never come. But the pain had only worsened, coming and going until it seemed a constant, twisting her body with its intensity, making her bite her lips and dig her hands into the straw tick of the bed to keep from crying out—she saw the granny woman shake her head, heard her tell Henry's mother that Nell should never have conceived, that she was too narrow to give birth, and too frail. But Deborah Sanders had only pushed the granny woman aside, saying she had brought many babies herself over the years, and that she was not about to lose her own daughter-in-law, or her grandchild.

"You push, honey—" she had told Nell, her face already drenched with sweat in the hot room. "You push with everythin' you got—you an' that baby's both Sanders; cain't nothin' get th' best 'a either one 'a you unlest you let it. Now, push! Push like the devil hisself has got a'hold 'a you! Push!"

She had pushed, had thought she would die, had prayed to see Henry one last time, to see the baby born and put into his arms before God took her, just as her mother had seen her put into her father's arms before she had died—she screamed aloud when the baby finally came, and Henry rushed into the room to see his son born into his mother's gentle and knowing hands, and to hear that first cry of life as Deborah Sanders lifted him by his ankles to slap him across the bottom. Henry collapsed to his knees by the side of the bed, taking Nell's hand in his, watching as their son was put into her arms for the first time, the baby screaming, red-faced, and angry at his entry into the world. Henry would not be moved again, staying with her even as they tried to make him go, touching her and their son, keeping her from heaven itself with the very love in his eyes.

As long as she lived, Nell knew she would never forget the feeling of holding that miracle in her arms for the first time, of counting the tiny fingers and toes, and examining the small, perfect body of the son she and Henry had made—and she would never forget the tears in Henry's eyes, the wetness on his cheeks, as he brushed the sweat-drenched hair back from her face. "We got us a son," he kept saying to her, over and over again. "We got us a son."

They named the baby Janson after her father, and Thomas after his, and their world had been complete within the three of them. Henry's mother said there would be no more babies, but, after the years alone, they had never expected even this one, and they accepted that one miracle was enough for any lifetime. They had each other, they had a son, and they had the land that would be his one day. They could want nothing more.

Janson had grown fast, a handsome young boy with his mother's dark coloring and his father's green eyes. He was a loving and happy child, with a bad temper when pushed, and, as his grandmother often said, more stubbornness and pride than was right in any man or boy. He loved the land from the moment he could walk, loved growing things, and the feel of the red earth beneath his feet; loved his parents, his grandparents, and his kin, but the remainder of the world he was often uncomfortable with. He was dark, and he was half Cherokee, and he was proud with a pride the world would deny him—Nell knew he often heard the same things she had heard in the years since she had left the reservation, but, whereas she had fought her battles with silence, and with the dignity her heritage had taught her, she knew her son often fought his with fists, and with a temper that was nothing less than Irish and inherited from his father's side of the family.

As Janson had grown into a young man, he had kept few friends, often alone it seemed, but never lonely; a young man often silent, but at peace with the earth and the sky and himself. He often reminded Nell of her father, and often of Henry, and often of herself—but Janson was Janson, and often even she could not understand him, though she had almost died to give him life.

There was a sadness within her now as she sat in the rocker by the side of the old bed, looking at the young man who had been stabbed and so badly hurt, remembering the baby she had nursed and held and touched—he was a grown man now, eighteen years old, older than she had been when she had become Henry's wife. There was a feeling within her that he had already been close with a woman, had already learned things that she and his father had not known until their marriage night—young people grew up so fast now days, she thought, too fast. She knew the stabbing had probably been over a woman—the wrong kind of woman—though Janson had not spoken a word of it, though she knew he would not. He would remain silent if asked, silent, and with that look in his eyes that said there were things in his soul that belonged to him alone—and she knew she would not ask.

He was proud, proud and stubborn and determined, traits that would make his life all the more difficult, even beyond what his coloring and heritage had already deemed that life would be—but she had known that from the start, from the time he had been that baby first learning to walk, slapping her hands away as she tried to catch him, falling, only to push himself to his feet and take a few tottering steps before falling again. She had tried to protect him, to keep him from hurting himself, even as he had learned, but again and again he had pushed her hands away, falling time and again, bruising his chin, hurting his elbow, fighting even as he cried—she had not seen him cry in years now, not since he had been a little boy, beaten bloody by bigger fellows because he would not perform a war dance when they demanded he do so. She had tried to protect him then as well, had tried to get him to tell her the names of the other boys so she could talk to their parents, but he had refused, coming home bloody and beaten day after day until they had at last found more interesting game—even then there had been no shame in him for a fight well fought, no defeat after a hard battle. Those were traits she could see in him now, the same pride, stubbornness and determination, and she knew she could expect nothing less of him, for he was a part of her, and he was a part of Henry.

The door opened quietly and Henry's mother entered the room—her mother, she thought, for she and Henry were long since the same. Deborah Sanders was dressed in a long cotton nightgown buttoned to the throat and wrists, her brown and gray hair hanging over one shoulder in a thick plait that reached to well past her waist, her round face kind and gentle as she looked at them, knowing they had not slept at all, and knowing it was only what they had to do. She walked to the side of the bed and reached to touch Janson's forehead lightly, his cheek, and then to check beneath the bandages to the wound that had bled so freely earlier, as Nell and Henry rose to their feet at the side of the bed. Henry reached out and brushed Nell's hand almost unconsciously, as he often did, and they waited.

Henry's mother came around the bed to them, placing a gentle hand first on Nell's cheek, then on Henry's, as she smiled at them. "He's gonna be fine, jus' like I tol' you," she whispered. "He's jus' got some healin' t' do, an' restin' t' get his strength back. It ain't gonna do him no good, you two gettin' yourselfs sick. You need t' get some sleep—"

"We will," Nell said, looking back to the bed, and to the young man who shifted slightly in his sleep as he lay there. "We will—" But she sat back down in the rocker, and Henry moved to sit again at her feet, lowering himself slowly as he leaned heavily on the arm of the chair, as he had not had to do in years past. He took her hand in his again and held it, intertwining their fingers securely. After a moment, Deborah Sanders shook her head and sighed, knowing there was no use in talking to them further. She turned and crossed the bare wood floor without another word, going out the door and closing it again quietly behind herself, leaving them alone again with their son.

Nell watched as Janson slept, thinking of the baby she and Henry had made, the child she had carried within her, thinking that time had passed too fast, and that the years had been all too quickly gone. She looked down at Henry, remembering the tall and handsome young man who had so tenderly told her about love, and who had even more gently taught her; the same man who sat beside her now, his brownish-red hair streaked with white, the wide shoulders bent from age and work, the once-smooth skin near his eyes lined from years of smiles—but the green eyes just as alive, just as caring, just as full of love now near fifty-seven, as they had been at twenty-five. Life was too short for love, she thought, too brief for commitment; the years all too soon gone, but the love grown only stronger still—surely death could not end that, and life could not begin it. It had to be there, forever, for always. That was what they had taught Janson, and she had to believe it herself now—suddenly, she had to believe it so very strongly herself.

She watched Henry, thinking of how he often spoke now of having grandchildren in the house, of Janson finding the right girl, bringing a bride to the land, giving them grandsons and granddaughters for the years ahead—but, as hard as she tried, Nell could not see that, could not see Henry with babies on his knee, babies with his green eyes and his caring, and that frightened her. There was an ache growing inside of her that would not go away, an ache even though she knew Janson would be all right and that his wound would heal—life seemed too short. So very short. And the sadness would not leave, no matter how hard she tried. She wanted to cry but would not let herself, for there was no reason. No—

Henry's hand tightened over hers and he looked up at her, and she realized with a start that he had been thinking the same things, feeling the same things, she had been feeling. She tightened her hand on his and smiled, nodding her head to tell him she was all right, and, after a moment, he looked away, back toward the bed, and to their son sleeping quietly there.

Nell turned her eyes toward Janson as well, the tears finally coming, spilling from her eyes and down her cheeks. She knew that, as long as she lived, she would never forget the look she had seen on her husband's face in that moment. Henry Sanders had been crying.

# 2

JANSON'S SHOULDER WAS fully healed by the time fall came and the cotton bolls burst open, paining him only on occasion now, when the weather was bad, or on days when he worked it too hard in the fields. He had not once seen Lecia Mae or Buddy Eason, or their father or grandfather, since the day of the stabbing, and he found that he was glad—not because he was afraid, for he held no real fear of any man, but simply because there were more important things on his mind, more important things that had to do with holding onto the land, and with selling their crop again where it could bring them the most money.

There was a surplus in the cotton market in that fall of 1925, more cotton coming in than buyers had a need for, and the going price per pound of lint had already dropped lower than it had been in either of the past two years—and the Easons were paying even less than that. There would be no more choice this year than there had been the last; they would have to sell out of the County if they were to hold onto the land, have to sell, and quickly, before there could be any further drop in price, a drop that could so very easily cost them the few cents per pound difference between being able to hold onto the land, and losing it.

Janson found that he was glad to be out in the fields again in that first week of picking the cotton, glad to be doing something, and not just sitting and waiting for his shoulder to heal, as he had been doing for so long—but it was tiring work, long days of dragging a pick sack behind him, picking until his hands bled from the dry hulls and his back ached from bending among the cotton plants, until his shoulder hurt and his feet were tired and he wanted only to go home and rest. There was trouble coming and he knew it, could sense it as he worked in the cotton fields, could see it in his father's eyes—Walter Eason could not let them sell their cotton out of Eason County this year.

But there was no choice. There was so little choice left for any of them now.

There were long hours in the fields that first week of picking the cotton, days that went from before sunup in the mornings until long after sunset at night, each of them dragging a long pick sack behind them down the never ending rows, Janson, his father, and his mother as well, for there was no money to hire pickers, and, even if there had been the money, there would also have been better uses for it as well. It seemed to Janson that those first days went on forever, days of emptying pick sacks into the cotton baskets he and his father had woven years before, tamping the cotton down, only to return to the rows again—after a few hours backs would be aching from the constant bending and stooping, fingers would be bleeding from contact with the dry hulls, and any neck not protected by hat or bonnet would already be painfully burned from exposure to the sun.

By the end of that first week, Janson was sore and exhausted. He was glad now that he had turned down an offer to supper that night at the home of one of the girls from church; she was a nice girl, very pretty, with long blond hair down her back to her waist—but at the end of that first week of picking cotton, Janson was too tired to even really care. His shoulders ached from the weight of the cotton sack he had dragged behind him all day, its wide strap slung across his chest and oftentimes pressing the healed wound in his right shoulder. His fingers were sore, a deep scratch in his left thumb from one of the cotton hulls, and his back ached—all he wanted tonight was rest and sleep. Tomorrow there would be church and kin and dinner with the girl's family after services—but tonight there was that old straw tick, and a rest he knew he so badly needed.

As darkness began to settle in that night over red fields now thickly starred over with white cotton, Janson and his father dumped the cotton baskets one last time into the overloaded wagon and started for home. The night was quiet around them, the sound of a motor car miles away in the distance the only thing that broke the stillness. There was a full moon, lighting the cotton fields and the bare-swept yard that led to the house; the smoke coming from the chimney of the separate kitchen, and the kerosene light showing through its windows, the only signs of life in the darkness.

Janson was exhausted as he sat beside his father on the seat of the old wagon. His mother had left the fields hours before to prepare supper for the family, but he wondered now if he would not be too tired to eat, stifling a yawn again as he stared toward the house and the old barn beyond. His pa was silent as he sat beside him, seeming to Janson somehow almost old for the first time in his life, his shoulders bent as he drove the team of mules—Janson knew he was thinking again of the work ahead, of the days of picking the cotton, and of the struggle that still might lie ahead to sell it as they knew they would have to. Things had been quiet around the place for the past several weeks; there had been no more broken windows, no slaughtered animals, but Janson knew it was not over yet. Walter Eason would know they had not been beaten so easily. Walter Eason would know, just as Janson knew. Walter Eason would know.

Janson's appetite returned as they entered the separate kitchen of the old house a short time later, the scent of baking biscuits and frying ham coming to him. There was good, strong coffee, potatoes fried in bacon grease, and turnip greens swimming in pot liquor, as well as fried apple pies for dessert—and Janson realized suddenly how very hungry he was, a hunger he had rightly earned from hours of hard work in the fields that day.

When supper was finished, he sat tired and contented in the flickering light of the kerosene lamps in the front room they used as a parlor. He rocked slowly in an old split-bottomed rocker, his head leaned back, his eyes closed, his mind thinking, dreaming. His father sat nearby, reading silently from the old family Bible, its worn and cracked leather cover open in his calloused hands. His mother was across the room, bent over the foot-treadle sewing machine that had sat here in the parlor for as long as Janson could remember, her voice, sweet and clear above the sound of the machine, singing the words of a song he had heard both her and his grandmother sing time and again.

On the floor beside her chair sat a specially sized and painted bow basket Janson had made and given to her on her last birthday, a basket now filled with assorted bits of cloth of odd shapes and sizes, quilt scraps she would soon be turning into warm cover against the cold Alabama winter nights. Her hands were busy at the sewing machine now, unable to be still even after the day she had spent picking cotton in the fields, her mind occupied with the remaking of an old shirt someone had given her—Gran'ma or Aunt Rachel, or maybe even Aunt Olive—remaking it into a shirt he or his father could use, and that the former owner would hardly recognize again once she was finished with it.

Janson listened to a dog barking a half-mile or so away in the darkness; listened to the sound of a train whistle off in the distance, a train going almost anywhere—such a lonely sound. He listened to the night outside, feeling the heat of the fireplace warm on his face, smelling the scent of the oak logs burning there. He heard his mother singing, and the sound of the sewing machine as long familiar as her voice—he kept his eyes closed, not having to look at this room to see it, for he had spent every day of his life here in this house. He knew every step of the way from where he sat through the house and out over the covered walkway to the kitchen, to the icebox that leaked water on the floor, or to the temperamental old wood stove that sometimes belched smoke back into the kitchen. He could find his way through these rooms in the dark or without sight, for this was his home, as much a part of him as his soul was. He knew the red land that rolled into pine-covered hills and woods, and the cotton fields he had worked for as long as he could remember. He knew the rise of land across the road, beyond the beginnings of the fields and the small apple orchard, the rise where the old oak tree stood, the place he liked to go to be alone, to think, to dream, or to just sit and look at the house and be. He knew every step of the way from the porch to the barn, to the smokehouse, or to the old shacks that had held sharecroppers long before his father had ever owned the land—if there ever had been such a time. He knew the rutted clay road and the woods, and every step of the way from here to his grandparents' house, or to the sharecropped land of any of his kin or neighbors, as well as to the Holiness church they all attended. This was his home. This would forever be his home.

He sat with his head leaned back against the rocker, his eyes closed, his mind dreaming—he loved this land, this place, and he knew he would spend the remainder of his years here, working the red earth as God had intended man to do, even as his own father did now. Someday soon he would marry and have sons who would work this land as well. He would find a good woman, a nice girl from a Holiness family, for the Sanders were a Holiness people; a woman very much like his ma or his gran'ma, a woman a man could depend on, strong and level-headed and a good cook—and pretty, with a nice figure and long hair; not one of these modern girls with their bobbed hair and their smoking, their face-paint and short skirts and oh-so-modern ways that made them something less than ladies. He would marry a good, old-fashioned girl; they would have a family, and they would have this land—and someday he would buy more land, maybe the next farm over. And he would never sell at Eason prices again.

He must have dozed, for he woke with a start at his father's cry. Henry Sanders was suddenly on his feet, sending the rocker he had been sitting in crashing over onto its side on the floor, the old Bible falling from his hands—he ran for the door, a horrified expression on his face, and for a moment Janson did not understand. Then he smelled it: Smoke, not the scent of wood smoke from the fireplace, but something more. And his eyes caught sight of the light reflecting orange and yellow onto the front windows of the house. Fire—

Within seconds he was out onto the porch beside his parents, a sick feeling in the pit of his stomach as he saw the unpicked fields ablaze, the cotton going up—all that work, all that sweat, all that hope, gone for nothing. His father had grabbed up a quilt from where it had lain sunning over a chair on the porch during the day, and he was already running across the yard toward the fields—Janson did not know how the other quilt got into his hands, but suddenly he was running as well, stumbling, falling, only to get back to his feet and run again, almost unmindful of the sudden, sharp pain that shot through his left knee at almost every step.

The fields were choked with smoke, with flying pieces of burning lint that singed his face and hands. He began to beat at the flames with the quilt, the thick smoke choking his lungs until he thought he would never breathe again, the sweat pouring into his eyes until he could see nothing but the heat and the fire and the hell around him. He gagged on the smell of the burning cotton, his lungs fighting for air until his chest hurt with the very effort to breathe. He was in hell and he knew it was lost, everything was lost, this field and perhaps the next—but still he fought on, beating at the flames with the quilt, only to see them rekindle again from the dry and burning plants nearby.

His mother was a few rows away, beating at the fire with the beloved rag rug that had lain in the parlor all these years, the rag rug that had once belonged to her own mother, a mother she had never known, it burning already in her hands as she swung it over her head and down into the flames again. Her long black hair had come loose from its bun, hanging now down her back and past her waist, swinging with her movements. Her face glistened with sweat, something near absolute panic in her eyes even over the distance, her long hair and dress both swinging too close to the flames each time she lifted and swung the rug—he started to yell for her to get back, to warn that she was too close to the fire, but suddenly something in her face changed. She threw down the rug and started to run, and for a moment Janson thought she had caught fire, that she was burning—then he saw. His father, a distance away through the hell, was clutching at his chest, seeming to fight for air, for breath, a look of pain suddenly constricting his features.

Janson threw down the quilt that was already beginning to catch fire in his hands and ran toward his father as well, a pain suddenly shooting through his left knee that was now too bad to be ignored. Fire shot up in front of him, moving down another row of cotton—but the cotton no longer mattered. Nothing mattered. Nothing but his father. And Janson already knew that he was dying.

Henry Sanders collapsed into his wife's arms as she reached his side, and for a moment it seemed Nell Sanders would fall as well with the added weight—but suddenly she was dragging him from the field, her face showing the strain, the muscles cording out in her neck with the effort. Janson reached her side and began to help, taking his father's other arm, hearing her voice, the same words, pleading over and over again:

"God, don't take him from me. God, please, don't take him from me . . ."

There was so much pain in his mother's eyes, so much fear, a fear that matched Janson's own as they reached the edge of the field and collapsed there, his mother's strength giving out, his own giving way with the pain that now filled his left leg. Nell Sanders was crying as she drew her husband's head onto her lap, her voice saying his name over and over again, her hands touching his face, tears streaming down her own—but Henry Sanders was already dead.

The burning field nearby cast the world around Janson into a hell of heat and smoke and writhing black shadows. Tears ran from his eyes and down his cheeks as he stared into the face of this man who had given him life more than eighteen years before, this man who had given him the dream of the land. His mother rocked back and forth on her knees, his father's head cradled in her lap, her face stunned, disbelieving, streaked with smut and tears and more grief than Janson had ever known before. He lifted his eyes from the nightmare before him, begging God to understand, to know why—

Then he saw. And he knew.

Sweat poured down his face and into his eyes to mingle with the tears already there. Burning pieces of flying lint singed his face and hands, the thick smoke choking his lungs, the strong odor of gasoline coming to him from the burning field—but still he saw clearly as the black car turned around in the road and started away. He saw clearly. And he knew.

It was the black, 1915 Cadillac touring car.

It belonged to Walter Eason.

THE GLOW of fire in the night sky soon brought neighbors and kin from nearby farms to help fight the blaze. As soon as Janson knew the fire was out and his mother safe, the church women and Gran'ma with her, he knew he would go after Walter Eason, would go after him to make him pay for what he had done, what he had caused—but his grandfather would not allow it, pulling him up short as he started to leave the blackened fields, as if the older man knew what it was he intended to do: Nell Sanders had already lost one man this night, his grandfather told him; she would not lose two.

Janson stood to himself in one corner of a chill room in his parents' home hours later that night, tears rolling from his eyes and down his cheeks as he watched his mother, his grandmother, and his aunts bathe and dress his father for the last time, preparing him for the burial that would come. His mother had not spoken for hours now, not since the moment Gran'ma had knelt beside her, one arm around her slender shoulders, tears streaming from her own eyes as she stared down into the face of her son.

"He's gone, child. He's with th' Lord now. Henry's done gone—"

Janson did not sleep at all that night. He lay awake in the darkness, remembering the big man with the gentle and calloused hands, thinking of all the things he would have liked to have said, all the things he would have liked to have told him—as dawn came he dressed and went out onto the front porch of the house, wanting to be alone, wanting to avoid the grieving and sympathetic looks of the kin and neighbors who had spent the night on chairs and pallets throughout the house, or who had sat up in respectful silence by the body of his father. He sat on the wooden steps that descended to the bare yard, staring out across red land burned black by fire, ruined fields, the destroyed crop, and it seemed to him as if the land was mourning as well.

The screen door creaked open behind him, and he turned to find his mother staring out across the fields as well, a distant and hurting look in her dark eyes. He rose out of respect as she moved toward him a moment later, stepping up onto the porch to take her hands in his, hands that suddenly seemed so small, and so very frail.

Her eyes were red and weak from crying, her face washed white with tears, her lips pale, their lines indistinct. He had never before looked into the face of loss, of grief such as she felt, and he knew somehow that her grief went much deeper than did his own, much deeper than even he could understand.

He held her hands tightly in his, searching in his mind for the words to tell her what it was he felt, somehow knowing all the while there was nothing he could do, nothing he could say, that might help to lessen her loss—but her voice came before he could speak, her words strong, determined, a fierceness in them as he stared down at her that he had never before seen in anyone in all his life.

"Your pa loved this land, and he loved me, and he loved you—and you make him proud—" she said, her hands squeezing his until his fingers ached. "Don't you let them take this land away from you, and don't you let them get the best of you—you're my and Henry's son; you're half him, and half me, and don't you ever forget that. Don't you ever forget it." She stared up at him, the strength in her matched only by her loss as she swayed slightly on her feet, her dark eyes never once leaving his face. "As long as they never beat you, they'll never beat him, and they'll never kill his dream. It's inside of you, part of you—and don't you ever let them touch it. You hold onto this place, and you be the man he taught you to be—and don't you ever let them beat you. As long as you live, don't you ever once in your life let them beat you—"

Henry Sanders was laid to rest in the quiet of the small country cemetery just beyond the Holiness church he had attended since Janson had been a small boy, laid to rest beside two brothers who had gone before him, and a great-grandfather Janson had never known. Within months of his death, Nell Sanders went to join him, laid to rest at his side, taken by the influenza in the cold winter months, even after having survived the epidemic that had taken so many in the years of the World War—but Janson knew the truth; he knew she died simply because she no longer wanted to live, no longer wanted to exist in a world where

Henry Sanders was no more. Her spirit had given in, and the influenza had taken her—and, even as Janson sat beside the two bare, unmarked graves in the small cemetery, the tears running down his cheeks and dripping onto the red earth, he knew his mother was where she wanted to be, beside his father again.

He and his gran'pa had gone to the sheriff with what he had seen the night of the fire, but, even these months later, nothing had been done about it, as he had known nothing would be done—there had been too many witnesses to say Walter Eason had not left his home the night of the fire, and that the Cadillac had never once left the carriage house. It had been a heart attack that had taken Henry Sanders' life, a heart attack brought on by the stress of trying to fight the fire, and it had been both the influenza and grief that had taken Nell Sanders—but still Janson knew the Easons were responsible. The Easons had set the fire that had taken more than half the cotton crop as it still stood in the fields, or had caused it to be set—Janson knew that; there was no doubt: the car, there where it should not have been; the fire, when there had been no cloud in the sky, no lightning that might have started the blaze; and the strong odor of gasoline in the burned fields—there was no doubt.

But, still, nothing would be done. Nothing in Eason County.

Time and again he started toward Pine in the weeks and months after his father's, and then his mother's, deaths, determined to make Walter Eason pay for what he had done, what he had caused. He knew the man could never have known the high price the fire would exact that night—but still he should pay, still he should—

But time and again he turned back. His mother's words would not leave him—". . . don't you let them get the best of you—you're my and Henry's son; you're half him, and half me . . . As long as they never beat you, they'll never beat him, and they'll never kill his dream . . . don't you ever let them beat you. As long as you live, don't you ever once in your life let them beat you—"

He could not allow himself to kill Walter Eason, though he wanted to badly. He was Henry and Nell Sanders' son, and they had raised no murderer. He would hold onto the land, and he would make his parents proud, and he would see to it that the dream they had held for so many years would never die—the Easons had never defeated Henry or Nell Sanders once in their lives, and they would not defeat their son even now. Henry Sanders had dreamed too long, had worked too hard, for land of his own, a crop all his own, a better way of life for his son and for grandsons he would never know—Janson would not lose that now.

But he was alone, eighteen, and with a farm to tend, a farm with fields devastated by the fire that had devastated his own life those months ago. He had picked what had been left of the cotton after the fire—prices were the lowest they had been all season, and over half the crop had been lost, but still he would not give up. He had taken the cotton out of the County for sale, and no attempt had been made to stop him—no words had been spoken, no threats made, but still Janson had carried a rifle beside him on the seat of one of the borrowed trucks that had been used to take the crop out of the County. He would have shot the first man who had attempted to interfere. He had already made that decision.

When spring came, he began to break up the red land again, working alone behind mule and plow from just after sunup each morning to the last minutes of light. He planted the fields, tended them, chopped out the weeds with a hoe when they appeared; worked and worried and sweated from well before daybreak until long after dark each day. He fended for himself, alone for the first time in his life, as often as not eating cornbread and turnip greens, or whatever else he could find left over from what his gran'ma or his Aunt Rachel, or one of the ladies from the church, had brought over days before, sometimes too tired at the end of the day to even bother to heat it up on the old wood stove, and often too hungry to really care what it was that he ate. The preacher had suggested to him that he marry, that he take one of the girls from the church as his wife, someone to take care of the house and look after him, to cook his meals and mend his clothes, and maybe even give him a son or daughter in the year ahead—but Janson could not consider that. There were nice girls in the church, pretty girls, and he knew there were one or two who might even have taken a fancy to him—but he could not think about marrying now. He lay awake often in the night, tired and sore from the hours of work in the fields, lonely in the old house, missing his parents, and remembering how they had been. It would have been nice to have a woman beside him, someone he could touch and pleasure with and talk to—but all he could think about now was the land. All he could think about was the home he felt each day that he was losing.

Somehow late each Saturday he found the time to wash his overalls, dungarees, and workshirts in the wash tub in the back yard, using hot water from the black pot on the wood stove, and strong lye soap his mother had boiled down the year before from hog renderings and potash dripped from the ash hopper in the back yard. He beat the clothes on the battling block out by the kitchen door, boiling the sheets and his two good white shirts in the huge black pot there, scrubbing his work clothes on the rub board until his fingers hurt and his knuckles were raw—and often doing it all by the light of the fire beneath the wash pot, the one kerosene lamp he had brought out from the house, and the light falling from the windows of the separate kitchen where he would go for supper when the work was finished. The clean clothes would hang on the wash line overnight, and would often still be damp the next morning when he would take down one of the two good shirts and his Sunday trousers, press them as best he could using the old black flat iron he heated on the back of the wood stove, and would often still be damp even hours later as he walked toward church in them, the old Bible with its cracked leather cover in one hand, and the only pair of shoes he owned in the other.

There was always more work than he could do in the days, and never enough hours to do it in, no matter how hard he tried. So he spent even more hours, worked even later into the darkness each day, refusing to give up, refusing to even acknowledge that defeat could exist—and he lay awake at night and worried, and listened for someone to come again this year to try to destroy the crop, to take the last hope there was left. To take his land.

But this year there was no interference, no broken windows, no killed animals. When fall came, his kin helped as best they could, spending hours in his fields in addition to their own, his grandparents, his Uncle

Wayne, and several of his cousins, picking his cotton as well as their own, trying to help him hold onto the land—but cotton was bringing less per pound of lint this year than it had in any year since 1921, less than he could ever remember it bringing before. There was a good crop, more cotton than the land had ever grown before—surely, even with the current prices, it would be enough to let him hold onto the land once it was sold. Surely—

When the cotton was at last picked, filling the bins in the barn, filling the two old sharecropper shacks on the land, filling even the spaces boarded in on either side of the front and back porches of the house with only narrow walkways left in between, Janson looked at it, and he worried all the more. Many farmers were saying their crops were going for less this year than it had cost to grow them—and there was the mortgage payment to meet, as well as the credit he had found it necessary to run at the store. His pa had always warned him against using credit—but even Henry Sanders had been forced to use credit from time to time. That was how they had gotten the land in the first place, the same damned mortgage that threatened to take it even now.

The cotton was loaded onto borrowed wagons this year for the trip out of the County. Janson knew any trouble they might find would come before they could reach the County line, and he was already prepared to meet it—the old rifle rested against his thigh this year as it had the last. The Easons would not take his land. Not even if he had to use the rifle. Not even if he had to kill someone.

It was not long after they left the land that morning, the wagons loaded heavy with cotton, that the black car began to follow them, always staying at a distance, never coming any closer, never any farther away; making no attempt to pass them on the narrow dirt roads, or to not be seen—but, as they reached the County line, it turned back, never once having attempted to stop them, or to halt their progress. The crop was sold, and Janson returned to Eason County—but he already knew it was lost. The cotton had not brought the money he needed. He was losing the land.

In the next days he sold off everything he could—two iron bedsteads;

the sofa, upholstered chairs and centertable from the parlor; the hog he had been fattening for slaughter; the milk cow—anything he could find that might bring him some little money, until all there was left were the things he could never sell: the rocking chair he and his father together had bottomed with smooth white oak splits for his mother, the foot-treadle sewing machine she had worked over on so many evenings, the old rope bed his parents had shared since their marriage, the chifforobe that had sat in one corner of their bedroom all his life, the old wood stove, the leaky icebox. He took every cent he could gather from the sale of the furniture and the crop, and he gave it to the bank, knowing it was not enough, but praying—He kept telling himself that it could not end this easily, not after all his parents' dreams, his own. Not after all the years that Henry and Nell Sanders had worked and saved to have this land, and to hold onto it for him. Not after his entire life spent here on this red earth, working these fields, not after seeing his parents die—not after the past year, after all the hard work, the long hours in the fields, plowing and planting and chopping the cotton; not after the work and the worry and the days upon days of picking the fields until his back ached and his fingers bled. Not after—

But the foreclosure notice came, the notice of auction—he did not have to be able to read them to know what they said. They meant he land was no longer his. His father's dream. His mother's. His own—he had lost the land.

It was only a few days later that Walter Eason came to the land, a cold, gray day with a heavy, damp chill in the air that clung to the skin like a wet coat. Janson had been working in another man's fields since before sunup that morning, clearing land for the next year's planting, earning the little money the work might bring him, for there was still the store charge to pay, as well as a long winter ahead, a long winter when he knew he would not be on the land. He was tired and hungry as he walked toward home late that afternoon, the money from the work now earned and in his pocket, but those few coins were soon forgotten as he rounded the side of the house to find the black Cadillac touring car pulled up into the front yard.

He stopped where he was just short of the front porch and stared, watching as the car door opened and Walter Eason got out, the old man's white hair a stark contrast to the gray and threatening sky behind him—for a moment Janson felt a muscle clench tightly in his jaw, his hands tightening into fists at his sides as he fought to control the rage that built inside of him at the sight of the man. Walter Eason stared at him for a long moment, as if he were assessing the situation, and the young man who stood before him, then he closed the door of the touring car, and made his way toward where Janson stood before the house.

It seemed a long time before either man spoke, as Walter Eason and Janson Sanders met each other's eyes over the short distance between them. A wind blown up by the lowered clouds and the threatening sky stirred the old man's white hair—but still he looked somehow unmoved as he met Janson's gaze. At last he spoke, his face seeming still unchanged. "I hear you've lost this place."

Janson did not answer, but only continued to stare, somehow remembering the words his mother had spoken to him on the old porch behind him those months ago—and also a day, over two years past now, when Walter Eason had stopped him and his father in town. He could almost taste the red dust the cars along Main Street had kicked up that morning, almost hear the horns of the Model T's, the Chevrolets, and the Buicks—and this old man before him, this old man who dared to come to the land even now.

"You'll have to be leaving here soon," Walter Eason was saying, staring at him now. "I want you to know there'll be a place for you in the mill, and in the village, if you want it." He paused for a moment, seeming to be waiting. "There's always work in the cotton mill for a good, hard-working boy like you—"

For a long moment, Janson said nothing. When he at last spoke, his voice was quiet, but filled with anger. "Get th' hell off my land—" he said, and Walter Eason's face changed almost imperceptibly. "This place may not be mine much longer, but, while it is, I want you th' hell off it—" He stared at the old man a moment longer, then turned and walked up onto the porch and in through the front door of the house he had lived in all his life, leaving Walter Eason standing alone in the front yard. It was then that Janson Sanders knew he had to leave Eason County.

He had not once thought of what he would do once the land was gone, once the farm was sold on the auction block, for that had seemed such an impossibility, even as he had held the notice of foreclosure in his hand—but now he knew it was a reality as unstoppable as fire or death or falling cotton prices had ever been. He knew he could not stay here now to see his home sold to another man, to see another man work the fields that had once been his own—he had to go somewhere else, to find work that could earn the money he would need to get his land back someday. The Easons had not beaten him, as they had never once beaten Henry or Nell Sanders in all their lives—Janson would return here; he would buy back his land, and he would pass his dream, his parents' dream, on to sons and grandsons of his own someday.

Two days later he stood on the low rise of land just beyond the small, winter-barren apple orchard and the beginnings of the red fields that in a few months' time would be broken by another man's plow, tended, picked—it was the same as if he were married, and knew his wife would lie with another man, for he had loved this land for so long, known it even more intimately than he had ever known any woman. He stood beneath the empty branches of the old oak, looking out over the fertile red land, an aching inside of him such as he had not known since the days that each of his parents had died.

Over his shoulder were slung his shoes, tied together at the strings to make them easier to carry; at his feet was his father's worn old leather portmanteau, the battered old suitcase containing everything he would take with him in the world—the faded and patched overalls, dungarees, and workshirts, his good trousers, and the two Sunday shirts, all equally showing signs of wear now, and his inexpert care and laundering. Stuffed in with his clothes were the few dollars he had, and the old family Bible, the only existing photograph of his parents carefully placed between its pages, a photograph from long years ago, before hard work and worry had served to age them both. Everything else had been sold in the past months in trying to hold onto the land, everything but the few objects that were too precious to sell, things that had belonged to his mother and father, things with too much meaning to ever allow them to go to strangers. Those few things he would ask his Uncle Wayne or his gran'pa to come for in a wagon before the auction, in hopes someone in the family could use them, or at least store them until they might be of need again—he would not be here then. Today he was leaving Eason County.

He took one last look around at the red land, the fields he had worked beside his father all his life, the woods he had played in as a boy, and at the old barn yearly filled with white cotton for as long as he could remember. He looked at the house with its wide, comfortable porch where his mother had sat in her rocker on so many Sunday evenings, and at the separate kitchen off to one side of the house, connected only by the covered walkway in between—home, but home no longer.

He stood staring at the house for a long time, remembering things he had not thought of in years, days long passed now, things his father had said, the way his mother had often smiled, the sound of the sewing machine now and forever stilled and silent in the parlor. After a time he left the rise, cut through the silent apple orchard and over the North Ridge Road just above where it ran past the house. He cut through the fields with their rows of dry and lifeless cotton plants waiting now only to be turned under for the next year's planting, and toward the woods. He never once looked back.

He went along the path long ago worn smooth by a man's steady step and a small boy's running feet, the winter woods silent around him, the green of the pines the only sign of life in the dead of the January cold—he would say goodbye to his grandparents, and then he would leave Eason County for perhaps a very long time. But he would be back. He would leave for now this place where his pride and his soul would not let him stay. He would go somewhere else—where did not matter, for it would never be home to him; nothing would ever be home again but that red land and that white house he could no longer call his own. He would go wherever it was that he might have to go, do whatever it was he might have to do, to earn the money it would take to buy his land back—and then he would return to Eason County, and he would make that dream a reality again. Even if he had to face hell or the devil or fight Walter Eason himself—he would have that dream.

After a time he came to the old Blackskillet Road, crossed a ditch at the side of the red clay expanse, then followed its edge toward the sharecropped land his grandparents had worked for as long as most in the area could remember. When he came within sight of the unpainted house, its tin roof long ago rusting and brown now, he realized suddenly that it was Sunday, for the preacher's four-year-old Chevrolet was pulled up before the narrow front porch of the tenant house, as well as his Aunt Olive's and Cyrus' Buick, and his Uncle Wayne's Tin Lizzie. There was to be a family dinner after services this Sunday, as on most Sundays, and the preacher and his wife had been invited to share the meal today, as had Janson. His gran'ma would be worried where he was, wondering why he had not been in church that morning—and now he would have to tell her he was leaving as well, leaving for perhaps a very long time, and that he would not see her again for possibly years after this day.

He stood for a moment and stared at the house, then made his way across the bare swept yard, past the preacher's car and the old Model T, and up onto the front porch. He knew he would be disturbing dinner with his late arrival, especially with company in the house, but he could not stop now. He could not go back to the land, to the house, for one more day, one more night, knowing it was no longer his. He turned the doorknob smoothly in his hand and pushed the door open, not bothering to knock, for he knew there was little need for anyone to knock at this door.

His cousin Sissy sat in a rocker in the warmth before the fireplace in the front room of the sharecropper house as he entered, the girl rocking a homemade ragdoll in her arms, her gentle face calm and happy. She looked up as he closed the door behind himself, smiling as she saw him, then quickly motioning for his silence, warning with a look that the doll-child in her arms was asleep. Janson smiled and nodded his understanding, then stood watching her for a moment, remarking again to himself how lovely she already was at twelve, her long blond hair hanging in curls down her back, her blue eyes large and expressive; she was already becoming a young woman—but her mind would forever be that of a child, as everyone in the family but Sissy herself already knew. He nodded again to her, saying goodbye in his own way, while taking care not to disturb the sleep of the carefully mothered doll in her arms.

He passed through the middle room of the house, glancing at the old iron bedstead that had sat there in the same position against the whitewashed far wall for as long as he could remember, a hand-pieced quilt neatly drawn over its corn shuck mattress, a chamber pot visible beneath the foot of the bed. Ahead, through the open door to the kitchen, he could hear the preacher's voice and his grandfather's, both raised in some religious discussion as they sat on wooden benches pulled up to either side of the eating table, the soft voices of the women in the kitchen almost drowned out by his gran'pa as he told the preacher for the second time that book learning did not necessarily mean that a man knew the ways of the Lord. Brother Harmon started to respond, a holding-forth tone in his voice that Janson recognized from long Sunday mornings seated in his sermons, but Gran'pa cut him off mid-sentence as Janson entered the room.

"Hello, boy, we missed you in church this mornin'—"

The kitchen smelled warmly of home: fresh-baked biscuits, country ham, and fried chicken, collard greens cooking in a black pot on the back of the stove, wood smoke, strong black coffee. There were deep dishes of good food on the table, black-eyed peas cooked with ham, potatoes yellow with fresh-churned butter, rich candied yams, and syrup cakes stacked with dried apples for dessert. The men sat on benches pulled up to either side of the table, enjoying his grandmother's and his Aunt Rachel's cooking, the preacher sitting across from his grandfather, Uncle Wayne and his three boys, Aunt Olive's husband Cyrus and their son Daniel. The younger people and the children were out back of the house, and Janson could hear their voices clearly through the windows and doors closed against the winter chill—they would be the last to eat, after the men, and then the women, were finished, and tempers were running high, and voices growing louder, as their empty stomachs growled and the minutes crawled by.

The women stood or sat at the edges of the room, seeing that the bowls and platters of food on the table remained full, or simply waiting. Sister Harmon, the preacher's wife, sat in a straight, split-bottomed chair away from the overpowering heat of the wood stove, her spine not once touching the seat back, her legs encased in thick cotton stockings, crossed primly at the ankles, and tucked away behind one of the chair legs as she talked in quiet tones to Janson's Aunt Olive. His Aunt Belle and Aunt Maggie sat only a few feet away, Belle with her arms folded beneath her large bosom, and Maggie with hers folded beneath her rather flat one, both pointedly ignoring the preacher's wife for some slight imagined in church long weeks before.

Gran'ma and Aunt Rachel stood near the wood stove, seeing to it that the men's plates never grew empty, and that no slight in hospitality should occur, as they discussed children or households, canning or kinfolks, or whatever else it might be that women discussed at such gatherings. Janson returned his grandfather's greeting, but did not take the time to explain why he had not been in church that morning, then he looked toward his gran'ma—she was staring at him, staring at him with a sad, rather-resigned expression on her gentle face. Her brown eyes did not shift to take in the shoes slung over his shoulder, or the portmanteau held in his right hand, and he realized suddenly that they did not have to—she had known all along he would leave, that he would have no other choice.

"When you wasn't in church this mornin', I knowed it'd be t'day—" she said quietly, staring at him. "I figured it'd be soon—you know yet where you're goin', boy?"

"I don't reckon' it much matters. I guess t' just wherever it is th' first train takes me—" They both knew he would not have money to pay for the fare, but that he would have to hop the train instead, waiting until it was picking up speed pulling out of the depot, then running to swing himself and his few belongings on board the first empty boxcar he might find—they both knew, but they also knew there was no way around it, just as there was no way for anyone to offer him money to pay for the fare instead. They both knew he would not take it.

"You'll let us know where it is you wind up?" she asked.

"Soon as I can—"

Gran'pa rose from the table, stepping around the end of the bench and coming toward him. "For once I was hopin' your gran'ma'd be wrong—why don't you stay on here, boy, an' help me crop this place?" But Janson knew his grandfather did not need him to help sharecrop the small farm. His Uncle Wayne had the next place over, and together he and Gran'pa, and Wayne and Rachel's three boys, worked the two sharecropped farms as one, splitting the work, and splitting the little annual return there was from the portion of the crops that did not go for use of the land. Janson knew his grandparents did not need another mouth to feed, more kin than there already was crowded into the small house, just as he also knew they would take him in anyway if he wanted to stay—but he could not stay. There was the land—his own land—and he could never forget that.

"Won't you stay on, boy?"

Janson shook his head. "I cain't—" he said, but explained no further. His grandfather looked at him for a long moment, then reached out to take Janson's hand in a firm handshake.

"If it's what you got t' do, boy."

Janson nodded. There was nothing else he could say.

He went to his grandmother, stopping for a moment to drop his shoes and the portmanteau on the bare wood floor at her feet before putting his arms around her. He hugged her briefly, and kissed the softness of her cheek, then looked down into the kind brown eyes, finding them now filled with tears.

"I'll be back in a couple 'a years," he said. "Soon as I—" He did not have to finish.

She nodded, placing a work-rough hand on his cheek as she stared up at him. "You may look like your ma, but you're just like Henry—"

And Janson understood.

She turned back to the wood stove, putting her mind to the worry that his stomach be filled, rather than that her favorite grandchild was leaving her. She fussed with the lid covering a black pot, lifting it with a folded pad of quilted material, then lowering it back into place without ever having looked inside. "You better eat somethin' before you go—"

"I ain't hungry. I made myself a big breakfast before I left th' house," he lied, knowing all the while that she knew he lied. His stomach was in knots, and he knew he would not be able to eat anything, not even if he had to.

She nodded again, then reached up to lower the door of the warming oven above the stove, reaching inside to take out something she had wrapped into a clean white cloth. She turned to put it into his hands. "Biscuits an' fried chicken," she said. "I knowed you'd get hongry later."

For a moment, Janson could only stare at the warm white bundle in his hands, then he bent and kissed her cheek again, smiling and nodding to her—there was no need for words. He knew she understood.

He gathered up his shoes and the portmanteau from where he had dropped them earlier, holding them in one hand as he turned to his uncle.

"Uncle Wayne, there are some things left at my—" then he stopped for a moment, realizing, "at th' house. Would you mind—"

"I'd be glad to, boy," his uncle said, knowing the words before they had to be spoken, and looking for a moment so very much like Janson's father.

Janson nodded, then looked around the room one last time, memorizing the sights and smells and feelings familiar from a lifetime—the wooden table worn smooth with use, the warmth of the wood stove, the smell of black coffee and good country food, the faces of his kin—there was nothing left to say. It was time that he leave.

They all walked him to the door: his gran'ma and gran'pa, his aunts, uncles, and cousins, even the preacher and his wife; and he told them goodbye one last time as they stood on the narrow front porch of the sharecropper house, the cold January wind whipping at their clothes.

"You take good care 'a yourself, boy," Gran'ma said, staring up at him with love and worry clouding her brown eyes. Her gentle hand squeezed his arm. "You try t' keep warm an' dry, an' let us know where you are soon as you can—you got any money?" she asked at last.

"I'm all right," he said, and she nodded.

"You jus' remember who you are, boy," she said. "You jus' remember who you are—"

Janson took one last look around at the faces of his kin, seeing the strength in them, and the weakness, knowing that what they were, he was also. Then he turned and left the porch, walking down off the narrow board steps and into the yard, crossing it toward the rutted clay road that would take him into town and to the train depot, and away from the only home he had known during the nineteen years of his life. As he topped the rise in the road that would cut off sight of the house behind him, he turned back for a moment to wave one last time, and to say goodbye. Then he turned and walked on, slinging his shoes over his right shoulder, the red clay ground cold beneath his bare feet—he was Henry and Nell Sanders' son, he told himself. And someday he would make them proud.

DEBORAH SANDERS stood on the front porch of the sharecropped house she had lived in for more years than she could count, staring at the red clay road long after the others had gone back inside to the kitchen and to the meal she had prepared for them. She smoothed her hands down over the front of the apron tied about her waist, her tears dried now, but the ache inside of her none the lessened—her grandson was gone now, gone from home and his kin and the only way of life he had ever known; and she was worried.

Janson was so like Henry—determined, stubborn, headstrong, with perhaps more pride than it was right for any man to have, and that same dream in his green eyes she had so often seen in Henry's, that same dream of a home and crop all his own. Deborah had seen her son work and struggle through his life for that dream—and she had seen him dead because of it, had helped Nell to prepare his body for burial, and had seen Nell die so soon afterward, ready only to be with him.

And Janson was of both his parents.

Deborah closed her eyes and talked silently with her God for a moment—there was no need for conscious words in her mind, for she and her Lord were of long-standing acquaintance. He would understand.

He would know. And He would look after her grandson.

She opened her eyes and stared at the road again, her mind no less troubled even after the prayer. Often neither God nor man made an easy life for a dreamer; she well knew that, as so many of their people through the ages had known it, from Tom's grandfather who had been killed in Ireland in the hard years before the Potato Famine had forced the family to flee to America, killed by the Protestant landlord of a tenanted farm for refusing to pay his rent moneys and still see his children starve; to her own ancestors, who had only barely survived the massacres of non-Catholics in France; to Nell's people, so many of whom had died in the forced march of the Cherokee west from the north Georgia mountains in the time of the Trail of Tears. They had always been a people with their own dreams, their own thoughts and ideals, different somehow by choice and birth from others, and willing to die for that difference if need be.

Janson held that same difference, that same stubbornness, and many of those same dreams, of the Irish, French, and Cherokee within him; and Deborah worried all the more as she stared at the road he had gone away on—so much blood had been shed in the past for dreams. So much blood.

Passages from the Old Bible came to her, verses about Joseph and his brothers, and the dreams that had plagued his life, making her suddenly cold even beyond the chill of the wind:

> And when they saw him afar off, even before he came near unto them, they conspired against him to slay him.
>
> And they said one to another, Behold, this dreamer cometh.
>
> Come now therefore, and let us slay him, and cast him into some pit, and we will say, Some evil beast hath devoured him: and we shall see what will become of his dreams.

Deborah Sanders stared at the point where the red earth and the blue sky met, her thoughts troubled—

". . . and we shall see what will become of his dreams."

# PART TWO

# 3

THE LANDSCAPE THAT passed outside the open doorway of the rail car that Sunday afternoon in January of 1927 was a mixture of green southern pines and red Georgia clay. Janson Sanders sat just within the open doorway of the boxcar, his back against the wall, feeling the train rock and sway beneath him as it moved along the tracks. He had no idea where the train was taking him, and in that moment it did not much matter—anyplace was fine, anyplace that was not Eason County.

He shivered with the cold and tried to pull his coat closer about himself, but knew there was little use. The frigid January wind that numbed his face, his hands, and bare feet, also cut straight through the worn old coat, his faded workshirt and dungarees, and even the old newspapers he had stuffed down inside his shirt against the cold, to leave him shivering anyway. He had considered for a time moving back into the recesses of the car, away from the freezing wind that blew in the open doorway, but had already decided against it—the cold was far preferable over the stench that filled a space usually occupied by cattle, far preferable, and also probably far safer.

He eyed again the two men who rode the rail car with him, glad again of the distance between him and where they sat. They stayed at the far side of the car, seated against the wall, away from the air and the light. They had been here, sitting much as they were now, when he had swung himself and his few belongings on board those hours ago as the train had been picking up speed pulling out of the depot in Pine. They had looked at each other, and then had begun to stare at him as he settled down with his back against the wall—as they stared at him even now, returning his look with hard eyes that showed little concern for him, or for the remainder of the world.

Some instinct born within Janson warned him to be on guard as he met their eyes. They seemed hard men, neither too clean, and neither with less than several days growth of beard on his face. The youngest was at least twenty years older than Janson's nineteen and one-half years; he was a big man, with huge shoulders bulging beneath a dirty coat, and huge hands and thick wrists extending far beyond the ends of his sleeves—but it was the older of the two who put Janson even more on guard. He was somewhere in his mid-fifties, with a body already going to fat, and a broad nose that looked as if it had been broken and poorly mended several times. He sat apart from the other man, drawing his looks on occasion without saying a word. His head was bare, the greasy black hair thin and sparse over the top of his large skull, but growing in thick mats down along the backs of both his broad hands—and somehow he made Janson even more wary than did the other, staring at him, squinting even through the darkness inside the car, never taking his eyes away even as the hours passed and the miles rolled by the train.

Janson returned his stare, knowing somehow that the two men were together, just as he knew they were not friends, for men such as these had no friends—rather they simply traveled together, as any predatory animal might travel in a pack. And, as Janson watched them, he felt as if all his instincts were on guard.

He turned his eyes out the open doorway of the car, some part of him still watching and alert for any movement one of the two might make, just as it had been from the first moment he had swung himself on board the train those hours ago—he wondered again where the train might be taking him. The land they were passing through seemed at times almost as red as the Alabama hills he had been born to, but it was flatter land, rolling only on occasion into the hills and curves his eyes were more accustomed to. There were pine woods, broken for broad expanses by winter-barren cotton fields; small towns, and what once seemed to him to be the edges of a big city, though he could only guess at that, for he had never been in a big city in all his life. From the height of the sun in the west, and the direction the train had been traveling, he knew they must now be somewhere in Georgia—Georgia, that seemed as good a place as any to start earning the money he would need to buy his land back.

He continued to stare out the open doorway, feeling the old leather portmanteau against his thigh, his shoes not far away. His stomach was growling and empty, but the smell of manure, urine, and sweat within the car, and the constant swaying motion of the train, had already combined to replace his hunger with nausea. The white-wrapped bundle of food his gran'ma had given him those hours ago before he had left Eason County had long ago grown cold, and it sat, still unopened, atop the portmanteau at his side, his hand resting on top of it. He knew he would have to eat soon, but not here, not in this stinking, swaying car. Once the train stopped, he would get off, find someplace warm, someplace the air was fresh and the ground steady, and then he would eat—besides, he had to urinate badly, and he could not bring himself to stand and relieve his strained bladder against the wall as he had seen one of the other men do.

He leaned his head back and closed his eyes for a moment, exhausted, numbed from the cold, sick from the smell. He had never felt so alone, been so alone, in all his life—but perhaps alone was better. No one to worry about. Nobody else to think of. Alone.

He was tired. There had been little sleep the night before, the decision to leave Eason County sitting heavily on his mind, taking the badly-needed rest from him—for a moment, he thought of home, of the white house on the red acres; the fields so rich, green with plants in the summer, white with cotton in the fall; the tall green pines, the rolling red land. He thought of his pa's booming laugh, his mother singing softly as she worked at the old foot-treadle sewing machine in the parlor, his gran'ma coming by to make sure he ate two messes of polk sallet each year to purify his blood, and the time she had drawn the fire from his arm when he had burned it so badly on the old wood stove several years back. For a moment, he could almost see it all, almost touch it all—home, his parents, the white house as it had been in years past, just as if nothing had happened. Just as if—

There was a sudden movement across from him, quick, furtive, and Janson realized with a start that he had been almost asleep. His eyes sprang open, and his muscles tensed, ready—

The younger of the two men was half raised onto one knee, the dark eyes above the tangled beard set on Janson's face. For a moment, the man stayed as he was, staring at Janson, then he slowly lowered himself back to a seated position, his eyes never once leaving Janson's face—they were hard eyes, eyes that put Janson even more on guard. He would not fall asleep again.

It was not long before the train began to slow, coming into a small settlement, then finally coming to a halt with a shudder and a high-pitched screech of metal just outside an old depot. Janson cautiously looked out, hearing the two men shift even farther back into the darkness within the car. He knew it was not safe to stay so close to the open doorway, there being too great a chance the railroad police might spot him with the train stopped here at the station, and even Janson had heard of what often happened to the transients found riding the rails, how they were often beaten, sometimes to within an inch of their lives, before they were thrown off the train—but something inside Janson told him even that could be far preferable to what could happen to a man even deeper within the darkness of that car. At least the railroad police were the law. There was no law alive within that rail car.

The old depot building was run down, the once-white paint on its walls now peeling and gray from the smoke of the many trains that had come through. There were several sets of tracks, going in several different directions, but few buildings, and even fewer people—probably a freight stop, Janson told himself, staying hidden as best he could at the edge of the doorway. This was not the sort of place he had thought to leave his free ride, but both the smell, and the companionship, forced the decision on him—there were other empty cars on this train, other trains going other places if he chose. He could get out into the fresh air, stretch his cramped muscles, maybe find someplace warm where he could eat—but he had to get out of here.

He gathered up his things, the portmanteau and his shoes in one hand, the bundle of food in the other, and glanced back at the two men. They did not move or speak, but only continued to stare at him from the darkness as he got to his feet, the muscles in his back complaining at the position he had been sitting in against the inside wall of the car for such a length of time. He looked out again, checking cautiously for any sign of the railroad police as well as for any people from the train or station house who might know he should not be here; then he jumped down into the loose dirt alongside the tracks and knelt there for a moment, waiting to make sure he was unobserved before hurrying on toward the woods that stood at a distance behind the depot—he did not know why he looked back, but he did, turning back as he reached the edge of the woods to see the two men jump down from the boxcar only seconds later, wait there for an instant, then hurry off in another direction. Janson stared after them for a moment. And for some reason he shuddered.

He made his way into the woods, stopping for a moment to make sure he had not been followed. He stood still, his eyes moving through the trees, his breathing quiet as he listened to the silence. Then, satisfied, he turned and made his way even deeper into the pines.

The temperature had fallen, the damp, chill ground uncomfortable now even to his toughened and calloused feet—but the air was clean and fresh, and the ground steady, and he decided to stay here rather than to risk going back toward the depot where he might find a warmer place to rest and to eat his food. He took the time to relieve his strained bladder, then happened on a rusting tin water bucket left discarded and forgotten beneath a tree, filled now with rainwater, and topped by a thin layer of ice and dead leaves. He knelt and brushed the leaves aside, then broke up the ice and washed his face and hands in the frigid water, washing away the stench from the rail car, and hissing through clenched teeth as the icy water hit his skin.

He settled down beneath a tree and unknotted the bundle of food his grandmother had given him those long hours ago, his appetite returning now at the sight of the biscuits and cold fried chicken wrapped in the white cloth. It had been sometime late the day before when he had last eaten, a supper of dry corn bread, cold turnip greens, butter beans, and fatback as tough as shoe leather, and he thought now that he had never been so hungry before in all his life as he greedily bit into a fried chicken leg and picked up one of the large buttermilk biscuits.

"You gonna hog all that food t' yer'self, boy?" a voice came from behind him, and Janson immediately froze, almost choking on the food in his mouth as he turned in the direction from which the voice had come, finding the older of the two men from the rail car staring at him. Janson moved into a low crouch, the food and his hunger both immediately forgotten—the man was alone, but Janson knew the other would be nearby. His eyes quickly scanned the woods near the man, his ears straining for any sound of movement through the underbrush.

"Ain't you gonna be neighborly, boy, an' offer t' share some 'a that food with a hongry man—"

A movement came from the woods to Janson's right, and his eyes quickly darted in that direction, then back again, as the older man quickly moved so there was no way he could keep his eyes on both men at the same time. He remained in a crouch, a nervous knot of fear constricting his stomach—he knew what sort of men these were, and he knew there was no mercy within either one of them.

"Why don' you let us get a look at what you got in that suitcase, boy?" the older man said, beginning to move forward, his dirty hands moving down along the thighs of his greasy trousers—Janson rose quickly to his feet, his muscles tensing, his back to the tree so the other man would not be able to get to him from behind. The older man froze, eyeing Janson cautiously. "You do what I say, boy, an' it'll be a mite easier on you—"

"Like hell I will—"

"We should'a took keer 'a him back there on th' train—" The voice came from the woods behind him, making Janson turn quickly in that direction—but the older man shifted, moving closer, drawing his attention back. There was a sudden, quick movement at the corner of Janson's eye, and he started to turn back—but it was too late; the big man was already on him, twisting his arm up behind his back, turning him to shove him chest-forward against the tree. His ribs impacted the hard wood with a pain that drove the breath from his body, and he struggled to breathe again, his cheek against the rough wood of the pine as the older man moved closer to stare at him.

The man looked at him for a moment, then down at the chicken and biscuits now scattered out over the ground. "Jus' look what you done, boy," he said, then bent to take up a fried chicken breast, making only a bare attempt to brush away the dirt and bits of dried leaves that adhered to it before biting into the flesh. He chewed thoughtfully for a moment, staring at Janson, cold grease shining now on his mouth and chin. "What you got in th' suitcase, boy?" he asked, then squatted cumbersomely at Janson's feet, holding the chicken breast between his teeth as he unbuckled the straps of the portmanteau and laid it open on the ground.

Janson struggled against the man holding him, having his arm forced even more painfully up behind his back as he watched the dirty hands go through his things, his clean clothes being shoved aside, the Bible thumbed through in search of anything of value—then there was a grunt of satisfaction as the man found the little money Janson had knotted into a handkerchief among the other things. The man spat out the piece of chicken and pushed himself to his feet, unknotting the handkerchief and counting out the few coins into one greasy palm.

"I tol' you he had some money, th' way he was holdin' ont' that there case—" the man behind Janson said, but the older man only grunted in response, shoving the money into one deep pocket of the dirty coat he wore. He turned to look at Janson again, and Janson started to struggle anew, only to have his struggle halted by the question the big man behind him asked. "We gonna kill him, Hoyt?"

For a moment, Janson could only stare at the older man, the muscles in his stomach knotting again—men such as these could kill him without a thought, and leave him here in the woods where it might be days, even weeks, before his body was found. But it was something more than that. He stared at the man, feeling a chill move up his spine.

"Meby—meby not—" the man said, and Janson heard the big man

behind him start to laugh—but there was no humor in that sound; it was cold, deadly, something less than human.

"You always did like 'em young—" And suddenly Janson understood. He started to struggle against the big man holding him, feeling a sharp pain stab through his right shoulder with the pressure on his arm. He twisted to one side, bringing his left elbow into sharp contact with the man's ribs, twisting farther to land a hard punch to his jaw. He lashed out with a foot into the groin of the older man, catching him off guard and sending him stumbling backward, clutching his crotch.

Janson stumbled as well and almost fell, his right shoulder hurting as he grabbed up the portmanteau and his shoes, trying to capture as much of his things as possible as he slammed the case shut and began to run, holding it against his side. He could hear the two men behind him, crashing through the underbrush and cursing—but he did not take the time to look back. His sense of direction was gone, but he could hear a train in the distance, and he ran toward that sound, hoping to reach the area of the depot before the men could catch him—but he had misjudged, coming into the clearing at a place he had never seen before, the tracks before him, and a slow-moving train gathering speed from the station blocking his way.

There was no choice. The men were coming closer, breaking into the clearing behind him. He ran toward the train, trying to match its speed, but failing—there was an open rail car doorway ahead—but the train was moving too fast. Too—

"Get him! Goddamn it, don't let him get away!" He heard the shout from behind him, the anger. He threw his shoes and the portmanteau in through the open doorway of the car, seeing the portmanteau open and his possessions spill out over the dirty flooring, his shoes bounce off the far wall of the car. He pushed as much speed from his legs as he could, demanding even more, feeling sharp rocks and bits of glass cut into his bare feet. He grabbed for the edge of the doorway, almost catching hold—if he lost his hold, or was unable to swing himself on board, he knew he would end up under the wheels of the train.

But he was dead to stay here anyway.

He grabbed for the edge of the doorway again, feeling his hands close over the wood and metal, feeling the power and momentum of the train jerk at his body as he finally caught hold. He swung himself forward, grabbing for the bottom of the doorway with his feet—for a moment, he lost his footing, hanging in mid-air, his hands slipping—then he was inside, landing with a hard jolt on his side on the wooden flooring.

He lay there for a moment, his heart pounding, the sound of the train loud in his ears. He forced himself to breathe, to think, to know that he was safe; then he moved to look out the open doorway of the swaying freight car, seeing the two men left far behind him now as the train gathered speed moving into the pines.

After a moment, he moved to sit with his back against the inside wall of the car, closing his eyes, and leaning his head back—for a while he could think of nothing more than that he was alive.

It was not until later that he realized what little money he had possessed in the world was now gone.

JANSON WAS sore and bruised by the time he woke on the hard floor of the rail car the next morning. It was not even daylight yet, and the car seemed damp and cold and lonely around him as he sat up in the darkness, trying to pull his coat closer about himself, seeking warmth he knew was not there. He had never been so cold or so hungry before in all his life, or so stiff and sore—but he knew he was lucky to even be alive this morning, lucky to have survived the day he had just seen.

He moved back out of the chill air that washed over him from the open doorway of the car, and sat cross-legged against a wall, closing his eyes against the darkness. The constant rocking and swaying motion of the train only increased the nausea that was already inside of him from his gnawing and empty stomach—he was so tired, having slept so little in the hours he had spent on the hard floor during the night. He had no idea where he was now, no idea in what direction the train was traveling in anymore without the sun or stars to use as a guide.

As light finally came, he moved to look out the open doorway of the car, finding the land the train was traveling through to seem strange and flat to his eyes already longing for sight of the hilly red land of Eason County. There were wide expanses of winter-barren fields, broken by woods, houses, towns, and settlements, but it all seemed strange and new and unknown to him. He wondered what he would do now, with the little money that he had had now gone. He could not ride the rails forever, living like the tramps and hobos, hopping boxcars from town to town, begging, stealing, barely even getting by. He had to find a place to start, work he could do to earn money, a place to sleep, food to eat—and, at the moment, food seemed of the most importance. It had been more than a day now since he had last eaten, and he knew now as he sat staring out the open doorway, his arms folded over his empty, complaining stomach, that he had never been so hungry before in all his life.

Soon the train began to slow, coming into the outskirts of a small town. There were neat rows of white houses alongside the tracks, stretching for streets away through a village, the large, brick cotton mill at its center belching lint and smoke through the quiet town. Even though this land was much flatter, it reminded him too much of Pine, too much of the Easons' cotton mill and the village, and memories came flooding back over him, renewing the hatred, and the determination—he would go back. The Easons had not beaten him yet, would never beat him. He would go back.

The train began to slow even further, drawing nearer to the depot—he would stay here for only a few days, find work that could give him food and a place to sleep, maybe even a little money. Then he would move on to some place less like Pine, some place that would bring fewer memories of a home he could no longer touch. Only a few days—

The train slowly came to a standstill at the depot, then rolled forward before finally stopping with a shudder alongside the platform. Janson moved back into the darkness within the car, not wanting to risk being seen before he could have the chance to leave the train. He gathered together his shoes and the portmanteau, then moved toward the doorway to risk a look out—but he quickly moved back. A man was making his way down the length of the train, checking cars as he went, pulling himself up to look inside each, and then moving on. He held a thick cudgel in one hand, which he pounded into the open palm of the other as he walked—only a few cars, and he would be at the one where Janson crouched hidden in the darkness. Only a few cars—

Janson risked another look out, seeing the man pull himself up into a car only a few distant. He knew he would be certain to be seen once the man reached this car, for there was no place to run, nowhere to hide. In a fair fight he knew he could hold his own with any man—but the cudgel changed the odds, and Janson Sanders would not easily submit to a beating at the hands of any man. He had only his two fists to defend himself with, but, even if there had been a weapon for his own use, he knew they were too close to the station. Others would come, and he would be beaten anyway.

He looked toward the woods that stood at a distance on the other side of the depot. There was a lot of open ground in between, but it was the only hope he had. He waited until the man had pulled himself up into the next car, then jumped down and started to run, holding his shoes and the portmanteau against his side. There was a shout and a curse from behind him, but he did not look back, keeping his eyes on the woods ahead as he ran, determined that he would not fall to that cudgel, determined that he would not—

He broke into the woods, low branches slapping at his face, brambles sticking his feet, vines almost tripping him—but he continued to run, hearing the man come crashing into the underbrush behind him. His side began to hurt with the effort, and he lost his shoes once only to have to stop and grab them up again, thinking that it seemed the man would never give up, that he would never turn back. A branch released too early lashed at his face and almost caught his eye; his left knee began to hurt again as it had not hurt since the night of the fire, threatening to fail him, threatening to end the flight—and then the sounds from behind him stopped.

Janson paused for a moment, listening, making certain, a cautious relief flooding over him as silence filled the woods. He limped over to a tree and dropped his things, leaning against its rough bark to catch his breath. After a time he looked around himself, realizing that he had no idea how to find his way out of the woods, or even how to find his way back to the depot. Then he sighed, picked up his things, chose a direction, and started to walk.

It began to rain long before he found his way clear of the woods, a cold, chilling rain that became a steady, icy downpour by the time he came to a clearing and found himself back at the edge of the town. He was soaked through to the skin, chilled, hungry, and hurting—and he already hated like hell this place he had found himself.

That was the longest day Janson felt that he ever lived through. He tried for hours, through the day and long into the evening, to find work he could do in exchange for a meal and a place he could spend the cold night ahead. He stopped at first one house and then another in the town, offering to chop wood or do chores, to do anything that might need to be done in exchange for food and dry shelter for one night—but at one house he was run off with a shotgun, at another a pan of dirty dishwater was thrown at him, chilling him only further. As afternoon came, he headed out into the countryside, believing that among the farm people he would surely find work, food, and a place he could rest—but dogs were set on him at one place, the door closed in his face at another. Sharecropping families said there was work to be done, but that they had trouble enough to feed their own. The more well-off farmers looked at him suspiciously and ordered him from their land. By evening he was tired and angry. It had been much more than a day now since he had last eaten, and he knew he would have to do something before darkness fell. He could not sleep out in the open tonight; the air felt chill and sharp, and the late afternoon sky looked right for a rare snow. He had no intention of freezing to death during the cold night ahead, not even if that meant having to put himself up in some farmer's barn for the night without the owner's knowing—but he had to do something about food. He would have to eat, and eat soon, and it would not be long before dark—

The house he chose was large and white, with dark-painted shutters on either side of its many windows. Electric light shone from within, and Janson could dimly hear the sounds of a radio playing as he crouched in the darkness, his eyes on the lighted windows. It was a big place, two stories, with six, tall white columns in the front, six matching ones in the rear, and a covered walkway leading to a large kitchen standing separate and apart at the back of the house. It was this latter structure that he watched now, seeing people go earlier to-and-fro over the walkway to the back veranda and in through a door to what had to be the dining room, a heavy-set woman in a dark dress with a bun of hair pinned at the back of her head, hurrying through the chill air with platters and bowls of what had to be steaming food. He could smell meats and gravy as he slipped closer to the house and spied in through the dining room windows—bowls and plates and serving dishes sat on the heavily-varnished table, heaped high with potatoes, beans, and corn. Nearby sat a platter covered with meat, another with what looked to be fresh-baked bread and creamy yellow butter; there was the smell of coffee, the sight of a deep-dish pie for dessert—his mouth was watering, and his empty stomach aching as he moved back into the darkness away from the house and waited for the lights to go out and the place to quiet down. He had come to a decision, a decision he had not wanted to make. Never once in all his life had he ever stolen from anyone—but tonight he would. Tonight he would steal food because he had to eat to live. Tonight he would become a thief.

He waited in the darkness, his resolve becoming easier with the passing minutes and with the smell of good food that came to him from both the house and the separate kitchen. He had known what he would have to do, had passed by the houses of the small farmers, and the shacks and shanties of the sharecroppers, until he had come upon this place. If he had to steal, then he would steal from someone who could afford it, from these rich folks, and not from some poor farmer or sharecropping family. These people, with their motor cars and their fancy clothes, their electric lights and running water and big table covered with fine china and silver—folks like these would hardly miss the little it would take to fill his stomach.

He crouched in the darkness, listening to the faint sound of a radio from somewhere within the house—no one should have so much, he told himself. Not the Easons, not these folks, not anybody. Not when all he wanted was those red acres back in Eason County, the old house, things to be like they used to be. Not when he was hungry and cold and tired and only God knew where.

After a time that seemed to him to stretch into forever, the big house grew still and quiet, and the electric lights downstairs shut out. He continued to watch until the light went out in the kitchen as well, waiting until the dark form of a woman emerged, and then blended into the greater darkness leading away from the house. Then he cautiously crept closer to the kitchen, listening, wary. He knelt for a moment near the back veranda, his eyes moving through the darkness, then he quickly moved up the few steps to the covered walkway and hurried toward the door to the kitchen. He paused for a moment, his hand on the doorknob—then he was suddenly inside with the door closed behind him, safe and alone.

He stood there for a moment, looking around the room in the darkness, thinking again of what it was he was doing—but the smell of food that still hung in the air spurred him to action. He made his way across the bare wood floor, past the kitchen table and some kind of fancy stove, his eyes on an open doorway at the rear of the room—he could see shelves of glass canning jars gleaming in the bare light that filtered through the single window beyond. There were barrels nearby, the smell of apples coming from them, bins of flour and meal, sacks of onions, and strings of dried pepper hanging from the ceiling. He closed the second door behind himself and made his way toward the shelves, kneeling in the darkness and taking up first one of the glass jars, and then another, trying to discern the contents: tomatoes, corn, jelly, what looked to be preserves, sweet pickles, relish, pepper sauce, peaches. His empty stomach aching, he tested the lid on one of the jars, straining against it, and finally feeling it loosen and unscrew in his hands. He stuck his fingers in the jar, smelling the scent of the peaches inside, taking out one of the halves with his fingers and shoving it greedily into his mouth—I'm a thief, he told himself, so hungry that he did not care as he licked the syrup from his fingers. I'll be damned if it's right for any man to go hungry, he thought, and stuck his fingers back into the jar for another peach half. I'll be damned if—

There was a sound from the kitchen, a creaking of the floorboards, and then the door flew inward, rebounding off the wall nearby, and then caught and held in a firm grip. Janson turned quickly, almost dropping the jar in his hands, almost choking on the food in his mouth. There was no way out—he knew he was caught.

"YOU PUT that jar down an' come on out 'a there where I can see you!" the woman demanded, her broad body effectively blocking the doorway into the kitchen, a large, black cast-iron skillet held raised in one hand as if she were intent on using it as a weapon. "Come on out 'a there, I tell you!"

Janson stood slowly, setting the jar of peaches down on the shelf nearby, his eyes moving to the room beyond her—he'd never make it. Even if he could shove her aside and get past her, she would yell and bring help from the big house. He would be caught, treated as a thief, when his only crime had been to—

She cautiously backed away as he moved forward, then again, moving toward the center of the room as they entered the kitchen. One of her hands moved upward, feeling in the air for something and finally hitting it, then pulling on a drawstring to flood the room with electric light from the bare lamp that hung suspended there at the end of a long cord from the ceiling. Janson raised a hand to shield his eyes from the glaring light, and blinked painfully, trying to adjust his sight to the sudden brightness in the room. When he could see again, he looked at the woman—she was tall and sturdily built, with a mass of iron-gray hair drawn into a heavy bun at the back of her neck. Her dress was loose and dark, pinned at the throat by a simple brooch; her coat plain and shapeless, hanging to within inches of the ugly black shoes on her feet. She stared at him as he lowered his hand, something in her eyes clearly saying that she did not trust him any more than the thief she thought him to be.

"I knowed I saw somebody movin' aroun' outside in th' dark," she said, lowering the skillet only slightly. "What you got t' say for yourself, boy? What's your name?—I don't know your face; you ain' from aroun' here."

When Janson did not answer, she raised the skillet again. "Speak up, boy, what's your name?"

"My name's Janson Sanders," he said, raising his chin slightly.

"'Janson Sanders', sayin' it all kind 'a prideful like—ain' nothin' prideful 'bout bein' a thief."

"I ain't no thief."

"Ain' no thief!—when I caught you in th' storeroom myself! It's a good thing I forgot my pocketbook an' had t' come back for it, or you'd 'a likely stole us out 'a house an' home! What you got t' say for yourself, boy, stealin' from good, hones' folks like—"

"Somebody like you'd 'a never missed what it took for me t' eat."

"Somebody like me! It don't matter who you're stealin' from, stealin's still stealin'—an' this place ain' mine; it b'longs t' Mist' Whitley, like most everythin' else aroun' here does. An' you better be glad it was me that caught you, an' not him; he'd 'a been likely as not t' shot you first—why didn't you just knock at th' door an' ask t' be fed if you was hongry?"

"I don't take no charity!"

"Don't take charity!—stealin's better 'n charity t' you, boy? That don't make too much sense!" she said, but Janson did not answer her, angry—he did not know whether more at her, or at himself. "Looks t' me like a strong young man like you'd be workin' for his way, 'stead 'a stealin' what other folks—"

"I tried all day t' find work I could do for food an' a place t' sleep, an' all I got around here was dogs set on me an' guns pulled on me an' I got run off folks land—" The words came out in an angry rush, and he immediately regretted them, seeing the look of pity that came to her face. She lowered the skillet and stared at him, but Janson only returned the look, lifting his chin defiantly.

"Where're you from, boy?" she asked. When he did not answer she raised her voice. "Don't do no good havin' a chip on your shoulder so big that folks can see it a mile away—now, where're you from?"

"Alabama," he answered her shortly.

"Folks ain' always like they ought t' be, are they boy?" she asked him, not seeming to expect a response. After a moment, she sat the skillet down on a nearby table and moved toward the fancy electric icebox that sat in one corner of the kitchen. "Miz' Whitley ain' never turned nobody away from her door hongry yet. You set down an' I'll see what I can fin' t'—"

"I done told you I don't take no charity!"

She turned an angry gaze back on him. "You better jus' decide real quick which is more important t' you, boy, your pride or your empty belly—"

For a moment he almost walked out of the kitchen, for he knew now that she would let him go. Then he heard her words, spoken back over her shoulder as if they were nothing: "Seems t' me like a man'd be a fool t' choose against a full belly, though."

Janson thought for a moment, and then moved to sit down at the kitchen table. When he looked back up at the woman again she smiled and nodded, then turned back toward the electric icebox without another word.

Her name was Mattie Ruth Coates, and she had been on the Whitley place for almost longer than she could remember, she told him a short while later as she sat watching him greedily sop up gravy with half an eaten biscuit. Within an hour Janson found himself accompanying her through the woods to the small house that she and her husband, Titus, lived in on Whitley land. He was offered their barn as shelter for the night, even given one of her hand-pieced quilts to use against the cold, and introduced to a thin, badly balding man—but by then he was too tired to even remember the name. He crawled onto a pile of hay in the barn and pulled the quilt over himself, and was asleep almost before he knew it.

He woke the next morning even before daylight, the air cold and chill around him, the warm quilt a welcome cover against the dampness inside the old barn. He got up and went out into the yard before the structure, wanting to see this place he had found himself, for he had been too tired to remember much of anything he had seen the night before.

The house sitting not far distant was small and unpainted, its rough boards weathered to silver-gray. The yard was bare and simple, swept free of grass and leaves, with rock borders marking where flower beds would bloom again in the spring. There was a well-tended winter garden behind the house, its rows of turnip and mustard greens stretching almost to the woods beyond, and fields of dry cotton plants going off into the distance. Janson looked until he found the well near the back porch of the house, and he drew a bucketful of water, then returned to the barn to bathe there in the chill air as best he could, using the frigid water, and a torn pair of underdrawers from his portmanteau as a wash cloth. He dressed and then rinsed out the clothes he had worn and slept in for the past two days, and slung them over a stall in the barn, to dry, possibly even to freeze, in the frigid air; then he went outside.

By the time the family was about, he had swept out the yard and begun to clean out the barn as repayment for the food he had been given and the shelter he had enjoyed for the night—as he had told the woman, he accepted no charity. He was served breakfast at the table just as if he were kin, and later, as Mattie Ruth and Titus Coates were off doing whatever work that rich folks like the Whitleys could find for them to do, he busied his hands again—chopping wood and stacking it near the back wall of the kitchen to dry; repairing a broken hinge on the barn door, and several shutters on the house; and was just completing the work on several chairs he had found on the back porch in various stages of being re-bottomed when Mattie Ruth Coates came home from the big house that afternoon to fix her husband's supper before returning to prepare her employer's meal.

When she saw all the work that had been done, she shook her head with amazement and looked up at him. "Lord, boy, your hands ain' been still a minute, have they?" she said, settling herself in one of the newly re-bottomed chairs to test it. "There ain' no reason somebody like you ought t' have t' steal t' eat, not hard as you work."

Janson looked at her, but did not respond, knowing there was reason in life for many things.

After a moment he said: "I was wonderin' if I could stay th' night in your barn again. I'll be gone by first light t'morrow—"

"You're welcome t' stay long as you want. I kind 'a hate t' see you go. It's nice havin' a young man aroun' th' place again, after both our own boys bein' killed in th' War—you goin' back home t' Alabama?"

"There ain't no reason for me t' go back. My folks're dead, an' my land's gone. I guess I'll just be movin' on; I got t' find work—"

"Well, if it's work you're lookin' for, you ought t' go talk t' Mist' Whitley. He wouldn't take you on t' crop, since you ain' got no family t' work as well, but he's always takin' on men for wages, farmhands an' th' like. If you want, my Titus'll walk up there with you after supper t'night—"

Janson looked at her for a moment, thinking—one place was as good as any other, he supposed, and a rich man like Whitley might even pay better than most. Besides, he still did not have any money, and he knew he would have to eat. He had already failed miserably at being a thief once; he did not want to be reduced to trying it again.

"I'll talk t' Whitley," he told her after a time, telling himself that it would not be for long. Once he had some money, he could move on to some other place. All he needed now was the money.

AS JANSON started toward the big house that evening, he found himself wondering at the older man who walked at his side. Titus Coates had spoken hardly a word to him since they had met the night before, just the barest "Mornin'—" or "Evenin'—" as they had passed, but there was something about the man Janson found he instinctively respected, something he liked and trusted, and he found himself wanting Titus Coates' respect as well. Titus would have to know that he had been found stealing, for his wife would have told him that—but there was nothing in the older man's manner to show he even thought of it as they left the bare-swept yard that evening and started up the road toward the big house.

"Th' folks'll be finished with supper by now," Titus said, staring at the point where the red clay road twisted darkly between winter-dead cotton fields ahead. "Mist' William'll say he's busy when we ask, but he'll talk t' us. He let a man go jus' th' other day an' he'll be needin' somebody."

"What's he like t' work for?" Janson asked.

"Well—" Titus fell silent for a moment. "He kin be a hard man t' work for, but he'll be right fair with you if you're doin' your job like you're suppose t' be doin' it. He'll pay you jus' like he says he'll pay you, an' he'll 'spect t' get his money's worth out 'a you in turn. Keeps my missus up there 'til all hours, cookin' an' cleanin' an' seein' after th' family; an' he keeps me runnin' here an' yonder, goin' int' town or all th' way up t' Buntain, an' even t' Columbus some, totin' packages for Miz' Whitley when she goes shoppin', or keepin' an eye on them two little gals when they're 'roun'; doin' chores an' keepin' th' cars runnin' an' fixin' things 'roun' here—he'll keep you busy, but you know how rich folks are—"

Yeah, I know—Janson thought, but said nothing.

"Now, Miz' Whitley, she's a gentle-like lady, givin' t' jus' 'bout everybody. She'd give th' last bite 'a food off th' table an' th' clothes right off her back t' somebody needin' 'em, if Mist' William 'd let her. Folks'll take 'vantage 'a that sometime, as folks'll do—'specially them four young'ns 'a hers. There ain' a one of 'em got a mind t' listen t' nobody, 'cept maybe Mist' Stan, 'a course, th' youngest. Th' two oldes' boys, Mist' Bill Whitley an' Mist' Alfred, now they do pretty much whatever it is they take int' their minds 'a doin', an' there ain' nobody that kin stop 'em—it comes from bein' spoil't all their lives, I'd say, always gettin' what they want. A good switchin' like th' ones I use t' give my boys'd done 'em both a heap 'a good a few years back. They both jus' like their daddy anyway, stubborn an' set in their ways, with tempers like shouldn't no man have; ain' scared 'a God Almighty or nobody else, I'd say—it's th' Whitley in 'em, same as in their daddy an' in his daddy 'afore him. Mist' Alfred's still young, but it's that Bill Whitley I sometime wonder about—"

For a moment Titus fell silent, and Janson glanced over at him. There was a peculiar look on the old man's face even in the darkness, and something of it stayed there even as he shook his head and continued.

"There ain' much I'd put past that Bill Whitley, boy," he said. "You jus' stay clear 'a him whenever you can. That one loves money, maybe even better'n his daddy does, an' he likes t' boss folks 'roun', tell 'em what t' do, even when he ain' got no business doin' it. Got a streak in him that—well—" Again he fell silent, and Janson looked at him. There was a sigh from the darkness, and the old man shook his head again. "Mist' Alfred, now that one's only a boy, even if he does think hisself full-growed a man. 'Bout your age, thinks he's real sharp with th' town girls, always dresses hisself up like a real dandy, an' he's got th' one reddest head 'a hair you ever did see in your life, an' a temper t' match it. Fancies all th' news 'a them gangsters on th' radio—that ain' good for a body, I'd say, listin' t' all that talk 'bout them crooks an' crim'nals bootleggin' liquor an' totin' guns an' sech way up North. You don't hear 'bout sech goin's on down here in Georgia where decent folks live, now, do you?"

His words paused for a moment, as if he expected Janson to respond, but Janson could think of nothing to say. He did not know anything about gangsters, or about criminals bootlegging liquor up North, and had heard a radio only once or twice in his life in the country stores back home. He knew that moonshiners and bootleggers operated stills in the backwoods in many areas; he and his father had even happened on a bootlegging operation once while hunting, and he had long ago been initiated to corn liquor himself—but he knew very little of the world the old man was talking about, of speakeasies and gangsters and the Prohibition agents everyone called "revenuers." He had not been raised in a world of radios, or even of electric lights and running water and telephones, and he realized for the first time in his life how very different the world was becoming now, a world where someone in Georgia could know what was going on up North, or anywhere else in the world, just by turning a radio dial.

After a moment he realized that Titus was waiting for a response, but he could still think of nothing to say. He glanced over at the old man, saying the first thing that came to his mind. "You said th' youngest boy ain't too much like th' other two."

"No, Mist' Stan ain' too much like nobody else in th' family, 'cept maybe he looks a good bit like his mama," Titus answered, seeming to be satisfied. "He favors Mist' Bill, too—but I'd say ways makes lots 'a difference in folks, an' Mist' Stan's shore different from th' rest 'a them young'ns in his ways. He's quiet an' all 'til he gets t' know you, but then he kin talk your arm right off, wantin' t' know th' whys and what-fors for everythin'—kin drive a body t' distraction sometime, but he's a good boy. Always got his nose in some book; don't never cause no trouble t' nobody. I doubt he's ever give his mama cause for one gray hair in all his life—not like them other two boys an' Miss Elise. With them three, it's a miracle Miz' Whitley ain' done white haired a'ready. An' Miss Elise ought t' know better, but she's spoil't an' all, like th' only'st girl's libles t' be in any family. She's pretty as a picture, with red-gold hair an' pretty blue eyes—but she's a Whitley through and through, stubborn like Mist' William, an' spoil't; an' that Phyllis Ann Bennett don't help matters none. She's always fillin' Miss Elise's head with all kinds 'a nonsense since she come back from spendin' a couple weeks in New York City with some cousin 'a hers back summer 'fore last. She even got Miss Elise t' bob her hair off—Lor', but Mist' William almost took th' roof off th' place over that!" The old man sighed and shook his head. "That Phyllis Ann ain' no kind 'a girl for Miss Elise t' be runnin' 'roun' with, her wearin' her skirts up t' her knees an' rollin' her stockin's down t' where anybody kin see th' tops of 'em, smokin' right in front 'a grown folks. I don't think her folks say anythin' t' her about her ways anymore; I don't guess they can—"

Again he fell silent as they walked along, and Janson found himself shaking his own head this time, imagining for a moment how William Whitley must have felt the day his daughter had come home looking like some city flapper, with her hair bobbed off and her skirts too short—he could almost feel sorry for the man, rich or not.

"Mist' William ain' too happy with Miss Elise bein' friends with that Phyllis Ann no more, but they ain' too much even him kin do about it. Them two little gals 's thick as thieves, an' they have been since they was jus' babies. After Miss Elise went an' bobbed her hair off, he packed her up an' sent her off t' some girls' school up in Atlanta where Miz' Whitley went when she was a girl, but th' next thing you knowed that Phyllis Ann was goin' too—not even Mist' William kin find a way 'roun' that daughter 'a his when her mind's sot on somethin'—" he said as they rounded a bend in the red clay road and came to within sight of the big house at a distance beyond the magnolias and the oaks that stood in the wide front yard. "I doubt if Miz' Whitley's had even one minute's peace in her mind since Miss Elise's been gone off up there with that little Bennett gal, worryin' about her even more'n when she was here. They ain' no tellin' what them two little gals 's liables t' get int' off up there on they own—" he said. "Ain' no tellin'—" And then he fell silent as they approached the house.

Janson stared up at the lighted windows before him, thinking of rich folks and their ways—what the world needed even less of, he told himself, was more fancied-up, bobbed-haired women, Miss Elise Whitley and her friend Phyllis Ann Bennett included.

He and Titus passed through the yard, trodding over the now winter-brown grass, and, as Janson stared down at it, he thought again of how much more pleasing to the eye the yards of the regular country-folk seemed: hard-packed clay swept free of grass and weeds, with uneven borders of rocks marking where the many flower beds would stand again in the spring and summer. There was absolutely no sensible reason, he told himself, for a man to sow grass in his yard, only to have to tend and cut it in the warm months—it could not be sold or eaten or made into clothes; all it could do was create more work for a man who had work enough already. It just did not make sense.

As they neared the house, Titus led him around toward the rear of the structure, and Janson went, though he felt his pride ruffle—for the first time in his life he realized there were front doors in this world he could not go to, houses he would not be able to enter as a man; that this was one of them, one of many.

The rear door of the house swung inward as they stepped up onto the back veranda, Mattie Ruth's ample form framed in the open doorway by the light falling from the wide hall behind her. "I seen you comin' from th' front parlor while I was straightenin' up," she said and stepped back to let them enter. "Everybody's done finished eatin' now; Mist' William's in th' library—"

Janson followed Titus in through the doorway, blinking to adjust his eyes to the brightness of the glaring electric light there in the hall. Very few times in his life had he ever been in houses lighted by electricity, and he did not like it, preferring by far the more-familiar muted glow of kerosene lamps, or even simple firelight, to the white, glaring brightness electricity created.

Once he could see better, he stared around himself with surprise at this place before him, from the waxed wooden flooring, to the walls papered with floral designs, to the heavily lacquered hall table against one wall, and the richly brocaded settee tucked in just opposite beneath where the staircase rose toward the back of the house and the floor above. At the far end of the wide hall stood double doors that opened out onto the front veranda, and, as Janson stared toward them, he noticed for the first time the transom of colored glass just above, as well as the matching glass panels on either side of the wide double doors, all inset with designs of blue and gold, and the frosted glass inserts in the doors themselves etched, he could tell even at that distance, with flower designs.

There were two identical crystal chandeliers of electric lights hanging from the carved ceiling at equal distances from the front and rear doors, and many doors opening off each side of the hallway, as well as a second, narrower hallway breaking off to one side of the house—Janson had never before in his life been in such a house as this, had never even believed that people could live in such a place. He stood just where he was, his eyes moving to the heavily framed paintings on the walls, the gilt-edged mirrors, and, at last, to the delicate what-nots of crystal and porcelain that sat on the hall table. He was almost afraid to move, afraid that he might break or damage something here in this fancy room.

"Y'all wait right here. I'll tell Mist' Whitley you're wantin' t' talk t' him," Mattie Ruth said, then moved down the hallway, stopping at a door to the right and tapping lightly. A gruff voice answered from inside, the words unintelligible, and she opened the door and entered the room, closing the door again quietly behind herself.

Janson followed Titus toward the center of the hallway, still amazed that people lived in such a place. He could hear a radio playing from one of the rooms at the front of the house, jazz music from an orchestra, finally interrupted by an announcer's voice, and, as he listened, he marveled again that he was hearing something from someplace far off, maybe even something from as far off as cities or even states away. After a moment, a young man of about his own age walked out the doorway to the right of the hall, stopped and stared at them for a moment, then walked toward where they stood near the center of the hallway.

Alfred Whitley looked at them for a long moment, his blue eyes moving from Titus, to Janson, and then back again, and Janson knew without having to be told who he was—the red hair and the fancy clothes left little doubt in his mind. "Titus, what are you doing here?" Alfred Whitley asked, his eyes settling on the older man.

"I come t' see 'bout findin' work for this young man here with Mist' William—Mist' Alfred, this's Janson Sanders: Janson, boy, this here's Mist' Alfred Whitley—"

Janson nodded his head, but the young man only stared at him in response. "Well, you've chosen a bad time. You'll have to come back tomorrow," the boy said, his voice taking on an authoritative tone as his eyes moved back to Titus. "My father is busy, and I just don't—"

"Turn that confounded radio down like I told you to an hour ago!" A tall, stoutly-built man in his sixties stood now in the open doorway to the library, Mattie Ruth just behind him. His mouth was set in an aggravated line, a disapproving look on his face—a look Janson sensed was often there. Mr. William Whitley looked from his son, to Janson, and then to Titus, making a point of taking his watch from his vest pocket and checking the time, as if to tell them all there were much more important things he should be doing. Alfred stared at his father for a moment, then, with a clear look of anger on his face, he retreated to the parlor without another word. After a moment the music from the radio died away.

"Titus, man, what in the name of God do you want at this time of night?" William Whitley demanded, clear annoyance in his voice and manner as he replaced the watch in his vest pocket and stared at the two men before him, an unlit cigar held securely between the index and middle fingers of one hand. "Well, speak up man!"

"Mist' Whitley, this here's Janson Sanders. He's needin' work, an' I was wonderin' if you might be needin' a extra hand 'bout now?"

Whitley stared at him for a moment longer, then turned his gaze on Janson, placing the unlit cigar in his mouth and clenching it firmly between his teeth. Janson felt as if he were being summed up with that look, assessed, and he did not like it—damn rich folks, he told himself, returning the stare.

After a moment, Whitley turned and walked through the door and back into the library, speaking back over his shoulder. "Make it quick, boy. I've got work to do—"

Janson waited for a moment, and then followed Titus into the library. He only hoped to hell he was not making the worst mistake of his life.

WILLIAM WHITLEY sat down at the cluttered rolltop desk in one corner of the library, shifting papers and a ledger that sat on the desktop before him, then turning back to the two men who stood near by—they would not be seated unless he told them to, and he would not tell them. He looked instead at the tall young man who stood at Titus Coates' side, impressed somewhat by what he saw. The boy was lean, but seemed powerfully built, without even a spare ounce of flesh on him. He looked as if he were accustomed to hard work, from the calloused hands, to the faded and patched overalls, to the thin but muscular frame that showed from beneath the old and tattered coat—but he met William's eyes with a directness that was unsettling.

William stared at him, his stare being met in return from pale green eyes that seemed oddly out of place in the dark face. He chewed down on his cigar, sensing a spirit of pride and dignity in the boy that he did not like—proud, independent men had a tendency to be trouble, and trouble was something that William would have none of.

He looked at Titus, deliberately speaking to him as if the younger man were not even in the room. "He sure is dark," he remarked, glancing again at the boy. "Looks like a Gypsy. I don't hire Gypsies—"

"I'm half Cherokee," the boy responded, just as if he had been addressed. "My ma was Indian, my pa white—I ain't no Gypsy." Then he fell silent again, continuing to meet William's gaze through the strange green eyes.

The boy doesn't know his place—William thought, staring at him. "Are you trying to get smart with me, boy?"

"No, sir."

"And you better not, boy." William continued to stare at him, unsure as to how to deal with someone such as this. Pride had no place in such a person. There was no reason for pride in faded overalls, sunburned skin, and calloused hands, no reason for pride in poverty—only in money and power and family name was there any reason for pride. This man had none of that, and yet there was as much pride in him as in the wealthiest men in Endicott County, of which William knew himself to be one—he owned more land, more property, worked more sharecroppers, produced more cotton; the Whitleys had been in Endicott County for generations, had carved this place out of the virgin forests, had held onto it through war and Yankees and carpetbaggers. The Whitley name meant something in this and the surrounding counties, and few men possessed such power, such prestige, as did William Whitley—Hiram Cooper did, perhaps Ethan Bennett, but few others.

William stared at the young man before him. "You're not from anywhere around here. I know everybody in this County."

"I'm from Alabama, Eason County—"

"That's a long way off—you in some kind of trouble, boy? Running from the law or something?" He peered closely at the boy; it paid to be careful.

"I ain't in no trouble. I just moved on."

"You're just passing through, then?"

"I aim t' stay, if I can find work."

"Do you have a family? A wife to help you crop, children you can put to work in the next couple of years—I expect my sharecroppers to have their children in the fields soon as they're old enough, boy, and I expect a good return for my half of the crop every year."

"I ain't married, but I been farmin' all my life. I can do most any kind 'a work around here that needs doin'."

William leaned back in his chair, considering. He could make use of the boy. It seemed as if he were strong and healthy and accustomed to hard work, and, as William questioned him further, he found him to be knowledgeable about cotton farming and the chores that had to be done about a place—but that air of pride bothered him.

William stared at him, making a decision. He had run a man off only a few days before, having caught him stealing, and had also had to deal rather strongly with several others. He needed a good man right now, a dependable farmhand; there were two new fields to clear, land to break up for cotton planting in a few months—and this boy could be handled, William told himself. There was not a man alive that could not be handled.

"Boy, I don't take no back talk and no trouble out of nobody—you get that through your head right now. I pay my hands good wages, and I expect good work out of them in return. You do what you're told to do, and you do it with no sass; and you remember your place and show respect where it's due—you got that, boy?" he asked, watching the man closely.

"Yes, sir, I got it—"

"All right, boy, you be out at the barn at sunup tomorrow morning and I'll give you a chance. I pay wages every other Saturday at quitting time—you got a place to live yet?"

The man shook his head.

"Well, there's a good room off the barn where you can sleep. It's got a cot and a wood stove and some furniture in it—the rent'll come out of your wages before you get them, so will the money for the store charge. I run accounts at the store for my people—I don't cotton to people who work for me doing their buying in town—" He stared at the man for a moment, seeing that he understood. "I'm good to my people, boy, and I expect them to show their appreciation in return—"

The man only stared, increasing William's irritation.

"I'm going to give you a chance, boy, but you give me one reason and you'll be sorry you ever showed your face around here, you got that?"

"Yes, sir, I got it—" the man answered. "I got it—"

William stared as the door closed behind the two men a few minutes later, satisfied that the boy understood what was expected from him. He turned and looked at the open ledger on the rolltop before him, then reached to shut it, needing a smoke very badly. He got up and crossed the room, going past the deep shelves of books that lined the walls, out into the hallway, and then through and out onto the front veranda of his home.

He lit his cigar and drew in on it heavily in the chill night air, watching the shadowy forms of the two men as they made their way down the long drive and toward the dark clay road that led away from the house. He was pleased with the decision he had made to hire the boy, though still disquieted by the look of pride and dignity that had been so apparent on the dark face. Proud men so often proved to be trouble—but William Whitley knew how to deal with trouble. He made sure it could never bother anyone again.

TITUS WAS quiet as they left the big house, Mattie Ruth having quickly told them goodbye at the back door, saying she would be home as soon as her work was finished. Now there was nothing but silence as they walked along, broken only by the occasional sound of their feet shifting in loose dirt and rocks alongside the hard-packed clay road, or the night sounds from the dead cotton fields, and then the woods, as they drew near, and Janson found that he was glad for the quiet.

He did not like William Whitley, of that much he was already certain. He did not like the man, or anything there was about him—but Whitley was a rich man, and all rich folks were alike, Janson told himself. Eason or Whitley, it did not much matter. They were all the same.

There was a sound from the large house behind them, a door opening and closing, and Janson paused for a moment and looked back just before the curve of the road could cut off sight of the house. Whitley stood on the front veranda of his home now, a bulky shape framed by the light of one of the parlor windows. There was a brief flame lighting his features for a moment as he lit his cigar, then he walked to the edge of the veranda, folding his hands behind his large buttocks for a moment and drawing in heavily on the cigar, the red glow of its ash dimly visible for a moment even over the distance.

Janson stood for a moment and watched him, thinking of the reasons he had to stay here, to work, to earn and save money—thinking of that white house on those red acres back home; of a tall, brown-haired man and a small, gentle woman he could never fail—and thinking of people like the Easons and the Whitleys, and somehow damning them all to hell somewhere in the back of his mind.

He knelt in the red dirt of the road and unlaced and removed his shoes, gathering them into one hand, and then straightening to meet Titus Coates's eyes. Neither man spoke. They just turned and started down the red clay road again, away from the brightly lighted house behind them, and into the chilly darkness of the January night.

# 4

Elise Whitley was in trouble. Again. Not that she was in trouble alone, for she rarely if ever was. Phyllis Ann Bennett, sitting at her side, seeming to try to appear mature and aloof and above the current situation, was in trouble just as deeply as she.

Eva Perry sat behind the wide expanse of her desk in the principal's office of the girl's school, considering the two girls over the tops of her eyeglasses. She rubbed her temples, trying to calm the pounding inside her head. She was in a horrid mood, having been awakened in the middle of the night only to be told these two were in trouble again. It had to be at least 11:30 P.M., if not even later, and she knew that she looked a fright. The heavy cotton nightgown she wore had to be her oldest, buttoned to the throat and wrists and covered by her most shapeless wrap; her long hair was twisted up in rag rollers, and there was not a touch of powder or rouge on her face—but at the moment she did not care. Her head hurt—but, then again, her head always seemed to hurt where these two were concerned. They were constantly in trouble: this time they had been brought back to the school by the police long after school curfew had passed, having been involved in a minor automobile accident while out driving with a number of boys from town; the previous week there had been a food fight in the dining hall, started by these two; less than a month before, a nighttime raid on the instructors' rooms, stealing undergarments and other unmentionables, only to later strew them out over the campus grounds; a few days before that an improper novel had been found in their possession, a novel so shocking the principal herself had seen to its destruction after severely lecturing both girls—always these two.

They were both sixteen now and ought to know better, both from good, old-Georgia families, families that had money and social standing—and both were spoiled, pampered, and petted, and a burden that had been gladly placed on Miss Perry's narrow shoulders by their long-exasperated families.

She stared at the two girls over the tops of her eyeglasses for a moment before pushing them up to the proper position on the bridge of her nose, then laced her fingers together and placed them on the desktop before her, leaning forward to look first at one girl, and then at the other, her eyes finally coming to rest on the girl to the right.

"Well, Miss Whitley, do you have something to say for yourself this time?" she asked, and watched as the girl glanced quickly over at her friend.

Elise Whitley was dressed in a straight, rather shapelessly-cut coat of the current fashion, over a low-waisted dress of a pale blue shade that was almost the same color as her eyes. Her hair was cut short, curling in at her cheeks below the dark cloche hat she wore, and was a rich, red-gold color that Eva had rarely seen before in her life. Her hands were quiet, folded tightly over the small purse in her lap; her rouge and lipstick a bit too obvious for a girl her age—but, then again, all the girls at the school were wearing it that way these days. She was not really a bad girl, Eva thought as she considered her across the desktop—if she could only manage to keep herself out of trouble for even a few days. If only—

"Well?" Eva prompted again, waiting for a response.

Elise Whitley looked quickly at her friend again, then back to the principal. "Well, we just—"

"Now, Miss Perry—" Phyllis Ann interrupted, a deliberate tone in her voice as if she were addressing a particularly slow child—a device Phyllis Ann employed quite often, and one which Eva heartily detested. "We were only—"

"Be quiet, Miss Bennett!" the principal snapped, feeling a muscle clench tightly in her jaw. She did not like Phyllis Ann Bennett, in fact, could find nothing even remotely likeable within the girl. Phyllis Ann was spoiled, self-serving, selfish, and vain, with a temper that was often unpredictable, and a manner of speech and behavior that constantly grated on Eva's nerves—"fast," Eva thought, not for the first time, for there was no other word she could find to describe the girl.

Phyllis Ann sat back in her chair, a look of anger in her dark eyes as they met those of the principal. Her legs were crossed before her at the knees, her kneecaps visible below the hem of her skirt, as well as the tops of the flesh-pink, rolled stockings she wore. She loudly popped the gum in her mouth and bobbed one foot up and down impatiently, but did not speak again—fast, the principal thought again. The girl had been behind almost all the trouble at the school since she had first arrived here months before—she cut classes; smoked cigarettes, both in her dormitory room and in the girls' lavatory; spread gossip, often outright lies, about the other girls, freely and without conscience; wore her skirts indecently short; and ran around with all sorts of young men. There were even rumors about the campus that she had been seen leaving a speakeasy late one Saturday night, though Eva could hardly believe that, even of Phyllis Ann.

It seemed all the girls were changing these days, shortening their skirts and bobbing their hair, wearing makeup, and wishing more than anything else they were Zelda Fitzgerald or Clara Bow, and many of those changes Eva could see little harm in. But Phyllis Ann Bennett was another matter altogether. Whatever she was involved in, Elise Whitley and many of the other girls at the school soon followed suit. She was a bad influence, trouble as the principal had never thought to have at her school, with her indecently short skirts, her cigarette smoking, and loose ways—fast, Eva thought again. She even doubted the girl was still a virgin, though she would never dare utter such a thought aloud.

"I was addressing Miss Whitley, Miss Bennett. I will get to you in a moment," the principal said, watching as the girl loudly popped the gum again and then tilted her chin into the air as if she considered herself to have been insulted. "You were about to explain why you were out riding in a motor car with a number of young men, when you were supposed to be in your dormitory here after curfew?" Eva prompted again, looking at Elise.

The girl glanced again quickly to her friend—for all the world, Eva could not understand how the two had ever become friends in the first place, much less how the friendship had endured over all the years she had been told it had existed. For all their pretensions, they were very different, and, although spoiled and often annoying, Elise Whitley could at times be a likeable girl—but she was just that: a girl trying very hard to be a woman, considering herself very mature and grownup and very worldly, but still nothing more than a child, not even yet knowing what it was to be an adult. Eva doubted if Elise had ever faced one hard truth in all her life, reared in the ivory tower of the Whitley name as she had been, and that bobbing her hair and shortening her skirts had probably been the worst act of defiance she could ever dream up—the girl had a lot of growing up to do if she were ever to be the woman she already considered herself to be, Eva thought; painful growing up if she did not end the friendship with Phyllis Ann Bennett, for it was the principal's considered experience that girls such as Miss Bennett always came to no good ends, and that they often took everyone else they knew down along with them.

"We went for a drive with some boys who just got a new car. I guess we forgot the time—" Elise Whitley said after a moment.

"You forgot the time—that is until these boys you went riding with ran this new car of theirs into an electric pole, and the police brought you back to the school because these boys had been drinking—" Eva looked at her for a long moment. "Do you realize how fortunate you are that those officers did not take you to jail right along with the boys you were with?" she asked, receiving only silence in response to her question, and thus getting the answer she had expected. She sighed and shook her head. "You're both sixteen now. You should be old enough to realize the dangers a young lady can find herself in when she's off alone in a motor car with a strange young man—especially if liquor is involved—"

"But we weren't drinking," Phyllis Ann interrupted. "And we weren't alone. There were two of us, and three of them; and they weren't strangers—"

"That very well might be the case, but we have a curfew here for a reason, Miss Bennett. A young lady just does not go off to all times of the night with—" But she let her words trail off, realizing they were being ignored by both girls. "Your parents have entrusted your well-being to us while you are at this school," she said more sternly. "For the time you are here, you will obey our rules, whether you see a need for them or not—am I understood?" She looked directly at Phyllis Ann, but Elise was the first to respond.

"Yes, ma'am—"

"Yes, of course," Phyllis Ann said, but her face spoke more truth than did her words—she would continue to do whatever it pleased her to do, just as she had always done.

Eva leaned forward, considering both girls again as she rested her arms on the desktop before her. "Your parents will be informed of your little misdeed tonight, and they will also be informed of this one fact, that if you are again found in one more infraction of our rules, one more food fight in the dining hall, or being caught out of the dormitory after curfew for any reason, or anything else along that vein, you will be summarily expelled from this institution—am I understood?"

The two girls looked quickly at each other, and then back to the principal—she was understood.

"For the next two weeks you will both remain in your room in the dormitory at all times when you are not in class. You will take your meals there, study there; there will be no recreation, and no radio—"

"You can't—" Phyllis Ann broke in, leaning forward.

"Young lady, you are in enough trouble as it is. I suggest that you remain silent—"

Phyllis Ann did not respond, but there was clear anger in her eyes as the principal sat back to consider both girls one last time. "I trust this will be the last time I will see either of you in this office again—" she said, dismissing them both—but, even as she watched the door close behind the two girls, she knew it would only be a matter of time before they would be back, and only a matter of time before they would again be a problem on someone else's hands other than her own. They never seemed to learn.

BY THE end of the first day, Phyllis Ann was already bored with the restrictions placed on them. By the end of the third, she was slipping out of their room to visit other girls on their floor, and by the end of the week she was leaving the dormitory itself. Elise envied her friend's daring, but she lacked the nerve to make such forays herself, staying alone in their room, worrying what excuses she could make should anyone check to discover that Phyllis Ann was not there.

But no one checked. The days passed and she was left alone, often for hours at a time, wondering where Phyllis Ann was, and worrying that Miss Perry or one of the instructors might come by to bring the wrath of heaven down on them both.

On the second Saturday of their punishment, Phyllis Ann was gone most all day, leaving Elise's nerves in a raw state by the time evening came. She had read until she finished the novel she had been reading, but lacked the concentration to begin another, had tried to write home—but her father was angry with her over Miss Perry's call, and her mother was worried she might get herself hurt or into trouble on such outings, or expelled if she were ever caught again, and her brothers would never write back. Out of sheer boredom she took up her knitting and tried to occupy her mind and not watch the clock on the table below the windows—where was Phyllis Ann? She'd get them both expelled, slipping out like this and asking Elise to cover for her. Elise had no intention of being sent home, expelled from school, only to have to face her father's anger; and the reception Phyllis Ann would receive at home would be even so much worse—no, thank you very much.

She swore under her breath as she dropped a stitch in the knitting, and then went back to pick it up again—she hated to knit, just as she hated to sew or to do most of the other domestic chores her mother had expected her to learn by the time she had entered her teens. She hated needlepoint and sewing, knitting, crocheting, and was notoriously bad at doing anything that did not strike her fancy, having long ago discovered that to avoid doing anything one did not want to do, one had often only to appear to be very bad at doing it.

She glanced up at the clock, listening for the sound of footsteps in the hall—Phyllis Ann, one of the other girls, the principal, one of the instructors. Phyllis Ann knew what would happen to them if she were caught out of their room—to both of them, for it would be clear that Elise was covering for her—but Phyllis Ann had a tendency to do whatever it was she wanted to do, no matter the consequences to herself or to anyone else. She had tried for half an hour to talk Elise into slipping out with her, and now Elise wished that she had gone—if she were going to be expelled, at least she could have had some fun beforehand.

She dropped another stitch, cursed again, more loudly and profanely this time, then flung the yarn and needles across the room, missing Phyllis Ann by only a bare few inches as she slipped in the door and closed it again quietly behind herself, one arm holding something hidden behind her back.

"Having a tantrum, are we?" Phyllis Ann asked, a vicious smile on her face as she came farther into the room.

"Yes, we are," Elise snapped, staring at her.

"My, my—it must come from being locked away here all day long, all by yourself—"

"Where have you been?" Elise was in no mood for the game—Phyllis Ann had gotten her into this in the first place; it had been her idea to go out riding with the boys, her idea to stay out as late as they had stayed out. "I've been sitting here having seizures every time there was a sound in the hallway, afraid old lady Perry would come by to make sure we were both here. I don't know what I'd have said if she had checked and found out you were gone—"

"You'd have thought of a convincing lie."

"Or maybe I'd have told her the truth, that you slipped out because you were bored out of your mind with staring at the four walls?"

"Of course not. You know you'd never squeal on me. You'd have thought up some excuse."

The conviction in her voice and in her expression irritated Elise all the more. "Well?" she asked after a moment, a little too sharply.

"Well, what?"

"Well, where have you been?"

"Into town. I went shopping—couldn't find a thing to buy—"

"That's fortunate, or how would you have explained a new dress in the chiffonier with supposedly no way you could have bought it?"

"We'd have thought of something." Phyllis Ann smiled.

Elise ignored the remark. "Where else did you go? What is it you're hiding behind your back?"

The other girl grinned and slowly brought out a small package wrapped in brown paper. "I came through the kitchen on my way in. Brought back the plunder—" she said, peeling back the wrappings to reveal two large pieces of chocolate cake that had recently been covered with a thick, dark icing, icing that now mostly adhered to the brown paper. "I felt sorry for you, sitting here all by yourself all day. I thought you deserved a present—" She sat down on the bed beside Elise, and the two set about enjoying the cake, eating it with their fingers straight off the paper, until the last bite was finished and the last bit of sweet icing licked from sticky fingers.

"Did you go anywhere else?" Elise asked, licking chocolate off her thumb, but receiving only a secretive smile in return.

After a moment Phyllis Ann rose and pulled a small book from a pocket of the coat she still wore, then shrugged the coat off and tossed it carelessly onto the back of a nearby chair.

"I thought you said you didn't buy anything—"

"I lied." Spoken easily enough. Phyllis Ann was good at lying.

"Is it—" Elise began, but did not have to finish; she already knew the answer from the look on Phyllis Ann's face. She accepted the small book, turning it over in her hands, already knowing what it was—a novel, like one of the many that made the rounds of the girls at the school, considered shocking by the instructors on the few occasions when they had been found, but gloried in by the students. Miss Perry had caught them with one a month or so before, and had burned it right before their eyes once she had read several of the passages— "risqué" she had called it, and Phyllis Ann had rushed to look the word up in the dictionary, disappointed to find out that it meant only slightly improper, when the girls considered the books to be so much more.

The novels were the most popular reading material on the campus, above French texts and the fine literature the girls were expected to read. Often they were little more than suggestive, poorly-written tales of young virgins in bustles and pantalettes, girls eager to be deflowered; other times they were the popular novels of the day—Fitzgerald, Samuel Hopkins Adams, Cabell—bestsellers, for it seemed everyone was interested in sex these days; at other times they were nothing less than pornographic, with little else but page after page of the sex act—Elise knew her mother would die of mortification if she even thought her daughter knew such novels could exist, much less that she had read one. But, at the moment, her mother's opinion did not seem to matter. The books were highly interesting, as well as instructive—besides, all the girls were reading them, and there could be nothing wrong with that.

"We haven't had it before, have we?" Elise asked, examining the cover and then opening it to skim through several of the pages.

"No, they said it was new—" Where Phyllis Ann got the books Elise did not know or care to ask. Phyllis Ann and several other of the more daring girls easily kept the school supplied, and it did not seem to matter.

Phyllis Ann took the book out of her hands and sat down on the bed beside her, opening the slim volume to a page at random and beginning to read, her lips moving silently with each word. Elise moved closer and read along, having to wait at the bottom of each right-hand page for her friend to turn to the next, for Phyllis Ann read much the slower of the two.

After several pages, Elise sat back, feeling her cheeks color with even the idea of—"I wonder if it's really like that?" she mused aloud.

"What, little girl—a man, or sex?" Phyllis Ann asked coyly, looking closely at her until Elise felt her cheeks grow even hotter.

"You know what I mean."

Phyllis Ann closed the book and moved to her own bed to stretch out on her back with her hands crossed beneath her head, staring up at the white-painted ceiling overhead. "It's all the same anyway, men and sex—and it's even better—"

"Oh, you wouldn't know—"

"Oh, wouldn't I, little girl?" Phyllis Ann looked over at her with clear meaning in her eyes—but Phyllis Ann was good at that.

"I don't believe you. You haven't done anything any more than I have—"

"I frankly don't care what you believe," Phyllis Ann said, looking at her again, and Elise did not know whether to believe her or not. She could say the most shocking things in the most convincing manner, whether they were true or not, until Elise never knew quite what to believe of her.

She decided now that it was best to change the subject, kicking off her shoes to stretch out on her stomach on her own bed, her arms crossed beneath her chin. She lay quiet for a moment, thinking. "I wonder if married people do it all the time?" she asked, staring at the headboard—somehow she could not imagine her parents "doing it," though she knew they must have at times in the past; she and her three brothers were evidence enough of that.

"They do it more with everybody else than they do with each other," Phyllis Ann said, and Elise looked over at her, shocked again. "That's why I'm never going to get married. I'll take rich lovers instead—men spend more money on their mistresses than they do on their wives, anyway—"

Elise stared at her for a long time, unsure as to whether to believe her or not. After a moment, she decided to change the subject again, resting her chin back on her crossed arms to stare at the headboard once more. "Oh, I'm going to get married," she said. "I'm going to have a big wedding, with all the trimmings and tons of flowers, and a beautiful dress—"

"And who shall you marry, little girl?" Phyllis Ann taunted, looking over with a smirk. Elise ignored the tone in her voice.

"Oh, he'll be tall and handsome, and rich of course. He'll be a college man, and a poet, and he'll write long, romantic letters to me if we're ever apart. He'll help Daddy in his business, and we'll build a big house on the hill not far from my parents' place—"

"And there'll be a baby every other year, and you'll get fat and old, and he'll leave you—"

Elise gave her friend an angry look, which seemed only to delight Phyllis Ann all the more.

"Everyone knows who you'll marry, anyway; everyone has always known who you'll marry—"

"And just who is that?" There was annoyance in Elise's voice—she already knew what was coming.

"Oh, he fits the bill, all right, little one—except for the tall and handsome part—and I doubt he'll ever write you love letters, for I've never heard him put two words together sensibly in the same sentence in all my life. But he's rich, all right, and he'll be a college man—"

"If you mean—"

"Everyone knows you'll marry J.C. Cooper—James Calvin—" Phyllis Ann said, a note of singsong in the last two words. "The County says you'll marry James Calvin. Your daddy says you'll marry James Calvin—" there was a sudden change in her tone, as if she were speaking to a very small child, "—and you're such a good little girl, you always do what your daddy says, don't you?"

Elise sat up angrily. "I have no intention of marrying J.C., and you know it!" But Phyllis Ann only laughed, and Elise knew that she had gotten the response she had wanted. Phyllis Ann was right anyway—everyone did think she would marry J.C. It had seemed a foregone conclusion in the County from the moment Hiram Cooper and his wife had produced a son, and William and Martha Whitley had produced a daughter. The Whitleys were the biggest cotton growers in the County, and the Coopers owned a half interest in the Goodwin Cotton Mill—it was a match made in heaven, or in the banks, a match that could not be passed up: Elise Whitley was to marry J.C. Cooper; her father said so—and he was determined to make sure that the marriage took place.

William Whitley intended to have the other half interest in the Mill once Hiram Cooper's partner, old Mr. Bolt, retired or finally died. The Whitleys produced more cotton than any other place in the County, and, once William Whitley owned a half interest in the cotton mill, with his daughter securely wedded to the other half, there would be no doubt in anyone's mind who was the most powerful man in all of Endicott County—if there was any doubt even now.

Elise knew everyone expected her to marry J.C.—that is, everyone but her and J.C. themselves. She and J.C. had been reared together, had played together as children, and she loved him just as she loved her brothers—they had climbed trees together, had gotten into fist fights, and had even broken the kitchen window once, which J.C. had taken the whipping for, though it had been she who had thrown the rock—dear, gentle J.C.; but she would not marry him. No matter what the County said. No matter what her father said. And no matter what Phyllis Ann Bennett said.

"I think James Calvin will make a perfect husband for you," Phyllis Ann was saying now, sitting up on the bed and grinning at her—oh, how Phyllis Ann had always loved to torment and bedevil J.C., which he had always tolerated with a characteristic good nature. She had even taken to calling him "James Calvin" of late, telling him he was much too mature now to go by the more-familiar "J.C." he had grown up with—how delighted he had been, how flattered; and how she had laughed at him behind his back for that delight.

"I have no intention of—"

"Oh, I think you'll make a perfect couple. He'll give you a houseful of little four-eyed Coopers—I bet you're really looking forward to the wedding night—"

"Oh, shut up!" Elise snapped, and Phyllis Ann began to laugh. Elise got up from the bed and started across the room for the door, but stopped short, remembering they were not allowed to leave the room even to go into the remainder of the dormitory. She sat down in a chair near the door instead, turning her eyes to stare at her friend again. Phyllis Ann laughed only all the harder, flinging herself back on the bed with her arms outstretched, and laughing until the mattress shook beneath her.

# 5

EVERY MUSCLE IN JANSON'S body ached as he walked toward the barn his second Saturday on the Whitley place. He was tired, tired through to his soul, he told himself, having struggled all day long against an iron pry, urging on a stubborn team of mules as they strained against their trace chains, doing everything he could to uproot a stump that had been firmly planted in the red Georgia clay for generations—that was still there, sitting dead center in the middle of a field he was clearing on Whitley's orders for cotton planting the next spring.

His back and shoulders ached from having thrown his weight against the iron bar all day, straining against it, even as the mules strained against the chains wound around the stump—even as the stump stayed in the ground, stubborn, immovable as the Earth itself. Blisters had risen on his palms early in the morning, only to be rubbed off and left raw and open as the day wore on. They hurt even now as he walked home in the growing darkness, but he paid them little heed. He did not have to look at them to know they were red and raw and even bleeding in places—they were a working man's hands. They had looked this way before. They would look this way again.

He left the road that led away from the Whitleys' store and cut across country, going through a section of the thick pine woods and toward the clearing where the barn and his small room stood. It was a drafty, lean-to affair he had been given in exchange for the rent just deducted from his wages. Haphazardly attached to the back of the building, with only one small window and a door that did not fit properly into its frame, it had already proven itself to be a cold place to sleep during the long winter nights. The black cast-iron stove he used to both cook his simple meals and to heat the one room did little to fight off the drafts that blew in around the door and in between the poorly-fitting boards in the walls—but the noisy and rusting tin roof that stood between him and the rain, and the ill-fitting walls that kept out the worst of the cold, were a welcome to him; and they were his, thanks to the rent that had been deducted from the wages he had just been paid. It was not a fine place such as the Whitleys lived in, this tiny room with only the one kerosene lamp for light, and the gaps in the walls that the wind whistled through at night, but it was his for now, and it would do—it would do until he could go home to his land and to that house he dreamed of most every night now. It would do.

He came clear of the woods and crossed a field of dry cotton plants, going toward the barn, and then around to the back and to the room that sat attached there. He almost stumbled over the single, cane-bottomed straight chair that sat just within the doorway as he entered, but righted it, then moved to light the kerosene lamp on the table at the side of the sagging rope bed.

The flickering yellow light showed bare, unpainted walls, an ancient chifforobe with a cracked and fading mirror, the narrow cot where he slept, the single chair, the splintery wooden table, the black stove—there were few other things lying about, just the Bible with its worn and cracked leather cover, the heavy, hand-pieced quilts Mattie Ruth had given him, the black, cast-iron skillet she let him use, the few clothes folded and put away in the chifforobe, and his shoes beside the bed.

He shivered with the cold and moved to build a fire in the stove, knowing it would be a time before the room would be warm and the heavy, damp chill in the air would be driven away. He kept his coat on and sat down on the narrow cot, thinking of what he would cook for his supper—bacon and eggs, for he was too tired to fool with much more. But it would still be a time before the fire in the stove would be hot enough to cook on.

He stuck one hand in the pocket of his coat and pulled out the few coins that were his pay for the work he had done since he had been on the Whitley place—ten days work, and he held it all in the palm of one hand, minus what had been taken out for the rent on this room, and for the charge he had been forced to run at the store. Doing chores for Mattie Ruth in the few hours he had free from Whitley's demands had allowed him her home cooking at times; chopping wood for one of Whitley's sharecroppers had given him eggs in return, butter, and a little flour, but still there had been food to buy, kerosene for the lamp, and thread to patch his overalls with. He had watched his charging carefully, worrying over every penny he knew would have to come from his wages in the end—how hard it had been to decide to part with even one of those few, precious coins, as he had to do today in deciding to place the telephone call to Eason County.

He knew his grandparents would be worried about him, wondering where he was, and if he was still even alive and well, but still it had been hard to part with even that little bit of money, knowing he could instead have put it away toward that dream that still lived inside of him—and it had been harder still, deciding to place the telephone call, when he knew he would have to ask for help, for he had never used a telephone before in all his life.

There had never been a telephone in the house when he had been growing up, such a contraption having been an extravagance far beyond the means of his parents or any of his kin in the County, and he had never had reason to use the one in the little store near their home. But for once in all his life he wished he had paid more attention when other people had been using the one that hung on the back wall in Garrick's Store in Eason County. He had almost changed his mind, waiting around in Whitley's store long after his wages had been settled up earlier in the day, wasting time, waiting for all the other farmhands to leave. Whitley himself had already gone back to the big house, having settled up accounts with his people for the past two weeks, and Janson had been left alone in the store with the storekeeper, Mr. Frazier, and with Whitley's youngest son, Stan. He had continued to wait, hoping the boy would leave as well, but a farm wife had come in to tie up the storekeeper instead, bartering with him in a loud voice over a trade of eggs for corn meal, and Janson had been left with little other choice but to either leave or to ask the boy for his help.

Stan Whitley was fourteen years old, five years Janson's junior, and, though Janson had seen him about the place over the past two weeks, he had never had any reason to speak to him during that time. The boy stared at him from behind round-rimmed glasses as Janson walked to where he sat on a tall stool pulled up before the counter, and Janson found himself suddenly certain the boy would laugh when he told what he wanted to do and asked him for his help—but Stan did not laugh. Not even a trace of amusement showed on Stan Whitley's face as he rose and went to the square, black contraption that hung on the rear wall of the store. He angled down the mouthpiece so that he could speak into it better, then picked up the receiver and turned the crank, waiting for a moment for the operator, then placing the call to Eason County.

After a moment Stan placed the receiver back into the cradle and turned to look at him, and Janson moved a few feet away, pretending to look at the tobacco cutter there on the counter as he waited the seemingly endless time it took for the operator to ring back with his call. He was afraid the boy would ask him why he had not written a letter instead of placing the costly telephone call to Eason County, especially since he had found it necessary to ask for help in even doing so—but, to Janson, it was far preferable that he let someone know that he had never used a telephone before, than to let them know that he could only barely read or write.

There had never seemed enough time to learn in his years of growing up, his having been out of school as much as in to help work their land; there had always been work to do in the fields, plowing and planting and chopping the cotton, picking it in the fall—he had attended school faithfully each day he had not been needed at home, from the time he had been barely old enough to be allowed through the school doors, until he had passed his sixteenth birthday; but still he had always seemed so very far behind, with no chance of ever catching up. The teachers had been too overworked, with too many subjects to cover and too many grades to teach in the crowded, two-room schoolhouse—and too many other students in the same situation as he, out of school too often to work the sharecropped and tenanted farms, and too far behind when they did return to ever have any hopes of catching them up.

He and so many others had been left back with the smaller children year after year, or simply passed on out of kindness, or out of a sheer sense of hopelessness at trying to teach the same material to the same pupil time and again. Now, at nineteen, he could read a few words, a few simple sentences; he could sign his name and figure in his head well enough to get by—and that was enough for anybody, he told himself. A man did not need more than that to get by in his life.

But he had sworn long ago that no other man, no other human being, would ever know that he could not read and write just as well as anyone else could. It was a matter of pride, of dignity—if he had nothing else left, he still had that.

The ringing of the black box on the wall broke into his thoughts, and he found Stan Whitley staring at him curiously as he looked up from the tobacco cutter on the counter. After a moment, the boy moved to the telephone and lifted the receiver to his ear.

"Hello—yes, Mrs. Huey, this is Stan—yes, ma'am—yes, all right—" Then the boy held the receiver out to Janson. "It's your call to Alabama."

Janson moved to the unfamiliar box, holding the receiver to his ear and leaning close to speak into the mouthpiece Stan had tilted up for him. "This is Janson Sanders—" He wondered suddenly why he was shouting; but it seemed the thing to do, so he continued.

"Go, on, ma'am, I've got the other—" an unfamiliar woman's voice began, but Janson's grandmother was already talking. She sounded strange, tinny and far off as he leaned toward the telephone; but it was unmistakably Gran'ma—and she was shouting as well.

"Janson—that you boy?" she shouted, making him hold the receiver away from his ear for a moment. "They come t' th' house an' said there was a telephone call at th' store for me all th' way from Georgia—you all right, boy? I knowed it had t' be you; praise th' Lord that we're hearin' from you s' soon—you been eatin' good, boy? You stayin' warm?"

It had been so good to hear her voice, but it had also made him think of home—not this place, with its drafty walls and its window shaking in its frame, but of a white house on rolling red acres, cotton fields as far as he could see, the sound of a sewing machine, the smell of wood smoke, the look of his father's face—

He closed his fist tightly now on the few coins in his hand, feeling them cut into his flesh—that was all he had now. That, and this room, and a lonely supper. And the cold night outside.

There was the sound of a truck's engine in the distance, coming up the rough road that ran before the barn, but Janson paid little attention. He shoved the money back into the pocket of his coat and got up from the cot to check the black stove, wetting a finger to touch to its surface, feeling warmth, but not hearing the accompanying sizzle that would mean the fire was hot enough to cook on. The chill in the room was just beginning to lessen now, but it would still be a time before he would be able to prepare supper—it was just as well, he told himself; he was not that hungry anymore. His mind was too filled with thoughts of Eason County, of home, of people he would not see again for a very long time, and of that red land he would have back only after many years of hard work and saving.

The sound was growing closer, drawing his attention, the truck cutting across country now and coming toward the barn. Janson thought he could discern individual voices, loud obscenities, and laughter from several men on the truck. Gilbert Baskin's voice could be heard well above the rest, his words louder, more obscene, being shouted well over the voices of the other men. Baskin was one of Whitley's hired hands, but the man did not do farm work; what he did for Whitley, Janson did not know, and he had enough common sense to realize he would probably be better off not to find out. Baskin was an unpredictable sort, liking his drinking and his pleasuring a little too much—what a man like Gilbert Baskin could be doing out in this direction so late on a Saturday night Janson did not know. What he did know was that, whatever it was, he did not like it.

He went outside into the darkness, seeing the weaving headlamps of the truck as it jounced over the rough terrain of the winter-dead cotton field nearest the barn. The voices yelled even louder as it came closer, and Janson heard his name called, but had little time to figure out what was being yelled at or about him as the truck veered to the right and seemed suddenly headed straight for him. He swore under his breath and jumped out of the way of the front wheels, hearing the truck come to a grinding halt only inches away, red dust being kicked up into a thick cloud around him by the sudden stop. He stared up at Gilbert Baskin where the man sat behind the wheel of the vehicle, Gilbert coughing on the red dust that now filled the air, but paying little attention to the threats and curses of the men on the back of the truck, men who had almost been tossed free of the vehicle by the abrupt stop.

"Damn it, Gilbert—you near ran me over!"

But Gilbert Baskin only laughed in response. "You sure jumped awful quick, boy," he said, and Janson realized he was drunk; they were all drunk. The truck almost reeked with the smell of liquor. "You got your wages today, just like the rest of us—we thought you might want t' go int' town for a little socializin' tonight, boy. We got the best looking women in all the South right here in Endicott County, and the best corn liquor, and plenty of both—here, boy, take a taste of this; you'll see what I mean—" Gilbert reached to wave an open fruit jar out the window of the truck, sloshing some of its contents out into the red dirt at Janson's feet. "Go on, boy. That ain't no busthead whiskey right there; that's good corn, some of the best made for three counties around—"

Janson stared at him for a moment, realizing the man was in no condition to be the judge of anything, much less of the quality of corn liquor. Janson had heard too much of busthead whiskey to not be wary of it, the poisonous corn liquor turned out by some of the back-country moonshiners, and by many of the new bootleggers who had gone into production since Prohibition had made bootlegging such a lucrative profession. Such men often condensed their whiskey through automobile radiators, used potash in the making, or did not strain it properly—at the very least, busthead whiskey, or popskull as many of the country people called it, well earned its name, causing violent headaches that often made the drinker pray for death. At the very worst, that death often came.

Gilbert waved the jar at him again, sloshing out more of the whiskey onto the ground. "Go on, boy. It ain't gonna hurt you. That's good corn liquor, made in one of the finest stills around here—go on, boy—"

Janson accepted the jar at last, looking past it and to Gilbert again. He was no stranger to corn liquor, the red hills where he had grown up having had their fair share of stills as well. Most young men in Eason County had their first taste of corn well before they entered their teens, and many were hardened drinkers by the time they had reached Janson's age—but Janson was not. On his own he seldom drank—corn liquor cost money, and money could be put to better uses.

He tilted the jar up and drank, then wiped his mouth with the back of one hand and handed the jar back.

"See, just like I told you," Gilbert said. "Hop on the back, boy; we're gonna take you int' town and show you some of the prettiest women in these parts—"

Several of the men on the rear of the truck shouted their approval, eager to get into town now as they passed a jar of corn liquor among themselves as well. Janson took a step forward, and then hesitated. "Wait a minute," he said, and then turned to go back into his room. He came back out only a second later, his shoes and socks held in one hand.

He jumped up onto the rear of the truck, and was almost tossed back out as the vehicle jerked into motion. He settled down between two men he recognized as farmhands he had worked with clearing land days before, and took a moment to pull on his socks and shoes, then accepted the jar of corn liquor as it was passed to him.

It was not long before he was not cold anymore.

THE BRICKED, downtown section of Main Street in Goodwin seemed lit almost as brightly as day when they reached town. There were cars still parked along the street, in front of the billiard parlor at one end of downtown, and near the drugstore at the other, as well as before the moving picture theatre that sat almost dead-center of town between the two. The wide double doors to the billiard hall were flung open to the cold night air as the truck drove past, and Janson could see the men inside through the blue haze of cigar and cigarette smoke that hung in the room, men who spent most every Saturday night there, playing billiards, discussing politics, avoiding their wives—and enjoying corn liquor and good bootleg whiskey in the back rooms, as well as the company of women who were somewhat less than ladies, so Janson had heard.

The street was brightly lit, with white globes of electric light sitting atop tall poles on one side of the street, the globes lighting the brick-fronted store buildings and sidewalks as Janson had never seen before. Pretty girls who looked almost like flappers moved along the sidewalk, going from the movie theatre to Dobbins' Drugstore at the far end of downtown, girls in straight coats and cloche hats, with short skirts and uneven hemlines and their hair bobbed off short like modern girls were apt to do. Janson watched them, admiring the slender calves beneath the knee-length skirts, finding himself surprised as one of the other men on the back of the truck began to call out things to the girls that he would never have dared to say to any woman, lady or not. He opened his mouth to tell the man to shut up, that he could not talk to a woman like that, but got only a few words out before the truck came to a sudden and unexpected halt before the drugstore, the brakes screeching in protest as Janson and several other of the hands were thrown against the rear of the cab with the suddenness of the stop. The men cursed and shoved against him and each other, threatening Gilbert as they got down from the rear of the vehicle and made their way into the drugstore, leaving the truck parked there alongside the street with one wheel up on the sidewalk.

After a moment, Janson jumped down from the back of the truck as well, feeling the effects of the corn liquor himself now. He made his way into the drugstore alone and found a stool to sit down on at the soda fountain, knowing the other men had forgotten his presence altogether. He watched as they settled in at stools and tables throughout the fountain area at the front of the store. Gilbert already had an arm around a blonde girl who had been sitting at a table alone, and several other of the

Whitley hands were already similarly occupied, but Janson did nothing more than just sit and watch, feeling suddenly very out of place.

Flat-chested flappers moved from the tables to the stools at the soda fountain, girls wearing short skirts and bobbed hair, with Kissproof lipstick and rouge on their faces, and rolled silk stockings down to their knees. They laughed and they talked and they flirted with the other men, loudly popping the gum in their mouths, or speaking so that half the room could hear:

"It's just like the one Clara Bow had on in her last picture . . ."

". . . it was a brand new Lincoln, and he banged up the whole right side . . ."

"A talking picture show—can you imagine that! Radio in the movies; I'll believe it when I see . . ."

". . . and she was wearing knickers, imagine that! Knickers, just like a man—"

The soda jerk picked at a pimple on his chin as he moved toward Janson to ask what he would have, but a short man with a paunch and a disagreeable expression stepped behind the counter instead, laying a hand on the boy's arm and nodding him toward another customer sitting not far distant. The man stepped up to Janson, wrinkling his nose as if there were a disagreeable odor in the place.

"What y' want, boy?" he demanded, staring at Janson, giving him the clear impression that he had to be the owner of the drugstore, Mr. Dobbins.

Janson stuck one hand in his pocket and pulled out his wages, staring at the little money in his hand for a moment as he debated on whether to spend even one of the few, precious coins and order a lemon phosphate, or whether to risk being thrown out of the drugstore as a loiterer instead. Dobbins pursed his thick lips together and nodded his head, as if he had received the answer he had expected, then started to speak—but, before he could tell Janson to leave, there was a shriek from a girl across the room, and the sound of a slap, setting Dobbins in motion around the end of the counter and toward the girl's table, making him forget all about Janson; and another of the Whitley hands was tossed out of the place instead.

The girl quietened back down as Dobbins pacified her and several of her friends with free ice cream sodas from the fountain, and Janson relaxed slightly, relieved at having been spared the indignity of having been publicly thrown out of the place. He shoved his wages back into his pocket and debated on whether he should stay here and wait for the other hands to leave so that he could hitch a ride back to the Whitley place, or whether to take off walking and just hope that someone might pick him up—but his eyes came to rest on a girl sitting only a few stools away at the soda fountain. She was pretty, probably at least quite a few years older than Janson, in her late twenties, with bobbed red hair and a tight green dress that did not quite cover her crossed knees. She had on face powder and lipstick and rouge, and, as she smiled, a slight dimple showed in her left cheek.

She stared at Janson openly, her fingers toying with the rim of the near-empty fountain glass of Coca-Cola before her. A tall, heavy-set man was leaning over her shoulder, saying something against her ear as he looked down toward her breasts—but she was paying him little attention. Her eyes were set on Janson instead; she smiled, and he smiled in return, and, after a moment, she stood and pushed past the heavy-set man to come and sit on a vacant stool next to the one where Janson sat.

"Hi," she said, the dimple showing in her cheek again. "I ain't seen you around here before."

"No, I don't guess you have." Janson smiled.

"My name's Delta; what's yours?"

"Janson Sanders—" He was going to say more, but the heavy-set man who had been trying to talk to her before was suddenly there, his hand on her arm, trying to pull her to her feet.

"Com' on, Delta; I ain't got all night—"

She looked up at him, anger showing plainly in her clear hazel eyes. "Go away, Les. I ain't goin' nowhere with you tonight."

"But you promised you'd—"

"I don't care what I promised," she snapped, jerking her arm free of his grasp. "You go away and leave me alone or I'll tell your wife about you, Les Jenkins."

"Now, sugar, you know you wouldn't—" he began, putting his hand on her arm again, but she only pushed it away.

"I mean it! Go away, Les!"

"You heard what she said." Janson rose to his feet, and the man turned to look at him.

"Wasn't nobody talking to you, boy."

"Maybe not, but she's done told you t' leave her be—"

"This ain't none of your business, boy. You just keep your mouth outta—"

"I'm makin' it my business—an' my name ain't boy—'

The big man's hands tightened into fists—he was ready to fight. But, then again, so was Janson.

"Now Les—" The girl's hazel eyes moved quickly around the room. "You behave. Just go on—"

"You heard what th' lady said," Janson told him, but suddenly the man snorted, and then laughed out loud, his ruddy face becoming only redder.

"Lady! She ain't no—"

But suddenly the girl's hand was on his arm, her tone somehow different. "Now, Les, you be a good boy an' go away, an' I'll let you call me tomorra' night—"

The man stared at her for a moment, and then glanced at Janson, seeming to consider the possibilities. After a time, he nodded his head, then retrieved his hat from a nearby stool, reaching up to put it on his head and adjust the brim. "Okay, tomorrow night," he said, and looked at Janson again before turning and crossing the fountain area going toward the front door of the drugstore. He went out onto the sidewalk, glancing back through the windows one last time, his heavily jowled face unreadable.

Somehow something did not feel right—but the girl turned to Janson again and smiled, the dimple coming back to her cheek, and the feeling was gone. All he could think of was that she had the prettiest red hair he had ever seen, even if she did wear it bobbed off too short.

SHE WAS not a lady. Janson knew that by the time they left the drugstore together, but it did not seem to matter. They went out into the chilly darkness, her arm firmly hooked through his—they were going for a drive in her motor car, she had said; but he knew what she wanted. She wanted the same thing he wanted. That was all that was important.

They got in her car and she let him drive. He choked the engine too much and it coughed and sputtered, but soon they were driving up Main Street, her warm hand resting on his thigh.

"Wait, hold on!" she said as they came abreast of the billiard parlor, and was out of the car almost before he could stop it. She went to a large, expensive-looking motor car parked alongside the street and quickly leaned inside, giving him a good view of silk-encased calves, and, for just a moment, even the backs of her knees, and the tops of her rolled stockings. She straightened up quickly and returned to the car with something in her hands, getting in and slamming the door after herself. "I figured Les would have some corn liquor stashed in his car, but I did even better'n that," she said, holding a bottle of gin up for him to see.

Janson started to protest, but suddenly her mouth was on his, her body pressed against him, her tongue sliding into his mouth. She looked up at him a moment later, rather breathless.

"Why don't we go to my place? I got some glasses for the gin—"

He nodded, but did not speak—he had known that was where they were going all along.

Her house was small and dark, sitting off on a country road a few miles from town. The parlor seemed gaudy under bright electric lights, the chairs and sofa upholstered in a worn brocade of some red and gold design, with a dark rug on the floor showing even darker stains in places. They sat on the sofa and had a drink, but she was soon in his arms, warm and soft, and willing. He had been with women before, girls, but somehow this was different. She was older, more experienced; forbidden, and yet exciting.

She led him toward the bedroom, toward a wide spindle bed that sat against one wall. Her dress was suddenly off, and he marveled at how full and round her breasts were in his hands. She was pulling at his overalls, his workshirt, as he unlaced his shoes and kicked them off; and then they were on the bed, and the world went away.

Her body moved beneath his as no woman's ever had before, her nails biting into the flesh of his back. She said things, did things, that no lady should—but it did not matter. His urgency came, the pleasure, and he strained forward, giving into the feelings. The tension mounted and peaked and he found release, collapsing into her arms, breathing heavily.

"Honey, get off 'a me. You're too heavy—" she said, pushing at his sweating shoulders, her voice sounding annoyed.

Janson rolled away, seeing her reach for the quilt at the foot of the bed and pull it up over herself—not out of embarrassment, he knew, but simply as a matter of course. He felt self-conscious now beneath her hazel eyes as they moved over him, and he reached for his underdrawers and sat up to pull them on.

"Honey, don't be gettin' ready to go an' all just yet. There's a whole lot more lovin' we can do tonight. I know some tricks I can teach you, how to last longer for a lady. You're no worse than any other young fella your age, s' eager an' all; you just got t' learn that it takes more sometimes for a lady to get what she—"

As Janson's eyes came to rest on her again, she seemed to realize she had said too much.

"Oh, don't get me wrong, honey. You sure got what a lady wants. It just takes learnin' to—"

But he was standing up, pulling on his shirt and reaching for his overalls. "I can find my way back int' town," was all he said.

"I didn't mean to get you mad at me." She sat up, letting the quilt drop from her breasts as she leaned forward. "Come on back to bed, honey. We got the whole night to love—"

Suddenly he was dizzy and his stomach hurt—love, this was not love. He did not even know this woman, and he wished now that he had never met her. Not being a lady was one thing, but she was something so much worse.

And, even worse still, he was drunk and he knew he was going to be sick. He fought down the nausea that rose to his throat, refusing to allow himself to be humiliated even further in front of this woman.

"Come on back to bed, James—"

"No, ma'am," he said, and thought—and my name's not James, though he did not bother to say it. He pulled the galluses of his overalls up over his shoulders and hooked them, then began to look for his socks and shoes, finding them under the bed. When he straightened up she was sitting up in bed, the quilt having fallen now to her waist. She held his coat in her hands.

"When you get ready for some more lovin', you just give me a call," she said as he took his coat in one hand, his shoes and socks in the other, and left the room.

"That ain't lovin'," he said aloud, but to himself, as he walked up the dark road a few moments later. He had not gone more than a few paces from the house before he collapsed to his knees by the side of the road and vomited silently into the ditch.

HE CONTINUED to retch long after there was nothing left to come up, then knelt there in the dirt at the roadside for a long time, allowing the cold night air to clear his head somewhat. He felt sick and alone, the memory of the woman's words bringing a burning embarrassment to his face now even as they had not before.

After a time he moved to sit in the winter-dead grass beside the road, taking the time to pull on his socks and shoes and shrug into his coat, feeling chilled now all the way through to his soul. He got to his feet and started down the lonely stretch of road toward town, shoving his hands deep into his worn coat pockets—then he froze, panic filling him. The money, it was gone. He turned the pockets of the coat inside out, then searched his overalls pockets—gone, those few coins that were his only pay for almost two weeks worth of work. Gone. Then suddenly he understood—the way the woman had held his coat in her hands, the look that had been on her face when he had straightened up from finding his shoes, and, even earlier, when she had first smiled at him in the drugstore—she had seen the coins in his hand. That was the only reason she had taken him to her home, to her bed. She had seen the coins.

Anger and shame fought within him as he clenched his fists and turned back toward her house—but he could go no farther. If he went back—but he could not strike a woman, so he stayed where he was in the road and stared at her house and cursed himself. Those few coins were so little. They would not buy her a dress. They were worth so little to anyone else—

But they had been worth the world to him.

He fought to control the rage building within him, knowing there was nothing he could do—and knowing she knew there was nothing he could do. Then he forced himself to walk on, toward town, toward that bricked section of Main Street, toward the drugstore, and the men who could give him a ride in the truck back to Whitley's place.

When he arrived, Main Street was deserted. Dobbins' Drugstore was dark; the moving picture theatre was dark; even the billiard parlor at the far end of the street was closed—and there was no sign of the truck or of the men from Whitley's. He was alone.

He sighed and looked up the long, dark stretch of road he had ridden down earlier, then sat down on the sidewalk to remove his shoes and socks—there was no more need for them tonight. Then he began to walk, cursing his stupidity every step of the way, swearing to himself that he would never again be taken, that he would never again trust anyone through the remainder of his life, no matter who that person might be.

The night was cold and he was shivering in the worn old coat long before he had covered the miles to Whitley's place and to the lonely, dark room that was now his home. The fire he had built earlier in the black stove had gone out, but he did not take the time to rebuild it. He shrugged out of the old coat and lay down on the cot, too tired and too sick to even bother to pull off his overalls and change into a nightshirt.

Outside the winter wind rustled the dead branches of a tree, whistling through the cracks in the walls and banging a shutter off somewhere in the distance. Inside there was only the sound of his own breathing, the beat of his own heart.

It was a long time that night before he slept.

# 6

THE SPRING RAIN HAD blown up quickly. Only a short time before the sky had been blue and the sun shining, but now all was gray and wet outside. Elise stared out the window in silence, watching as the rain washed away the remnants of what had been a beautiful late-April day. Water stood now in muddy red puddles on the campus grounds, hanging in droplets from the shrubs outside the window, and running in narrow, red-stained rivers alongside the streets. Girls in pale spring dresses ran from the dormitory to their classrooms, holding folded Atlanta newspapers over carefully crimped bobs, laughing and giggling and splashing in puddles of water as if they were still no more than children. Elise watched them, envying their carelessness, their minds without trouble or worry or thought beyond new chiffon stockings or the latest shade available in lipsticks. Such a short while ago she had been much as they were now, worry free, with little more than the discontents of children—but in these past hours she had come to realize how the world could change, and, though she knew she could still stop it, she also knew she would not.

She sat in the antechamber outside the principal's office of the boarding school, in a richly-upholstered chair that for all its luxury could not seem to sit her comfortably. Her eyes stared out the window, watching the rain as it washed down the glass and soaked into the closely clipped lawn outside, somehow looking but still not seeing—Phyllis Ann was in there now, talking with the principal. If she would only tell the truth, tell what had actually happened—but Elise knew she would not.

Phyllis Ann would lie, or she would remain silent, whichever she thought would better suit her purposes; and Elise would be called in to answer questions she did not want to answer, make choices she did not want to make—choices she should never have to make.

Only the day before, everything had been fine. Elise had studied through the afternoon and late into the night, using a small, shaded lamp after lights-out had been called on their hall, studying for a history examination that was due in Miss Jackson's class that following day. Phyllis Ann had come in long after curfew had been called on the school grounds, having gone out riding with several of the boys from town after Elise had refused to go; and she had gone directly to sleep—Elise had reminded her of the examination, and of her near-to-failing grade in the class, but Phyllis Ann had not seemed concerned. She had only groused about the light and the late hour, and then had gone to sleep, as if she had not one care in the world.

But, still, when the examination had begun that next morning, Elise had been surprised to see her friend referring to a small bit of paper she kept hidden in her hand. Elise had stared in open disbelief until Phyllis Ann's angry glance made her turn her eyes away—Phyllis Ann was cheating, when Elise had never before seen anyone cheat in all her months at the school. The other students knew better, for they all knew that cheating garnered the most immediate and the worst possible punishment—expulsion, with no defense heard, and none to be given.

About a half-hour into the examination, Phyllis Ann had dropped her notes—it had been an accident, a clumsy movement of a hand, a shifting of papers, sending the small scrap of cheat notes onto the floor between Phyllis Ann's desk and Elise. The two girls had looked at each other nervously, that small scrap of paper lying like a damnation between them. Neither could bend to pick it up, for Miss Jackson's sharp eyes would be sure to catch such a movement, and she would then demand to see what it was that had been retrieved from the floor—but they both knew the notes could never remain where they were.

Miss Jackson moved about the classroom, first up one aisle and then down another, pausing at the front or rear for just a moment, and then moving on. Elise's eyes met Phyllis Ann's in a desperate nervousness. Phyllis Ann would be immediately expelled if the notes were found, packed up, sent home—Elise could see the fear clearly written on her friend's face, not at the possibility of expulsion itself, but at what she knew could happen to her once she reached home. Ethan Bennett, Phyllis Ann's father, was well known to have a violent temper, and Elise herself knew he had beaten both his daughter and his wife on more than one occasion in the past—she had seen the bruises, the bloodied nose, the blackened eye, even the fractured collarbone from when he had slung Phyllis Ann against the stair rail on her tenth birthday. Elise could little doubt the reception Phyllis Ann would receive at home—or the honesty of the fear that now filled the other girl's eyes.

Miss Jackson started up the aisle that passed between the girls' desks, and Elise found herself praying fervently to a God she hoped was there—please, let her go on by. Please, God, just let her go on by—

The teacher stopped before their desks, and Elise sat, almost holding her breath, as she stared down at the words she had written only moments before on the examination paper. She dared not look up to know for certain—

Miss Jackson bent, picking up the small scrap of note-covered paper from the floor between them. It was a long moment before she spoke, staring down at the cheat notes in her hand. "Miss Bennett, Miss Whitley, would you please come with me."

They had followed her out into the hallway and directly to the principal's office. There had been only one brief moment when they had been left alone in the antechamber, one brief moment, and hurriedly whispered words.

"If we stick together, she can't do a thing to either of us—" Phyllis Ann had said, clinging to her arm, her fingers biting into the flesh until Elise's wrist hurt. "She doesn't know who had the notes—if you don't talk, and I don't talk, she can't prove a thing. She won't expel both of us, knowing one of us hasn't done anything wrong—you've got to stick with me. It'll be all right; you'll see—"

The door had opened before Elise could say a word, but she knew that

Phyllis Ann expected her to remain silent, that Phyllis Ann believed—

Elise sat now wondering if for once in her life she might not disappoint her friend—but she knew she could not. If she told the truth, if she told that the notes had belonged to Phyllis Ann, then her best friend would be immediately expelled from the school, sent home—and Phyllis Ann would go back to Endicott County to face her father, and her father's temper, and a hell that Elise could only imagine. But, if she remained silent—

Elise stared out the window now, at the rain washing away the self-assurance of a world she thought she knew. If Phyllis Ann was wrong, then they both could be expelled, sent home in disgrace—but she could not let herself think about that, about going home now to face her own father should everything go wrong. Damn you—Elise thought. Damn you for putting me in this situation. Something inside of her told her that she should protect herself, that she should tell the truth, that she should make the other choice—

The door to the principal's office opened and Phyllis Ann walked out. The girl stopped for a moment, looking at Elise, the fingers of one hand toying at the long strand of beads that hung about her neck, a clear confidence in her eyes that her friend would never betray her—damn you, Elise thought again, staring at her as she rose to her feet. Damn you for knowing me so well.

EVA PERRY sat behind her desk, looking at Elise Whitley as the girl sat with her head lowered, her eyes staring down at the hands folded quietly in her lap—Elise looked frightened, worried, more ill-at-ease than Eva had ever before seen her in all the months she had been at the school, allowing the principal at least the brief hope that she might be able to get the truth out of her. But she knew she would not. She had known that from the moment Elise had walked into the room, had read it in her eyes, and, for once in her life, she wished she did not know girls of that age so well, for she would have liked nothing more now than to hear Elise Whitley speak the truth.

Phyllis Ann Bennett had been the one to cheat; Eva knew that, just as surely as she also knew she could do nothing without proof. The cheat notes had been so hastily scribbled as to make the handwriting unrecognizable, and their position on the floor could have laid either girl to blame, but Eva knew, of the two girls, that Phyllis Ann would have had to have been the one using the notes. Elise was too good a student to have a need to cheat, and, besides, the girl was not even the type to think of employing such a device. But Phyllis Ann Bennett was another matter altogether. There was not much in this world the principal would put past a girl like Phyllis Ann.

"Well, Elise?" Eva prompted, hoping against her own instincts that the girl would tell the truth and admit it had been her friend using the notes—but something in the girl's expression dashed that hope. Elise would remain silent, or she would deny any knowledge of the cheat notes altogether as Phyllis Ann had done—but there had been an underlying nervousness behind Phyllis Ann's denial, a poorly-concealed fear that had spoken the truth, and a twist to her words that had said she would very much have liked to have laid the blame at Elise's feet, if she had only known how to do so. But this girl before her now would protect her friend, even at a risk to herself and her position as a student at this school, with all the blind and often misled loyalty of youth. Somehow Eva could respect that loyalty, much as she at the same time pitied the girl who held it.

She sighed, shifting in her chair, suddenly feeling much older than her forty-two years would allow her. "Well, Elise, is there something you want to tell me?"

The girl remained silent, her eyes set on the hands in her lap. She straightened a fold in her skirt, then clasped her fingers together, seeming to realize suddenly that they were trembling.

"Tell me what happened. Who was using the cheat notes? Was it Phyllis Ann?" She knew those words had placed her beyond a boundary she should never have crossed. She should never have prompted the girl with such a question—but it was done now. She watched Elise, feeling that the girl might be close to tears. Eva knew this had to be the hardest thing Elise had ever gone through, making the choice to either protect herself, or to protect her friend at a risk to herself. The two girls had grown up together, and were closer than many sisters—it would be a hard decision for any sixteen-year-old to make, and Eva could see the cost of that struggle on the girl's face even now.

"You aren't helping Phyllis Ann, you know," she said, her voice softening. "It never helps to protect someone when they do wrong—"

Elise's eyes rose quickly to meet hers. "I never said—"

"I know, but it was Phyllis Ann, wasn't it?"

Elise looked at her for a moment, and then averted her gaze again. She seemed to realize her eyes told too many secrets. Eva had already read the truth in them.

"I don't have anything to say." The girl's voice came quietly, her hands trembling in her lap even though her fingers were clasped tightly together.

Eva got up from her chair and went around the desk to sit where Phyllis Ann Bennett had sat such a short while before. She moved the chair closer to Elise, looking at the girl with a motherly affection she felt toward many of the students at her school—she knew she would never have a child of her own; time and the death in the World War of the tall, red-haired sergeant who would have been her husband had seen to that. But she had these girls, and something she could give the world in the lives they led, and the things she could teach them. She took both Elise's hands in her own, knowing somehow she had to get through to the girl, that whatever decision Elise Whitley made this day would affect the remainder of her life.

"Look at me, Elise," she said quietly, and the girl's blue eyes rose to meet hers. Eva smiled. "That's better. Now, you and I have to have a serious talk. I know Phyllis Ann is your best friend, and I know that you want to protect her if you can, but this is one case where you can not protect her, not if she's done something wrong. Elise, you've got to realize one thing. If you don't tell me the truth, if you don't tell me who it was using the cheat notes, I'm going to be forced to treat you both just as if you both had been cheating—" She paused for a moment, hoping to see some spark of understanding in the girl's eyes. "Do you understand what I'm saying?

Do you want to be punished for something you haven't done?"

Elise lowered her gaze again, but did not speak.

"You're too good a student; you don't need to cheat—I know that; you know that; and so does that selfish little friend of yours out there." There was a flicker of something in the girl's expression that Eva hoped was understanding. "Don't you see that Phyllis Ann is only trying to protect herself; that's all she ever does. She doesn't care about you or that you'll be hurt by all this. She's only concerned about herself, nothing more, nothing less, just as she always is—" She paused again for a moment, letting her words sink in. "You have to think about yourself this time. You have to tell me the truth—who was using the cheat notes?"

For a long moment the girl did not speak. She withdrew her hands from those of the principal, and clenched them tightly in her lap as she stared down at them. When she spoke, her voice was forced, but steady. "I don't have anything to say, Miss Perry—" she said, her eyes rising to meet those of the principal at last, fear in them, but also decision. "I don't have anything to say—" And Eva knew she had lost.

But she knew it was perhaps Elise Whitley who had lost most of all.

ELISE SAT with her hands pressed together in her lap a few moments later, trying to calm their trembling. She had made her decision, and she knew now that she would have to live with it, no matter what consequences it might bring. Phyllis Ann was beside her now, sitting in the chair so recently vacated by the principal, a well-masked nervousness apparent beneath the seeming disinterest on her face. The girl toyed with the long strand of beads she wore, one foot bobbing up and down absently as she sat with her legs crossed, the tops of her rolled stockings visible below the edge of her skirt—she had smiled at Elise when Miss Perry had called her into the room, had smiled at her with a calm self-assurance, and with an absolute belief in her loyalty; and for once in all her life Elise cursed her for that belief. It was all up to Miss Perry now. Everything was up to Miss Perry. And, not for the first time, Elise felt a shadow of doubt.

"I guess I've known all along that this day would come," the principal was saying, settling herself behind her desk again after having closed the door. "You both have been in and out of trouble almost continuously since the day you first came here. I had just hoped that—" She paused for a moment, then shook her head. "Well, it doesn't matter now. It's over with, finished—"

Over with, finished—Elise's heart gave a start. But surely she did not mean—

"You have left me with no other alternative but to expel both of you from this school effective immediately—"

Elise's throat tightened. She had known it could happen, but she had never really believed—Phyllis Ann had said everything would be all right if only they would stick together; that Miss Perry could never expel them both, knowing that one was innocent of any wrongdoing. Phyllis Ann had said—

"I will notify your families of what has happened," the principal was saying. "You will have until the end of the week to—"

"No!" Phyllis Ann shouted, rising suddenly to her feet. She reached and with one movement of her arm slung things from the desktop before her, sending water and dispossessed flowers from the vase there over the floor and the varnished wood of the desk, soaking a stack of students' files, and staining the front of her own dress. She leaned across the desktop, holding a finger only inches before the principal's face. "You can't expel me! I won't let you!"

Miss Perry did not move, but her eyes narrowed in anger, her hands clenching on the ruined desktop before her as if to keep from striking the girl. When she spoke, her voice was quiet, but steady. "I can expel you, young lady. And I have—"

"My daddy helped you build your goddamn new gymnasium, and to stock your library. He won't put up with you throwing me out like—"

"This school got along perfectly well without your father's money before, and it will do so again—"

Phyllis Ann's hand tightened into a fist before the principal's face, and, for one moment, Elise thought she would strike the older woman—but the girl reached instead to sling the wet files from the corner of the desk, her bobbed hair suddenly wild about her head, spittle gleaming at one corner of her mouth. "You goddam fat-assed old whore! I won't let—" She lunged suddenly across the desktop. Miss Perry tried to stand, but only stumbled backwards instead, knocking her chair over and landing with a hard jolt against the wall. Elise froze for a moment, then was suddenly on her feet, grabbing Phyllis Ann's shoulders and holding her back. Phyllis Ann screamed with rage and spun toward her, her jaw clenched, her fist raised—

For one brief moment, Elise could do nothing but stare at that fist, then she slowly brought her gaze to her friend's eyes, seeing a stranger there before her now for the first time. Phyllis Ann's chest rose and fell with heavy, angered breathing. Elise could feel her shoulders trembling beneath her hands—never before in all her life had she truly known what it was to be afraid of anyone. She did now.

"Are you going to hit me, Phyllis Ann?" she asked, hearing her own voice shake. "Are you going to hit me?"

Phyllis Ann stared at her for a long moment, then slowly lowered her fist, letting her arm drop to her side. Elise did not take her eyes from those of the girl before her, did not release the hold she held on her shoulders. She felt a trembling now fill her own body—from shock, from fear, from nervousness, from anger; she did not know which.

"We're going to our room to pack now, Miss Perry," she said, her voice continuing to shake. "We're going to our room to pack—"

Phyllis Ann did not speak. After a moment she pulled free of Elise's hands, turned to look at the principal one last time, then walked toward the door without another word, leaving it open behind herself as she walked through and out into the room beyond.

Elise took a deep breath, trying to calm her racing heart—none of this was supposed to have happened. Everything had gone wrong. They were not supposed to be expelled. Phyllis Ann had said—but Phyllis Ann had almost struck her, had almost struck her with an anger so like that of the father Elise had been trying to protect her from. My God, how could everything go so wrong, Elise wondered, so completely wrong. She had remained silent only to protect Phyllis Ann, for she had known that to speak would have meant Phyllis Ann's immediate expulsion—now they had both been expelled, and Elise wondered if she would ever be able to forget the sight of that fist that had been raised against her, that fist of the person she had gambled everything for. Gambled everything for, and lost.

She shivered and hugged her arms, suddenly cold. She looked toward the flustered principal, wanting to say something, to apologize—she turned without a word and started toward the door. She had made the wrong decision; she knew that now—by God, how clearly she knew it. But there was nothing she could do. Nothing. It was a decision she would have to live with. It was too late for anything else. There were no other choices left.

MARTHA WHITLEY sat on the brocaded sofa in the front parlor of her home that April afternoon, the needlework in her lap all but forgotten. She stared across the room at her husband, William, where he stood by the writing desk in the corner, the candlestick of the telephone clenched tightly in his hand.

"Yes, I understand, Miss Perry," he said into the mouthpiece, a forced-calm tone to his voice that only served to tell Martha that something was very wrong. She stared at him, unable to take her eyes away, knowing that the principal of Elise's school would never have called all the way from Atlanta without good reason. Her mind raced, going over all the things that might happen to a girl of sixteen away from home for the first time, her stomach tying itself further into knots with each thought. She laid aside the needlepoint she had been working on and rose to her feet to cross the room, but stopped a few feet short of William, seeing the look of anger, of pure rage, on his face, and she wondered what it was that Elise might have done to earn such a response.

"Yes, Miss Perry, I quite agree," he said, anger in the gaze he now directed at his wife, his dark brows lowered, knit together. The knuckles of the hand holding the telephone began to turn white as he clenched it even tighter. "Yes, it's unfortunate this had to happen, but I can see you had no other choice but to expel both girls—"

Expel—Elise had been—but what could she have done to—

"When will she be coming home?—yes, I see. Yes, I'll be meeting the train. Thank you very much for calling, Miss Perry. Yes—goodbye—"

As soon as the receiver was replaced in its cradle and the telephone set back down in its usual position on the writing desk, William turned on her, anger filling his dark eyes. "Elise was—" she began, but got no further.

"You should be pleased with your daughter this time!" he yelled, staring at her. "Giving in to her all her life, spoiling her—she's managed to get herself expelled from that fancy school of yours for cheating."

"Cheating—but Elise—"

"That's what that damn principal said. Elise and Phyllis Ann are being sent home—they found cheat notes that could have belonged to either girl, and neither one would say who had used them, so they expelled both girls—"

"But, they had to belong to Phyllis Ann! Elise would never—"

"Don't you think I know that, woman!" he shouted, and she fell silent. "It's that damned Phyllis Ann again, always putting fool ideas into Elise's head. Elise is just covering up for her—you just wait until I get my hands on that daughter of yours; she'll tell me the truth or I'll—"

"You won't lay a hand on that child!"

"That's what's wrong with her now! You coddling her and spoiling her all her life—but this time it's going to stop! She's sixteen now, and it's about time she started to act it. That's what you sent her off to that school of yours for in the first place—"

Martha stared at him for a moment longer, and then turned and went back to the sofa to take up her needlepoint again. She sat down and angrily jabbed the needle through the fabric, but refused to say a word. It had been his idea to send their daughter off to school in Atlanta, his idea, and not hers, but of course it would do no good to remind him of that now. Martha had agreed only reluctantly, not wanting to send her only daughter so far away from home, but hoping the time away from Phyllis Ann Bennett would do Elise good. The two girls had been friends from the time they had been little more than babies, and, though Phyllis

Ann had always been selfish and self-possessed, the friendship had never presented a problem—until Phyllis Ann had returned from spending a few weeks in New York City with a cousin more than a year before. She had come home with a new wardrobe, a new bobbed hairstyle, and a new and rather shocking manner. The girl had become only more spoiled and self-concerned the older she had gotten, and now she had become daring as well, unconventional, flaunting herself in a manner that was totally unbecoming, and saying things in a way that Martha knew was more often than not meant only to shock.

What was even more horrifying was the way Elise now seemed to want to emulate her friend, wanting to copy her new manner and appearance, to be shockingly modern, as so many young girls were trying to be now days. The short skirts, the bobbed hair, the rolled stockings, the lipstick—William had been fit to be tied when he had seen his daughter.

They had sent Elise off to the same boarding school Martha had attended as a girl, hoping she might settle down and get the new and radical ideas out of her head in her time away from home. Then Phyllis Ann had enrolled there as well, and they had been forced to content themselves with the idea that perhaps the school would have a beneficial effect on both girls.

But it had not.

Now they were both being sent home, expelled, disgraced, accused of cheating. Martha knew her daughter well enough to know Elise would never have been the one to cheat, as did William—but still she worried at the reception Elise might receive from her father once she reached home. William could be bad-tempered, unpredictable; Martha could only hope there would be time for his temper to cool before Elise could arrive.

William was pacing back-and-forth before the marble fireplace now, and Martha looked up from her needlepoint to watch him, wondering what was going on in his mind. Worrying—sometimes she almost did not trust her husband.

He stopped in his pacing for a moment and turned to stare at her, something in his dark eyes that made her uneasy.

"What is it, William?" she heard herself ask almost before she thought.

He remained silent for a moment, continuing to stare. "This just might work out after all," he said, his eyes never leaving her. "It just might." He stared at her for a moment too long for comfort, and then turned and left the room, going out into the hallway and toward the back of the house, the door to the library closing behind him only a moment later.

Martha stared after him for a time, letting her needlepoint come to rest in her lap for a moment. The look she had seen on his face just before he had left the room would not leave her mind—there had been no anger there, no rage, as only a moment before; there had been only something very close to determination.

And, somehow, that worried her all the more.

J.C. COOPER stood in the front parlor of the Whitley house the next morning, nervously waiting for William Whitley to come downstairs. He pushed his glasses up off the bridge of his nose and shifted from one foot to the other, knowing he had gotten here too early—William Whitley had called the evening before and had asked him to stop by here for a moment on his way to school this morning. J.C. would be graduating in only a matter of weeks, and he ought to know well enough by now what time school began, which was more than an hour from this, but he had wanted to get this over with. He had slept very little the night before, worrying, dreading this meeting—he did not like William Whitley; in fact, he could barely even abide the man. Whitley terrified him, with his aggressive personality and his plans for J.C.'s future—but J.C. could never seem to tell him no. That was why he was here an hour early to a meeting he did not even want to attend.

He pushed his glasses up again and shifted to the other foot, waiting, wishing he were anywhere else on the face of the Earth other than where he was at this moment—what could Whitley want of him? But he knew what Whitley wanted; what it was he always wanted.

William Whitley entered the room behind him, with a slam of the door and a loud: "Hello, son!" to the boy.

J.C. jumped slightly, startled, and pushed his glasses up again. "Hello, sir."

Whitley came toward him and clasped him on the shoulder, his round face even more florid than usual. J.C. looked at him, and became only more nervous—the man was smiling. J.C. did not like his smile; it always looked more like a leer.

"Have a seat, son; have a seat." Whitley motioned to a richly brocaded settee nearby, and J.C. sat, then cringed into the back of the sofa as Whitley sat down beside him and slapped him on the knee familiarly. "I've got some good news for you, son, some really good news."

"Sir?" J.C. rubbed his knee unconsciously—he hated to be called "son," especially by this man. It never boded well.

"Really good news—Elise will be returning home soon. This school nonsense of her mother's did not quite work out as we had hoped. The two girls should be home in only a matter of days—"

J.C. sat forward, suddenly attentive. "Phyllis Ann and Elise are coming home?"

Whitley's smile changed into a broad grin. "They sure are, boy. They sure are."

J.C. was smiling now as well. This news was worth facing even this man for—Phyllis Ann was coming home, after so many month, and she would be here in only a matter of days.

Whitley was watching him. "I knew you'd want to be the first to know, son," he said. "I knew you'd be glad to have Elise back home again."

"When will they be here?" J.C. asked, ignoring the tone in Whitley's voice, the meaning. He knew it well enough by now.

Whitley's grin broadened even further. "Why, you're an eager one, aren't you, boy?" he laughed, slapping J.C.'s knee again.

J.C. ignored the familiarity, too wrapped up in his own thoughts and feeling to care what it was the man did. He had been in love with Phyllis

Ann Bennett for as long as he could remember. She had been the one beautiful, unattainable dream before him all his life, from the time he had been a little boy first pulling her pigtails for attention, and getting beaten up by bigger boys for doing it; to the feverish dreams he had about her now most every night. When she had gone off to school, he had felt as if the world would end—what if she met someone else in Atlanta and fell in love? What if she decided to never come home at all? What if—

When she and Elise had come home in December for the Christmas holidays, he had almost wept with joy. He had seen her at church, had watched her from the choir all during the time he should have been listening to the sermon, and had even gotten a moment to speak to her at the Christmas party Whitley had thrown; a party supposedly to celebrate the season, but in reality, as everyone there knew, designed to throw J.C. and Elise together for at least a time.

But he had seen Phyllis Ann, had talked to her, had watched her through the evening. She had smiled at him, had tweaked his cheek, had called him "James Calvin"—he knew she was making fun of him; he always knew. But it did not matter. He was in love with her; she could make fun all she wanted.

Then she had gone back to Atlanta, and his world had stopped again—but now she was coming home. She was coming home, and now he might have the chance to tell her how it was he felt, the courage to—

"I was thinking you might like to come with me to meet the train Friday," Whitley was saying.

"Yes, I'd like that," J.C. answered, almost without thought—Friday; it seemed like such a long time away. Such a long time.

"Good . . . good . . ." Whitley's grin was self-satisfied. He sat back and sighed contentedly. "Well, son, let me tell you that I'm glad to see how happy you are about this. But, then again, I knew you would be. I knew you would—" He smiled and nodded complacently. "You have my full blessings in this, boy. Sixteen's a good courting age for a girl, and it's a good marrying age, as well." He patted J.C.'s knee and nodded, almost fatherly. "You get a girl when she's good and young and you can train her up to be the way you want her to be—it makes for a good wife, marrying young—"

J.C. stared.

"Yes, I think it's about time for you and Elise to start planning that wedding of yours. And, like I said, you've got my full blessings, son, my full blessings." He patted J.C.'s knee again, then startled him with a loud laugh. "Who knows, boy! You and Elise might make me a grandfather in a year or two!" He clasped J.C. across the shoulders and gave him a hug that was meant to be fatherly.

J.C. squirmed out of the embrace and swallowed hard. He pushed his glasses up off the bridge of his nose and stared at Whitley—he should have known this was coming. It always came—but he had never before been given outright permission to marry Elise, or to be the father of her children; and he did not want it. He could never marry Elise—Elise was quiet walks and playing together as children and telling her things he could never tell anyone else; she was the sister he had never had—but Phyllis Ann was passion and fire and love and all the things J.C. had dreamed about all his life. He wanted Phyllis Ann, loved her, needed her—but William Whitley planned an altogether different future for him, just as he always had. J.C. swallowed hard and tried to force the words to come, the refusal—but silence filled the room, broken only by the ticking of the mantle clock, until Whitley spoke again.

"I'm really glad we had this talk, son," he said. "Really glad." And J.C. Cooper felt as if his fate had been sealed.

# 7

THE PLOWSHARE CUT through the rich Georgia clay, splitting it aside in waves of fertile red. The man and the animal at work in the field moved almost as if they were one, sweating and straining against the plow in the hot noontime sun that late April day as William Whitley watched from the relative shade of the interior of the Ford Model T he more often than not persisted in driving. He puffed at his cigar and took another drink from the corn liquor he had brought with him—it was a very rare occasion when he drank, but this was a special day. Today he was celebrating—today he was celebrating the future.

Rarely in his lifetime had he been more pleased with himself than he was at the moment, and the talk he'd had that morning with J.C. Cooper had put the final touch on his day. He had taken a potential problem, a potential liability, and had turned it to his advantage—how furious he had been with Elise for her having managed to get herself thrown out of school and sent home months ahead of schedule, but he realized now that it was probably the best thing that could have happened. There was no need to wait the more than two years it would take before she graduated from school for her to start her life with young Cooper, and Martha's dreams of college for the girl were completely out of the question anyway; education was wasted on a girl, and, besides, William had much more important things for his daughter in mind, things that had little to do with school books and learning.

Elise would marry J.C.—William had known that almost from the first moment the nurse had told him Martha had delivered a girl those sixteen years before. Elise would marry J.C., and in doing so she would guarantee her father the things he had wanted for more years in his life than he cared to remember.

J.C.'s family was of the old, landed southern gentry, proud, wealthy, of even higher social standing than William's own—but that was not the reason William wanted his daughter to marry J.C. Cooper. The Coopers owned half of the Goodwin Cotton Mill, and, as such, were a part of the most profitable business venture in all of Endicott County, and for several counties around. William might grow more cotton, work more sharecroppers, own more land, than did anyone else in the County—but it would take a share of that Mill, a fifty percent partnership, to guarantee him that he was the most powerful, the wealthiest, man in all of Endicott County. For years William had tried to buy into that partnership, but neither Hiram Cooper, nor his aging partner, old Mr. Bolt, would sell—then Cooper had produced a son, and Martha had given William a daughter, and William had seen the opportunity. Sooner or later old Bolt would retire and sell, or simply die, and his share of the Mill would finally come up for sale. With Elise married to J.C., William would be guaranteed the first chance at that share—and it was a chance he would have, even at the cost of his right arm, or his daughter, if that need be the case.

Elise could do far worse than young Cooper for a husband anyway, William told himself. The boy was from a good family; he would be wealthy, well-educated, and tolerant; and he would never lay a hand on her in anger or in violence. William had been pleased, and more than a little bit surprised, to see how excited and eager the boy had been that morning at the knowledge that Elise was coming home so soon, and he could almost pity the boy as well, for, once William had his daughter off his hands for good, she would then be J.C.'s problem—his problem, then and forevermore.

William knew J.C. Cooper would present no problem of himself in the weeks and months to come, but Elise could be another matter altogether. She could take it into her head to do just about anything. She had no interest in J.C.—William knew that—but still he was not about to let the whims of a sixteen-year-old girl ruin the plans he had so carefully laid for so many years. Women never knew their minds in such matters anyway; they talked of love and courtship and romance, when marriage was more often than not best a partnership, a merger, a profitable business arrangement for all parties concerned—but Elise's opinion in the matter was of little concern anyway. For once in her life she would do exactly as she was told, even if William had to beat her daily to keep her in line—it was all for her own good anyway, he told himself, studying the glowing tip of his cigar for a moment. It was all for her own good. William would soon have his troublesome daughter off his hands once and for all, married to his choice of husband—and someday his grandsons would own the Goodwin Cotton Mill, thanks to his foresight now. Elise would thank him then; he knew that. She would thank him then.

William took another drink from the corn liquor and returned to watching the plowman at work in the field, fancying for a moment that he could almost hear the creak of the wooden hames and leather collar, the patient plodding sounds of the mules's hooves on the soft, red earth. The animal snorted and brayed, its ears moving back and forth in rhythm to its slow steps as it pulled the plow down the newly cut furrows. The man seemed to handle the animal well, keeping tight control over the plow lines looped about his shoulders, issuing the monosyllabic commands the mule best understood: "Gee," or "Haw," for direction, with "Whoa" at the end of a newly plowed row, then "Git-up" with a slap of the plow lines to start the animal down the next.

The man's forearms below the rolled-up sleeves of his faded workshirt showed muscles knotting beneath dark-tanned skin. A crushed and battered hat shaded his face and neck from the direct noonday sun, its sweat band already showing through dark stains of perspiration. He wore faded and patched overalls, and a shirt that looked as if it had originally been a guano sack, as did many other of the farmhands at work in the lower part of this field and in others—but there the resemblance ended. The overalls, though faded and worn, had been clean when the work had begun that morning, the shirt mended. The man's skin was darker than that of any other of the sunburned farmers at work in the fields, his hair black and straight—he still looks like a Gypsy, William mused to himself, watching as Janson Sanders guided the mule onto unbroken ground and began to cut a new furrow into the red earth, the man handling the plow and the animal with the patience and knowledge born from years of experience.

William had never had an Indian on the place before—but, then again, Janson Sanders seemed different from most men in a great many ways. William had been pleased almost from the beginning with the boy, more pleased than he had ever thought he might be. At first there had been the worry that the boy might present a problem of himself with that pride that seemed almost inborn in him, but, in the almost four months since, William had been pleasantly surprised to have found himself with one of the best farmhands he had ever had on the place. The boy did not say much; he kept to himself and did his work, and he had made few friends in the months he had now been on the place—and that had taken on important meaning in the past few days.

William puffed at his cigar and watched the boy through the haze of blue smoke that hung within the car, noting how he handled himself, as well as how he handled the plow and the animal. Janson Sanders was a strange one, staying mostly to himself in the little time he was not working, doing odd chores for Mattie Ruth and Titus Coates, or for other people in the area, earning whatever little money it might bring him, taking in eggs or meal, kerosene or lard or butter when there was no money to be had. He seemed to take on whatever extra work he could find to do—cleaning out a barn or a chicken coop, mending a roof, cutting stove wood, splitting rails for fencing, plowing, clearing land—the kind of work seemed to matter very little to him, the pay all important, whether that pay be money, or fresh meat, or even flour.

William had wondered often what it was the boy might do with the money he earned from his wages and from the numerous other odd jobs he could find for himself to do. He seemed to spend very little on himself, buying only the bare necessities at the store, trading work for them instead whenever possible; he did not even seem to have a woman to spend it on—he could even have it all buried in the barn, William mused to himself, thinking over the possibilities. But the boy earned his pay; he did his work and kept his nose clean, and he could do with the money whatever he wished—he could bury it, or burn it, or do whatever it was that someone like him might choose to do with it, for at the moment that mattered very little to William Whitley. That mattered so very little.

William took another drink from the corn liquor, and then sat for a moment considering the sunlight as it glinted off the surface of the whiskey remaining in the jar—it was good whiskey, distilled from the finest corn mash in the area, made by one of the last of the good, old-time moonshiners still left alive in that part of Georgia. It was a dying art, whiskey-making, as William well knew. It had been killed by the Women's Christian Temperance Union and Prohibition, and all the shouting preachers who sought to tell a man he could no longer have a drink; killed by the bootleggers themselves, in their greed for profit at the cost of quality in the years since Prohibition had made stilling such a lucrative business, until many a bootlegger nowadays would no longer even drink the liquor he himself had made—but William did not worry about the quality of the corn liquor he drank. There would be no violent headaches from it, no sickness, no death, as from much of the bootleg that was sold these days. The corn liquor in that jar was possibly some of the best in that part of Georgia; and William should know—the corn and malt it had been distilled from had been grain grown on his own land, and the old man who had done the stilling had been one of his own people; even the copper in the still and the rock in the furnace belonged to him. If Prohibition had done nothing else in the past seven years, it had at least made a much wealthier man of William Whitley.

William swished the corn liquor about in the jar and turned his eyes back to the boy at work in the field—but his mind did not return to anything so trivial as a farmhand's money, or the minor irritations often caused by a headstrong and disobedient daughter. He now ran one of the largest and most profitable bootlegging operations in his part of the state. In the more than seven years since Prohibition had come into effect, the government's efforts to stop the sale, transportation, and production of alcoholic beverages in the United States had taken his small liquor sideline and had turned it into big business. He was now clearing more money from the bootlegging than he did from cotton production or from any other of the legitimate businesses he operated in the County. Liquor was money these days—just ask the speakeasy operators, the owners of the low-class smoke joints, the bootleggers, the gangsters running the liquor business up North, the revenue agents, the Southern country sheriffs. Liquor was big business and big money, and William would have a share of that business, and of its profits—but William Whitley was no fool. Only a fool nowadays would be involved in the direct stilling of liquor, and in the transportation or the sale of alcoholic beverages in the United States now in the 1920's. The Volstead Act and the Prohibition laws made that dangerous, and the revenuers, though ill-funded and often inept, could make powerful enemies once they were on to a bootlegger—but William did not consider himself a bootlegger. He was a businessman involved in the liquor trade. He had men to do the stilling, men to run the liquor across the County line hidden beneath the false beds of trucks, men to handle the sale of the whiskey to the owners of the speakeasies and the smoke joints, or to other men who would only cut and re-bottle and bootleg the liquor on to someone else. In the past years, William's eldest son, Bill, had taken on more and more of the business side of the operation, until now William was only rarely involved with the bootlegging at all—but even Bill was little involved in the direct operations of the liquor trade. There were other men to take that risk, men who were well paid for the chances they took, men like Franklin Bates, and the farmhand Gilbert Baskin.

Tall, thick-necked, absolutely bald, with massive hands and massive arms and massive shoulders, Franklin Bates had killed at least one man in the past; William knew that, for Bates himself had told him that upon coming to the place years before. William had no idea where the man had come from, and only the barest idea as to why he had left there, but still he trusted Bates completely. The man had no family and no friends, no woman except for the hours in which he needed one, no conscience, and it seemed no regrets. He did his work and was paid well for it—he belonged to William, just as surely as did the massive house or the cotton fields or the liquor stills that made him only more money. Through the years Bates had served him well, keeping peace on Whitley land and in much of Endicott County, seeing to it no one crossed William, and seeing to it that those who did often lived to long regret their actions. Together with Gilbert Baskin, he had made the stilling operation one of the largest in that part of the state, one of the most profitable, and one of the busiest, as well as one of the most despised.

Gilbert Baskin had not been on the Whitley place as long as had Franklin Bates or many other of the farmhands, but he had long since proven himself more valuable in many ways than men who had been on the place years longer. He had a liking for money and little conscience as to how he earned it, as well as a talent for getting any job done quickly and in the least-obtrusive way possible. William had started Baskin out years before hauling liquor across the County line for sale, but had soon moved him into other phases of the operation—purchasing supplies, sugar, jars, and sheets of copper in Buntain and even up in Columbus; taking corn or malt to the mill to have it ground for use in the mash; helping in the actual stilling and cutting of the liquor, and in the important preparation of the corn mash the whiskey was distilled from; as well as delivering the product out of the County to the seldom-spoken men who William did not trust, men who had made him only richer in past years.

Baskin had been one of the few men ever allowed close to the whiskey-making itself, the old man handling the actual stilling having refused to allow but few men through the years close to his operations. Old Tate had been making corn liquor on Whitley land for as long as William could remember, and he was a cantankerous old fool William knew he had to humor whether he liked it or not. The man was of indeterminable age, and he was one of the best of the old moonshiners still left alive, having made whiskey through most of the years of his life. He had survived war with the Yankees and life with at least four wives that William knew of, as well as the fathering of a brood of twenty-three children, all grown, many dead now—Tate had little left of his life but the whiskey-making, and it was something he took pride in. He would allow no popskull to leave his stills so long as he lived, and he would allow no man close to the operations unless he could trust him to uphold the quality of the 'shine he had been making for so many years. He had at last grudgingly accepted Gilbert Baskin. He accepted few others.

Baskin had proven himself valuable time and again through the years, especially in the searching out and elimination of the stilling operations of other moonshiners in the area, threatening many into halting production, reporting others to the sheriff or to revenue agents, as well as in cashing in on the customers then left without a source of supply. William knew that without Gilbert Baskin he would never have been in the position he was in now in the liquor trade; his operation would not have been so big or so lucrative—he might even have gone the way of the many bootleggers he had forced out of the business over the years. But it seemed now that Gilbert's usefulness had come to an end. Gilbert Baskin had become a liability, and liabilities were something William knew were better done without. Something better gotten rid of.

He had known it was coming for some time now; Baskin was just too fond of his liquor and his women, just too free with his money and his talk. William had known—but still that had not lessened the surprise he had felt when Sheriff Hill had come by the house that morning not long after J.C. Cooper had left, come by with what had amounted to a quiet and friendly warning. Baskin was spending money too freely, running his mouth too often, drinking too openly, and annoying good, decent girls from nice families throughout the County—people were starting to talk, to speculate, to wonder about things that should not be wondered about. Gilbert Baskin had too much money for a farmhand, and too free access to liquor for anyone—he had made himself a danger to the entire bootlegging operation, a danger to the Whitleys' good name, and a danger to William himself.

But Gilbert Baskin was a danger to no one anymore.

As soon as the sheriff had left, William had called in the two people he trusted most, his eldest son, Bill, and Franklin Bates—Gilbert Baskin had been driven to the depot and put on a train bound for Montgomery, and told, rather convincingly William was certain, that if he were ever to show his face in Endicott County again, he would not live long enough to see the other side of the County line.

Now that danger was passed. Gilbert Baskin had left the County, and the talk would soon die down—but that left another problem. There would have to be someone to take Baskin's place, someone to go for supplies and run liquor and do the dirty jobs not fit for Bill or even for Franklin Bates to do. Bootlegging liquor was not the safest or most certain of professions, and the men on the front line were the ones who accepted all the risks—there were the revenuers and the other bootleggers, and the hard feeling from deals gone sour and deals long past; there were men William had forced out of the business, and men eager to grow in the business, and men who bought the liquor but who no man could trust. William could not risk his son or a man with the proven value of Franklin Bates—and, yet, running liquor took a certain kind of man, a man with little to lose, a man with a liking for money and with little conscience as to how he might earn it; and a man with the courage to do what he had to do, no matter what that might be, to get the job done.

William took another drink of the corn liquor and wiped at his mouth with the back of one hand, his eyes never leaving the young man at work in the field—Janson Sanders could be that sort of man. Unlike Gilbert, Sanders had little to do with anyone else on the place other than Mattie Ruth and Titus Coates, and, on occasion, to William's dislike, William's own son, Stan. He stayed on Whitley land and went into town only rarely; he had few, if any, friends, and no woman it seemed he might go talking too much to in a moment of passion. If the boy drank, it was not so anyone would notice, and he seemed to run his mouth very little—and, best of all, he had exhibited a liking for money, and a willingness to do whatever it took to earn it, and yet still did not spend it too freely or too openly. The boy was strong, and he seemed to be smart enough—but it did not take brains to drive a truck load of bootleg whiskey across the County line, or to know when to keep his mouth shut. The boy could very well prove himself as capable as Gilbert had been in driving a truck and in hauling 'shine out for sale, and even in other things he might be called on to do in the future. Right now all William needed was someone to bring supplies in and to handle runs of corn liquor over the County line to the speakeasies and the smoke joints and the bootleg distributors William rarely dealt with personally. Janson Sanders very well could be that man—but, first, William had to be certain. Too much was riding on the choice: William's reputation, his good name, the profits from the stilling, the safety of the entire whiskey-making operation. The boy would have to be tested, proven. If he could prove himself, all well and good. If not—

If not, Janson Sanders would regret the day he had ever come to Endicott County. He would regret that day for a very long time indeed.

THE QUIET of late afternoon settled in over Whitley land hours later that day, bringing with it a slight chill in the air of winter trying to hold on into the new spring of late April. The smell of wood smoke filled the air, and the odors of cooking and good food from the nearby kitchen as Janson unloaded firewood near the Whitley's back veranda, stacking it into high, symmetrical piles to dry at easy access from the wide steps, or from the covered walkway that led to the separate kitchen standing at a distance from the rear of the house.

Stan Whitley sat nearby on the wide board steps that led up to the center of the walkway, talking, as it seemed to Janson he had been doing for hours. The boy had come out to where he had been cutting firewood earlier in the afternoon in the heavily-wooded area bordering the Whitley cotton fields, and had ridden back to the big house on the wagon seat beside him, talking, it seemed, almost without stop—but it was a familiar sound, the boy's voice droning on, changing in pitch and timbre, his hands moving as he talked, the late-afternoon sun glinting off the round lenses of his eyeglasses as he moved and spoke and then sat down again.

Janson halfheartedly listened to him as he worked, fond of him in a big-brotherly sort of way that he had never felt toward anyone before in all his life, though he could still never quite forget the boy was a Whitley. He still did not know how they had ever become friends in the first place, for he was five years Stan's senior in age, and many years his junior in book learning and education—but they were friends, friends as Janson had known but few times in his life. It seemed almost as if the boy looked up to him, almost as if he saw no difference between them, though Stan wore fancy clothes and expensive shoes and shirts that would have cost Janson several weeks worth of wages. Stan often came out to the old lean-to room off the barn where Janson lived in the hours after supper was finished at the big house, where they would sit and talk for hours until the boy would have to go home to do schoolwork or to go to bed; or Janson would teach him to carve or to make baskets from white oak splits, and Stan would tell him stories about places and things that Janson would never even dream to see. Usually he enjoyed the boy's company, enjoyed the way he could use words to make them say more than the words themselves were—but today he was distracted, his mind on things other than conversation as he unloaded the wagonload of firewood that Mrs. Whitley had already paid him cash money to cut and to bring to the house.

Janson got an armload of wood from the back of the wagon and jumped down into the newly greening grass that grew there in the yard, grass that was so carefully tended and looked after, and that Mrs. Whitley had already paid him twice to cut with the wooden-handled push mower that was kept in the storage shed out behind the kitchen. He carried the wood toward the stack he had already begun near the covered walkway, hearing Stan continue on, as he had been doing for much of the past hour, about the sister who had been sent off to school up in Atlanta in hopes that it might somehow turn her into more of a lady. He already knew from Stan that the girl was now being sent home in disgrace, having been caught cheating on some kind of test up at that fancy school—rich folks, Janson thought, still only half paying attention to what the boy was saying. Elise Whitley had all the money in the world; she would never have to work even one day in all her life, or worry about where the next day's bed or meal was coming from. She could have anything in the world she wanted—all she had to do was go to school and try to learn to act like a lady. But she had been caught cheating on a test instead, when her only work in life was book learning and looking pretty and getting an education that most other people would be grateful for—rich folks, Janson thought again, growing irritated at the idea of someone who so easily had so much, but who appreciated it so very little.

But the girl was a Whitley, he reminded himself, and he could expect nothing less from a Whitley. None of them seemed grateful for the life they had, though they each of them had the world. Stan was the only one of the lot he could even abide, except for Mrs. Whitley, of course, who he reasoned was not really a Whitley anyway, for she had only married into the family. She often gave him extra work to do when he was free of the farm chores that earned his wages and took up most of his time, paying him in cash money for cutting firewood or mowing the lawn, weeding spring flower beds or painting a fence, or doing whatever else she might find that wanted doing. She seemed a fine lady, gentle spoken, with usually some bit of fancy needlework or prissy sewing in her hands—and she paid in cash, which was rare among the farm folk who usually hired him. Janson could little abide her husband, and he often found himself wondering how someone like William Whitley had managed to marry so fine a lady as Mrs. Whitley—but it was the Whitleys' oldest son that he liked even less.

Bill Whitley plainly rubbed Janson the wrong way, and it was clear Janson had the same effect on him, for the two had almost come to blows several times already in the months he had been on the place. The man liked power, and he also liked to abuse that power—there was something not quite right about Bill Whitley; what that was, Janson could not put a finger on, but he despised the man, and knew without question that the feeling was more than mutually shared. There seemed to be very little of Mrs. Whitley in her eldest son, and a great deal of his father—but there was something more, and it was that something that made Janson wary of the man, cautious, more cautious than he was even with Whitley himself.

Whitley's second son, Alfred, was little like either of his parents, or even his older brother. He was very near to Janson's age, but, to Janson, Alfred Whitley seemed so much younger, often even younger than did Stan. He was a slick-hair, fascinated with the gangster news on the radio, blaring loud jazz music through the open front parlor windows in the rare times when he was at home. He drove his motor car too fast, and dressed purposefully like a fop, in his blue serge suits and wide trousers, with a gold watch chain always hanging out of his vest pocket, and his hair slicked back and shining with Glostora—he had even come home drunk, so Stan had said, on several occasions, to his mother's utter horror and his father's absolute disapproval. Janson knew that Alfred Whitley played at being a man, trying very hard to act as he thought a man should act, dress as he thought a man should dress, behave as he believed a modern man should behave, without ever having taken the time to really understand what that behavior should be. He often made a loud and deliberate show of temper and rebellion, and seemed always into one scrape or another, always hiding from some girl's father or angry older brother. Alfred was a boy, spoiled, self-willed, with everything he had wanted all his life, and, though Janson had not met or even seen Elise Whitley as of yet, he knew she had to be very much the same as her brother Alfred. The things he had already heard about her left little doubt—and Janson did not like spoiled children, even pretty ones, as he had heard Elise Whitley to be.

He started back to the wagon for another armload of wood, still paying little attention to what Stan was saying—there were many more important things on his mind than the troubles a spoiled rich girl could manage to get herself into. There was the wood to finish unloading, and a quick supper to cook and eat before he went on to other work that had to be done this evening—work that was now causing a growing uneasiness within him.

William Whitley had approached him earlier in the day just as he and the other hands at work in the fields had taken their dinner breaks for the sandwiches of cold pork sausage or pressed meat, or biscuits and ham, or cold fried chicken they had brought with them earlier to the fields to eat. Janson had just sat down to himself beneath a tree at the edge of the field he had been plowing, uncovering the dinner bucket he had left there earlier in the day, and opening the lid on the pint jar of buttermilk he had left in the shade to remain cool through the morning, when Whitley had walked up, a big cigar in his mouth, and had stood staring down at him.

"You want somethin'?" Janson had asked, annoyance clearly in his voice as he stared up at the man—he did not like being forced to look up to anyone, especially not a man like William Whitley. He had been plowing since shortly after sunrise that morning, and he was hungry now, with little time to rest or to eat before he would have to return to the fields and the plowing still left to be done.

Whitley stared down at him for a moment, taking the cigar from his mouth before answering. "You interested in earning some extra money, boy?" he had asked at last.

"Yeah, I'm interested," Janson said. Whitley had taken him on for extra work before, hiring him to sweep out the barns, patch a roof, or clean out the chicken house; usually the dirtiest work Whitley could find that needed doing. The man oftentimes wanted to pay in food that was not always fit to eat, or wanted to apply the work against the small charge Janson had run at the store, but work was work, and there was always the chance he might pay in cash money this time, or at least in food that was fit to be eaten or traded for something else he could use even more. There had not been one offer of work, or of money, that Janson had turned down in the months he had been on the place—he had saved, scrimped, done without; and had worried over every single penny he had been forced to spend for food or for kerosene or matches or anything else he could not get in trade—it was worth it, worth anything, when he saw the money he had knotted into an old sock and hidden in the back of a drawer in the splintery old chifforobe in his room. Each Saturday that he received his pay that was the first place he went with his wages, or with any other cash money he could make from extra work or from selling what he was paid in trade; and he sometimes sat alone at night and counted it in the light of the single kerosene lamp in his room—not a fortune, but money he had earned, money he had saved, money he had worked for, money that would help him to buy a dream one day. Or, more properly, to buy one back.

"What you got that needs doin'?" Janson had asked, chewing into a biscuit of cold ham, ham he had taken in trade for more than two days' work bottoming chairs for one of the local sharecroppers. He expected that Whitley would give him work much as he had given him before, farm chores, repair work, but was surprised when Whitley spoke again.

"I'm going to send you on an errand, boy. There's something I want you to pick up for me in Buntain."

"What's that?"

Whitley stared at him for a long moment, not speaking. "I want you to bring back a load of sugar for me, boy—"

"Sugar?" Janson stared at him. Surely he had not heard right. Any kind of sweetening a man could want was already available right here on the place—sorghum, molasses, wild honey from bee trees in the woods or from gums kept out back of the main barn, cane syrup cooked down the previous fall in the syrup kettle out near the cane mill, white sugar that could be store-bought right on the place, or from the grocery stores in Goodwin or from the other County towns. He had even seen sacks of white sugar being unloaded at Whitley's own store just a few days before, along with tin cans of peas and beans, colorful cloth sacks of flour, bolts of cloth, men's overalls, ladies bloomers, and everything else that had come in on the big truck from Columbus. Surely he had not heard—

"Yeah, sugar—and don't you go asking too many questions, boy, or telling anybody what I'm sending you after. You can drive a truck, can't you?"

"Yeah, I can drive."

"Good, I'll have a truck waiting for you by the barn at dark. You'll pick up the sugar and come back by the route I give you—it don't much matter to me how you get there, but you come back just like I say, you got it?"

"Yeah, I got it," Janson said, staring up at him.

"There'll be a tarp in the back of the truck; you cover the sugar up and tie it down good before you head back—and you remember to keep your mouth shut, boy—"

Janson stared at him, comprehension slowly coming—sugar, and a large quantity of it if he would need a truck to haul it in, being bought quietly out of the County, brought in after dark. Suddenly he understood. There was only one thing that much sugar would be needed for, only one reason it would have to be purchased so quietly, and brought in under cover of darkness—Whitley was bootlegging, and he would be using Janson to make a haul of black market sugar. With the Prohibition laws so strict, and revenue agents it seemed everywhere, that much sugar could never be bought openly; it could arouse too many suspicions, start gossip—and William Whitley could not afford gossip.

Janson could tell from the look on Whitley's face that the man knew he had made the connection. "You do good at this, boy, and there'll be more work for you in the future. You could be earning yourself some extra money pretty regular—that is if you can keep your mouth shut and do what you're told to do."

More work—hauling sugar that would be used in stilling corn liquor, maybe even being called on to haul bootleg whiskey itself later on. The Prohibition laws were tough; a man could end up in jail real quick if he got himself involved in moonshining, if he did not get himself shot first—but the money, and the chance for more in the future. Moonshining was a dangerous business, with the sheriff and the revenue agents and other bootleggers all constantly after your tail—but the money—

"How much?" he asked, looking up at Whitley, not really liking or even trusting the man—but the amount he was told did much to wipe away the remainder of that thought. More money than he could earn in weeks of farm work, and the promised chance for more in the future—he accepted the run without a second thought and watched as Whitley walked away, satisfied in that moment that he had made the right decision, the only decision.

But that was hours ago, and now he was wondering. Moonshining could be a good way for a man to end up in jail, if he did not get himself killed first. Between the revenuers and the sheriff and the other bootleggers—Janson wondered now if he had not made the worst decision of his life. Even considering the money—but a man could not spend money, and he could not farm his own land, if he was in jail. Or buried.

But he had given Whitley his word, and this time it would be nothing more than sugar he would be hauling, he told himself. He would not have to take on more work in the future, more hauls, if he did not want to, and hauling sugar could not be against the law. Hauling sugar could not be—

He kept telling himself that even now as he carried another armload of wood from the wagon to the stacks near the covered walkway. There was nothing illegal about hauling a truckload of sugar—but if he were stopped, if the truck was searched, there were questions he would be asked, questions about a load of black market sugar he would probably not even be able to prove he had a claim to. Some sheriff or sheriff's deputy would think it was stolen, or, even worse yet, probably make the same connection he had made—but he had given his word, and never once in all his life had Janson Sanders ever gone back on his word. It was a matter of pride, a matter of being the man he was. It would be nothing more than sugar this time, one haul, one run—but, even as he told himself that, he knew he would take on those other runs if they were offered to him, no matter what it was that he might be called on to haul. He would do it for the money. For what the money could buy him.

Stan had gotten up from the wide board steps that led up to the center of the walkway, and he now moved back and forth between the wagon and the growing stacks of firewood, carrying small loads of the wood and handing it to Janson to stack with the much larger loads he carried. The boy continued to talk on about his sister, but Janson now heard hardly a word, his mind on the meeting scheduled with Whitley just after dark, and the haul that would come later—and the other work that might come soon enough. He did not want to get involved in running corn liquor, not for the rightness or wrongness of the act, for his desire for the money well overcame that, but he could not help but to worry over what might happen to him if he were caught tonight with such a large amount of an ingredient known to be needed in moonshining, or, later, with an even more damning cargo. He kept assuring himself that little could happen to him for being caught with a load of even black market sugar—but to be caught with a load of bootleg whiskey—

He suddenly realized that Stan was waiting for a response to some question asked or some comment offered. The boy stood with a small load of firewood in his skinny arms, the redness of a setting sun glinting off the round lenses of his eyeglasses. The sleeves of his expensive and well-laundered and pressed shirt were rolled to above his elbows, and a dark smudge of dirt shown on the front just beside where his suspenders went up over his shoulder—his ma'll tan him for that, Janson thought, realizing how peculiar it looked to see a Whitley working, a Whitley doing physical labor as if he were one of the farmhands or sharecroppers.

Janson took the small load of wood from the boy's arms and stacked it with what he had carried from the truck, then turned to look at him again. "You better go back and sit down. Them fancy clothes of yours ain't much for workin' in."

Stan obeyed, going to sit down again on the steps of the covered walkway, then resumed what it was he must have been saying in the first place. "Anyway, I'd be worried if I were Elise, coming home now to face Daddy—I've never seen him so mad in all my life as he was when he first found out she had been expelled. I'd be plenty worried—"

So would I—Janson thought, but said nothing. He had seen Whitley's temper often enough over the four months he had been on the place, had seen him curse and threaten and verbally abuse the farmhands, the sharecroppers, even his own sons—but the girl rightly deserved it, Janson reminded himself. She had been given her life on a silver platter, all she could ever want in the world, and was still spoiled and blind and willful enough to not even care. Janson had little patience for spoiled, petted children, and little sympathy when they got what they rightly deserved—Elise Whitley had probably well earned what her father would give her, earned it several times over. A good, sound spanking would probably do the girl a world of good, even if she was sixteen now and "full-growed t' be a woman," as Titus Coates had told him.

Janson's attention began to stray again, his mind occupied with his own thoughts as he moved back toward the wagon for another armload of wood.

"Daddy'll be meeting the train day after tomorrow. Elise and Phyllis Ann—I've told you about her, haven't I?" Stan interrupted himself to ask.

"Phyllis Ann?—yeah, you told me—"

"Well, anyway, Daddy'll be meeting the train, and Elise won't be too happy with the surprise he'll have waiting for her."

"Surprise?" Janson asked, still only half paying attention. He jumped down from the back of the wagon with another armload of wood and started toward the stacks near the walkway.

"Oh, yes—a surprise in the form of J.C. Cooper. Daddy's taking him along to meet the train. Elise will be furious."

"I thought your sister liked J.C.." Janson had seen J.C. Cooper at a distance only a few times; he seemed a decent enough fellow, spoke rarely—and seemed scared of his own shadow. Janson could little imagine him with the flirtatious, bobbed-haired, lipsticked little flapper he imagined Elise Whitley to be, with her bold, modern ways—but, then again, he could hardly imagine J.C. Cooper with any woman.

Stan shrugged his shoulders. "Elise likes him well enough, but she won't want to marry him, which is what Daddy wants. She won't want to marry anyone just to please Daddy."

"Then what's your pa wantin' her to marry him for?"

"For the cotton mill. J.C.'s daddy owns part of the mill, and Daddy wants to be partners with him in it—anyway, Elise won't want to marry J.C.—"

"Sounds t' me like it'd do her good t' get married. Maybe a husband an' some young'ns'd settle her down—"

"I think she'd scare J.C. to death if he tried to settle her down."

"Well, then that's his own fault. If he's man enough, he'll handle her."

"Elise would never agree with you on that. She's very modern, you know, very independent—"

"That's what's wrong with th' world, independent, bobbed-haired, modern women," Janson remarked absently, stacking wood on a pile, and then turning back toward the wagon.

Stan shrugged again. "Well, Elise is very independent. She'd be furious with any man who tried to settle her down, J.C. and Daddy included."

"Then, if you ask me, she needs t' get married," Janson answered, somewhat more than distracted now. "A man could do her a lot of good, get some 'a th' flighty ideas outta her head—sounds t' me like a sound spankin' wouldn't do her no harm either—"

Stan laughed, but Janson did not even break stride as he walked back to the wagon for another armload of wood. There were much more important things on his mind than the marriage plans for a spoiled rich girl. He had enough worries of his own over the planned haul of what he knew would have to be black market sugar tonight—and the possibilities of what he might be called on to haul in the future. Besides, Elise Whitley sounded to him like more trouble than he would wish on any man, J.C. Cooper included. If J.C. wanted to take her on, and her father in the bargain, then perhaps he was more of a man than Janson would ever have given him credit for being.

And perhaps he was more of a fool as well.

THE TRUCK jolted and bounced over the rutted, back-country roads a few hours later, the dim headlamps picking out only a few feet of red clay road before the front tires. Janson gripped the steering wheel with both hands, straining forward, trying to see any hazards in the road before the truck could hit them—if he were to break an axle, or ruin a tire out here in the middle of nowhere—

He had hoped that the weight of the heavy cloth sacks of sugar that now lay beneath the tarp covering the back of the truck would help to reduce the pitch and sway of the vehicle over the worst of the ruts, but it had done little good. He was headed home now, over the route that Whitley had given him, the roads he had been traveling for the past hour some of the worst he had ever seen, rough, rutted, completely washed out in places. His palms sweated against the steering wheel as he fought to keep the truck on the road and still avoid the deepest of the ruts; but it was not just the worry over breaking an axle or ending up in one of the ditches alongside the road that concerned him—what would he say if he were stopped, if the truck was searched to reveal the large, cloth sacks of sugar that lay beneath the tarp over the back? How would he explain hauling such a large amount of sugar over these back roads at this time of night? It would be more than obvious to some sheriff's deputy that so much sugar would be needed for only one reason. Only one—

The possibilities of ending up in one of the ditches seemed to be growing by the minute, the road before him becoming progressively worse. The truck jounced over the deepest rut yet, throwing him against the inside of the driver's door, and he held his breath for a moment, praying, until he was certain the tires were still sound and the truck still in running condition. He slowed to make a turn onto a second, seemingly even worse road, glancing back as he made the turn, thinking for a moment that he saw the lights of some sort of a vehicle bob into sight on the road behind him. He forced himself to continue on at the same speed, trying to concentrate on the road, but found himself glancing back over his shoulder, slowing, watching as he came into a straight—the lights were there again, and again a few minutes later as he came into another straight. The nervousness that had been sitting in the pit of his stomach for hours was now growing—he was being followed. He knew that it was impossible, that no one could know—but, still, he was being followed. He was certain of it.

He gripped the steering wheel harder in his sweating palms, forcing his eyes to concentrate on the few feet of rutted clay road that the headlamps picked out before the truck—he just wanted to get off these damned roads and back on Whitley land. He just wanted—

He risked a look back over his shoulder again, seeing the lights bob into view, just coming around a curve—they were closer now. The truck hit a deep rut, throwing him against the door, and he tried to make himself watch the road before him, and not behind—goddamn it, they were closer. He pushed down fully on the accelerator, hearing the truck's engine whine and complain—but the damned thing could blow up if it wanted to, so long as it got him off these roads first. So long as it—

The lights were growing closer as he glanced back again, gaining distance as he tried to force even more from the tortured machine, the steering wheel becoming slippery in his sweating palms now. He fought to control the truck as it bounced over the deep gullies washed in the roadbed, its frame squeaking in protest as it careened along the rough clay road at speeds neither it nor the road were ever meant for—forty miles an hour, forty-five, the heavy load of sugar shifting beneath the tarp over the back, increasing the pitch of the vehicle into a curve, the tires sliding in loose rock and dirt, almost losing everything as he came out of one curve and went into another. The lights grew even closer, showing now even inside of the truck, all semblance of innocence now gone, and the knot of fear tightened even further in his stomach—he had been followed. He had been followed; and now—

The truck slid into a sharp curve, coming to within inches of the ditch—suddenly all control of the vehicle was gone, the tires skidding in loose dirt and rocks at the roadside, a huge oak tree looming before the headlamps. Janson jerked the wheel in his hands, slamming his foot down on the brake. The truck skidded wildly, the rear end seeming suddenly independent of the front. He yanked the wheel in the opposite direction, praying and cursing all at the same time, feeling the truck jerk, recover for a moment, then go wildly in the other direction. He fought the steering wheel, clenching it in his hands until his palms hurt, struggling to keep the truck on the road as it recovered and finally came out of the curve, the oak tree going by only bare inches away.

He forced himself to slow, to breathe, damning the driver of the other vehicle as it slid into the same curve, recovered, and then sped on, closing the gap between them even further as he glanced back again. He pushed at the accelerator, then slowed as he came into another curve. The heavy load beneath the tarp shifted again, worsening the sway of the vehicle and throwing him against the inside of the door with the force of the turn. He pushed the accelerator down again, the truck recovering, coming into a straight—and then slammed his foot down on the brake as the headlamps picked out a car across the road ahead. The truck skidded for a moment, then finally came to a halt, the tires throwing up a thick cloud of red dust that choked the air around him.

Janson sat, staring at the car just yards ahead that blocked the roadway, its headlamps dark. He fought down the urge to jump from the truck and take his chances in the nearby woods—sheriff's deputies, revenue agents, bootleggers; whoever it was, they might be more likely to shoot a man if he ran. And then it was too late. The car following him ground to a halt on the rear of the truck, and two men emerged from the car ahead, one of them training a flashlight in Janson's direction—he was caught. He could still take his chances in the woods—but he could not make himself move. He could only grip the steering wheel so tightly that his knuckles turned white, watching as the two men ahead slowly approached the truck. There was a sound from the vehicle to the rear, a door opening, its lights now out as well—but Janson's eyes stayed on the men before him, settling on one as he came even with the truck and peered in the window.

William Whitley stared at him with a half-amused, half-pleased expression on his face—the goddamn son-of-a-bitch, this was a test, Janson thought, realizing suddenly that he was shaking. The goddamn—

"You're white as a sheet, boy—did Bill put a scare into you, running you like that?"

Janson took a deep breath and let it out slowly, trying to force a control over the anger that raged up inside of him. He turned loose of the steering wheel with hands that ached from released tension—the goddamn son-of-a-bitch, this was a—

"You stupid half-breed—" Whitley was quickly shoved aside and the truck door yanked open. Bill Whitley reached in to grab Janson by the shirt collar and pull him from the vehicle, then turned to shove him hard back against its side. "You about lost that whole load back there, and almost got me killed just trying to follow you—you goddamn—"

Janson shoved him away, clenching his hands into fists, ready to fight the man. "What the hell were you doing on my butt like that anyway!"

"Did you really think we'd trust you with a truck and that much money? I was betting you'd head straight for the state line; everybody knows you can't trust an Indian, not even half-breed trash like—"

Something snapped within Janson. He went after Bill Whitley with a fury he had not known since the day he had almost killed Buddy Eason in that carriage house back in Eason County almost two years before. He grabbed Bill by the shirt front, turning and slamming him hard back against the side of the truck. "You goddamn son-of-a—"

But he was suddenly grabbed from behind and thrown backwards into the red dirt of the roadbed, William Whitley standing over him, staring down. "You watch your mouth boy—" he said, his eyes never leaving Janson's face in the darkness.

Janson stared up at him for a moment, and then slowly got to his feet, dusting off the legs of his faded dungarees. He saw Whitley motion away the third man, who had stepped up to intercede, turning to stare as Franklin Bates moved a step away, his hand still resting on the gun tucked into his belt, and Janson realized suddenly how close he had come to death in those moments.

After a moment, William Whitley spoke back over his shoulder to his son. "Bill, take the truck on to the house and get somebody to unload it."

Bill Whitley stood staring, unmoving, his eyes never leaving Janson.

Whitley's voice rose. "I said go!"

For a moment Bill Whitley did not move; then he slowly turned and got into the truck, slamming the door behind himself. His eyes met Janson's again for a moment just before the truck started away—there would be another time.

As the truck slowly maneuvered around the car blocking the road ahead, Whitley turned toward Bates. "Franklin—"

There was a sound of acknowledgment from the big man, a slight lift of the head, but no words. He continued to stare at Janson, his hand never leaving the gun in his belt—Janson had wondered for months what a man like Franklin Bates might do for Whitley. Now he knew.

"Take my car on to the house. I'll take Bill's Packard; the boy'll ride with me. We've got some talking to do."

Bates nodded without a word, then dropped his hand from the gun at his waist. He turned and started toward the car that blocked the road, never once looking back. Soon Janson was left standing alone in the middle of the rutted clay road with William Whitley.

"You did good, boy," Whitley said, staring at him with eyes that Janson could not read in the darkness. The man reached into his pocket and pulled out a roll of bills, counted off several, then shoved the remainder back into his pocket. "You've earned this money right and proper tonight, boy—and there's more where it came from, if you can keep your mouth shut and do what you're told to do without asking too many questions." He held the bills out toward Janson. "There could be some extra work for you pretty regular. You can be earning yourself some good money, boy, if you're interested—"

Janson stared at the bills in Whitley's hand, the reason he had taken on the haul of sugar in the first place. His suspicions that he had walked into a bootleg operation were only stronger—why else the need for such secrecy; why else the need to test him as they had done tonight. William Whitley was a bootlegger, and Janson was—

He took the money held out to him, crumpled it into one hand, and shoved it into his pocket—if anything, he was no fool. Whitley was offering him money, more money than he could make in years of working as a farmhand. If he wanted his land back, it would take money, and a lot of it. Whitley was offering him a chance for that money, and Janson knew that he would be a fool to turn that chance down—no matter what it was he might be called on to haul.

"Yeah, I'm interested," he answered, meeting Whitley's gaze levelly. "I'm interested."

THE FOLLOWING day crawled by with a nervousness growing in the pit of Janson's stomach. He was to meet Whitley behind the big house at dusk—there would be work for him to do tonight.

As the afternoon hours came and the sun began to lower toward the tops of the pine trees in the west, throwing the yard and the fields into long, slanting shadows, Janson could little think of anything else but the meeting to come, and the possibilities of what he might be called on to do that night. He knew what Whitley was—common sense told him that—and, as dusk began to settle in over the fields, he had to fight the urge to grab his things and head straight for the County line. It was only the thought of the money that kept him walking toward the Whitleys' big house, and not toward his room off the barn and then the road out of town.

Whitley and Bill were both waiting for him behind the separate kitchen, near a truck that Janson had never seen before. Franklin Bates was at a distance from them, hunkered down by a tree in the yard, his eyes on Janson as he approached. Janson looked at him for a moment, then toward Whitley and Bill, his eyes finally settling on the truck—there seemed something not quite right about the truckbed, even in the failing light. But he had little time to pay attention as Whitley spoke.

"You're late, boy."

"I was plowin'. I had t' take th' mule back t' th' barn an' see to it she was fed," Janson said.

Whitley stared at him, but it was Bill who spoke first. "I figured you'd be headed for the County line by now. I always did hear that Indians were cowards, as well as thieves, drunkards, and liars—"

Janson took a step forward, ready to wipe the smug look from the man's face, but Whitley stepped between them. "That's enough of it between you two. There's no time for that now. You've got a job to do, boy, if you're interested."

Janson stared past him to Bill for a moment—the time would come. He knew that. But right now there was work to do, money that he could earn. "I'm interested," he said, bringing his eyes back to Whitley. "What kind'a job?"

Whitley stared at him, shifting the cigar to the other side of his mouth. "There's something I want you to take into Buntain for me."

"What's that?"

Whitley looked at him for a moment, then turned to hook his hands beneath what appeared to be the truckbed, and lifted—but Janson already knew. The false bed came up, revealing a space beneath, the fading light glinting off the surface of the glass jars of bootleg liquor concealed there. Whitley reached to lift one from its nest, then held it out toward Janson.

"You know what this is, boy?" he asked.

Janson had known, but still he had not been prepared—corn liquor, bootleg whiskey, moonshine. He had the sudden impulse to tell Whitley that he had made a mistake, that he wanted out—then he saw the look on Bill Whitley's face. The man thought he would run, even now.

He said: "Yeah, I reckon' I know what that is."

Whitley nodded, seeming satisfied. He replaced the jar of corn liquor back into its nest before lowering the false bed back into place. "That's your load, boy. The wood covering makes it look like an empty truckbed at night, unless someone gets real curious." He considered Janson for a moment, the cigar clamped between his teeth. "Well, boy, you want the haul or not? There's good money to be made delivering corn liquor for me. I could be giving you extra work a couple of times a week, taking corn liquor into Buntain and other towns outside the County, bringing back sugar and other supplies." He stared at Janson for a moment. "Well, boy, are you interested?"

Hauling bootleg liquor. Running against the law and the revenuers and other bootleggers. Maybe ending up in jail, maybe shot. Hauling black market sugar had been bad enough; did he really want to—

"How much?" he asked, forcing all other thoughts away. "How much'll you pay?"

He had plenty of time later to wonder if he had made the right decision, as he jolted over rutted, back-country roads with a truck load of bootleg liquor.

# 8

THE SCENERY THAT SPED past the train early that April afternoon in 1927 was a montage of everything that home was to Elise Whitley—the tall, straight pines; the newly plowed fields red to the Georgia sun; the neat, white houses bordered by spring flower beds; the automobiles hurrying along busy country roads; the handsome young men in wide-legged trousers, the girls on their arms in pale, low-waisted spring dresses and new cloche hats. Elise stared out the window at the passing landscape, not wanting now to recognize the landmarks that would mean she was nearing home—but they came anyway: Dunn's Grist Mill, the Pinckney settlement, the old colored church at the edge of town. For once in her life Elise Whitley did not want to go home, though homesickness had followed her through much of the past months as she had been away at school, with only the single trip home at Christmas, and the rare trips to Atlanta by her family—but now she did not want to go home. She did not want to see her family and the friends she had not seen in months, did not want to go home to the place she had spent most all her life—her father would be meeting the train at the station. That was a meeting Elise Whitley could well do without.

She stared out the train window, wondering at the reception she would find waiting for her, and knowing that it would not be a pleasant one. There had been only a single telephone conversation in the days since she had been expelled, a single telephone conversation terminated abruptly when her father had hung up on her mid-sentence. Since then, there had been only silence from Endicott County; her father would have forbidden her mother, Stan, and Alfred to call, and Elise had not dared to place a call herself. He would never have accepted a telephone call from her, and would have become angry with anyone else who had done so. For the first time in her life, Elise felt alone in the world, felt as if she had been divorced from the family that had loved and sheltered her all her life—which was exactly what her father had intended that she feel.

In the moments before he had hung up on her on the phone, he had called her a fool. Elise was beginning to wonder now if he were not right.

Phyllis Ann sat beside her as the train neared Goodwin, the girl's eyes staring into space at something Elise could not see. A slight crease wrinkled her usually smooth and thoughtless forehead, her brown eyes set on a point near the front of the car, her fingers toying with the long strand of beads she wore—she was unusually silent now, compared with the spiteful and acid-tongued creature Elise had left the school with that morning. Phyllis Ann had criticized the school, criticized the instructors and the other girls, even called Miss Perry something to her face that Elise would not even dare to repeat—now she sat staring into space, her words silent, her eyes showing a concern that Elise told herself she could understand. She knew that, no matter the reception she herself might receive at home, Phyllis Ann could expect something so much worse—Ethan Bennett would see to that. Ethan Bennett would amply see to that.

In the days since the expulsion, an uneasy truce had existed between the two girls. They were cordial to each other, often even formally so, and it had seemed on occasion almost as if nothing had ever happened—but that fist that had been raised between them stayed there still: silent, ghost-like, ever present. Elise continued to see it in her mind, and felt she would see it through the remainder of her days—perhaps her father had been right. Perhaps she truly was a fool.

The familiar landmarks moved past the train, bringing them only closer to home. Elise glanced over at Phyllis Ann—the girl looked worried, almost frightened. Elise suddenly found herself very glad that she was going home to William Whitley, no matter how bad his temper might be, or how angry he was with her at the moment, instead of going home to a man like Ethan Bennett. Phyllis Ann had told her so many things—but it was more than that. Elise herself had seen the bruises, the blackened eyes, the remnants of a badly bloodied nose. Ethan Bennett often beat his wife, only slightly less often beat his daughter, and Elise lived in horror of the man—not for herself, for she knew she had little to fear from him, but instead for the girl who had been her best friend all her life. She knew one day Ethan Bennett was going to kill someone; she could only hope that someone would not be Phyllis Ann.

She reached over and patted her friend's hand reassuringly—for they were still that, friends, even after all that had happened between them. They had known each other for too long, shared too many secrets, too many fights, too many heartbreaks, done too much growing up together, for the friendship to end so simply. Phyllis Ann did not look at her, or even acknowledge the touch, and Elise understood, or at least told herself that she should—she knew she could never really understand the things that went on inside her friend's mind, especially not in matters concerning Phyllis Ann's father. And perhaps there was no one who could understand that.

Elise placed her hand back into her own lap and turned to stare out the window again —almost home, the countryside now as familiar to her as a long-known family face. Her father would be waiting for her at the depot—how she wished she could delay that meeting. But there would be no delay, no matter how much she might want it.

The train began to slow, coming into the station, and, after a moment, she saw her father waiting on the platform, J.C. Cooper beside him. She gathered together her things and waited for Phyllis Ann to move from her seat so she could get out into the aisle—she was not ready to face her father yet. But there was no choice. There was little choice left for any of them now.

As they reached the rear door of the car, Elise glanced back for a moment to see a look of fear cross Phyllis Ann's face, and she understood—she too had seen Ethan Bennett waiting on the platform, standing alone at a distance from her father. Pity filled Elise, and she reached back to squeeze her friend's arm reassuringly. "It'll be all right; you'll see," she said softly.

As she stepped down onto the platform, an eerie feeling came over her—those had been the same words Phyllis Ann had used to reassure her they would never be expelled. The very same words.

MARTHA WHITLEY moved about the front parlor of her home a short while later, tidying the placement of the velvet-upholstered chairs about the centertable in the midst of the room, adjusting the heavy, yellow curtains held back from the windows by tasseled cords, running her hand over the cool marble of the mantelpiece for the hundredth time. There was little to do to occupy her hands or her mind this day, little to keep her from thinking, or from worrying.

She moved to one of the tall front windows that faced out onto the broad expanse of yard, the drive, and the red dirt road beyond, knowing that it was not yet time for William to return from the train station with Elise. She had not seen her daughter now in months, had not even spoken to her in days, not since William had forbidden anyone in the household from calling Atlanta following the one conversation he had with Elise the day she had been expelled.

Martha stared out the window for a moment, then moved to the heavily brocaded sofa to sit down, and to wait. Her hands grew restless and she got up to get her needlepoint from across the room, then returned to the sofa to try to occupy her mind with the long-familiar work of her hands—but it was hopeless. Her usually small, delicate stitching became large and uneven. She angrily threw the needlework down beside herself on the sofa, then sat and stared at it for a moment, surprised at her own actions. After a time she took it back up, carefully picked out the bad stitching, and began again—damn you, William, she thought, then felt immediately guilty with the silent words. It was so like him to think he could plan other people's lives to suit his own purposes. He had been doing it for years with their sons, and he had been doing it to Elise all her life. He would marry his daughter off to Hiram Cooper's son, without regard to Elise's feelings in the matter. He had even forbidden Martha from going with him to meet the train this morning, because he was taking J.C. Cooper with him instead.

"Elise is going to start doing what I say, and she's going to start today," he had said before leaving for the train station. "I won't have you interfering, filling her head with more nonsense. She is going to marry J. C., even if I have to beat her black and blue to see that she does—it's for her own good anyway. He's a fine boy; he'll make her a good husband—"

And you'll be closer to getting your hands on the mill—she had thought, but had said nothing. She had given in, had stayed home, not wanting to make Elise's reception any more unpleasant than she already knew it would be—she would see her daughter soon enough; and there would be time later to worry over how they might delay William's plans.

Her hands moved the needle through the fabric with little conscious involvement of her mind, her usually smooth brow furrowed on other matters now. She stuck her finger and a drop of bright red blood stained the delicate stitching, but she hardly noticed—she was worried over what Elise might do once William made clear his intentions that she would marry J.C. Cooper, and marry him soon. William had never once made secret his hopes that his daughter and J.C. would one day wed, and had taken every opportunity in the past to push the two together—but he had never before stated it with such finality that they would marry, and marry soon, no matter Elise's feelings. Martha was not worried that William might actually physically hurt the girl as he had threatened to do, for he had never once struck any one of the children through all the years, no matter his threats—but there were other things he could do. And there was not much she would put past her husband. He would be determined to have his way, and determined to do whatever he had to do to have it.

Elise was not one to easily control her temper; she had enough of her father in her to assure that. She readily spoke her mind, often without thought, and especially when she was angry—she did not want to marry J.C. Cooper, and had never once made secret her feelings for the boy over the many years they had known each other. She thought of J.C. just as she thought of her brothers—they had grown up together, had played together as children, fought just as Elise had fought with her brothers, and had even discovered together that boys and girls were different one afternoon out behind the kitchen in the year that Elise had turned three.

But they were not in love, and they never would be—damn William for knowing that, and for not thinking it mattered.

J.C. was a nice-enough young man, from a good Georgia family, a family that had been in that part of the state for generations longer than the Whitleys had. He would have money and property, and the best education that his father could buy for him, as well as the Cooper name and standing in the County—but, even if he and Elise had been in love, Martha knew she would have had reservations about the choice of him as husband for her daughter. He was not at all the sort of man she hoped Elise would spend her life with, though she did not yet know what sort of man she hoped that would be. Elise had plenty of common sense, though she was often plagued by a hasty nature. She had the intelligence and strength of character that would make her a strong woman one day—but she was still but a child now, only sixteen, not yet ready to be faced with life and marriage and children. J.C. Cooper had no interest in marrying Elise, any more than Elise had in marrying him, but Martha knew he would lack both the strength and the courage to speak his mind and put a stop to William's plans—that would be left up to Elise, and to Martha. Martha would not easily have her daughter forced into a loveless marriage. Not now. Not ever. No matter how badly William might want it, or for whatever reasons.

She sat her needlepoint down and got to her feet to cross the room to the front windows again, then stood staring out, looking across the broad expanse of yard toward the quiet road. William would be home soon with Elise, and then the struggle would really begin. For the first time in her life, Martha Whitley knew she would be on the opposite side from her husband, and that worried her. She knew William all too well. He would do whatever it was he had to do to get what he wanted.

And William Whitley was not one to lose too often.

ETHAN BENNETT had not spoken a word since leaving the train station that afternoon, and somehow his silence frightened Phyllis Ann more than any yells or curses could ever have frightened her. She cowered against the inside of the car door, as far away from him on the front seat as she could possibly get, trying to make no move or sound that might draw his attention. It seemed almost that he had forgotten her now, almost as if he had forgotten her presence, her very existence—he stared straight ahead through the windshield of the LaSalle, his eyes fixed on the road ahead, his hands clenching the steering wheel in a grip that turned his knuckles white. Phyllis Ann stared at him, praying that her breath would make no sound, praying that the car would go off the road and into a tree, or over the embankment and into the deepest part of McGarrett's pond—if he did not kill her today, then it would be some other day, for some other reason, if he needed one at all. At least that way she would see him die as well, know that for even that one moment he had suffered just as she suffered—she would gladly burn in hell for all eternity just to have that moment. She had been living in just another sort of hell all her life anyway.

He had been drinking, and rather heavily. He stank of it, as did the car. An empty flask lay on the seat between them, drained even before he had reached the train station—he was drunk, but, then again, he was always drunk. Not an amusing drunk, like the boys she knew from Atlanta, who were more like playful kittens when they had been at the gin, but an ugly drunk, prone to beating both her and her mother, as well as anyone else who might happen into his way.

He drove like a madman on the way home, taking the LaSalle around curves at speeds even its powerful engine was never meant to handle, causing Phyllis Ann to cling to the door all the more desperately to keep from being thrown over against him—God, don't let him remember I'm here, she prayed. God, don't let him—

She stared ahead at the tall, white house as it came into view around a curve, the six fluted columns across the front gleaming white in the sunlight, the lines elegant and regal, almost like the palaces she had dreamed of as a child—but there were no palaces, no knights in shining armor, no fathers kind and protective and gentle. Life was not sweet and soft and smelling of roses and sunshine—it was hard, with sharp edges, and teeth that could cut and wound; it came quickly and passed fast, and you had to grab hold to get the most you wanted, whether that be pain or pleasure, love or joy or sorrow. She stared at the house, feeling as if she had been cast back into some pit, for hell lived for her within those beautiful walls—don't let him remember I'm here. Please, don't let him remember—

The car turned off onto the long, graveled drive that led up to the front of the house, then went off onto the smooth lawn, cutting up turf and destroying spring flower beds before finally coming to a rest only inches short of the wide front steps. Phyllis Ann was thrown into the dash by the suddenness of the stop, and recovered herself only slowly, sliding back onto the seat and pushing her short, brown hair back from her eyes to look up—he was looking at her now, a muscle clenching in his jaw. He was looking at—

He was out of the car almost before she knew it, slamming the door shut behind himself. She stared in horror as he came around the LaSalle to her side, knowing what would happen, knowing he would—he yanked the car door open even before she could move, reaching inside to drag her from the seat, twisting her arm, hurting her wrist. For a time he only stared down at her, a muscle working in his jaw, then he began to drag her toward the front steps, jerking brutally at her arm as she resisted, his fingers digging into her flesh. She heard her own voice begging, pleading—but it was no use. He dragged her across the brick-floored veranda, in through the front doors and into the wide hallway that ran the depth of the house, finally releasing her with a shove that sent her sprawling onto her back on the hardwood flooring.

The heavy door slammed shut behind him, and for a moment he stared down at her, his black eyes filled with anger. She could hear her mother sniffling from the open parlor doorway to her right, and she turned her eyes in that direction, hoping for interference, hoping for help—but she knew she was alone, alone though her mother stood only that short distance away, clinging to the parlor doorframe. An ugly bruise already shown along one side of Paula Bennett's face, a face that had once been lovely before long years of beatings and fear had aged it—Phyllis Ann was alone, alone with him no matter what he chose to do, for her mother could not interfere. They both knew he would very easily kill her if she did—but, then again, he would probably kill them both one day.

Phyllis Ann began to slowly slide backwards across the floor, pushing with her hands and feet, putting as much distance as possible between herself and her father. He started toward her slowly, his hands clenching and unclenching at his sides, his eyes black and filled with rage.

"You stupid little bitch—" he said, his voice so low that for a moment she had to strain to hear it. "You damned stupid little—"

"Daddy, please, you don't understand. I—"

"Don't understand!" his voice exploded at her. "Don't understand why you went out of your way to make a fool out of me. To have the entire County laughing, thinking I didn't raise you any better than for you to get yourself thrown out of that school for—"

"No—it wasn't like that. I never meant—"

"After everything I've done for you. After—"

"No, please—" She shook her head, continuing to slide backwards. "You don't—"

"You're going to be sorry you ever thought about cheating. By the time I'm through with you, you're—"

Her back came up against the wall; she could go no farther. "Please, Daddy—please, don't—" She managed to push herself to her feet, sliding her back against the wall, her hands flat against its surface, until she was standing. She looked quickly past him, licking her lips that were suddenly dry—if she could get past him, make it to the door—

She shoved hard against him as he reached for her, and tried to run—but he caught her, grabbing her roughly by the shoulders and slamming her hard back against the wall again. Her head struck with force, making her knees buckle and her senses swim—she was crying, crying so hard that she could not breathe, crying so hard that she choked on her own tears. He drew her away from the wall and slammed her back into it again, then again, cursing her, calling her names that she had never—

"After everything I've done for you, tried to raise you right, teach you right from wrong—" He stared down at her, the muscle clenching again in his jaw, his dark eyes going over her, as if seeing her fully for the first time. "Look at you, coming home dressed like some cheap, speakeasy floozy—" He took her dress by the sleeve, bunching the fabric in his hand. "Going around looking like some painted-up whore—is this the way I raised you to dress? Is this—" She could hear the dress fabric tearing, the sleeve separating from its seam—suddenly something gave way within her. She shoved hard against him and managed to pull away, stumbling, falling against the nearby hall table. Her mother's favorite china figurine toppled from its surface and crashed to the floor, breaking into tiny slivers of nothing around her.

She picked up a heavy book from the tabletop and flung it at him, then another, seeing it strike a glancing blow against his rib cage. She grabbed up another and attempted to throw it, but he blocked it with his arm and slammed her back against the table—he was a madman. He was a madman, and now he was going to—

He slapped her hard, backhanded, across the face, and then again, his arm rising to—a sheer desperation took over within her, a pure instinct for self-survival, for life. She heard herself screaming the words even before she consciously thought them, screaming the words, over and over again: "It wasn't me! Elise was the one who cheated! It wasn't me!"

His hand stopped only inches from her stinging face, and he stared at her, his breath fetid in her nostrils—for a moment she was afraid that he had not heard, that he had not—

"Elise—" he said at last. "Not—"

"Yes, Elise—" she said, her gaze locked with his—he had to believe her. He had to—

"It wasn't me, Daddy. You know I wouldn't cheat. You raised me better than that, didn't you?"

He stared at her. "I raised you better than—" Some degree of normalcy had returned to his voice, some degree of control. "I should have known—" he said, almost to himself. "William Whitley's girl, and not mine." He reached out an almost gentle hand to pat her hair, and she almost cringed away, but he did not even seem to notice. "Never my little—"

"Never me—you know I wouldn't do that, don't you, Daddy?"

He looked at her for a moment longer, and then released her to move a step away. He straightened his coat and vest, then looked toward his wife where she still stood cringing against the wooden frame of the open parlor doorway. "Paula, you'd better feed the girl. She's lost weight since she's been away."

Paula Bennett seemed almost to tremble beneath his gaze for a moment. She released the doorframe only reluctantly, then moved into the hallway, seeming to go no closer to her husband than she had to.

"Come, child," she said, quietly, her voice almost at a whisper. "Dinner's already on the table." She took Phyllis Ann's hand and gently drew her away.

Ethan Bennett turned and walked through the door and into the parlor, then stood looking around the room for a moment before going to take up a bottle of gin from where it rested on the bookshelf in the corner. He crossed the room and collapsed onto a velvet settee, stretching his long legs out before him. His wife came into the room only a bare few steps, remaining what seemed a safe distance away. "Ethan, will you be—"

"No," he said, and turned up the bottle of gin to drink, not bothering with a glass. She hurried from the room, back to the comparative safety of the hallway, and Phyllis Ann glanced up at her, looking away from the torn sleeve she had been examining.

"He ruined my dress."

"I'll have it fixed for you, dear," her mother said, glancing from her back into the open parlor doorway.

"I don't want it fixed; I want a new one."

"Then we'll buy you a new one—but go on up and change now. We'll talk about it later. The cook has dinner waiting."

Phyllis Ann started toward the wide staircase that curved from the rear of the hall to the bedrooms on the floor above, feeling almost pleased with herself at how she had handled the situation—it was over now. Her father had someone else to blame at the moment, and she was safe. Tomorrow, if he was sober, he would feel guilty; he would buy her a new dress, perhaps even two. He was in there drinking now, and would be very drunk by nightfall. He would probably leave later, going into town to blow off steam before returning to the house to sleep it off. He might beat up one of the mill hands in town, or one of his own sharecroppers, maybe even some hobo down by the railroad tracks if one happened to get in his way. There was even a chance he might go to the Whitley place intending to confront Elise—

She paused for a moment, turning her eyes toward the telephone that sat on the hall table nearest the staircase. She considered calling to warn Elise, but quickly decided against it. Elise would be mad that she had laid the blame at her feet—and, besides, Elise had always been the strong one. She could take care of herself.

Phyllis Ann Bennett stared at the telephone only a moment longer, and then started up the wide staircase, the only concern remaining on her mind being the style of the dress she would buy.

# 9

ELISE WHITLEY SAT ON THE white-counterpaned bed in her room that afternoon, staring across the bright rug to the trunks she was supposed to be unpacking—but she hadn't the heart to unpack now; she hadn't the heart to do much of anything but sit and stare and wish that she were anywhere else other than where she was at the moment.

She had known all along that her reception at home would not be an easy one, but still she had not expected to feel as she did now those hours ago when her father had met her at the train station. She had expected that he would be angry, furious with her in fact, and at first she had been pleasantly surprised at his attitude—he had seemed fatherly, almost affectionate, as he kissed her cheek and stepped back to admire her dress.

"My, but don't she look pretty, J.C.!" he had said, taking her off guard. He stood with one arm around J.C.'s shoulders, looking at her with obvious pride in his expression—this was nothing as she had expected him to be, and at first she had been unable to do anything but stand and stare, wondering what it was that he was up to, for she knew her father never did anything without a reason.

"Y—yes, you look very nice, Elise," J.C. had stammered out at last, his cheeks coloring slightly as he fumbled with his glasses and moved a step away from her father. His eyes kept straying away, his mind seeming to be occupied elsewhere, and Elise followed his gaze, finding him watching Phyllis Ann and the cold, almost silent, reception she was receiving from her own father.

"I couldn't keep this young fellow away once he heard you were coming in by train this afternoon—"

"That's very nice of you, J.C.," Elise said, looking again at J.C.—but his eyes never left Phyllis Ann, and Elise again felt a pang of worry for her friend, and for what might very well happen to her now that they were home.

Her own father had seemed in a good humor as they left the train station, laughing, joking as she had rarely heard him joke in all her life—but she already knew it was all for J.C.'s benefit. She sat between them on the front seat of the Ford, her father taking up more room than was necessary, just so that she would have to sit even closer to J.C.—she knew what was happening, knew that her father was again trying to thrust her and J.C. together, just as he had tried to do so many times in the past. He had never once made any secret of his plans for her—but they were plans Elise was determined she would have none of.

She stared through the front windshield throughout the ride home, feeling as if her teeth might be shaken from her head at any moment by the rattling, bouncing Model T her father persisted in driving—how she hated that car, but she knew that she could have expected nothing less than for him to have come to the station to pick her up in the ugly, balking thing, instead of in the Studebaker Big Six President, or even in Bill's Packard. Why her father insisted on driving the ugly, black monstrosity of a motor car she could not understand, for he could well afford to drive a Cadillac, or a Stutz, or a new Packard, or even a lovely new LaSalle such as the one Phyllis Ann's father drove—Elise knew he thought it made him appear frugal, money-wise; but in her opinion it only made him look tight, and more than a little bit stingy, which was more often than not her opinion of her father anyway.

J.C. sat beside her, cringing away as a deep rut in the clay roadbed bounced her over against him. He seemed to be a thousand miles away now, staring out the window of the car at something that seemed to hold his interest—he had fled almost as soon as they reached the house, nearly falling down the front steps in his haste to be away. Her father stopped him in the front yard before he could reach his car, yelling out from the veranda in a commanding voice:

"We're expecting you to supper tonight, son—"

"Y—yes, sir—" J.C. had answered. "I—I'll be here—" But his face clearly said that he would rather be anywhere else on the face of the earth other than at the Whitley house that night.

Her father's attitude had changed the minute J.C. was gone. They were left alone in the wide hallway, her mother having left them to check on the preparations for dinner. Elise watched him as he closed the heavy front door on the sound of J.C.'s car driving away, noticing a peculiar set to his shoulders as he turned to look at her again.

"What have you done to J.C. to scare him so?" she asked, but he did not answer, staring at her instead for a long moment, a hard, almost calculating expression in his eyes.

"You've got to be more inviting to the boy," he said at last. "You said hardly more than two words to him on the drive home."

For a moment, Elise could only stare at him. "Inviting?"

"Hell yes, inviting!" he yelled, taking a step toward her. "You've got to pay a man some attention, show him a little life, flirt with him—"

"I have no intention of flirting with—"

"I don't give a damn what your intentions are; I'm telling you what you're going to do. You are going to pay that boy some attention, be nice to him, flirt with him—and you're going to be married to him before this year is out—"

"I am not going to marry—"

"Oh, hell, yes you are!" he yelled, cutting her words off. "For once in your life, you are going to do what I tell you to do. You thought you were real smart, getting yourself thrown out of that school—well, I think it's about time you—"

"I am not your property to be bargained off in a business deal!" she yelled, enraged. "I'll choose the man I marry, when I choose to marry, and I'll do it with no help from you!" She turned and started toward the staircase, but he grabbed her by the arm and spun her back around to face him.

"You'll do what I say, even if I have to beat you black and blue to see that you do it!"

Elise lifted her chin, meeting his gaze—it was a familiar threat, but one he had never carried through on. "Go ahead and do it; I still won't marry J.C.!" she yelled, but his face only hardened all the more. When he spoke again, his voice was quiet, his hand hurting her upper arm as he held her still before him.

"You are going to be nice to that boy; you're going to show him some attention, get him to court you—and you are going to marry him. I'm tired of you always causing me trouble, thinking you can do anything you want, never listening to anyone—you are going to marry J.C. Cooper, and then you'll be his problem—"

"And you'll be one step closer to owning part of his daddy's mill!" She threw the words at him, unable to stop herself, but he only stared at her, a set, determined expression on his face.

"That's not any concern of yours," he said, the inflection of his voice never changing. He released her with a slight shove that sent her toward the staircase. "Now, get upstairs and unpack. Put on the prettiest dress you've got and fix yourself up; the boy'll be back here for supper in a few hours."

For a moment Elise only stared at him, not moving.

"Get going, goddamn it!" he yelled, taking a step toward her, and she turned and ran up the stairs, for once in all her life unsure as to whether he might not actually strike her.

Now she sat staring at her trunks these hours later, unwilling to get up and cross the room to them to begin to unpack, for, once she finished her unpacking, she would have no choice but to go back downstairs. She had been called down to dinner what must now have been hours ago, but had not left her room—she just wished she had never come home. She had no intention of marrying J.C. Cooper, not even if there was some way that her father could make him ask her. J.C. was not in love with her, and, though he was dear and sweet and one of the best friends she had ever had in growing up, she was not in love with him either. She could not imagine spending the rest of her life with him, sleeping beside him, touching him—no, she would find some way to change her father's mind. There had to be something she could do, something she could say that would—

But she knew her father too well. William Whitley wanted the cotton mill, and he would have it, even if he had to have it at his daughter's expense.

She sighed and got up from the bed to cross the room to the first of her trunks. There was no use in delaying any longer. In her father's current mood, he would never allow Mattie Ruth to come up to help her, and it was unlikely he would even allow her mother to come and keep her company, for, if he would, Martha Whitley would already have been up to see her daughter. Elise was being left alone to think—but she had been thinking for hours now, and could still come to only the one conclusion; she could not marry J.C. Cooper, no matter how badly her father might want it. It was her life, her future, and she was not going to spend it with J.C.—it was 1927 after all, and parents no longer had the right to arrange marriages for their daughters, barter them away in matters of state or business or custom. That was archaic, something from a barbaric past when women had been nothing more than property to be used to the greatest advantage by husband, father, or lover—and Elise Whitley was none of that past. She would make her own decisions, choose her own husband, live her life exactly as she chose to live it—and damn any man who tried to tell her differently. After all, that was the manner of things these days. That was the reason why young flappers were being arrested the country over in their one-piece bathing costumes, why they were smoking and drinking and carrying on in all manner of ways—they were very much the same sort who had won women the vote only seven years before, the same girls who now had cut their hair and shortened their skirts and brought out their rouge compacts.

Elise Whitley prided herself that she was that sort of girl. Her father and any other man be damned, she would live her life as she chose to live it—the only problem was, her father was accustomed to having his own way. Very few times in his life had he not gotten exactly what it was he wanted—he expected it. And William Whitley could be very hard to get around. Very—

There was a sound outside her door, and then a light tap, and her brother, Stan, stuck his head into the room. "You want some company?"

he asked, with a smile that made her suddenly feel as if she had come home. She laughed, motioning for him to come in.

"Sure, if you're not afraid Daddy will—"

"He just left to go into town with Bill," Stan said, not having to hear the remainder of the thought. He came into the room to lightly touch her cheek with his lips, then went to sit down on the bed, watching her as she began to unpack. He seemed so much more grown up now than he had the last time she had seen him, even taller, though that had been the matter of only a few months before. He watched her for a moment through his round-rimmed eyeglasses, as she began to take dresses from one of the trunks and put them away in the tall chiffonier that stood against one wall of the pink, rose, and white room; then he began to talk, telling her of all the things that had happened on the place in the time since she had been away.

It felt so good just to hear his voice, so familiar—for a time it seemed almost as if she had never been away, never had to make the awful choice between herself and a life-long friendship, never had to go through the embarrassment of being asked to leave the school, never had to come home to her father's impossible demands—why couldn't he just understand? Why couldn't he just see? He was her father; he had to want the best for her, and, surely, he had to realize that J.C. was not that "best." He knew that she did not love J.C.; that J.C. did not love her—the mill was his dream, not hers; and, for all she cared, the damned thing could rot to the ground. In fact, at the moment, she wished that it would. Wished—

Stan was saying something that broke into her thoughts, dragging her attention back to the conversation. "—says he thinks you ought to marry J.C., that having a husband and children might settle you down—"

"Settle me down—who said that!" she demanded, stopping halfway across the room with a dress over her arm. She turned back to stare at her brother—settle her down, indeed! How dare anyone suggest that she needed settling down!

"Janson—Janson Sanders. He's a new hand Daddy hired back during the winter."

A farmhand! A farmhand had dared to suggest— "Just who does

this farmhand think he is?" she demanded angrily.

Stan shrugged. "He's my friend. We talk a lot. He's taught me all about—"

"And this farmhand thinks I need settling down, does he?" Elise asked, interrupting her brother's words.

Stan nodded. "He said that he thought a man'd do you good, get the 'flighty ideas' out of your head, as he calls them. That, if J.C.'s man enough, he'll be able to handle you—"

"Handle me?" she yelled. Handle her—as if she were some spoiled child to—

Apparently someone needed to teach this farmhand some manners—flighty ideas, indeed. The man needed to be shown his place, taught some respect for his betters. Of all things, for a farmhand to—

"—he said that he didn't think a good spanking would do you any harm, either—"

"He—oh—!" Elise yelled, furious. "How dare—" She stamped her foot and slung the dress she had been carrying across the foot of the bed, too angry to even finish the thought. "Just exactly where can I find this farmhand?" she demanded.

Handle me, indeed—a good spanking—need a man to settle me down, my foot! This farmhand had the unmitigated nerve to—oh, but he was going to find out he was not dealing with a small child. He was going to well find that out before she was through with him. She would put this Janson Sanders in his place.

THE MAN must have sensed her presence, for he turned and met her eyes the moment she rounded the corner of the barn that afternoon. He had been at work before the small room Stan had told her he lived in, chopping stove wood with some sort of ax, his shirt discarded in his supposed privacy and hanging over the back of a nearby cane-bottomed straight chair. He seemed immediately taken aback at the sight of her, moving to take up the faded workshirt and pull it on over the crossed galluses of his overalls. "I'm sorry, miss. I figured I was by myself, an'—"

"Mr. Sanders?" Her voice sounded harsh, just as she intended it to.

"Yes, ma'am. I'm Janson San—"

"I would like to know just exactly who you think you are?" she demanded, then watched as a look of confusion came to his face, a face darker than she had ever before seen on any white man.

"Ma'am?"

"Telling my brother that you think I ought to marry J.C. Cooper, that you think a husband would get what you call the 'flighty ideas' out of my head, saying that you think I need a good spanking—just exactly who do you think you are to say something like that about me?"

"I reckon' I know who I am," he said, buttoning up his shirt and returning her stare.

"Well, in case you need reminding—you, Mr. Sanders, are a farm-hand—" She flung the words at him with as much derision as possible, and watched him raise his chin defensively. "How dare you presume to meddle in my life?"

"I wasn't tryin' t' meddle in your life," he said, his eyes never leaving her face.

"I'll have you know that I can handle my own affairs on my own, without any help from someone like you, thank you very much—"

"Seems like you're doin' real good at it, too, since you just managed to get yourself throwed out 'a school all by yourself—'thank you very much.'" He gave her own words back to her, making her only angrier.

"You don't know anything about me or my life! How dare you—"

"I guess I've seen enough spoil't young'ns in my life t' know one when she's standin' right in front of me," he said, interrupting her words as he stared at her. "It'd probably do you good t' marry J.C. Cooper; that is, if he'll have you—who knows, he might not be too interested in raisin' a spoil't brat for a wife, once he thinks about it—"

"How dare you!" Elise gasped. "I could have my father put you off this place for talking to me like that!"

But he only stared at her in response, the green eyes oddly out of place in the dark face. "Git on back up t' th' big house where you belong, Miss Whitley," he told her, reaching again for the ax handle. "I ain't got time t' fool with you. I got work t' do—" He started to turn back to his work.

When she did not move, he looked back at her. "I said, git!" he said louder, taking a step toward her, and she scrambled away, actually afraid for a moment that he might strike her.

She was surprised to hear him mutter: "Rich folks—" as she walked away, and so furious that she did not care what it was he meant with the words.

"IS THERE something wrong with the food, Elise?" her mother asked a few hours later as the family sat around the large table in the dining room of the great house.

Elise looked up from the plate she had only barely touched all through supper. "No, it's fine."

"You'd never know it, to see how you're picking at it now."

"I guess I'm just not hungry," she answered, then watched as her mother's eyes flicked first to J.C., and then to Elise's father. Martha Whitley fell silent, and Elise forced herself to eat a bite or two of the meal Mattie Ruth had prepared for them before her mind wandered away again, too filled with her own thoughts to be concerned with food.

Her grandmother's antique lace tablecloth decorated the table before her; the lovely Coalport china that was usually displayed in the glass-fronted china cabinet in the corner sat now at each place setting, her mother's best pressed-glass water goblets—but the elaborate preparations for his benefit seemed to be lost now on J.C. as he sat at Elise's side, his eyes on the almost-untouched plate before him. He had hardly eaten a bite throughout the entire meal, and actually looked even more uncomfortable than Elise felt, if that were even possible. Her father was watching them both, smiling contentedly to himself every so often—he had enough food in him now to make him more affable than he had been earlier in the day, and he was now putting on his best airs for J.C.'s benefit. At least, perhaps, supper would end in peace.

Her brothers seemed unaware of the tension that sat at the table. Bill had a section of folded Columbus newspaper before him, from which he made occasional comments about some recent and rare remark President Coolidge had made. Alfred was eating too fast, afraid he would miss some radio program, and Stan was talking, as he always seemed to be doing, though he knew the others at the table only rarely listened.

Elise picked at her own food, her mind occupied with things other than conversation—she could not stop thinking about the ill-mannered farmhand she had argued with earlier in the day. She had almost told her father how the man had talked to her several times already since returning to the house, but somehow she found she could not—how dare anyone talk to her in such a manner. The man had called her a spoiled brat, had said that she needed a man to settle her down, someone to get the "flighty ideas" out of her head, and had even told her brother she could do with a good spanking—no one had ever spoken to her in such a manner in all her life, and now to have a lowly farmhand of all people to—

But she could not tell her father. He would tell her she should know better than to have anything to do with one of the farmhands or sharecroppers on the place, and she could not bring herself to tell him that the man had said he thought she ought to marry J.C.—no, thank you, she had enough problems on that front already without adding the opinions of a farmhand to her father's arsenal. Of all things for a farmhand to—

He could not be more than a couple of years older than she was, and yet he had talked to her as if she were a small child today, had called her a spoiled brat—it infuriated her even now, to think that someone so far beneath her had dared to—

The mention of Janson Sanders's name dragged her attention back to the conversation going on around her. Stan was staring across the table toward their father, light from the cut-glass chandelier above the table reflecting off the round lenses of his eyeglasses. "Janson's teaching me to tell the weather from the signs, that smoke going to the ground means it's going to rain, and smoke rising means it's going to be dry—"

"That's all nothing but superstition," Martha Whitley said, delicately cutting the meat on her plate with a knife and fork as she glanced up at her son.

"I don't know about that. So far the boy's been right most of the time—" William Whitley began, but Bill interrupted before he could finish the thought.

"That's about all that damned Indian's good for—"

Elise's father started to respond, but Elise cut him off mid-sentence, not even taking the time to think. "He's an Indian?" She had never met an Indian before, or even seen one, and, somewhere in the back of her mind, she had not even really believed they existed any longer, at least not outside reservations and the movies. But Janson Sanders was an Indian, or at least so Bill had said, and he really looked as she thought an Indian might look, so dark, looking much like the pictures she had seen in books and in the movie theatres, with that black hair, and those cheekbones—but weren't Indians supposed to be savages, living in tepees, wearing breechcloths, murdering people. That was the way they had been shown in the movies, and in the books she had read.

"He's half Indian," Stan answered, delighted to at last be the center of conversation at the table. "His mother was a full-blooded Cherokee Indian, from a reservation and all, but his daddy was white—"

"Full-blooded or half-breed, he's still nothing but a damned, useless Indian," Bill said, interrupting his brother's words. "It's a miracle he hasn't stolen us blind already, the goddamn thieving—"

"Bill Whitley!" Elise's mother's face had gone white at her son's words, her Baptist soul aghast at the blasphemy spoken. She cleared her throat loudly, her cheeks slowly beginning to stain with embarrassment.

"When did you get to be such an expert on Indians, anyway?" Alfred asked, seeming only to want to prolong the confrontation. He smiled with self-satisfaction at the look on his brother's face. "He's the only Indian we've ever had around here."

"Everyone knows what they're like. They're all still a bunch of thieving, dirty savages, even after having lived with white men all these years."

"That boy's no savage. He's a good, God-fearing boy—" their mother began.

"He's a 'Holy Roller'—" Alfred snorted, but fell silent as his mother's look fell on him.

"He's a goddamn savage!" Bill snapped.

Before his mother could respond, William Whitley's voice broke across the table. "That's enough!" and everyone fell silent. "We're putting on a bad face for our guest here. J.C. will be thinking that it's us who are the savages." He smiled in J.C.'s direction for a moment, and Elise could almost feel the boy cringe away. Then her father turned back to Bill. "Besides, the only reason you're so against the boy is because he won't take any of your bluster."

No, he wouldn't—Elise thought to herself. From what she had already seen of Janson Sanders, he would never back down from her brother, and he would not be afraid of him, as so many of the other farmhands were. She saw the look of anger in her brother's eyes, but knew he would not dare to respond—their father would never allow it.

"The boy's a hard worker, and he earns his pay, which is more than I can say for most of the men on this place."

"He's weeded the flower beds for me, and mowed the lawn several times," Martha Whitley said. "He's very well-mannered, considering who he is. I don't think I've heard him say more than two words—"

"He has a lot to say," Stan protested. "He talks to me all the time."

"You shouldn't spend so much time around that boy." A stern expression came to William Whitley's face as he stared at his youngest son. "It doesn't look right, your being friends with someone like him, especially not with that boy. He's only half white—"

"But he's all right, Daddy. He's taught me all about growing things, and foretelling the weather by the signs, and about wild plants you can eat, and the ones you can use for medicine—"

"That's all nothing but superstition," his mother said, "old wives tales. He ought not teach you that nonsense."

"But he knows all about it. Really, he does; his grandmother taught him. And he's all right, really he is, even if he is only half white. He's my friend—he's okay, don't you think he is, Elise?"

Suddenly Elise felt as if every eye in the room was on her. She swallowed hard and glanced around the table.

"How would your sister know anything about that boy?"

Elise opened her mouth to speak—she did not know what she was about to say, and she never had the chance to find out. "Elise went to see him today. I told her something he said, and she didn't like it. She said she was going to talk to him," Stan said, looking toward her again. "You did go talk to him, didn't you?"

"Yes, I did, but—" she answered, knowing that she had to change the subject, and change it quickly, before someone could ask—

"What was it he said that you didn't like?"

She was going to say that it was nothing, just a misunderstanding, but Stan blurted out the truth even before she could speak. "He said he thought she ought to marry J.C., that having a husband and some children might settle her down and get the 'flighty ideas' out of her head—he said that he didn't think a good spanking would hurt her any, either."

William Whitley stared for a moment, then roared with laughter, slapping his knee beneath the table. "That's damned out of line, but it's just like the boy!" he laughed. "He doesn't talk much, but, when he does, he says just what's on his mind. Those people usually do."

Who 'those people' were Elise did not know, and at the moment she did not care. She had never been so horribly embarrassed in all her life.

"Maybe you ought to listen to the boy's advice, Elise," her father said, still chuckling, looking from her, to J.C., and then back again. "It sounds to me like he's speaking good, common sense. It'd do you good to get married, settle you down—and, if you behave yourself, J.C. might even let you get by without the spanking."

Her face was burning with embarrassment—she only wanted to get out of this room. Janson Sanders had made her the center of this joke, had caused her this embarrassment—and he had only given her father one more weapon to use in his drive to marry her off to J.C.. She was absolutely furious, her hands twisting the linen napkin in her lap into knots. Damn him! Damn that ill-mannered—

She glanced over at J.C.. The boy looked absolutely horrified, pink to his ears, almost choking on the food in his mouth. She had to get them both out of there before anything else could be said. She had to—

"If you'll excuse me," she said, sliding her chair back and setting her now wrinkled and knotted linen napkin on tablecloth beside the plate she had only barely touched all through the meal. "J.C., would you like to go out and sit on the veranda with me?" she asked, wanting only to get them both out of this room and away from her father.

"Yes, I—I'd like that." He looked unbelievably relieved and grateful, pushing his glasses up from the bridge of his nose as he got to his feet.

Elise saw her father's complacent smile as she rose from her chair—he thinks I'm going along with him, she told herself. He thinks that he's won, that I'm going to marry J.C. without a fight—damn that Janson Sanders, it was all his fault, Elise told herself. The damned, ill-mannered farmhand.

ETHAN BENNETT sat in the front parlor of his home that night, trying to drink himself into a stupor. He sat on the velvet settee, staring at the light as it reflected through the half-empty bottle of whiskey on his knee. The house was quiet; Phyllis Ann had gone out, and Paula had gone upstairs long ago—but his wife held little interest to him. He wanted only to drink and forget, to sink into the blackness he could so often find at the bottom of a bottle.

But tonight that nothingness would not come. His mind refused to stop working; his thoughts refused to stop coming, so he just sat and continued to drink, getting only drunker—but still that nothing would not come.

It was all Phyllis Ann's fault. The confrontation with her earlier had only served to clear his senses and somewhat counteract the alcohol that had already been in his bloodstream. It was all her fault, the damned, ungrateful little bitch, getting sent home from—

But, no, it was not Phyllis Ann's fault. She had said something—yes, it was Elise Whitley who had gotten her sent home. It had been Elise Whitley who had done whatever it was that had gotten Phyllis Ann thrown out of school. It had all been Elise Whitley's—

He knew the entire County had to be laughing at him, laughing at how he had allowed William Whitley's daughter to take his Phyllis Ann down the road to ruin—Phyllis Ann had done nothing wrong; she was a good girl. He had raised her to be a good—

Elise Whitley was a bad sort. He should have realized that long before. All the changes in Phyllis Ann—but it was not too late even now. Whitley's brat had to be shown she could not ruin his daughter's good name and get away with it, that she could not make him the center of jokes the County over, that she would have to pay for—

He turned the bottle up and drank from it again, long, burning swallows that brought tears to his already watery eyes—Elise Whitley needed to be taught a lesson. She needed to be taught a lesson indeed for what she had done to his family. If her father was not man enough to give her what she deserved, then Ethan Bennett was. Then Ethan Bennett was—

He got unsteadily to his feet, swayed and almost fell, the room shifting slightly around him. He steadied himself against the settee for a moment, then began to slowly walk toward the door, knowing what it was he had to do—Elise Whitley had a lesson coming to her tonight. A lesson she would remember for a very long time.

A very long time indeed.

THE NIGHT was calm and quiet, the silence broken only by the sound of crickets in the front yard. Elise sat in a wicker chair on the front veranda of her home, staring out across the yard toward the dark road, thinking. The light from the parlor windows behind them fell onto the veranda, dimly illuminating J.C. where he sat nearby in a chair that matched her own—they had never in their lives had trouble talking, not from the time they had been small children together. Now there were no words to say and silence hung over them, a physical silence as real as the barrier her father had placed between them, a barrier of pressures to make a long-standing friendship more than it could ever be.

"Damn my father!" she said aloud, but quietly, without thinking, then laughed at the shocked expression that came to J.C.'s face. She reached out and took his hand, smiling. "Well, it's how I feel."

"I guess he just wants what he thinks is best for you."

"Best for him, you mean. He doesn't give a whit for what I want, and he never has—but it won't work. He can't make us get married if we don't want to."

For a moment J.C. looked unbelievably relieved. "I was afraid we wouldn't be able to get out of it," he blurted out, then sat blinking at her from behind his glasses, aghast at his own unthinking words. "Oh, Elise, I didn't mean it that way. I—I didn't mean that I didn't want to marry you. I—I don't, but—I mean—it's just—"

She laughed at his discomfort and squeezed his hand. "Oh, J.C., calm down. I know what you mean, and I don't want to marry you either. You're one of my dearest friends, but I don't love you, at least not in that way."

He smiled tentatively.

"I do love you, but like I love my brothers, and I don't want to lose you as a friend."

"Your father, he wants us to be more than that—Elise, what are we going to do? It's not just him; it's my father as well. He's pretty set on it, too. We can't go on just trying to ignore them both forever."

"I know." She sighed and sat back, thinking. There had to be a way to end the marriage plans and still keep peace in both families. But, try as she might, she could think of nothing.

"Well, we'll think of something; don't worry," she said, wishing she could feel a little more assured herself.

J.C. looked less than convinced—she knew that she would lose the little peace of mind she had left if she had to look at his sad expression much longer. She stood. "It's getting late, J.C.. You better go on home. Us being alone like this can only make matters worse."

"Yes—yes, of course, you're right." He stood, fidgeting with his glasses. She walked him down the front steps and to his car, then stood watching as he drove away.

The quiet of the night closed in about her as the car turned out of the drive and into the dark road, then disappeared among the cotton fields that led away from the house, the sound of the crickets now seeming to have fallen silent as well. She sighed and looked back up at the house from where she stood just before the front steps, the tall, brightly lit windows throwing patches of light onto the curve of the drive and the smooth lawn around her—she could not go back in just yet. Her father would be waiting for her, waiting to find out if anything had happened between her and J.C., waiting to find out if his plans were working.

The night air was chill and she hugged her arms for warmth as she turned and wandered slowly out into the yard, thinking. There had to be a way to put a stop to her father's plans. She had no intention of marrying J.C., no matter how much trouble it might stir up in her family, or in his.

"Oh, why can't things just be easy and simple?" she wondered aloud, hearing her own words as she reached the old oak at the edge of the yard and stopped beneath its branches. Life seemed so uncertain now. So very uncertain.

She looked up into the dark branches overhead, wondering how old the tree was, how long it had stood in this spot, how many Whitleys it had seen come and go, how many changes in how many lives. She felt as if she were almost between stages in her own life now, not a girl anymore, and not quite a woman, uncertain about life and the future itself. She sighed and looked back toward the house standing at a distance across the yard—it was like waiting for the other shoe to drop; she knew something would have to happen. She knew—

She also knew that, whatever that something was, it would change her life forever.

ETHAN BENNETT parked his car a short distance down the red clay road from the Whitley house and walked the remainder of the way. He did not want to announce his presence, his intentions, too soon. Elise Whitley would not have the chance to get away, to deny him the lesson she had coming—she had to learn, had to be shown that she could not take advantage of his little girl, use her, and then make him the butt of jokes the County over for what she had done to Phyllis Ann.

He stopped at the edge of a field of young cotton plants as he neared the house—then he saw her, standing beneath a large tree not too far distant, alone, unaware that her judgment stood so close at hand. He turned up the bottle he had brought with him and drank—she had grown up, matured, since the last time he had seen her. He remembered her as a skinny girl, all arms and legs, with long, red-gold braids, and freckles across the bridge of her nose. Now she had the body of a young woman, rounded and soft. And waiting.

He licked his lips and took another drink, feeling his penis begin to harden in the crotch of his pants. He had not touched Paula in months, and the girl he kept in town had not had anything to do with him in the weeks since she had seen his LaSalle parked in front of Delta White's house one Saturday morning—it's not good for a man to do without, he told himself, his hand straying unconsciously to his crotch. He might just do more than teach her a lesson. Once he finished punishing her, he might just teach her a few other things as well. That was all they wanted anyway, he told himself, being batted about a bit, and then bedded good and hard.

He wiped the back of his hand across his mouth and started forward, almost stumbling over his own feet for a moment, then catching himself and continuing on, his eyes never once leaving the girl—Elise Whitley would never forget this night, he told himself. This night, or the lessons she had coming.

# 10

THERE HAD BEEN THE sound of movement behind her, harsh breathing, the feeling of being watched—Elise turned, fear rising to her throat as she saw a man approaching her across the narrow expanse of yard edging the cotton field near where she stood. She took a step away, prepared to run toward the house that stood at a distance across the yard—then she recognized him, the sparse moonlight filtering through the branches of the tree overhead throwing his face into sharp planes of light and darkness.

"Mr. Bennett, what are you doing here?" she asked as he stopped before her, his eyes on her in a way she did not like, edging her voice with caution as she spoke again. "Mr. Bennett—"

"Don't Mr. Bennett me, girl. I know what you're about—"

"What I'm about?" She took a step backwards, away from him—she had seen too many times the results of his rages: the blackened eyes, the swollen lips, the purplish bruises, on Phyllis Ann and her mother; but never in her life had she ever had reason to fear him herself. His violence had always seemed restricted to his own family—but somehow she was afraid now. His eyes moved from her face and down her body—she could feel the look more than see it, but she knew it was there. She shivered involuntarily, suddenly cold, and took another step away, hugging her arms for warmth. "I don't understand. Maybe we should—"

"Don't give me that innocent look of yours; it won't help you any now."

Her eyes moved to the whiskey bottle held in his right hand. "Mr.

Bennett, you've been drinking. You don't know what you're saying. You just go on home, and we'll forget you ever—"

"Did you really think I'd just let you get by with it?"

"Get by with what?" She could hear the fear in her own voice, and she prayed that he could not hear it as well. She took another step away, looking again toward the brightly lighted house—but his words stopped her.

"You think you're so good, don't you, acting like you're so innocent and pure—but I know the truth about you. Phyllis Ann told me, do you know that? Phyllis Ann told—"

"Phyllis Ann—"

"She won't lie for you anymore. Everyone in the County will know the truth, that it was you and not my baby that cheated—"

The full import of his words hit her. "But that's not true! It was Phyllis Ann who—"

Suddenly, he was on her, grabbing her by the arm and shoving her hard back against the tree, the whiskey bottle sliding from his grasp. Her head struck with such force that for a moment her senses swam and her knees began to buckle—but he held her upright, pinning her against the tree, his free hand coming down over her mouth before she could make a sound.

"You hush your lying mouth about my little girl," he hissed, his face close against hers. His breath, hot on her cheek and stinking of liquor, made her want to vomit—she could hardly breathe, the hand over her mouth almost closing off the supply of oxygen. She stared up at him, horrified, somehow knowing, still unprepared—

"Don't you think I know what it is you want, anyway?" His body, close, crowded hers; the smell of stale sweat, of liquor, filled her nostrils—she gagged against his hand, feeling hot tears begin to sting her cheeks. "You're just like the rest of them, no matter how innocent and good you try to act. All you want is a man between your legs to—"

She began to fight him, clawing at his face, striking out with all the force there was in her. She managed to struggle away from the tree, only to be shoved hard back against it again, her head striking with even greater force than it had the first time, her knees trying to give way beneath her. The painful grip on her arm was released, and for a moment she thought she might be able to break free—then there was a tearing sound, as the front of her dress was ripped downward to the waist. She tried to scream against the hand covering her mouth, but little sound came out as he fumbled inside her torn neckline for her breasts. His hand left her mouth, only to knot in her hair and force her head back. His mouth came down over hers, his tongue forcing its way between her lips as he pinned her back against the tree, one knee pushing its way between her thighs through her skirt. She clawed at his eyes, gagging as his tongue touched hers—she wanted to die, prayed to die, rather than to—

Suddenly, the pressure of him holding her back against the tree was gone. She sank to the ground, her lungs greedily taking in deep drafts of the clean night air, her senses so addled for a moment that she wondered if God had not actually answered her pleas with the release of death—then Janson Sanders was kneeling beside her, a concerned expression in his eyes as he said the same words, over and over again: "I'm here; you're all right now. I'm here—"

She looked toward the form of Ethan Bennett where he lay on the ground, and she began to shake, realizing what had almost happened, what would have happened, if—

For a moment she thought she saw movement, then was certain, her heart almost stopping within her as she saw the man slowly regaining his feet, reaching for a jagged half of the whiskey bottle broken sometime during the struggle with her, grasping it by the unbroken neck, turning toward them—

And Elise began to scream.

MOONLIGHT GLINTED off the jagged edge of broken glass as Ethan Bennett moved what was left of the liquor bottle in Janson's direction. "You're a dead man for—" But then the man's eyes moved toward Elise Whitley, and back again, something in his face changing. "Go on, boy, this ain't none of your business."

Janson did not speak, moving instead to stay between the broken bottle and the girl behind him. He stared past the weapon to the eyes of the man holding it—there was violence there, violence and rage and something more.

"I said go on, boy!" Bennett's voice rose. "Or I'll take care of you before I—"

"You ain't gonna touch her," Janson said, feeling the man's body tense with rage even over the distance. The bottle moved again, its sharp edge catching the sparse light—the girl's screams were loud in his ears. He knew he would die tonight before he would let any man hurt a sixteen-year-old girl.

There was a yell of rage as Bennett lunged at him, the bottle coming to within inches of Janson's chest as he leapt away. He went in low at Bennett, reaching up to block another sweeping arc of the weapon, somewhere in the back of his mind amazed at the man's sheer, drunken strength.

For a moment the jagged glass began to lower toward Janson's face. He twisted away, trying to free himself, only to have his left arm captured and pushed up behind his back, such force behind the movement that he thought the bone would shatter at any moment. His right arm strained to keep the bottle away, the muscles aching as it was forced lower and lower, the shattered edge finally touching his throat with a stinging sensation as it was drawn along the skin—he was afraid to move, afraid to breathe, his free arm useless now to counteract the pressure of that jagged piece of glass.

Time slowed as he stared at the open horror on Elise Whitley's face. He could think of only one thing, over and over again: God, don't let her see this. God don't let her see—

Ethan Bennett's breath was hot in his ear, each word spoken clearly, as if to make certain he understood. "I'm going to slit your throat for interfering with me, boy. And, when I'm through with you, I'm going to take my time going at that little girl right here on the ground. I'm going to—"

Pure hatred and fury rose within Janson. He screamed with rage and released his hold on Bennett's wrist, feeling the glass cut into his skin as he twisted to one side and brought his elbow back into sharp contact with the man's ribs. Lowering his head, freeing the arm held pinned behind his back, he twisted to land a hard blow to the man's jaw, then another.

Bennett stumbled backwards, then went down, the broken bottle falling from his grasp—suddenly Janson was over him, the jagged remainder of the whiskey bottle held in his own hand, its sharp edge already cutting into Bennett's throat. He stared down into the man's eyes, knowing he was about to kill this man who had—

Then he caught sight of Elise Whitley where she sat beneath the oak tree, her hands trying to hold together the torn top half of her dress, a look of horror on her face. He caught sight of—

He released Bennett and stood to go to her, knowing he could not kill even this man before a girl's eyes—but, before he could reach her side, her family was suddenly there, surrounding her, her screams having finally reached over the distance to the house, bringing Whitley, her mother, her brothers, and Franklin Bates. Someone took the broken bottle from him, and he released it without struggle, never knowing who it was who had taken it—she was safe now, her family there, her mother holding her as if she were a small child.

Alfred Whitley froze for a moment as he reached his sister's side, then lunged for Bennett, his hands closing over the older man's throat where he lay on the ground. "You goddamn—"

"No!" his father shouted, dragging him back, leaving Bennett choking and coughing. "I said no! Let the sheriff have him." He shook the boy as he continued to struggle. "I said no!"

Alfred stared at his father for a moment, the fury still obvious on his face, then he yanked free and went to his sister, kneeling at her side to turn an angry look back up to Whitley. Janson watched as Martha Whitley, Stan, and Alfred helped Elise to her feet and led her toward the house, Alfred unbuttoning and taking off his own shirt to drape it across her shoulders over the torn dress. Janson stared until they left his sight.

As soon as they had entered the big house with the girl, Whitley turned toward Bennett, grabbing him by the shirt collar to drag him from the ground. "I ought to kill you, you goddamn son-of-a-bitch. I ought to—" He stared at the man for a moment, then doubled him over with a hard fist to his stomach. Ethan Bennett gagged and went to his knees, gasping for breath as Whitley turned away.

"Franklin, take him to the barn to wait for the sheriff," Whitley said, and the big man nodded, but did not speak. He reached to drag Bennett from the ground again, hitting him hard in the face as he began to struggle, bloodying his nose and splitting his lip before dragging him away. Bill Whitley followed at a short distance, walking slowly.

Janson stared after them until they left his sight, William Whitley beside him. "I should'a killed him," he said quietly, staring after the man who had tried to hurt Elise Whitley, the man who had tried to kill him.

"Somebody will someday," Whitley said.

"I hope it's me," Janson said, never turning his eyes to see Whitley's approving nod. "I hope to hell it's me."

SOMETIME LATER, Janson stood just within the wide, brightly lit entry hallway that ran the depth of the first floor of the Whitley house—he had not been invited here; he had just simply come, following William Whitley, and had not been asked to leave. He had no idea what time it was, or how long he had been standing here, but still he would not leave, not until he knew for certain that Elise Whitley was unhurt.

Her parents were upstairs with her now, and the doctor, who had come from town to give her something to help her sleep, had already left. Stan Whitley sat on the lower steps of the wide staircase that rose to the second floor, his elbows on his knees, his head in his hands, a worried and concerned expression on his young face. Alfred sat to himself not too far distant, on a brocaded settee tucked in against one wall of the wide hallway, his lowered brow showing an anger such as Janson had seen but few times in his life. Bill Whitley and Franklin Bates had returned to the house long before, and Ethan Bennett had been turned over to the sheriff—Janson knew the hour was late, but still he continued to stand, to wait, as he would wait until someone could tell him that the girl had not been hurt.

There was a sound on the stairs, and Janson looked up to find

Whitley descending from the floor above. He straightened from where he had been leaning against the frame of one of the open parlor doors, and waited. Whitley patted Stan on the shoulder as the boy rose, and looked at his second son as Alfred met him at the bottom of the stairs.

"Is Elise—"

"She's okay," Whitley said. "She's been pretty badly shaken up, but she'll be all right."

An angry muscle clenched in Alfred's jaw, his hands tightening on the carved newel post before him. "That son-of-a-bitch ought to be killed for what he—"

But his father cut him short. "Sheriff Hill has him now. He'll see to it that—"

"The law won't do to him what he deserves for what he tried to do to Elise! He should be—"

Bill Whitley interrupted his brother's words, entering the hallway from the front parlor just opposite where Janson stood. "He already got something of what he deserved before we turned him over to the sheriff."

"'Got something of—what did you do?" Whitley demanded, but Bill only shrugged, returning his father's stare.

"It doesn't matter. Sheriff Hill has him now, and maybe he'll handle the rest without doing any further damage to this family's name—"

Janson tightened, anger filling him. "Your sister almost got raped t'night, an' you're worried about your goddamn family name!" he yelled, taking a step forward, his hands clenching into fists at his sides.

Bill turned toward him, as if suddenly noting his presence there in the hallway. "Who the hell do you think you are to be telling me what I should be concerned about—and what are you doing here, anyway? You don't have any business—"

"Who th' hell I am is somebody that's worried about your sister—looks t' me like you're more worried about you!"

"You goddamn half-breed—" Bill lunged at him, but Whitley stepped between them, holding his son back.

"That's enough of it between you two!" he yelled. "Tempers are running high tonight, and I won't have any punches thrown here in this house."

Bill only continued to stare at Janson, his body tensed.

"Now, Bill, go on, and you boys, too," Whitley said, releasing his eldest son and looking toward Stan and Alfred. "I want to talk to Janson alone."

After a moment, Stan quietly pushed Alfred up the stairs, but Bill stood unmoving, staring past his father to Janson.

"I said go—" Whitley gave Bill a slight push—for a moment, Janson thought Bill would strike the older man. Bill's body tensed, as if ready for a fight, his right hand tightening into a fist—he stared at his father, something in his eyes that Janson could not read; and then he seemed to force a control over himself, looking at Janson, and then back to Whitley again. He turned and left the wide hallway without another word, slamming the heavy front door behind himself.

Whitley turned his eyes toward Janson for a long moment. "I want to thank you for what you did tonight, boy. If you hadn't come along—" He fell silent. "I appreciate it, boy," he said, reaching back to pull a thick wallet from the rear pocket of his trousers, then opening it to begin to count out bills from it. "And I want to pay you for—"

"No," Janson said, not even taking the time to think.

"No?" Whitley's eyes rose to meet his.

"I didn't do it for no pay. I did it for her. You keep your money. I won't take no pay for helpin' her."

Whitley stared at him for a long moment. "You sure, boy?" he asked.

"I'm sure."

Whitley replaced the bills in his wallet and shoved it back into his pocket. "If that's the way you want it, boy," he said, "but it's not soon I'll forget what you did for us tonight—"

For her—Janson thought, but said nothing. After a moment he said: "Now that I know she's all right, I'll be goin' on." He turned and started for the door.

"Well, like I said, I appreciate it, boy."

Janson paused for a second, but did not turn back. He went on through the door and pulled it shut behind himself, then walked across the veranda, down the front steps, and out into the night.

JANSON SLEPT very little that night. Each time he would drift off, it would only be to awaken again, thinking he had heard Elise Whitley call his name. As dawn came, he got up and dressed, pulling on his least-frayed shirt and the only pair of dungarees he owned that had no patches, then made himself a breakfast of fried eggs, bacon, coffee, and hard biscuits rewarmed from the day before. He sat on his narrow cot and tried to eat, thinking about the girl, and about the things he had said to her the day before. After what she had gone through last night—

For the first time in his life, Janson Sanders knew what it was to feel sorry for something he had done. He should never have said the things he had said to her, not to any girl. He would probably not be thrown off the place now, not after having been able to help her the night before, but still he should never have said the things he had said. He should never.

It was a Saturday, and he had the morning free. Most of the other hands on the place had been in the fields since before daybreak, but Whitley had told him there would be no farm work for him this day. There would instead be a haul of corn liquor to be made all the way to Columbus that night, and he was supposed to be resting—but he could not rest; he could do nothing but sit and think about Elise Whitley and know that he had to see her.

He left his room and made his way across the fields toward the big house, smelling the heavy odors of manure and sun-baked earth around him. He stopped at the edge of the woods and on impulse gathered a large handful of spring wildflowers, then cut across the red clay road and through the rows of cotton to the yard of the big house.

It was quiet; Whitley's Ford was gone, as was Bill's Packard, but Janson paid little attention as he walked across the yard, up onto the wide veranda, and to the front door. He knocked, and then waited, looking down at the wildflowers he held in his hand, and then beyond them, to the worn and cracked shoes on his feet, the only pair of shoes he owned, the pair that no amount of cleaning and polishing would ever remove the scuff marks or red dirt from. He suddenly realized what a ridiculous sight he must make, coming to the front door of this big, fine house, in his threadbare clothing and cracked shoes, with his wildflowers gripped in worn farmer's hands—wildflowers, for a girl who could have hothouse roses anytime she might want them, simply for the asking. He had the sudden impulse to leave, but the door swung inward before the impulse could become action, and he found himself looking into the surprised face of Martha Whitley.

Elise's mother looked him over, and then quickly masked her surprise with a kind smile, inviting him in just as if it were a common occurrence for one of her husband's farmhands to come calling at her front door.

"I thought that Elise—that Miss Whitley—" he corrected himself, realizing suddenly how very forward he was being, "might like these—do you think she might be willin' t' see me, even for just a minute?" he asked, feeling so very awkward now that he stood within the wide hallway, the heavy front doors with their frosted glass panes now closed behind him.

Mrs. Whitley smiled. "I think she would like very much to see you, to thank you for what you did for her last night. Why don't you wait in the parlor. I'll tell her you're here."

He nodded, and watched as she went toward the stairs, then turned and went through the open doorway she had indicated to the right, stopping just inside to stare around himself at the room before him.

It was the most elaborate room he had ever been in in all his life, more elaborate than he had ever imagined any room might be. Patterned paper covered the walls, with small yellow and gold flowers on tiny green stems over its surface. Heavy gold curtains hung over the tall windows, held back by braided cords with fancy gold tassels hanging from their ends. Delicate lace doilies covered many of the rich wood surfaces, and a gold and brown rug lay on the floor, on which sat mahogany furniture with polished surfaces and richly brocaded upholstery. A sofa, two chairs, and an upholstered rocker rested against the walls, with an old-fashioned center table and velvet-seated chairs in the center of the room. An elaborately-tooled piano filled one corner, a tall secretary another, and a writing desk fronted by a delicate lady's chair filled a third. The mantle piece was of marble, topped by a chiming mantle clock, and, within the fireplace below it, stood firedogs shaped like marching men.

Janson stood just within the doorway of the room, afraid to move or touch anything, for fear that he might break or soil it. He stared up at the crystal chandelier hanging from the center of the ceiling, amidst the cherubs and fleur-de-lis surrounding its base, watching the light reflecting off the thousand tiny prisms—how could anyone live in a room, in a house, such as this. How could—

Then he caught sight of a portrait of Elise Whitley hanging on a wall not far distant from the piano, and he moved into the room so that he could see it better, then stood staring up at it. She had sat for the artist here in this room, wearing a pale blue dress with some bit of lace at the collar—she might not want to see him, he thought. He had been rude and insulting when they had met, and he could now only be a reminder of what had almost happened to her the night before—but he had to see her, to apologize to her for the things he had said.

It would be the first time in his life that he had ever apologized for anything.

ELISE SAT staring into the oval-shaped mirror above her dresser, the quiet room of pink and rose and white reflected behind her—she did not feel safe, did not feel quite as easy or at home as she should have felt in this lovely room that had sheltered her all her life. Her parents had brought her here immediately after the attack the night before, and she had not once left the room since—there had been a drugged sleep throughout the night, a drugged sleep she had vaguely awakened from several times to feel that she was not alone, that she was not safe, only to drift back under that hazy veil of sedative again, carrying that feeling back into sleep with her. There had been nightmares, demons chasing her through the rooms of the house, demons all with Ethan Bennett's face and his hands and his body. She kept remembering his words: "Phyllis Ann told me . . . that it was you and not my baby that cheated—"

You and not my baby that—

Phyllis Ann had lied, had caused all this. In order to save herself from whatever it was her father had intended for her, she had turned him on Elise instead—Phyllis Ann knew her father; she knew what could happen. Phyllis Ann knew. And Elise could not stop thinking that it had been her best friend, the girl she had risked everything for—

Phyllis Ann had been in her nightmares as well. She had stood to herself, safe, laughing. "It was Elise who cheated. Elise did it—" she said over and over again to the demons. "It was Elise—"

When Elise had remained silent only to protect—

There was a tap at the door, and Elise jumped, startled. "Who is it?" she called out, taking up the ivory-handled hairbrush from the dresser top and clenching it in her hands so tightly that the bristles cut into her palms—it was good to feel something real and solid, to leave behind the nightmare demons she had lived with through the night.

"It's me, dear," her mother said, opening the door to look in at her. "You have a visitor."

"A visitor?"

"Yes, Janson Sanders is downstairs. He would like to see—"

Elise sat forward, suddenly attentive as she laid the hairbrush aside. "He's here? Now?"

"Yes. He wanted to know if you might—" But Elise was up and already past her, through the door down the hall to the stairs that descended to the first floor. She stopped on one of the lower steps and took a deep breath, trying to calm the beating of her heart—she knew what a sight she must have made, rushing past her mother as she had done, but there was nothing she could do about that now. She smoothed a hand over her bobbed hair, and then made herself walk more slowly as she descended the remaining steps and crossed the wide hall to the front parlor where she knew he would be waiting for her.

The door was open and she saw him standing there, staring up at the portrait of her that hung on the wall—suddenly she felt very safe, very protected, just in seeing him. He would let nothing harm her, nothing touch her, not so long as he was here. He had saved her the night before, and—

"Mr. Sanders?"

He turned to look at her, his eyes taking her in at one glance, and then settling on hers with an intensity that was almost unsettling. He did not smile as she approached him.

"I'm glad you're here. I wanted to thank you for—"

"There ain't no need for thankin' me," he said, not allowing her to finish. "I didn't do nothin' last night more'n anybody else'd 'a done. I just wanted t' come by this mornin' t' make sure you were all right."

"Yes, I'm fine, thanks to you. And I do need to thank you. You might even have been killed when—"

"Like I said, there ain't no need." He stared at her.

"But, there is a need. If it hadn't been for you—" Her words fell silent, and she shivered involuntarily. She hugged her arms to herself, suddenly cold from within, and turned away. After a moment, his voice came again, from very close behind her, his words quiet.

"You're okay, Elise. Ain't nobody gonna hurt you now—"

She turned to meet his eyes, finding them filled with concern. After a moment, he seemed to draw away from her, as if realizing what he had said.

"I mean, Miss Whitley—"

She smiled. "Elise, not Miss Whitley. I think you can call me Elise after—after last night."

He looked at her for a long moment, but did not return her smile. "Elise," he said after a moment, and she nodded.

She looked down at the wildflowers he held in his hand, knowing somehow that he had forgotten them. "These are lovely. Are they for me?"

"Yes, ma'am. I thought maybe you'd like 'em."

"Oh, yes, I do. They're beautiful." She gathered the flowers into her hands and smiled down at them. "Thank you."

"They ain't nothin' but wildflowers I found out by the woods," he said, seeming almost to shrug as she looked up at him.

"Well, they're beautiful."

He looked at her for a long moment, and she remarked to herself for the first time that he really was rather handsome, with the black hair and high cheekbones, and those green eyes. "I just wanted t' come by an' make sure you were all right," he said.

"I am, thanks to you."

But again he seemed to ignore her thanks. There was a small gesture of his hand, as if he did not know what to say. "I wanted t' tell you, too, that I know I shouldn't 'a talked t' you like I did yesterday. I had no right. I shouldn't never said any 'a th' things I said t' your brother, an' I shouldn't 'a said any 'a th' things I said t' you. I was outta line an' I know it, an'—well—I'm sorry."

Elise looked at him for a moment, sensing that this was a man who rarely apologized for anything said or done in his life, and realizing that he was not very good at, or very comfortable with, the words. "I shouldn't have said the things I said to you, either," she told him, then smiled. "Why don't we just start over?" She offered her hand to him. "Friends?"

He stared at her hand for a long moment, and then reached out and took it, lifting his eyes back to hers. "Frien's," he said at last, though he sounded almost uncomfortable with the word. Elise looked at him as he held her hand in his, knowing she had never felt so utterly and completely safe in all her life, protected, as if no one and no thing could ever touch her again, not so long as he was near.

The moment was broken by Stan's entry into the room. Elise drew her hand back, embarrassed at her brother's curious stare. Janson quickly excused himself, looking ill-at-ease, and left.

"You were looking at him awful funny," Stan said as she turned to look at him.

"And you ought to mind your own business." She walked past him and out the door, still holding the wildflowers in her hand.

One of the front doors at the near end of the hall stood open, and she went to close it, but stopped instead with her hand on the knob, watching as Janson Sanders crossed the wide yard toward the road. He stopped for a moment and looked back, and their eyes met over the distance. Elise raised a hand on impulse to wave, but he simply stared at her for a moment longer, and then turned and walked away.

She continued to watch him until he left her sight, going down the red dirt road, across the fields, and toward the old barn where he lived, and then she closed the door and leaned against it, looking down at the small bouquet of wildflowers she held in her hand. For a time she fancied she could still almost feel his presence around her, in the wide hallway, throughout the rooms of the house. And she knew she was safe.

That feeling of security stayed with her through the day and into the early evening. She sat in the front parlor sometime shortly after darkness had fallen, a favorite book of poetry open on her lap—but her mind was not on poetry, on words she knew and loved so well that she could almost quote them by heart. Her eyes kept straying toward the vase of wildflowers she had placed on the center table in the midst of the room, wildflowers Janson Sanders had given her—he was so unlike anyone she had ever known before. He might even have died last night in protecting her; but he had not, and she was safe now.

She looked toward her brother Alfred where he knelt across the room trying to adjust the tuning of a radio program he had done nothing but talk about all day, hearing him curse rather less than quietly as the hiss and crackle of static filled the air around them—they were perhaps not that far different in age, Janson Sanders and Alfred, and yet Janson seemed so much older somehow, as if he had lived more in his nineteen or twenty years than anyone else could possibly have lived. He seemed so worldly, so mature, as Alfred only thought himself to be with his posturing and his temper and his theatrics—Alfred was radio programs and illegal gin just for the sake of its being illegal; he was fascination with Al Capone and gangsters, and with young flappers who had somewhat less than savory reputations; he was trouble and fights and even having been arrested once more than a year ago in a raid of a speakeasy in Buntain.

Elise watched him for a moment, noting the studied slouch of his shoulders, the expensively cut trousers and shirt that were worn with such a practiced disdain, the fair skin so like hers that burned all too easily in the sun—somehow she could not picture Janson Sanders here in this room, doing what her brother was doing now, or even sitting here as she was, and she found herself wondering what kind of man he really was, for she truly had never known anyone even remotely like him before in her life. She wondered if he liked the movies and the glamourous but silent stars all her friends so wanted to be like—handsome Douglas Fairbanks and John Barrymore, Tom Mix and his Westerns, Charlie Chaplin and Buster Keaton, Greta Garbo, Mary Pickford, and Clara Bow. She wondered if he could talk for hours about Babe Ruth and the "Manassa Mauler" Jack Dempsey, as could most of the young men she knew; she wondered if he was fascinated with flagpole sitting and dance marathons, with crossword puzzles and jazz music, with radio and scandals and Sigmund Freud, with bathtub gin and automobiles—and, even as she wondered, she knew that she should not, for he was a different sort of person than she was, and not at all the sort of young man she should find herself interested in.

She turned her eyes back to the slender book lying open on her lap, and read again the same words she had read already a number of times tonight:

> Unlike are we, unlike, O princely Heart!
> Unlike our uses and our destinies.
> Our ministering two angels look surprise
> On one another, as they strike athwart
> Their wings in passing. . . .

Her attention was drawn away as Bill entered the parlor from the hallway, and then crossed to the sofa against the wall just opposite, never once looking at her or at Alfred, as if not acknowledging either of their presence in the room. He sank down on the brocaded pillows and finally brought his eyes to her, and Elise looked away, somehow uneasy under the stare he directed her way. He reached to unbutton his vest, then turned to glare at Alfred.

"Turn that goddamn thing off if you can't get the station!" he ordered, and Alfred turned an angry look his way, but, after a moment, the radio fell silent. Alfred moved to sit in a nearby chair, glaring at his older brother from beneath lowered brows, but Bill seemed hardly to notice, stretching against the back of the sofa and relaxing as he waited for supper to be called.

"It was hell today," he said, beginning to look as if he were comfortable. "I had to argue with that fool at the bank for almost an hour; I thought I'd never get out of there—and you'll never guess who I saw when I stopped by the drugstore on the way home. Ethan Bennett was sitting at the fountain having a cup of coffee, just as if he had never spent last night in jail. The sheriff must have had to let him go on bond—you should have seen that son-of-a-bitch's face; Franklin and I did him up pretty good last night when we—"

But Elise did not hear the remainder of his words. A cold chill went over her, the feeling of security suddenly gone, and she found herself hugging her arms for warmth even in the stuffiness of the room. She wished suddenly that Janson Sanders was here, for she knew she would feel safe if only—

Her eyes came to rest on Alfred where he sat across the room, and another feeling came over her, a feeling that frightened her even more than did the first, but a feeling that she could somehow not put a name to. She stared at him, seeing a muscle clench in his jaw, seeing something fire behind his blue eyes that she could not understand. His hands tightened into fists so hard that his knuckles stood out in white relief across their backs, his eyes hardening, making him look as if he were a different person from the brother she had loved all her life, making him look like a man intent on murder, a man she would be frightened of, though she liked to think that few things in life frightened her.

He stood and crossed the room without a word, going to the writing desk in the corner, standing with his back to her as he opened a drawer and lifted something out—but Elise knew what was in his hand even before he turned, for she knew what was kept in that drawer, and suddenly she realized all it was her brother was capable of.

"Alfred—no—" She stood, the book of sonnets falling from her lap—but he only stared at her, their father's pistol in his hand, the pistol that was always kept loaded and ready in the top drawer of the writing desk. Alfred stared at her. When he finally spoke, Elise heard more fury in his voice than she had ever heard from him in all her life.

"They're not going to let him get by with it." His voice was quiet, deadly, and somehow that frightened her all the more.

"He's only out on bond. He'll stand trial. He won't—"

"They can't do to him what he deserves for what he tried to do to—"

"But, you can't—" She took a step toward him, but froze as he motioned with the gun.

"I'm going to send Ethan Bennett straight to hell where he belongs; then they can do what they want!"

"Alfred!" But he was already out the door and into the hallway. She heard one of the heavy front doors slam, and she knew that, if someone did not stop him, her brother would either commit a murder, or be killed himself tonight. She looked toward Bill, but he only stared at her in response, as if he did not understand, or possibly even care, what it was that might happen.

She was through the hallway, out onto the veranda, and down into the yard even before she knew how she had gotten there, catching hold of Alfred's arm before he could get into the big Studebaker parked before the house—but he only jerked free, prying her fingers from his arm and shoving her away, and she was left standing alone in the drive before the house, a cloud of red dust being kicked up around her by the tires of the departing car. She stared after it for a moment, panic filling her, knowing that someone would have to stop her brother before he could reach town, before he could reach Ethan Bennett, before he could—

She looked up toward the lighted windows of the house, knowing there was no one within those walls who could or would help her—her father was gone, and neither she nor their mother nor Stan could drive. Bill would do nothing—but she had to have help. Someone had to stop her brother before he could kill Ethan Bennett, before he could be killed himself. Someone had to—

Janson Sanders—

She was running from the yard even before she thought, running through the edge of the cotton fields and the woods toward the old barn and the room Janson Sanders lived in—he had to be there; he had to help her, if no one else in the world would help her. She caught her foot once and fell, knocking the breath from her body and badly skinning an elbow—but she hardly even noticed. She ran on, kicking the high-heeled shoes from her feet for fear that she might fall again, running now in her bare stocking feet alone, though rocks and twigs quickly tore through the silk to bruise her tender skin—let him be there. Please, God, just let him be—

A dim light shown through the single window of the room attached to the rear of the barn as it came within sight. She almost fell against the door as she reached it, then pounded on it so hard that it shook within its frame, screaming out Janson Sanders's name over and over again. She collapsed into his arms as the door opened, seeing a thousand different things cross his face in the moment before he understood her words.

"Alfred—Mr. Bennett's free; Bill saw him in town at the drugstore. Alfred went after him—oh, you've got to stop him; he's got Daddy's gun. You've got to stop—"

He took her back to the house, walking quickly with her through the woods and the edge of the cotton fields, holding to her arm all the while, and left her there on the veranda, starting toward Bill's Packard as Elise heard the front door open behind her.

"You goddamn half-breed son-of-a-bitch, I won't have you in my—" But as soon as Bill left the veranda to stop him, Janson hit him hard, sending him into the dirt. He turned and got into the car without saying a word, looking back up at her one last time as he backed the car up and started toward town.

As soon as he was gone from sight, Elise sagged against one of the huge white columns that supported the veranda roof, all the strength leaving her body—Alfred would be all right now. Janson Sanders would find him, stop him, before he could get to Ethan Bennett, before he could kill the man, before he could be killed himself, before he could be thrown in jail for murder or assault, or for—

Bill got up from the ground, knocking the red dirt from the legs of his white trousers, cursing, calling Janson things such as she had never before heard in her life. She stared at him for a long moment, knowing for the first time in her life what it was to truly hate, though he was her own brother.

"You goddamn, selfish—" she began quietly, seeing him turn to stare at her, a surprised look coming to his face. "You goddamn—" but she could not finish the words. She turned and walked into the house, slamming the heavy front door behind herself, leaving him standing alone in the red dirt of the drive.

JANSON PUSHED the Packard for all it was worth those minutes later, demanding even more from the powerful engine, trying to hold the big car in curves at speeds he had never driven before—but it was not fast enough. He knew that Alfred Whitley had gotten too much of a head start on him, that he had already had too much time. If Bennett was enough of a fool to have stayed where Bill had seen him, Alfred would have found him long before Janson could reach town, long before Janson could stop him—but he had to stop him; someone had to stop him, before Alfred Whitley could commit a murder publicly, or be killed himself.

Janson held tightly to the steering wheel, struggling to keep the car on the road and out of a ditch at the speed he was driving. He cursed Alfred Whitley with almost every breath—as long as he lived, he knew he would never forget the look he had seen on Elise Whitley's face as he had driven away. The girl had already been through so much in the past two days, and now, if someone did not stop her brother in time, she would have to go through even more. Alfred was hotheaded, bad tempered, just stupid enough to go after Bennett in public with a gun, and just stupid enough to wind up in jail, or possibly even shot himself, because of it. There were better ways to take care of Ethan Bennett if the law let him off, better ways her father would likely take care of later if he had to, but not like this.

The car went wild into a curve and Janson fought to control it, almost ending up in a deep gully alongside the roadbed. He swore under his breath as the Packard recovered, seeing the headlamps of another vehicle coming toward him on the narrow road. He honked the horn to warn the other driver aside, but the man gave him no leeway, almost forcing him from the road instead as the truck neared and then passed with only bare inches to spare. The other driver braked hard, almost going off the road and into a ditch—

William Whitley—

Janson jammed on the Packard's brakes, almost off the road himself, then yanked open the door to lean out and yell over Whitley's cursing: "Alfred's gone after Bennett with a gun!"

Whitley's words fell immediately silent, an awful look of understanding coming over his face even in the darkness. "Where at?" he demanded.

"In town. The drugstore—" But Janson did not wait for Whitley's response. He got the car in gear and got it back on the road, headed toward town. He had to stop Alfred Whitley.

JANSON REACHED town before Whitley did, the man left somewhere behind him—the area before the drugstore was too quiet, Main Street too still, but Janson already knew what was happening. The Whitleys' Studebaker was parked on the brick pavement before Dobbin's Drugstore, Bennett's new LaSalle as well. Alfred had already found Ethan Bennett.

He drove the Packard up onto the sidewalk before he could stop it, badly nicking the fender of another car, but he hardly noticed. He was out of the car almost before it could stop, leaving the door open behind him as he headed toward the glass windows at the front of the drugstore—there were people crowded back against the soda fountain, people crowded back against the walls beyond small tables where sat half-eaten sandwiches and dishes of melting ice cream. In the middle of the luncheonette area stood Alfred and Bennett, the boy slowly shifting back and forth from one foot to the other as he held a gun on the older man. There was a nervous perspiration broken out on Alfred's upper lip, among faint reddish hairs that were supposed to be a mustache. His face was flushed, and, as Janson entered the drugstore, he could tell the boy's hands were trembling—if someone yelled, Alfred might very well wheel and fire from sheer panic. Someone else in the room, some woman or young child, could be hurt, could even die—Janson began to slowly inch his way past the front windows and toward the soda fountain. If he could reach Alfred—

"Now, you put that gun down, boy," Bennett was saying in a tone that was meant to be soothing, one hand stretched out before him toward the boy—his face showed dark, ugly bruises, and his lower lip was nothing more than a crusted red gash where Franklin Bates had split it the night before. One of his eyes was almost swollen shut, and the other was very nearly black—Bill and Franklin had done him justice. Janson only wished they had killed him instead. "You know you don't want to hurt me, boy. You're just confused right now. You don't know what really happened last night. Your sister—"

"You shut your dirty mouth about my sister!" Alfred yelled, his hands visibly shaking now. His courage was beginning to leave him before the very real possibility of killing a man, even a man like Ethan Bennett—but every word that Bennett said now only brought him closer to death, only increased the likelihood of the boy pulling the trigger. The man was just too stupid to know it.

"Alfred, you've got to know the truth, boy. Your sister didn't get anything more than she was asking—"

"Shut up!" Alfred screamed, enraged, and for a moment Bennett fell silent, his eyes on the gun in Alfred's hands. "You tried to hurt Elise. You tried to—you're going to pay for what you did. You're going to—"

"Give me that gun, boy! I'm not playing with you anymore—give me that goddamn gun!" Bennett took a step forward, but froze as Alfred leveled the gun at his chest.

"Stay back! I mean it!"

Bennett stared at him for a long moment, a look of nervous fear coming to his face as he licked the busted and swollen lips. Across the room a child began to cry, a small voice begging to go home. Mr. Dobbins and an elderly man tried to intervene, but fell silent as the gun moved in their direction for a moment, Alfred seeming very close to the breaking point now. Bennett's eyes darted to Janson where he moved slowly along the edge of the soda fountain, and some degree of understanding seemed to come to his face—if it wasn't for what Elise Whitley has already been through, I'd let him kill you, Janson thought. I'd kill you myself.

Bennett's eyes moved back to the boy. "Alfred, I've known you all your life. I know you can't really believe—"

Only a few more steps—Janson told himself. If he could get his hands on the gun, disarm the boy, then it would be over. If the law did not make Bennett pay for what he had done to Elise Whitley, what he had tried to do, then they would make him pay: her father, Alfred, Franklin Bates. Bennett would not get off scot free. He would pay—but not like this. Not like—

"Alfred!" Whitley's shout as he entered the drugstore startled the boy. Alfred turned, the gun turning with him. A lady screamed, and Janson moved quickly—but it was not quickly enough. Bennett was already on the boy, trying to wrest the gun from his hands. They struggled for a moment, knocking over chairs and a table as they fought—and then there was the sound of a gunshot, its reverberation filling the air around them.

For a moment there was absolute silence. Alfred Whitley took a step back, his hands to his chest. There was a startled, disbelieving look on his face, a look that turned to horror as he drew his hands away and looked down at them. They were covered with blood.

He stumbled slightly and collapsed to the floor. There was a strangled shout for a doctor, but Janson never knew the voice—Whitley was already kneeling beside his son, trying to pull the boy's head to his lap. Tears were coursing down the big man's cheeks, fear and horror there as Janson had never seen before.

"You're going to be all right, boy. You're going to be just fine. You're going to be—"

Alfred looked up at him, tears filling the blue eyes that seemed suddenly so like those of Elise Whitley. "Daddy?" he said softly, reaching up a bloody hand to touch his father's face.

"Don't try to talk, boy. You're going to be just—"

"It doesn't even hurt, Daddy," the boy said, and closed his eyes, his hand dropping from his father's face, leaving a bloody handprint there. "It doesn't even—" There was a rattle deep in Alfred's chest, and then again, louder. He lay still for a moment, taking one last breath. And then he was silent.

Bennett's voice rose loud above Whitley's, above the sound of a child crying across the room, and of a young lady weeping nearby, drowning out all else. "It was self defense! All of you saw it; you saw him come after me with the gun! It was—"

Janson turned and hit him hard in the mouth with the force of all the anger and pain inside of him, sending him stumbling backwards, knocking over chairs and tables in his path before finally coming to rest on the floor across the room. Then he knelt by Whitley, putting a hand on the big man's shoulder, crying with him as Whitley rocked his son's body in his arms, unable to speak as he heard the man say the same words over and over again:

"Open your eyes, boy. You're going to be fine, you hear me. Listen to your daddy now, you're going to be just fine—"

JANSON LEFT the Packard where it sat half on the brick pavement of Main Street, one of its front tires up on the sidewalk. He drove Whitley home in the truck, silently respectful of the older man's grief as Whitley stared out the window beside him at the passing night. Whitley's tears were dry now, but Janson knew his hurting was none the less—sometimes grief went beyond tears, beyond feeling. On the back of the truck, beneath a blanket someone had brought out from the drugstore, lay the body of Whitley's second born. Alfred Whitley was going home for the last time.

Janson stared ahead through the windshield at the few feet of red dirt road that the headlamps picked out before the truck—how can I tell her I couldn't stop him? How can I—

Elise, her mother, and Stan came out onto the veranda as the truck pulled up before the big house. There was silence as he and Whitley got out, as Elise, her mother, and younger brother descended the wide steps to the yard. She came to stand before him, looking up into his eyes in the darkness, and for a moment he could not speak for the fear he could see on her face. He could not be the one to tell her—

"You weren't able to stop him?" she asked quietly.

Janson slowly shook his head.

"Alfred's dead, isn't he?"

No words would come to him because of the pain he could see in her eyes. But she needed no words. She knew. She came into his arms, the tears starting to move down her cheeks, and he held her, his own pain at seeing such grief almost more than he could bear. He heard himself saying mindless, comforting words, trying to ease her loss, all the while knowing there was nothing he could say, nothing he could do, that would ever help.

He heard Martha Whitley cry out, saw her collapse into her husband's and Stan's arms as she saw the body of her son beneath the blanket. He heard Whitley saying that it had been quick, that there had been no pain, that the boy did not suffer long—but he could only think about the girl in his arms, of the hurt she was feeling, of—

He caught sight of Bill Whitley standing near one of the tall white columns at the edge of the veranda. The man's face was unreadable, his eyes on Janson and his sister, and a cold chill moved up Janson's spine—there was no grief on the man's face, no—

Elise Whitley was warm in his arms, crying quietly against his chest as he held her, and he turned his attention back to her, hurting for her pain and grief, wishing there were something he could do to lessen her hurt, something—

Whitley and Stan led Mrs. Whitley up the steps to the veranda, supporting her, half carrying her, as her knees sagged and she leaned against her husband. Bill gave her only a slight glance as they passed him, not offering to help, not moving to open the door, not speaking—then his eyes moved back to Janson and Elise, and Janson felt the cold chill return. He held Elise only more tightly to him, and returned the stare—Bill Whitley's face was no longer unreadable. There was nothing but cold hatred there.

## II

ELISE PASSED THROUGH the days in a haze of pain and grief, feeling nothing more inside herself than a terrible ache of emptiness that it seemed nothing could ever fill again. She had never known loss before, had never known tears of grief and hurting, had never known anything that her father's name and influence could not set right again in the world.

But this William Whitley could not set right. This he could not even deal with himself—Elise had heard him crying like a child behind her parents' closed bedroom door, had heard her mother's tears as well. She had gone to them hoping to find comfort, hoping to find someone who would be strong to let her cry. Her brother was dead and she was hurting, blaming herself in the times when she was alone, for Alfred had gone after Bennett only to revenge and protect her—and she was alone often in those first days, crying into the pillows in her bedroom until there were no tears left. Everywhere she looked, everything she touched, reminded her of Alfred, reminded her of the boy he had been, the man he would never be. She needed her family, needed her parents and Bill and Stan, needed to know they did not blame her, even as she blamed herself—but they were not there for her, not there even for each other; they were each involved in their own grief, each hurting in their own way, each somehow and completely alone even in the times when they were together.

Her father was working too much, immersing himself in business, her mother moving about the house as if she were not even the same person she had been before, talking about Alfred sometimes almost as if he were still alive, almost as if he were still the small child he had been long ago. Stan was spending too much time alone, reading, forgetting, withdrawing into the worlds of others to escape his own. He rarely talked to her, or to her parents, or to anyone—but she could see the hurt in his eyes, the pain, the grief, and she turned away, unable to deal with his hurting anymore than he or her parents could deal with her own.

Only Bill showed no pain. Bill, who said everything right and wore his mourning as if it were a cloak. There was no hurt in his eyes, no pain, no grief. It was as if Alfred had never been, had never existed, had never died, in his world—and Elise sometimes felt as if she had lost two brothers that night instead of one.

There was only one person who seemed to be there solely for her, only one person who was not involved in his own pain and grief, but who seemed concerned only to lessen her own. In those first days of grieving and loss, Janson Sanders became the one constant of caring, understanding, and support in her world.

He would sit with her for hours, letting her cry when she needed to, or talk when she felt like it, letting her grieve and mourn, and heal. He sat in silence as she talked, letting her tell him about her brother, about a boy she would always remember, always love. He did not say the stupid things everyone else said when she cried, did not tell her that her brother was with God or in a better place, but instead he just sat in quiet sympathy, respecting and allowing her her grief. Many of her friends had turned away now, embarrassed at her pain: young people she had known all her life, her own cousins, even J.C., the pressure for them to wed gone now for the time being in light of her family's loss—they could deal with her pain no more than her family could. They no longer came to call on her, no longer asked her to visit—but Janson Sanders was there to fill the place they all left. The place they all left, and more.

He began to call on her each day, coming to the side door and knocking softly, spending with her whatever time he could find free from farm chores and from the work he did for her father. At first it seemed as if she talked to him only of Alfred, remembering days long past, just as her mother did, but gradually she found him leading her away from the memories that were at once so bitter and yet so sweet—she found herself telling him things she had told no one else, about Phyllis Ann and the reasons they had been asked to leave the school. She told him of the choice she had made to remain silent, and of the betrayal she had found in Bennett's words that night—Phyllis Ann had lied to save herself, just as Elise had remained silent such a short while before in trying to protect her. Elise's silence, her lie of omission, had resulted in her own brother's death—if she had only told the truth in the principal's office that day, if she had only let Phyllis Ann face the consequences of what she herself had chosen to do, then Bennett would never have come after her, and Alfred would never have gone into town with the gun, and—

Elise cried and she confessed, and Janson told her it was not her fault, that things that had been done could never be undone, and that Alfred would not have wanted her to blame herself for something she could never have foreseen, something she could never have prevented. And, slowly, she began to heal.

Her days came to revolve around his visits, around whatever time he could find to spend with her. She had rarely left the house since the day of Alfred's funeral, afraid she would run into Ethan Bennett—he was still free, awaiting trial for the attack on her, and she was terrified. He would never face judge or jury for killing her brother—self-defense they had called it, for there had been too many witnesses to say Alfred had intended to kill the man, too many witnesses to say Bennett had acted only to save his own life. But Elise knew differently. Alfred could have killed no one, not even the man who had attacked her. He had been nothing more than a hot-headed boy. A boy who would now never have the chance to become a man.

Somewhere in the back of her mind sat a fear that Bennett would come after her again. She was afraid to leave the house, and did so reluctantly only when she had to, avoiding going shopping in town, or for the long walks she had always enjoyed taking. Only when Janson was near did she feel safe, and only gradually did her fears begin to lessen. She built her days around him, waiting for the time when she would hear his tap at the side door, as eager as a child for the simple gifts he would bring her: a penny's worth of candy from the store, chewing gum, a ribbon, a small basket he had made, a figure he had carved from wood. She would receive him in the sewing parlor at the back of the house, for her mother would not allow him in either of the two front parlors—he might have cotton poisoning on his clothes, or red dirt on his feet, and, even if he did not, he was still a farmhand and only half white, her mother said, and he could never be allowed to forget that. They would sit for hours, talking, listening to the radio, just being together, and it would be Elise who would forget—he was her friend, the one person who had been there for her when she had needed someone the most, and that was all that mattered.

They went for long walks together, or sat in the shade on the back veranda and drank lemonade, or took small picnic dinners into the woods and ate in the meadow clearing there. Often Elise would take along a book of poetry and read to him for hours on end as he sat and watched her, or he would gather wildflowers and bring them to her, telling her the names of each and showing her where it grew. What they did never seemed to matter; it only mattered that they could be together, that she could spend time with him, be near him.

At first her parents did not object to the friendship, too involved in their own pain and loss to see or even to care. They were grateful to Janson for how he had fought Bennett to protect her, and grateful for all he had done to try to stop Alfred the night he had died. Her father knew she was safe when she was with him, for, though Ethan Bennett was free and walking the streets of the County, he would not dare to come near her so long as Janson Sanders was nearby.

In those first days her father had often had Janson drive her about to the places she needed to go, into town to shop, or to choir practice at mid-week, even to church services when he and her mother could not attend. By the time the early days of summer came and her father did voice an objection to the friendship, it was already too late—Elise already cared too deeply for Janson Sanders to give a whit what her father said or thought about anything. There could be no harm in their friendship, no matter that her mother did say that it was unseemly and that people might begin to talk—to Elise it did not matter. Janson Sanders was her friend, and—and he was growing to be so much more.

In the weeks and months she had known him, Janson had never once tried to touch or even to kiss her, seeming content with their relationship as it was. But, as the warm days of June passed, Elise began to realize she wanted more from him than friendship alone. She was falling in love with Janson Sanders. And she knew it.

At first that knowledge had surprised her—how could she be in love with someone so different from she, someone who had no family, no money, no background, no home other than the lean-to room he slept in off the barn, none of the things that she had grown up thinking one could normally expect from life. They were so different, and yet—and yet there was something inside of him that was so very like her. He made her angrier at times than any other human being alive, and happier. He seemed to know how she thought and felt, often without her having to speak. And, as the days passed, she was beginning to know desire—the way he looked, how she felt when she was near him, how she thrilled if even he touched her hand. She wanted him, and she lay awake often at night wondering what it would feel like to kiss him, to touch him, to share with him the most intimate thing a man and woman could share.

And, yet, the things she felt also somehow frightened her as well. She had never felt this way before, had never dreamed it possible to feel this way, to care so deeply for someone, to feel such desire—and yet be so unsure and afraid. He was so unlike her, so different from the man she had dreamed of all her life, and yet she could not imagine spending the remainder of that life with anyone else.

But Janson was a farmhand, a farmhand with little prospect in the future of ever becoming anything more than what he was now. He would never be able to give her the kind of life she wanted, the kind of life she had always had. He could not give her a home, or surround her with beautiful, wonderful things; he could barely even provide the necessities of life for himself, and even that could be taken from him at a moment's notice, for her father would surely drive him from the place the minute he were to ever learn how Elise truly felt about this farmhand. Janson Sanders had nothing, at least nothing to her eyes accustomed to wealth and luxury and beauty and more than she could ever want.

But that seemed to matter less and less to her as the days went by. She loved him. She loved him for all his difference, and not in spite of it. She loved him, and she wanted him, even though his pride and his intensity sometimes frightened her, and his quiet introversion oftentimes left her feeling as if she did not know him at all. She did not understand him, and the distance he kept between them served to confuse her all the more. He rarely spoke of himself or of the place he had come from in Alabama, or of anything that had gone on in his life before the day he had first come here to Endicott County those months ago. She rarely knew how he thought or felt about anything, except nature and the land and growing things. What she had learned about him she had learned from Stan, for Janson seemed to talk more freely with her brother than he ever could with anyone else—he had come from the hilly regions of Alabama, had had a farm there but had lost it. His parents were dead, and he was alone, though he had kin in Alabama, and relatives spread throughout the South. His mother had been Cherokee, and his father's people mostly Irish; and his pride went back for generations.

Stan said Janson spoke often of his grandparents who were sharecroppers back in Alabama, of his gran'pa who planted by the signs and knew everyone in the County by name, and his gran'ma who could draw fire and stop blood and cure sick people with nothing more than belief and prayer—they sounded so far distant, so unreal, so divorced from the modern world of automobiles and electric lights and telephones and running water. And yet Janson was a part of their world, of a world he seldom spoke of, of a world she knew nothing about.

By late June, it no longer seemed to matter to her who or what Janson Sanders was, that his skin was darker than hers, or that his life had been so far different from her own. The only thing that mattered was that she loved him, wanted to be with him, and that somewhere in her dreams she held a belief that he had to love her as well, a belief that they could be together—how that could be, in the manner of fantasies and children who have had all they have wanted all their lives, she did not know. The only thing she knew was that she wanted him, and that she would have him. The remainder she trusted would take care of itself.

On a warm summer morning late in that June of 1927, Elise sat before her dresser, critically staring into the mirror at her own reflection. She considered herself for a moment, assessing—her hair was a warm red-gold, bobbed into the most recent fashion; her eyes blue, darker than the sky, but unlike any other shade she knew; her skin soft, fair, flawlessly perfect. She knew she was pretty; enough young men in her life had told her that until it was something she did not doubt—but Janson had never told her she was pretty, and it was only from him that she wanted to hear the words. Many times in the past weeks she had turned to find him staring at her, and in those moments she had been certain he had been about to speak; in those moments his eyes had been readable, his feelings clear. In those moments she had known—Janson Sanders did think of her as a woman. He looked at her the way she wanted a man—the way she wanted him—to look at her.

And yet he would never speak of what she often told herself he felt. He would never let her closer, never let her get to know the man inside of him, never really let her see his thought or his feelings or his dreams, seeming determined to remain as silent and as unknown to her as a closed and unread book. He seemed to enjoy the times they spent together—she knew she could not be wrong about that—but still there remained that barrier between them, a barrier he had placed there himself, a barrier she could somehow not cross.

She picked up the ivory-handled brush from the dresser top and began to run it through her hair, considering again something she had been thinking of in the past several days—if Janson knew how she felt, he would have to respond. He would have to tell her how he felt, have to tell her that he loved her—and he had to love her; she knew he had to. There was no doubt within her of that. It made no sense to have to wait weeks and months in order for him to declare his feelings first. This was 1927, after all, and a woman no longer had to act demure and senseless and completely devoid of feelings until a man spoke, just to protect a reputation of the sort older people revered so highly. That was a good way to end up an old maid—and she was young and pretty and thoroughly modern, she had no intention of becoming an old maid as well. Janson would respect her openness. He might even be grateful for it—after all, even if it did not matter to her that he was a farmhand, it might matter to him. He could be afraid to show what it was he felt for William Whitley's daughter, afraid she would turn him away, afraid she might even have her father put him off the place, when he could be no more wrong.

She smiled at her reflection in the mirror, satisfied with the decision she had come to—today, she would know.

It took her over an hour to choose the dress she would wear, and she finally settled on the first one she had laid aside, a cool white cotton that had almost no sleeves, a waist that fell somewhere about her hips, and a hem that barely even touched her knees. She slid on her favorite pair of silk stockings, daring flesh pink in the lightest chiffon, and then rolled them down to her knees, securing them with garters and then checking to make sure the seams were straight in back. She took an hour to do her face: Winx to darken her lashes, Kissproof Lipstick and Rouge, face powder advertised as that being used by all the smart Parisiennes, perfume; then she smiled at her reflection, noting how blue and sparkling her eyes were, how happy she looked, how pretty she was. Today Janson would see her as a woman; today he would speak at last. She was certain of it—even if she had to be bold and flirtatious and even tell him outright how she felt. He would speak at last.

She made her way down the staircase to the first floor, then stopped for a moment in the wide entry hallway, trying to calm her heart and strengthen her courage. When she finally left the house a half-hour later, she carried a bow basket over her arm, a bow basket containing a picnic dinner she had watched Mattie Ruth prepare for them both—cold milk in a quart fruit jar, fried chicken and biscuits, potato salad, and gingerbread still warm from the oven of the Kitchenkook gasoline-fueled range her father had recently bought for the kitchen over her mother's protests for an electric range. She would surprise Janson, go to where he was working in the fields, and share the picnic dinner with him beneath the shade of some tree during his dinner break. She already knew how she would tell him what it was she felt—also within the basket was a book of poetry, a book wrapped in brightly colored paper and tied with a string. She would give it to him once they finished eating, ask him to read to her from it—so many times in the past she had read to him from other books; but this time it would be his turn. She had chosen the book, the verse, carefully: "How do I love thee? Let me count . . ." Today he would know how she felt.

She almost lost her nerve a short while later as she reached the edge of the field and saw him plowing there behind a mule down the long rows of cotton—he looked so distant there, sweating at work such as she would never know, and perhaps she looked at him in that moment with her eyes and not her soul for the first time in those months: his skin was sunburned, his overalls old and faded, and his frayed workshirt stained with perspiration beneath the crossed galluses. He worked with the red earth as if he understood it, as if it understood him—how could she feel as she did, and yet he be so different from her, so different from anyone she had ever known before. Had she really never looked at the farmhands and sharecroppers on the place, and, if she had, would she have found people as simple in needs and yet as complex in nature as he was? Suddenly she felt uncomfortable in her cool white summer dress and her rolled silk stockings—what did he see when he looked at her? Did he really see her as a woman, or was she only deceiving herself? Would he laugh at her gift and her feelings, turn her away; would he—

Her courage failing, she turned to leave, but he had already seen her. He pulled back on the plow lines looped about his shoulders and called: "Whoa, Nicodemus—" to halt the mule, then raised his arm to wave to her. She could almost feel his smile over the distance, his delight at seeing her, and her courage returned.

"What're you doin' out here?" he called to her as she crossed the field toward him, stepping carefully over the rough, uneven ground between the rows where the plow had already turned the red earth aside.

She lifted the light brown basket slightly and motioned with it. "I brought our dinner. I thought we might have a picnic—"

"That sounds nice, but I cain't quit right yet t' eat."

"That's all right. I can wait." She made her way back across the field to spread out the blanket and sit beneath the shade of a tree at the edge of the woods, watching him as he guided the mule down the long rows, watching him as the hot sun beat down around him, baking the red earth, baking his shoulders beneath the faded and worn material of his workshirt. She looked at the cotton plants growing lush and green in the rows—it would be laying by before long, and he would have more time free to spend with her, at least for a while, time free of the constant work in the cotton fields and the constant demands of her father. The church bazaar to raise money for the children's home would be coming up in a few days, and the Independence Day celebrations were not too far distant—perhaps by then she and Janson would be more than friends alone. Perhaps by then he would be her beau—what a wonderfully old-fashioned word that was, a word from her grandmother's time, but it was a word that stuck in her mind. She smiled to herself, imagining long walks with him, holding hands; the feel of his arms around her, his kiss; the knowledge that she alone would hold his heart—she lifted her chin and bolstered her courage. Nothing would ruin this day.

He mopped his face and neck with a torn handkerchief as he made his way across the field to her, looking happy but tired. The crushed hat in his hand was soaked through with perspiration, as was his shirt; red dirt stained his feet and the frayed hems of his overalls—but Elise hardly noticed. She saw only his smile, the delight in his eyes as he looked at her, the handsome curve of his jaw. She already had the picnic basket emptied of food, the meal spread out on the blanket before her, and he joined her beneath the shade of the tree, sitting down nearby, smiling at her. She had carefully patted her hair and wet her lips—she could see the effect in his eyes, in the way he was watching her. Today he saw a woman before him.

"Are you hungry?" she asked, smiling.

"I sure am—"

She had planned to wait until they had finished eating before giving him the book, but she could not contain her eagerness. They had only just begun to eat when she knew she could wait no longer. "I have a present for you—"

"A present—for me?" She had played the moment out in her mind a thousand times—she would give him the gift, would see the delight in his eyes that she had thought of him. He would unwrap the present, and she would ask him to read aloud to her, to read the sonnet she had chosen. He would open the book, read—and then he would look at her, and in that look they would both know. After this day, her life would never be the same again.

She took the wrapped package from the bow basket and handed it to him. He turned it over and over in his hands, almost wondrously, looking at the colored paper, seeming for all the world like a small boy on Christmas morning—just as she had known he would.

"You shouldn't 'a got me nothin'—" he said, smiling up at her.

"You're always bringing me presents. I wanted to give you something for once—aren't you going to open it?"

"I kinda hate t' bother it; you've got it wrapped s' pretty an' all." He began to fumble with the paper, finally untying the string and carefully beginning to fold the wrappings back. "This's th' first present anybody's give me in years—" He grinned delightedly up at her, and then looked back down as the paper fell away to reveal the book that lay beneath.

A peculiar look passed across his face, and was so quickly gone that she was unsure as to whether she had actually seen it or not. He turned the book over in his hands again, seeming unsure as to what to do with it, what to say, then he smiled up at her with a smile that seemed to be almost forced. "It's real nice. Thank you—"

No—this was not right. This was not the way that he was supposed to react. This was not—

Elise forced a control over the moment's panic rising within her. She brought her most flirtatious smile to her lips. "Don't you like it? It's my favorite; I've always adored Mrs. Browning."

"Mis Browning—"

Something was very wrong. She could feel it. She moved closer to him, purposefully brushing against the sleeve of his workshirt—but he only moved away. A hurt feeling filled her—what had she done wrong? What had—

She reached and opened the thin volume on his lap. "Poetry, like we read before—"

He seemed so distant, so—"Poetry, oh, yeah."

This was not the way that it—the way that he—was supposed to be. If anything, he was only more distant, only more—"But, this is special poetry. It's—" She searched her mind for the words, but could not find them. How could she tell him how she felt? How could she tell him what he had come to mean to her over the past months? It was all there on the pages before him, in words beyond anything she could say, if only he would look; if only he would—

"Now, you can read to me sometimes. And, you'll have your own book—" Her mind raced: what had she said wrong, done wrong? What had she said that could have offended that damnable pride and independent nature? Her heart was written plainly there on those pages before him, her love, her feelings, if only he would read. How could that offend him? Surely, he had to see, had to—

She took a deep breath and marshaled her courage, determined not to have come this far only to fail now. "There's one that I really like—" She moved closer to him and felt him move away again, but she refused to allow that to stop her, leaning only closer to him and flipping the pages in his lap, feeling the strength of his body so near to hers. He would know how she felt, even if she had to tell him outright. He would know. "Here, this is it—"

But he only stared at the page blankly. A muscle twitched in his jaw.

"It makes me think of you," she said—the words were there on the page before him. Everything she felt—couldn't he see. Didn't he know? "Why don't you read it to me?"

"You—you read it t' me—" He tried to push the book into her hands, but she refused to take it.

"No—" She placed her hand on his arm and smiled up at him. "I love your voice; it's so strong and masculine. I've read to you so many times. I'd like to hear you read to me for once—"

His arm was warm beneath her hand—but he did not look at her, or even at where she touched him. He stared down at the book in his lap, clutching the sides of it in his hands until his knuckles turned white. For a moment there was only silence. The muscle twitched again in his jaw as he gritted his teeth. He kept his dark head bent and his eyes fixed on the page before him. For a moment something close to shame and embarrassment flickered across his features—shame and embarrassment, where she had never before seen anything but pride.

When he finally spoke, his voice was so quiet that she had to strain to hear it, his words forced, filled with pain. "I—I cain't read it—"

For a moment she could only stare at him, not comprehending. "What do you mean, you can't—" and then comprehension slowly came. She stared at him, realizing what she had done.

"I cain't read it," he said again, louder, his voice carrying a choked sound. He closed the book slowly, got to his feet, and moved a few steps away, never once looking at her. She stared at his back, not knowing what to say, what to do.

"I—I'm sorry. I didn't know," she said quietly after a moment, but he only lowered his head and shook it slowly back and forth, standing with his back toward her. She stood and went to him, placing her hand on his arm, wanting nothing more than to undo the hurt she had caused him, the embarrassment, the pain. She wanted to put her arms around him, to hold him and tell him that it was all right, that it did not matter, but she knew she could not. She could only stand there with her hand on his arm, staring up at the profile she loved so well. "Janson?" But he did not lift his eyes. "Janson, please look at me—" She moved to stand before him, putting her hands on the crossed arms that held the book now to his chest. She looked up at him, but still he would not meet her eyes. "Janson, it doesn't matter—"

"Yes, it does." His voice was tinged with anger as he finally looked at her. There was so much hurt in his eyes that she felt a stab of pain go through her. "It does matter, when some little kid can read an' I cain't—"

"But that's only because someone taught them. Didn't you go to school?"

"Yeah, I went, when I wasn't needed t' work in th' fields or t' pick cotton. I tried t' learn, but I was always s' far behind—I don't know, maybe I'm just slow—"

"You're not slow. You just didn't have time to learn then, but you can learn now." A rush of maternal instinct filled her. She wanted to take away the cause of his embarrassment, the cause of his hurt pride, so that he would never have to feel shame again. "I could teach you—"

But anger flared behind the green eyes. A muscle clenched in his jaw. "I get along just fine like I am! I ain't gonna be taught like I was some back'ards schoolboy!"

"I didn't mean—"

"I know what you meant," he said, his feelings coming out now in a rush of hurt pride as he stared at her. "You comin' here, battin' your eyelashes, at me, flirtin' like you thought I was somebody—I don't need your help, Miss Elise Whitley, an' I don't need you tryin' t' wrap me aroun' your little finger jus' 'cause you think that's th' way every man aroun' here's got t' be. If anybody needs some learnin', I'd say it was you an' not me, 'cause you sure don't know how t' act like a lady ought t' act—"

She could only stare at him with absolute surprise, forgetting his embarrassment, forgetting his shame, forgetting all the things she had meant for this day. "How dare you!"

"If you're s' 'shamed t' be aroun' a ignorant farmer like me, then why don't you just go on back t' your uppity family an' your uppity friends, 'cause I sure don't need nobody like you meddlin' in my life—"

Fury filled her. "Well, I don't need you either!"

"That suits me jus' fine." He turned and started away.

"You're a damned, stubborn fool, Janson Sanders!" she yelled after him, filled with anger.

"An' I was right th' first time I ever met you," he said, turning back for a moment. "You ain't nothin' but a spoil't brat of a rich girl—an' you cain't even talk like you was a lady!"

"How dare you!"

But he only ignored her indignation. "You jus' go on back t' your fancy life, Miss Whitley. You won't have t' worry about spendin' no more 'a your time with no ignorant farmhand," and he angrily turned and started away again.

"Oh!" she yelled furiously, then stamped her foot in impotent rage at his retreating back. She knelt and began to shove the remnants of her lovely picnic dinner back into the bow basket—how could she have ever believed herself to be in love with someone like that! Stubborn, stupid, ill-mannered—

She was too furious to even notice that he had taken the book of sonnets with him.

"GOD-ALMIGHTY—feed that fire easy, boy!" Tate warned in his sharp old voice, poking Janson in the ribs with one long, bony finger as he stood hovering just over his right shoulder that next morning. "You got t' feed th' fire easy, not git it t' hot t' fast when you're b'ilin' th' beer—"

Janson sidled away from the poking, and continued to feed the fire just as he had been doing all along, avoiding a long stream of tobacco juice that Tate spat onto the ground nearby. He had been making liquor deliveries for Whitley for a little over two months now, and for the past several weeks had been brought into the stilling operations as well, working with the ill-natured old moonshiner to whom it seemed he could do nothing right.

Tate made a disgusted sound as he stared at him, then moved aside to sit atop an overturned barrel placed to one side of the large copper stills there in the midst of the woods—but Janson paid him little attention this morning. He straightened from where he had been feeding the fire in the furnace beneath the nearest still, his eyes moving to the smoke drifting upwards, through the log framework and branch covering of the shelter beneath which the stills were located, his mind ticking off the minutes until the fire would be burning hot enough so that it would no longer produce so much smoke. He knew the heavy drift of smoke from the midst of the woods would only increase the likelihood of the detection of the stills and the men operating them—and Janson did not want to be caught operating a moonshine still, anymore than he wanted to be caught hauling corn liquor. He and the old man usually began the operation well before sunup, to allow the darkness itself to hide the smoke—but not this morning. This morning there had been delay after delay, and now it was broad daylight, and the smoke was drifting up above the trees—goddamn it. He could already see himself spending the night in the County jail.

After a time that seemed to Janson to stretch into forever, the fire began to burn well, and the smoke began to dissipate. The cap of the copper still had been sealed on with thick rye paste, and the beer within was boiling well. Janson allowed himself to relax for a moment, keeping an eye both on the fire, and on the old moonshiner who was watching him as well.

"Back in my day, we made pure corn, not none 'a this sugar whiskey like now days—" Tate said, sneering toward the barrels of sugared mash that waited nearby to be processed in the stills, just as he had done on numerous other occasions over the past days as they had tended the mixing and working of the mixture of corn meal, ground malt, sugar, and raw rye that had fermented to become the beer now boiling in the stills and filling the barrels. Janson paid little attention to what the old man was saying, having heard it all several times before in the past days, until he could almost have repeated it back word for word if he had chosen to do so.

Steam from the boiling beer in the still finally passed through the long arm attached to it to hit the contents of the thump barrel nearby, starting it to bubbling. Janson sat back to wait. He listened to the dull sound coming from the barrel and looked out through the woods, leaning his head back against the tree, smelling the distinctive odor that always hung over the stilling operation. He knew this was the most likely time of the run that they might be caught, for the sound could be heard for a good distance into the woods—but his mind could not stay with the danger of detection, or the chances of ending up in jail in violation of the

Prohibition laws. His mind wandered back to Elise Whitley, and to the confrontation he'd had with her the day before, just as it had been doing all morning long.

Damn her—

He should have known better than to have let himself have anything to do with her. He should have known—but, still, when she had turned to him after her brother's death, he had been unable to help himself. She was just a girl, and she had been through so much—the attack, then the death of her brother; she had needed someone, and he had let himself be needed. He had let himself—

In the weeks and months since her brother had died, he had tried to help in whatever way he could. He had felt sorry for her, felt somehow responsible and guilty in a way he could not explain—and he had felt something more. It had been in those moments the morning after he had fought Ethan Bennett to protect her, those moments spent in the front parlor of her great house, as he had worn his threadbare clothes and cracked shoes, with his wildflowers for a girl who could very well have laughed at him—but she had not laughed. She had just been a girl that morning, treating him with kindness, even with respect. He had allowed himself to care about her, to think about her as someone other than William Whitley's daughter, as someone—

She bobbed her hair and wore makeup; she was rich and petted and so unlike anything he had ever known in his life. He had been surprised at his feelings, but he could not fight them—he cared about William Whitley's daughter. He cared about her in a way he had never cared about anyone in his life, and as the days passed, he had realized those feelings would not go away. She was nothing like him, nothing like the people he had come from. When he looked at her he saw the rolled stockings and the short skirts, and he knew what his mother would have said—

But he loved her.

That had surprised him more than anything in his life. He loved Elise Whitley. He loved her, and he knew he could never let her know—how could he tell her, with her fancy book learning and her family's motor cars and her big fine house, that he dreamed of taking her back to Eason County, that he dreamed of taking her to that small white house on those red acres, that house with no electric lights and no running water and even no indoor water closet that she might use. How could he tell her that he dreamed of taking her home to meet his gran'ma and his gran'pa, of walking down Main Street in Pine with her on his arm, of making her Elise Sanders—she would only laugh at him, call him a fool.

And perhaps he was.

When she had begun to flirt with him the day before, he had been almost unable to believe the evidence of his eyes and ears—Elise Whitley, smiling at him, surprising him with a picnic dinner, looking so pretty in her white dress; Elise, treating him as a man and not just as a friend. And she had brought him a present—but that had been the end of it all.

He felt a hot flush of embarrassment even now, knowing she knew that he could not read. She had even offered to teach him—as if he were some ignorant, backwards schoolboy that needed to be taken on in charity. But he was a man. And now that man knew. He knew, and in that knowing was the end of those dreams. Elise Whitley would never be his. She would never see beyond his patched clothes and his calloused hands and his country ways, to see the man beneath, a man with all the pride and feelings of any man. She had flirted with him, and she had done so simply because she thought he was the one man in the County not in love with her already—what a fool she was. At least he had that part of his pride left; at least she would never know how much he had loved her.

Still loved her.

Even as he thought the words, he damned himself for the feeling. How could he love someone like her. Someone so rich and spoiled and uppity. He knew he had said things to her that he should never have said to any woman—but she had deserved it. She had made him look as if, feel as if, he were something less than a man; she had made him tell her something that no one else had known, that no one else had any right to know. He had wanted to fling her book in the ditch at the edge of the field, had wanted to fling it in the water of the creek that cut across Whitley property, but somehow had been unable to. He had been unable to throw it away, destroy it, as he told himself he wanted to—it now sat on the small, splintery wooden table by the cot in his room, reminding him of what she was, of what he was, and of what happened to the dreams of fools. He was lucky to have found out about her now, lucky to have realized the truth. She could never have been his, and feeling the things he had been feeling for her would only have led to the destruction of his dreams, of all he had ever cared about, even to his very soul. They were far too different, and perhaps they should never have become friends in the first place—it did not do for a man to reach after things he could never have, dreams he could never touch. He was better off on his own, better off to find a girl more like himself, a girl familiar with country folk and their ways, a girl who was not afraid of hard work or doing without, a girl who would give a man sons and daughters, who would raise them as they ought to be raised, and not act spoiled and selfish and like a child herself. It was better to find a girl like that—instead of spending his days thinking about Elise Whitley. A man would be a fool to waste his life thinking about a girl he could not have, a girl he would be better off not to—

He came out of his reverie to Tate's cursing at him. The thumping in the barrel had quit, and the surge of liquid had begun, flowing from the end of the worm and onto the ground there beneath the condenser. Janson got to his feet and quickly placed a jug beneath the worm to catch the liquid, then looked up at Tate, seeing the old man turn away, cursing him still as he uncovered a barrel of beer to use for the second run.

Damn her—she would ruin even this for him. There were few jobs that would pay him as well as moonshining for Whitley did. His dreams might mean nothing to her, but they mattered a great deal to him. He needed the money to buy his land back, to be able to go home as a man—and to be able to get as far away from her as he possibly could. She had destroyed his pride, had made him feel shame as no other person ever had in his life—but he still had his dreams. He still had his dreams, and he would make them—

But in that moment he realized that he had allowed Elise Whitley to become part of those dreams. And, even as that realization came, Janson Sanders called himself a fool.

PHYLLIS ANN Bennett stood at the front window of her bedroom that afternoon, staring down at the long, graveled drive that led up to the front of her home. Carson Edwards, the eldest son of the Baptist minister, had kept her waiting now for ten minutes—ten whole minutes, just as if she were nobody. He was late in picking her up, and he would be sorry; oh, he would be so very sorry—there would be no quick drive to some deserted spot on a back road, some kisses, a little petting, and then straight to what he wanted. No, he would beg before he would lay her back today. Oh, how he would beg, and for more than ten minutes alone.

She glanced at her wrist watch, then began to drum her fingers along the edge of the window frame—it was just like Carson to keep her waiting, just like him and that entire family of his. They had stuck up their collective noses at her a dozen times in the past two months since she had returned from school, all because of what Elise had told on her father, all because of Alfred Whitley having managed to get himself shot—but she had shown them. Her father had practically ruined her life over those two months—no one invited her over any longer; no one introduced her to handsome young relatives; no one asked her to go shopping, or to the movie theatre, or to parties; and few of the good-looking men in the County had anything more to do with her now than just to share a bottle of gin and some fun in the back seat of a motor car. It was all Elise's fault; Phyllis Ann knew that. Phyllis Ann's father had never tried to rape Elise; that had been nothing more than Elise's overactive imagination, and probably her hopes as well. He had almost been killed by some hired farmhand on the Whitley place, had been beaten black and blue by Bill Whitley and Franklin Bates, and Alfred Whitley had even tried to shoot him, all because of what Elise had told—but Alfred had only gotten himself shot instead, and now no one would hardly speak to Phyllis Ann, or invite her over, or ask her out, as if she really gave a damn what her father had done to anyone.

But she had shown them. She had gone after Carson Edwards with a single-mindedness of purpose she had shown few times in her life. The son of the Baptist minister could come in handy for so many things. Association with him could remove the taint from her name, and divorce her in the minds of so many from what everyone thought her father had done. She might even marry Carson, though she had never really considered before that she might marry anyone until she was too old to really care if she ever had any fun again—he was good-looking enough, though he was old, practically twenty-five already, and he was not as good in bed as she would have liked, but that was what love affairs were for anyway. Besides, it would be worth marrying him just to see what a fit that cow of a mother of his would have the very thought of her precious boy marrying the County bad girl. It would be worth marrying him indeed.

Phyllis Ann glanced again at her wrist watch and then paced across the room toward the full-length mirror that stood near her bed. She stopped for a moment, admiring her reflection, her impatience at being kept waiting forgotten as she turned sideways to admire the flat chest, the slim hips, the boyish figure that everyone so envied now days. Her dress had been carefully chosen, barely touching her knees at all, her stockings rolled down into garters beneath it. She smoothed a spit-curl of bobbed hair down against a rouged cheek, and then swung the long strand of beads that hung about her neck—all she needed now was the white cloche hat that waited on the bed, the gloves, and her new handbag to complete the picture. Carson would be at her feet—but he was practically at her feet anyway. He had been more difficult than she had ever thought he might be to start with, wary, because of the things that had been told about her father, but she had taken care of that. She had run into him time and again, seemingly by accident, had practically thrown herself at him—they had been seeing each other for over a month now, but today was the first time they would be out together in public. Carson would be taking her shopping, maybe even to the movies, before they found some quiet place to park his car, share some bootleg whiskey, and have some fun.

She nodded with satisfaction at her reflection in the mirror, hearing Carson's Oldsmobile at last turn into the drive before the house—there had been no doubt in her mind whether or not he would not show. He would never dare to stand her up; no man would dare to stand her up. She would leave him standing downstairs for a while to teach him a lesson for making her wait, and then she would make him buy her something expensive in apology. Something very expensive.

She put on her cloche hat and took up her gloves, slowly beginning to smile to herself—oh, yes, her plans were well under way.

THE KNOCK sounded at the front door for a second time. Ethan Bennett cursed under his breath as he set his drink aside and pushed himself to his feet—damn Paula and Phyllis Ann, they were never around when you needed them, never around when they were supposed to be. It was not a man's place to have to answer the door in his own home; that was what women were for, one of the few useful things they could do in life, other than satisfy a man's needs and get pregnant even when you did not want them to—Paula and the girl both knew that, and, if they had forgotten, he would make sure they never did again.

He started for the door, and then turned back to take up his glass, allowing himself another generous swallow of the bootleg whiskey as he entered the hallway. The knock came again just as he reached the door, and he cursed as he started to swing it inward—the damn fool must think he was deaf or something; somebody ought to—

But the thought ended there, incomplete, and died, as he found himself staring into the face of the young fop son of the Baptist minister. The boy stood there on the front veranda, flawless in a white linen suit, a look of barely concealed dislike on his face as he met Ethan's eyes, and for a moment Ethan wanted nothing more than to hit him—over the past two months almost everyone in the County had slighted him at one time or another, but none so badly as had the Baptist minister and his family. After all the years Ethan had been a member of that church, after all the money he had given, all the time he had wasted in Matthew Edwards' long-winded sermons, the son-of-a-bitch had dared to have him removed from office as a deacon just because of that little bitch, Elise Whitley, and her brother—and now Carson Edwards stood at his front door, just as if nothing had happened, just as if Carson's father had never stabbed Ethan in the back, just as if—

"What the hell do you want?" Ethan demanded, blocking the doorway with his body. "If you're out drumming up people to go to that goddamn church of yours, you better—"

"I've come to pick up Phyllis Ann. We've got a date." The boy's chin lifted defiantly, as if daring Ethan to throw him off the place.

"A date—hell no you don't! My daughter's not going anywhere with you!"

"Phyllis Ann agreed to—"

"I don't give a damn what she agreed!" Ethan shouted, cutting off his words. "You're sure as hell not taking my daughter anywhere, not after the way you and that goddamn family of yours has treated me! That son-of-a-bitch father of yours turning me out as a deacon—and now you've got the nerve to come to my house sniffing after my daughter! Get the hell off my property, boy, before I beat your ass for you!"

Carson's face had blanched, but now it began to redden. He shifted his stance, clenching his fists at his sides. "Now, you listen—"

"I said get!" Ethan shouted, and then on impulse slung his drink in the boy's face, watching with satisfaction as the bootleg whiskey soaked into the fine white linen of his suit. For a moment he thought the young fop would stand and fight, but then the boy seemed to think better of it, turning on his heel and striding across the veranda and down into the yard without another word.

"And I better not see you out here again, or I will beat your ass for you!" Ethan shouted after him, still standing in the open doorway. Suddenly he was shoved aside, as Phyllis Ann reached the door in time to see Carson get into his car and slam the door shut behind himself.

"Carson, wait!" she yelled, but the boy only looked back at her for a moment, a look of clear anger on his face, and then turned away, jerking the car in gear and starting to back down the drive.

Ethan yanked her back from the doorway, slamming the door shut behind them so hard that the glass panes rattled in their frames.

"What the hell do you think you were doing, saying you'd see that boy!" he shouted. "I told you not to have anything more to do with any of them!" He shoved her backwards, down the hallway, toward the wide curved staircase at the far end. "And look how you're dressed, showing yourself off like you were some cheap little whore for him—you know all he wants is to stick it in you! Him and that whole family of his, thinking they're so high and mighty, passing judgements on me—but that doesn't matter to you, does it? All you want is what's between that boy's legs. All you—"

He grabbed her arm, holding her before him, watching as a look of fear passed across her face. She began to pry at his fingers, trying to free herself, but he would not allow it, shaking her soundly to silence her words as they came.

"I'll teach you to betray me, you little—" He slapped her hard, backhanded, across the face, sending her cloche hat spinning across the floor. "Damn little tramp—" He slapped her again, and then again, hard, stinging blows that left her face red and his hand stinging. One blow struck her across the nose, sending blood spurting across the clean white cuff of his shirt and down over the lower half of her face—suddenly she seemed to go wild, no longer just struggling to break free, but lashing out to hit him across the face instead, yelling with rage. She clawed out and dug her nails into his cheek, scratching him deeply from the ear downward to his chin.

He yelped with surprise and shoved her away before she could do any further damage, his hand going to his scratched and bleeding face. She fell backwards against the staircase banister and clutched at it for support, breathing heavily, her bobbed hair wild from the struggle, falling into her face. He stared at her for a moment, wary of the look of sheer self-preservation in her eyes.

"Get your ass up those stairs, and don't come down again until I tell you to!" he ordered, keeping his distance from her. She did not move, but continued to clutch the banister instead, her chest rising and falling, her eyes fixed on him. "I said get up those stairs!" he yelled again, taking a step toward her.

She straightened up quickly, and he froze, but she only stared at him for a moment, and then slowly turned and started up the stairs, making a deliberate show that she was no longer afraid of him.

He stood clenching his fists at the bottom of the staircase, shaking with rage as he watched her ascend. When she left his sight, he slammed his fist hard into the wall, leaving a mark on the wallpaper and making his hand and arm ache, and then he turned and kicked over a nearby table for the pain in his hand.

"Damn little bitch!" he shouted to the empty hallway—but she would pay for it, and she would pay dearly. He would see to it—oh, how he would see to it.

PHYLLIS ANN sat on the bed in her room a short while later, her knees drawn up to her chest, her back against the headboard. She had heard her father leave the house already, had heard the front door slam and the LaSalle start down the graveled drive toward the red dirt road—she hoped he was drunk enough to drive into a tree and kill himself. Her life would be so much simpler if only he were dead.

She looked down at her dress, now rumpled and stained from the bloody nose. It had been so fresh, so pretty, only half an hour before, and she had been so lovely in it, all ready to meet Carson, ready to put her plans into motion, ready to regain her rightful place in the community—but all that had changed now. Her father had ruined her plans, had managed to undo everything she had already accomplished—stupid fool, he had already ruined his own life; now he would ruin hers as well. The goddamn stupid fool.

The violence she had met with today was nothing new to her. It had been an ordinary part of her life for as long as she could remember—but today something had changed. Today she had backed him down, had even managed to hurt him a little—how good it had felt to see that look of pain in his eyes, that look of wary distrust. How good it had felt just to hurt him for once as he had hurt her so many times in the past.

She hated him now even more than she had ever thought it possible to hate him, more than she had ever hated him before. She needed all those people he now despised, all those people of social prominence in the County, all those people who could make her life be again as it used to be—all those people who were now shocked and scandalized by what he had done, by what Elise had told about him, and by the way Alfred Whitley had gotten himself killed. Carson had been the first step in getting her life back as it should be, back as it had been before when she had been the most popular girl in the County, the most envied, the most wanted, and the most despised by the other girls just for her looks and her flair and her sex appeal. But her father had ruined that; he had interfered, ruined her plans. It had been hard enough to sway Carson to her charms this time; she knew she would have no chance at him again, no chance at any of the men in the County who might be of use to her, not once Carson told everyone what her father had done today, not once—

Then her mind hit upon another thought—Elise. Elise had started all this, had caused it. Phyllis Ann knew her father had never tried to rape the little bitch; that had all been Elise's imagination, some bid for attention, and look at all the trouble it had caused. The least Elise could do now was make amends, undo the damage she had done to Phyllis Ann—and Elise would do it. As one of the Whitleys, as the one making the accusations in the first place, Elise could set everything right again—oh, why had she not thought of this before! She knew she could not trust Elise, for her one-time friend had long since proven herself a self-serving little liar in the past months, thinking only of herself—but Phyllis Ann could handle her; she had always handled her. There had never been one time in all her life that Elise had not done exactly as Phyllis Ann had wanted, and this time would be no different. No different indeed.

Phyllis Ann got up from the bed and went to her dresser mirror, then flinched as she saw her reflection. Her nose had quit bleeding now, but blood had dried beneath it on her upper lip, and an ugly bruise was just beginning to show beneath her right eye. She stood considering her face for a moment, and slowly she began to smile—hadn't Elise always been concerned about the violence Phyllis Ann lived with. A bruise or two might be just what it would take to bring out the streak of maternal sympathy that Phyllis Ann knew existed within her. Elise would never be able to turn her back on her old friend when she was in such obvious need of help. Never.

Phyllis Ann continued to smile at her reflection for a long time—Elise Whitley would be putty in her hands. She always had been.

# 12

ELISE SAT ON A CUSHIONED straight chair behind her table at the church bazaar that Saturday morning, fanning herself in spite of the shade of the cottonwood tree beneath which her table was located. The day was hot and sticky, and her light summer dress already clung to her from perspiration—but the day was only just beginning, her table still laden with plates of cookies and candy, boxes of fudge, and cakes of all varieties, from lemon pound to chocolate to coconut, that Mattie Ruth and the part-time girl from town had been baking for days. There would be a long day ahead of her before she could go home to find some cool place to rest; a long day, and too much time to think.

She watched the people move about the church grounds, listening to the sound of Saturday morning traffic as it made its way toward the cluster of store buildings downtown. The sound of jazz music started up from a Victrola in the church basement nearby, and for a moment it seemed as if the day might improve for at least a time, but then the preacher marched across her line of vision, headed toward the building, a look of stern disapproval on his face. After a moment, the music fell silent and the preacher reappeared, followed by several young people who looked as if they would rather not have been caught, and the day settled back into silence above the sounds of traffic and the hum of the voices of those at the bazaar.

Elise stared past the plates and boxes of sweets on her table, thinking of the days of delicious smells that had surrounded the area of the kitchen during their baking. She had so looked forward to this day, to sitting behind her table and talking to the people as they stopped to buy her cakes and fudge and candy, to seeing the new dresses the church and town girls would be wearing—and, most of all, to the time when Janson Sanders would come to her table to buy one of her cakes, as he had promised. They had planned a picnic supper for later, once the bazaar was finished, and slices of the cake for dessert—but now that would never be, and she knew it. She watched the boyishly shaped girls passing by in their light-colored dresses, all of them looking much like pale, immature butterflies on the arms of their young men in light summer suits, and she felt as if she were the only person alone today.

She was being kept busy at her sales, and the large display of cakes and sweets that had burdened her table was growing smaller by the minute, for Mattie Ruth's baking was well known as some of the best in the County—but Elise was finding it difficult to even be civil to the many people as they stood and chatted about their neighbors and the weather and the other church members. Her mind was not on the gossip, or on the summer dresses, or even on the news that Alice Marsh had just given birth after only five and a half months of marriage—her mind was on Janson Sanders instead, as it had been for days now.

She had not seen him except at a distance since the argument several days before, and she was still angry. She had not intentionally set out to insult his damnable pride—and yet he had said that she did not know how to act like a lady, had called her a spoiled brat. Well, if he wanted to act that way, then let him. She did not need him anyway. She did not need—

And, even as she told herself that, she realized she had never before missed anyone so much in all her life. He had grown to be such a normal part of her days, and, even though she was no less furious, to her anger she was also no less in love—stupid, stubborn, ill-mannered farmhand; it was not her fault that he could not read, not her fault that he had seemed so determined to be insulted, no matter what it was that she had meant. Well, if that was the way he wanted it, then he could certainly have it that way. He could certainly—

She caught sight of him standing at a distance across the churchyard. He was with another of her father's farmhands, someone she had seen before, but whose name she could not recall. They were both dressed in what was probably their best, Janson in a clean white shirt and dungarees, his hair combed back and groomed as neatly as she had ever seen it—he was looking at her, and for a moment their eyes met across the distance; then he turned away, back to the girl behind the table where he stood, and Elise felt a hot flush of anger spread to her cheeks—at him, at herself, at the girl he was talking to, she did not know which. She looked away, furious—how dare he come here after—

But her eyes strayed back to him, and she watched as he bought a cup of lemonade from the girl behind the table, and then stood talking to her as he drank it. It was only Rachel Cleary that he was talking to, the daughter of a small farmer from there in the County, a short girl with a large bosom and wide hips, and long blond hair that hung to somewhere past her waist. Elise had paid little attention to Rachel, had hardly spoken to her a dozen times in her life, though both girls had grown up in the same church and within a number of miles of each other—but, then again, few people in the church had much to do with the Clearys, for they really had no business attending the largest Baptist church in the County. They were only farm people; they had no farmhands or tenant farmers, and they produced little more than a few bales of cotton each year. Rachel was not smart or pretty, and neither was either of her two sisters—but Rachel looked pretty now as Janson talked to her, smiling up at him until a dimple showed in her cheek. Elise had hardly wasted a thought on her in all her life, had paid her little mind—but now she suddenly despised her, despised everything there was about her, from her dimpling smile to the figure that was too well-rounded to ever be in fashion.

Elise snapped at the buyer who came up to her own table with money already in hand, and then hardly paid any attention as the woman walked away muttering about the manners of modern youth—she was too distracted, too irritated at the attention Janson was paying to Rachel Cleary to even care. He had no right to smile at another girl like that, no right to laugh at some silly, empty-headed remark she might make, no right to stand there looking so handsome and so distant, spending time with someone else. He had behaved stupidly, had acted like a child, and it should be him, and not Elise herself, feeling alone and lonely at this moment. She had nothing to feel sorry for. She had done nothing wrong—and if he was too stubborn to admit that he had behaved like a fool, then that was his problem. She had been insulted, yelled at, and it should be him to apologize—to say that she did not know how to act like a lady, indeed! She would show him that he mattered nothing to her at all; she did not need him anyway. She never had. And she had never loved him. That had been a silly, schoolgirl dream—and she was no longer a schoolgirl; she was a woman now. She was a woman.

She snapped shut the lid of the cigar box that held the money from her sales, and sat back against her chair, folding her arms across her chest and giving Rachel Cleary an assessing look—she was not even in fashion, with her tight-waisted dress that showed off her bosom and hips and more than covered her knees, with her cotton stockings and long hair, and her figure too ample to ever be in style. If Janson thought she was pretty, then Elise had certainly never had any business being attracted to him. No business, indeed.

There was a sound from behind her, which she ignored, her attention focused on the pair talking at the other table, then came the sound of her own name: "Elise—" and she turned to find Phyllis Ann Bennett standing just behind her.

The entire right side of Phyllis Ann's face, from just beneath the eye and down along the cheekbone, was swollen and bruised. Her lower lip was puffy, one eye nearly black. Elise felt a stab of alarm at her appearance, at the beating she must have suffered—and then memory came flooding back: the weeks and months of hurt and grieving, the look on her mother's face when they had lowered Alfred's coffin into the ground, what Bennett had tried to do to her—the lies; the selfish, self-serving interests of this girl in setting that madman on Elise in order to protect herself. Elise felt the anger and disgust well up inside of her. She clenched her fists at her sides, trying to calm their shaking—Phyllis Ann dared to face her now after all she had done, all she had caused. No words would come. She could only stare, rage filling her, daring the other girl to speak first.

"Elise, I'm so glad I found you. I need your help; you've got to—"

"My help!" The rage exploded. She wanted to slap Phyllis Ann, but instead forced a shaky control over her anger as she rose to her feet, clenching her fists only more tightly at her sides. "You would dare to ask for my help after what you've done! After—"

"Can't you forgive and forget about something that—"

"Forget! Forget that you were the cause of your father trying to rape me! Forget that he murdered my brother!"

"But, I need your help. My father—"

"I don't want to hear about your father! You know that he told me what you said, that it was me and not you that cheated, me and not you that got us thrown out of school—"

"I never meant for—"

"I don't give a damn what you meant to do! You lied to save your own neck, and made him come after me instead! Do you think I'd help you after it was you that caused my brother's death?"

"He came after Daddy with a gun. It was self defense; there were witnesses—"

"I don't give a damn about the witnesses! It was murder, and you were the—"

"You can't blame me for that! And look what he's done to me now, just look—" She brought a hand to her face, to the bruises, to the evidence of the beating she had suffered, wincing slightly as her fingers touched the battered cheek. Tears welled up in her eyes, and her swollen lower lip quivered. "You've got to help me. You've got to—he's going to kill me—"

For a moment Elise saw before her again the girl she had grown up with, the girl she had loved almost as a sister, the girl she had shared her deepest secrets with, her most treasured dreams, and something of her weakening must have shown on her face, for Phyllis Ann began to slowly smile, a look of satisfaction coming to her eyes.

"I knew you'd help me. I knew—"

Elise stared at her, seeing her clearly perhaps for the first time in her life, understanding. "You and your father can both rot in hell for all I care," she said. "You deserve each other."

She stared to walk away, started to leave her table and her plates of cakes and candies, started to get as far from Phyllis Ann Bennett as she possibly could—but an angry hand grabbed her arm and held her back, the nails biting into her flesh, and she was hauled around to face the cold, angry, hate-filled eyes. "You will do what I say—" The words came as a statement, a demand, hissed out between barely parted teeth, all pretense at vulnerability now gone—there was nothing left within this creature of the girl Elise had grown up with, the girl who had been almost a sister to her. There was nothing but hate and rage and determination. "You will do what I say—"

"Let go of my arm, or I swear I'll black your other eye for you—" Elise threatened, barely controlling her own rage—this girl had caused her brother's death, had caused her to almost be raped, and now—

"You don't have the nerve. You always were a coward." The nails bit even more deeply into her arm, now out of nothing more than sheer cruelty. Elise could see the pleasure in her eyes, the satisfaction at the pain she caused.

"You're just like your father," she heard herself say, unable to stop the words, all the while knowing what would happen.

"You little bitch!" Phyllis Ann's free hand clenched into a fist, flying upwards, and then starting down toward Elise's face. Elise braced herself for the blow—but it never came. A strong male hand grabbed Phyllis Ann's arm and held it back, a male voice saying:

"You better let go 'a th' lady, an' right now—"

Elise looked up into Janson Sanders's green eyes, feeling the painful hold on her arm being released. She rubbed at the aching nail marks reddening her wrist, seeing Phyllis Ann's angry glare as Janson released her with a slight shove.

"You better get on out of here," Phyllis Ann said, open contempt for him in her eyes. "This isn't any concern for the likes of you."

"I'm makin' it my concern—an' I think it's you that better git outta here."

"How dare you talk to me like—"

"I said git!" he said, taking a threatening step toward her, "before I forget you're a woman—"

Phyllis Ann stared at him for a moment, and then shot a look at Elise, a look that said clearly that this was not the end. Then she turned and left, walking toward the edge of the church grounds without ever once looking back. Elise stared after her, seeing several of the church people turn to look in her direction, seeing the embarrassed looks on the faces of those who had seen and heard, and who had not interfered, and then she turned back to Janson, finding his gaze on her. For a moment their eyes met. Then he looked away.

"You all right?" he asked, his voice gruff.

"Yes, I'm fine. Thank you—"

He simply nodded, and then turned to walk away. For a moment the anger welled up inside of her again—if his damned pride was that important to him then let him be that way. She had nothing to apologize for. She had done nothing wrong. And she did not need him anyway. She did not need—

"Janson, please wait—" she heard herself call even before she thought, and then watched as he stopped and turned back to look at her—she did need him.

And she knew she always would.

FOR A long moment he just stood there staring at her—why would he not at least say something, make it easier.

"You want somethin'?" he asked at last.

"Yes, I wanted to thank you for—"

"I don't need your thanks." His voice cut through hers.

"Yes, I know, but—"

"I couldn't just stand there an' watch what she was doin'."

"But, I want to—"

"I said I don't need your thanks!" His voice rose, his green eyes clouding with anger. He turned and started away again, but her voice stopped him.

"Janson, please wait—" she called, going toward him, and he turned back to look at her. "Can't we at least talk?"

"I don't know as we got anythin' t' talk about." That damned, insufferable pride. Couldn't he at least—

"I think we do."

"What about?" he demanded, his voice rising in anger, in hurt feelings. "About how ignorant an' uneducated I am? Well, I don't need your pity, Miss Whitley!"

"I'm not offering you pity. I never meant to hurt your pride. I didn't know that—"

"Well, you know now!" he yelled, silencing her words.

"Yes, I know now—" she said, more quietly, and he looked away. After a moment she heard his voice again, much quieter, but no less filled with emotion:

"I may not can read as good as you, but that don't mean I'm not a man."

"I know you're a man. I never meant to hurt your pride or to embarrass you."

Anger rose behind the green eyes again as he looked at her. "I told you I don't need your pity!" He turned and started away, but suddenly she was beside him again, her hand on his arm, staying him.

"What I'm trying to say is that I'm sorry I—that—" She looked at him for a moment. "I'm sorry," she said simply.

He sighed, looking away. After a moment he spoke, not bringing his eyes back to her. "I guess I shouldn't 'a got s' mad at you. You couldn't 'a knowed. An' I guess I said some things I shouldn't 'a said—"

"I said some things I should never have said as well. Can't we just forget that it happened, and let things go back to being the way they were before?"

He turned to look at her, something unreadable in his eyes. "I don't know as they can."

"Why not?"

He stared at her for a long moment, and then looked away. "I just don't know as they can."

"Why—because I know you can't read? That doesn't matter—"

"It's more 'n that. It's—" His voice trailed off and his eyes met hers again. "You an' me are 's different. I don't know as how we could ever be frien's."

"We were friends before."

"Yeah, but—"

"But, what? What's so different now?"

He stared at her for a long moment. "It's just different."

"What's different?"

He moved so that her hand fell from his arm. "It's just different. You're a lady, an' I'm a—"

"A—what? A farmer? A hired man who works on my daddy's place? What does that matter? We're the same people we were a week ago."

"Yeah, but that was before you knew—" His words fell silent.

"Before I knew you couldn't read? That doesn't matter."

"It matters t' me."

"Why?"

He stared at her. "It just does."

She sighed and shook her head—why did he have to be so stubborn and stupid, so proud, so mule-headed—and why did she have to love him so much. "Janson, I need you in my life. You're the best friend I've ever had. I don't want to lose that because of a stupid argument."

He looked at her for a long moment—there was something going on behind his eyes that she did not understand. Something—

"I don't want t' lose it either," he said at last, very quietly. " I don't want t' lose it either—"

And, even as he said the words, Elise saw something in his eyes that she understood at last. It was resignation.

ELISE WHITLEY and Janson Sanders—a black rage filled Phyllis Ann Bennett as she drove the coupe down the rutted clay road away from town that morning. The window beside her was down, blowing her bobbed hair wildly into her eyes. She pushed the accelerator even further, tasting the raw, red dirt being blown into her face by the wind—goddamn them. Goddamn them all.

Elise had turned her back on her—Elise who had followed her blindly for years. And that farmhand—oh, yes, Phyllis Ann knew exactly who he was, just as she knew who every other reasonably good-looking man in the County was, even those beneath her attention, such as that half-breed Indian. He was the one who had almost killed her father the night of Elise's supposed attack, the same one who had broken her father's nose after he had found it necessary to kill Alfred Whitley—goddamn them. Goddamn them both for what they had done to her. Elise had failed her, insulted her, and the farmhand had even dared to threaten her harm—but they would not get away with it. She would make them pay. She would—

She rounded a curve in the road to find an elderly Negro man walking along the road's edge toward town. She honked the horn of the coupe, warning him out of the way, but he only froze, staring first at her, and then at the ditch alongside the roadbed. The coupe brushed him as it passed, sending him stumbling onto his knees at the side of the road. Phyllis Ann did not stop or even slow, pushing only harder at the accelerator—the goddamn nigger, she thought, should have gotten his black ass out of the way. The goddamn—

They would pay. They would all pay. Elise, and the farmhand, and all the people in the County who had snubbed their noses at her. They would—

They were nothing anyway. Nothing at all. Like the nigger. Like the farmhand. Nothing—but she would make them pay. If it was the last thing she did in her life, how she would make them pay.

# 13

IN THE WEEKS FOLLOWING the bazaar, Elise never once mentioned his failing, never once suggested that she teach him to read, but somehow to Janson that only stressed the differences between them, only stressed that she was William Whitley's daughter, and that he was nothing more than one of her father's farmhands. In some ways they had grown only closer over those weeks, even as Janson had fought to keep her at a distance in his mind. He knew he could never have her, could never love her, as he wanted to, and that dreaming of her was the one sure way to destroy all that he was—but still he could not stop loving her, could not stop wanting her, no matter how hard it was that he tried. She was somehow part of him in a way he could not explain, in a way he could not fight, and, as the days passed, he was growingly coming to understand that he did not want to.

He sat on the steps leading up to the rear veranda of the Whitley house that first Sunday afternoon in July, staring out across the wide yard, past the kitchen, and to the woods beyond. He was waiting for Elise, waiting for her to finish Sunday dinner with her parents and with J.C. Cooper, waiting for her, as he had been waiting for more than half an hour now. He toyed with a blade of grass he had pulled from the smooth lawn, staring out toward the woods where he knew he would feel more at home than he did waiting here behind this great house—he had promised to spend the afternoon with her, had promised to take her for a walk in the woods, had promised even to teach her to weave a basket from white oak splits later if she wished—but now he knew he would have to break those promises, would have to break them, just as he had been forced to break so many promises to her lately. And he knew she would not understand.

Laying by had finally come that year, bringing with it the long waited-for rest from the before dawn to sometimes long after dark work of the sharecroppers and farmhands on the place. At last there was time to court and socialize, to visit kin or tend their own gardens, to attend the revival meetings at the bush arbor set up at the edge of town, or the all-day singings held on Saturdays at the little Holiness church out in the country—but Janson did not have those hours free, though the cotton fields now stood lush and green, and there was little work left to be done there until the bolls would burst open and the back-breaking work of picking the cotton would begin. Whatever hours he found free from the plowing, chopping, and poisoning of the cotton were quickly taken up by the bootlegging operation, by the making and hauling of the corn liquor that gave him the money he could put away in the back of the old chifforobe in his room.

The Fourth of July celebrations coming up had only increased the demand for corn liquor throughout the area, and William Whitley was determined to meet that demand, claiming more and more of Janson's hours for the stilling and distribution—and putting a distance between Janson and Elise that not even their differences had been able to. Elise wanted to spend time with him, wanted to go for picnics and walks and drives in the country, wanted to sit with him in the back parlor and listen to programs on the radio, or just spend hours talking about the thousands of things they could find to talk about, claiming his hours sometimes almost as if she were his girl and they were courting—but he knew they were not courting. Never again had she flirted with him as she had done that day; his temper had ruined that, his temper and his pride. He knew she had flirted only because he was a man, and only because it was in her nature to want every man to be a little in love with her—but he could often not help but to wonder what might not have happened that day if he had not lost his temper, if he might not have gotten a kiss on the cheek, maybe even on the lips, before she had come to her senses.

But it did not do to wonder about such things. It had not happened, and it never would. She was going to marry J.C. Cooper; Janson knew that, though she herself had never spoken of it. J.C. had taken again to calling at the Whitley house, being invited to dinner after church on Sundays, or to big family suppers at mid-week; and Janson had even overheard Whitley telling someone that the wedding would take place within a matter of months—but Elise never mentioned it, and Janson could somehow not bring himself to, not wanting to think of her married to someone else, to anyone other than himself. And he knew that would never be.

All she wanted was his friendship, time they could spend together; but time was the one thing he could often not give her, and it was the one thing he could never explain—how could he tell her there were things he had to do, places he had to go, that he could never tell her about. Instead, he gave her excuses, lies, reasons why they could not be together, even as he saw the disbelief in her eyes. She could never know that he was involved in a bootlegging operation, that her father was running a bootlegging operation, even though he knew the lies were only forcing a growing distance between them. She knew that he was lying, knew that he was involved in something more than he would tell her, for he could see the knowledge in her eyes—but it was a truth she would be better off never to know. He knew what he did could not matter in the slightest to her, but still he could not be the one to shatter the image she held of the father she had loved all her life. She could never know that it had been bootleg whiskey to buy her father the big house and the fancy cars and all her pretty clothes—little girls were entitled to their dreams after all, entitled to their dreams, even after they had become women.

He sat staring out across the back yard, hearing the sound of J.C. Cooper's car start up in the drive before the house, and, after a moment, drive away. He wondered if Elise had kissed him goodbye, wondered if she had been in his arms for a moment, but forced the thought away, knowing it was better that he never know. He tried to think of what he would tell her, what excuse he would give to explain why he could not spend the afternoon with her as he had promised he would. It had been only a matter of hours before when William Whitley had stopped by his room on his way to church that morning, had stopped by to tell him that there was a truck load of corn liquor to be delivered to Buntain that afternoon—a daylight run of bootleg whiskey across the County line was a dangerous thing to take on, but Whitley had left him with little choice. Janson would either have to make the delivery, or get the hell off Whitley land—and that was something he could not do, not so long as Elise Whitley was here, not even if she were going to marry someone else.

Through the open windows of the great house behind him, he could hear Elise's voice calling to her mother somewhere within the rooms, and a pang of guilt went through him that he would have to disappoint her again, lie to her again, as he had lied to her so many times in the past weeks. He stayed where he was on the steps of the rear veranda, knowing she would find him here when she was ready, for this was where he always waited when they were to meet.

The rear door of the house creaked open behind him, and he stood to meet her, feeling another stab of guilt at the sight of her, and at the disappointment that came to her face at the first sight of his expression. "You've got to go somewhere," she said, not even waiting for him to speak. "We're not going to spend the afternoon together."

For a moment he could think of nothing to say, no excuses to give her, as he stared at the set and disappointed look on her face. Finally he managed, "I'm sorry," but could say nothing more.

"What is it this time?"

"Work, your pa—"

"Work, what kind of work?" she demanded. "Today's Sunday, Janson, and it's laying by. What kind of work could you have to do today?"

"Jus' work," he said, turning away, his voice short as he fought to control his temper—it was for her own good anyway. Damn her, why could she never leave anything alone? Why could—

There was a peculiar note in her voice as she spoke again: anger, irritation, and something more. "If there's someone else you'd rather be with, you can tell me outright, you know. I'm not a child—"

He turned back to look at her. Her chin was set as she met his eyes. "Somebody else I'd rather be with?"

"Yes—don't you think I know you've got a girl in town? If it wasn't something like that, you'd tell me. If it wasn't—" Then she suddenly seemed to note the amusement that came to his face, which seemed to irritate her all the more. "Don't you laugh at me, Janson Sanders! I am not a naive child who has to be protected from the world, no matter what it is you seem to think! I know you've got a girl in town—why else would you go off at all hours of the day and night, and never be able to tell me or anyone where it is you're going! Well, you don't have to tell me fairy stories to cover it up any more. I know that there are things that you—that a man—that—" Suddenly she seemed at a loss for words. She stared at him for a moment longer, her mouth still open, then her face flushed and she looked away.

Janson laughed outright at the look on her face, unable to stop himself, and her eyes came back to him angrily.

"I ain't got no girl in town," he said, trying to keep from smiling. "It ain't nothin' like that."

"Then, what is it? Where are you going?"

"I cain't tell you."

"Why not?"

"I jus' cain't, an' it don't really matter. There're jus' things sometimes that a man's got t' do that he cain't tell nobody about—" he said, and she looked away again. When she looked back there was accusation in her eyes. "I done told you, it ain't nothin' like that—"

"Then what is it?" For a moment they only stared at each other, neither speaking. "Sometimes I feel like following you just to see—"

"Don't you ever do that!" His voice, in his surprise and agitation, was harsher than he had intended it to be—Elise, stumbling onto the bootlegging operation. Elise, finding out that he and her father were involved in selling bootleg liquor. Elise, finding out—

He watched her chin raise defiantly, her eyes determined. "You can't tell me what to do."

He crossed the short distance between them, going to where she stood near the closed rear door of the great house, then stopped to put his hands on her arms and stare down at her. "I shouldn't 'a yelled at you. I'm sorry—" Why was one or the other of them forever saying 'I'm sorry'— "An' I'm not tellin' you, I'm askin'—you cain't never follow me. You've got t' promise me that."

For a moment she only stared up at him. "Why? What is it you're involved in?"

How could he tell her? How could he explain—"You've just got t' promise me."

She searched his eyes, standing so close for a moment that he could have bent to kiss her—then she moved so that his hands fell from her arms and walked a few steps away, to stand with her back to him, staring out across the wide back yard. He could read a stubborn determination in the set of her shoulders—she would know what it was that he was hiding, no matter the cost to herself. No matter—

"Promise me, Elise—" he said, moving to stand just behind her, unable to touch her again. "You got t' promise me—"

When she turned to look a him, there was distrust in her eyes.

"Promise me—"

She was silent a moment longer, and then her voice came, quiet, reluctant, carrying with it a note of that same distrust. "Okay, I promise."

He smiled, relief flooding him. The words had been pulled from her against her will, perhaps even against her better judgement, but she had given them, and she would not go back on them now. She was safe from finding out about him, about her father, about—

"I suppose you'll have to 'work' all day tomorrow as well, Fourth of July or not?" she asked, stressing the word as if it were a curse.

"No, I ain't got t' work."

"Then, can we spend part of the day together tomorrow at least?"

"I thought you were goin' t' th' big picnic outside 'a town with your folks—" Somehow he could not mention J.C. Cooper, though he knew J.C. had been invited to share the day, and the picnic, with the Whitleys during the big Independence Day celebrations in the meadow clearing just south of town the next day.

"Yes, but afterwards, as soon as I can make my excuses?"

"Sure, we can spend some time t'gether."

"The entire day, just as soon as I can get away from my father and J.C.?"

Janson found himself smiling—she wanted to spend the day with him, with him and not with J.C. Cooper, or with anyone else. "Sure, th' whole rest of th' day, if you want t'—"

He left her shortly there on the back veranda, not wanting to end the time with her, but knowing that he had to. He cut around the corner of the house and across the wide front yard toward the clay road, then across the fields toward the barn where the loaded truck waited for him. The false bed of the truck seemed all too apparent in the daylight, the cases of corn liquor hidden beneath it all too easily discovered by some sheriff or revenue agent if he were to be stopped and questioned. How would he ever be able to explain that to Elise—I couldn't spend the Fourth of July with you as I promised I would because—

That was one explanation he hoped he would never have to make.

As he made the long trip into Buntain over the rutted clay roads that afternoon, one thought kept coming to him, one question—had that really been jealousy he had heard in Elise's voice when she had accused him of having a girl in town? Had it really been jealousy, and not just her irritation at believing he was treating her as if she were a child—how embarrassed she had been when she had managed to tangle herself up in her own words, how flustered, when he knew that she could not even understand what it was she was accusing him of, for an unmarried girl her age should not even know of such things. Could Elise really be jealous? She had wanted to spend the day with him tomorrow, with him and not with J.C. Cooper or even with her own family. Could Elise really be—

His mind was so filled with possibilities that he could give little thought to the increased risks he was taking on by making the daylight run, the risks of being found out, arrested, and jailed in violation of the Prohibition laws. He made the delivery, then started for home—could Elise really have been jealous? To be jealous of some other girl she thought he was carrying on with, she would have to care about him, and care about him as more than a friend. Was it really possible that Elise—

As he sat over his solitary breakfast in his room that next morning, he could not stop thinking about Elise, about the things she had said to him the day before, the way she had behaved—and about the dreams he had lived in through the night. He had dreamed they were married, that he was taking her back home to that white house on those red acres in Alabama, that he had held her and loved her for hours on a creaking rope bed in one of those long-familiar rooms—how beautiful she had been, part of him then even as she was not now, sharing with him, touching him, telling him that she loved him. Somehow those dreams did not seem an impossibility now as they had just the day before. Somehow he could let himself think, let himself wonder, if she might not really—

There was a knock on the rickety door to his room and he got up to answer it, smiling to himself, somehow happier in that moment than he had been since that day years before when a fire in a cotton field had begun the destruction of all that he had loved. He swung the door inward, telling himself that it might be Elise—but William Whitley stood glaring at him from just outside the open doorway, a look of anger, of impatience, on his jowled face. And Janson knew this day would be nothing as he had imagined it might be.

LESS THAN an hour later, William Whitley stood behind the old barn on his property, not far from where the lean-to room sat attached to the structure. He shifted the cigar in his mouth and folded his arms across his chest, staring at the man held before him. "Didn't I tell you never to show your face around here again, boy?"

Gilbert Baskin was struggling against the two men who held him between them. There was a trickle of drying blood showing already at one corner of his mouth, evidence to his reluctance at being asked to accompany the men who had been sent into town to bring him to this meeting. "You don't own me, you goddamn son-of-a-bitch! I go anywhere I want t' go!"

William's teeth clamped down on his cigar. He took a step forward, clenching his hands into fists at his sides. "You smart-ass son-of-a-bitch, I own you or anything else I say I own around here. I ran you out of this County—did you think I'd let you get by with coming back here now?" He had thought himself rid of this problem, had never thought the man brave enough, or stupid enough, to ever come back to Endicott County—until Bill had seen him in town earlier in the day. This man had jeopardized the entire bootlegging operation those months ago, had jeopardized everything William had worked so long for—and now here he was back again, an even greater threat than he had been before. Before he had only been a stupid man. Now he was a stupid man with a grudge.

William forced a control over his temper, his eyes moving from Baskin, to the two men who held him between them, touching for a moment on his son Bill, and then finally settling on Janson Sanders. Sanders had been an improvement over Baskin almost from the first moment William had brought him in to take the man's place in the stilling operation. He did his work without comment, kept to himself for the most part, and didn't flash his money around, though William paid him quite well. The only real problem with the boy was his friendship with Elise. William had never been pleased with the idea of his daughter making friends with the half-breed farmhand in the first place, especially not since he was using the boy in the bootlegging operation. He had even briefly allowed himself a worry that some sort of romantic interest might develop between the two—but the idea of his daughter and the half-Cherokee dirt farmer had been so laughable that the worry had been short lived. Elise was grateful to the boy for his having fought Ethan Bennett to protect her, and grateful for all he had done to try to stop Alfred the night he had died; she felt safe with him, knowing the boy would not let Bennett or anyone else harm her, for he was one of William's people, owing his livelihood and his life to the Whitley family—it was nothing more than that.

But it had gone on long enough. In the past several weeks William had done everything possible to discourage the relationship, keeping the boy busy, and keeping Elise occupied elsewhere as much as he could—

she spent altogether too much time with the farmhand, and not enough with J.C. Cooper. She had J.C. to think about, after all. J.C., and William's future.

There was only one thing about Janson Sanders that worried William now. There was still something within the boy that he knew he did not control, something he might never control—there had been a moment's hesitation that morning, a moment's reluctance, when William had sent him into town with Bill and Franklin to bring Baskin back to the place. That hesitation worried William—the boy was too proud, too independent. He had to learn once and for all that William was not a man to cross, not a man to anger—and he had to learn what could happen to any man who did anger him.

Just as Gilbert Baskin had.

He brought his eyes back to Baskin, chewing down on the cigar in his mouth for a moment before speaking. "Maybe I should have had you taught a lesson those months ago, boy, instead of just having you run out of the County. Nobody crosses me without having to answer for it—" His eyes moved back to Janson Sanders for a moment. "Nobody." He nodded his head toward Franklin Bates where he stood nearby waiting. "Teach him a lesson—" he said, stepping out of the way as Bates moved forward. His eyes settled back on Janson Sanders. "Teach him a lesson he won't ever forget—"

ELISE RAN down the stairs and into the wide hallway that ran the depth of the main floor of the house, stopping for a moment to admire her reflection in the heavy mirror that hung there between the doorway to the company parlor and that of the first-floor bedroom. She turned first this way then that, smiling to herself, finally giving approval to the picture she made. She had spent all morning getting ready, choosing her dress, crimping her hair, doing her makeup—today was the Fourth of July, Independence Day, the day she was certain her life would change forever. There was to be a picnic in the large meadow just south of town this morning, and a dance in the basement of Town Hall tonight. At least half the County would be turning out for the festivities—but half the

County did not matter. What mattered was that Janson Sanders would be there; that he would be there, and that he had promised the day to her.

She had lain awake half the night trying to think of a way out of having to spend the early part of the day with her parents and with J.C., but, try as she might, she could think of no reason that would excuse her from the picnic without also excluding her from leaving the house for the remainder of the day. She would have to spend the morning with them—but, as soon as she could slip away, she would have the afternoon and the evening with Janson. The day was theirs; he had promised her that. There would be no mysterious 'errands' for him to go off on, no secret 'work' that he could never tell her about. He belonged to her for the day. And to her alone.

She spun happily around, hugging herself. There would be the dance tonight, following the picnic and the hot dogs and the patriotic speeches. A group of young people from the County had made arrangements for musicians to come all the way from Atlanta, over the objections of many of the older people that jazz music, and even the already-outdated Charleston, not to mention bobbed hair and hip flasks and the blatant sexuality of rolled stockings and short skirts, were morally corrupting. Elise had attended dances at the Town Hall before, had often been one of the most popular of the young flappers there, dancing with more of the County boys than did any other girl in attendance—but she had never before looked forward to any dance as she looked forward to the one tonight. She knew she would not be able to dance publicly with Janson, for her father would never permit that—but there was always the chance she might get him off into some quiet corner, or even into the darkness outside Town Hall. He could be so awfully old-fashioned about some things—but still she might talk him into a private dance, just the two of them, alone in the darkness, something old-fashioned and slow, so that he would have to hold her. She could flirt with him—not too much, for she well remembered his reaction the last time she had flirted, and she would not have him think she was not behaving like a lady again. She would let him know that she did care about him, was interested in him as a man, without ever having to say a word. Once the music was playing, soft and low in the background, and she was in his arms, close against him, she knew it would have to happen—he would lean to her and kiss her and—

And after tonight he would forget all about that other girl in town.

No matter what it was he said, she was certain he had a girl, someone he would not tell her about—what else could take him away at such peculiar hours and times? What else would he not be willing to tell her about?

But she refused to think about that today. Today he belonged to her, and only to her, for this one day alone. She would make him forget that other girl, all other girls—she knew they were meant to be together, and he would know it as well before this day was through. He had to love her; she could feel it—women always knew such things, she told herself. Janson had to love her, and that other girl, whoever she was, was nothing more than a diversion because he did not believe that Elise felt exactly as he did. But, tonight, once she was in his arms—

Her father would be furious, but she would not let herself think about that now. She and Janson would be married—how that could be, in the manner of those who have had all they have wanted in their lives, she did not consider. She wanted Janson, and she was determined to have what it was she wanted.

She smiled happily at her reflection in the mirror, thinking of all the days ahead, thinking of the green of Janson's eyes, the curve of his jaw. She felt she could never wait an hour or more to see him, to begin this day that she would remember forever—if she could just steal a few moments with him now, under the pretext of telling him where and when to meet her later. He would be in his room, getting ready for the picnic—it would be so easy, just slip out the back and over to the barn. Just a moment with him, to renew his promise that his day belonged to her today. Just a moment—

She slipped down the wide hallway toward the door that opened out onto the back veranda, glancing back once to make sure that her father was nowhere within sight. She went through the door and closed it quietly behind herself, then crossed to the steps that led down into the yard—her father would have a fit if he caught her. He had seemed so strange earlier when he had told her not to leave the house until time to leave for the picnic. But seeing Janson even for a moment would be well worth the risk. Her father might scream and yell, but even he could not ruin this day for her. This was her day, Janson's day, and nothing would spoil it. Nothing.

With that thought in mind, she slipped quietly around the edge of the house, across the yard, and toward the barn, knowing this day would change her life forever.

THERE WAS a sick feeling in the pit of Janson's stomach as Franklin Bates stopped before them. Gilbert Baskin was struggling in his grip now, struggling, not out of defiance as before, but in fear, a film of perspiration beading over his upper lip. Bates took a step forward, flexing his massive hands before knotting them into fists, and Janson turned his eyes away, the sickness rising to his throat for he knew what was about to happen.

William Whitley stood just a short distance away, his back turned toward the work about to be done on his order, a thin wraith of smoke rising from his cigar as he finally lighted it. Janson stared at him, realizing for the first time how dangerous the man could be—he was a man who could do anything, anything at all, if he were only pushed far enough. Janson's eyes moved back toward Bates, and then to Gilbert Baskin who dragged at him as he tried to back away—and then he caught sight of Bill Whitley, and a cold chill moved up his spine. The man was smiling, a cold, hard excitement in his eyes—he's enjoying this, Janson told himself. My God, he's enjoying this.

The first blow almost collapsed Gilbert to the ground, his knees sagging beneath him. He dragged at the two men holding him, struggling to free himself. His words were incoherent now, pleading, begging, all defiance gone—but there was no use. The second punch collapsed his knees beneath him, almost pulling Janson and Bill down as well. A trickle of fresh blood appeared at the corner of his mouth from where he had bitten his jaw to keep from crying out—this isn't right, some part of Janson kept saying. This isn't—

Franklin knotted his fists for another blow, his face absolutely impassive, business-like—this has gone too far, Janson thought. Gilbert was shaking his head back and forth, spittle drooling from his mouth and down over his chin—too—

"That's enough!" Janson heard his own voice over the sound of Gilbert's near-incoherent pleading. Franklin's eyes flicked to his for a moment, and then moved toward where William Whitley stood at a distance, Bates hands still tightened and ready before him.

Whitley had turned back toward them, surprise, something near disbelief, in his eyes as he took the cigar from his mouth and stared at Janson for a moment. "What'd you say, boy?"

"I said he's had enough." There was anger building inside of Janson—there were many things in this world he would do for money; but this was not one of them.

"You goddamn coward!" Bill Whitley said, his voice filled with anger and hatred from where he stood just at Gilbert Baskin's other side.

"Shut up, Bill!" Whitley snapped, but his eyes never left Janson. "I'm the one who'll decide when he's had enough, boy—" he said, clear threat in his words.

"He's had enough." Janson kept his gaze locked with Whitley's as he supported Gilbert Baskin's sagging body. He knew he was walking a thin line; one misstep and he could meet with what Gilbert had received—or even worse. Whitley was no man to provoke; he had well learned that this morning—and he knew he might have already gone one step too far.

Whitley's jaw clenched, his eyes filling with anger as he stared at Janson. "Boy, don't nobody—"

But a shocked female voice cut through his words, silencing him as quickly as a slap. "Oh—dear God—!"

Janson turned quickly in that direction—but he already knew. Elise stood at one corner of the barn, her eyes taking in the scene before her, and then settling on his own. He felt he could never take the weight of that gaze, and of all that it said. There was accusation there in her eyes. Accusation, and a sudden, horrible understanding.

ELISE FELT as if she herself had been delivered a blow, so great was the shock—her father, Bill, and Janson—oh, dear God, Janson—Gilbert, looking so battered, so hurt. What she saw said everything—what kind of men were these, to be able to hurt another human being so easily, so without feeling. Her father, her brother, the man she loved—Janson, her Janson, holding another man for a beating—

"Oh—dear God—!" was all she could say, staring at him.

"Elise, go back to the house!" Her father's face was set, drained of color, as her eyes came back to him.

"No! I won't! What in the name of—" Her voice was pleading, demanding—it could not be as it seemed. Not her father, not Bill—not Janson. Her eyes moved to Gilbert as he was released, as he sagged to the ground—no man could have deserved this. No man. "What are—"

"Go back to the house!" Her father's voice rose in anger.

"No!"—please, God, let me be dreaming, she begged. Let this all be a nightmare—but this was no nightmare. It was all too real, in all its ugly, glaring truth. And suddenly she understood—all the times Janson had left her, had gone places he could not tell her about, done things he could not tell her about, had been times like this, times when he had done terrible things for her father just for the money it could bring him. Just for the money. Her eyes moved back to Janson, and she stared at him in disbelief—Janson, hurting someone, helping her father to hurt someone. Janson, but not the man she had known, never the man she had known. A stranger inside of him, a stranger who wore his face and had his voice. A stranger who mocked and angered and frightened her. "Why? Daddy—Janson—how could—"

"I said, go back to the house, goddamn you!"

"No!" She screamed at her father for the first time in all her life, feeling as if she wanted to cry—but the tears would not come. They stayed locked inside of her, hurting far worse than any she had ever shed.

The color returned to her father's face in a rush. His cheeks reddened, and he clenched his hands into fists angrily at his sides. Janson's eyes seemed to dart quickly to him, and then back to Elise. His voice suddenly came, even more commanding than her father's had been.

"Get back t' th' house, Elise!"

Her chin rose, defiance suddenly flaring within her, defiance stoked by shock and hurt—how dare he not be the man she had thought him to be. How dare he present her with this mocking stranger behind the face she had loved so well. How dare he—

"Get t' th' house!" His voice rose, a stern look in his eyes that allowed no disobedience. "Now!"

Suddenly she wanted nothing more than to get away, away from this place, away from her father, away from Janson. She needed to be alone, needed to think, to sort it all out in her mind. She felt as if she had been slapped cold, hard in the face by something she had not been prepared for, something she could never have been prepared for. She turned and ran—toward the house, toward the shelter of her room, toward the comfort and safety she had always known. Her mind was filled with Janson, a Janson she had never known before, a Janson she did not like—and a Janson she did not want to love.

But into her mind crept the one thought as she ran toward the road, the fields, and the house beyond, momentarily crowding out all others, and bringing with it a stab of bittersweet pain—there had been no other girl in his life. The days he had been gone from her, days so secretive and mysterious, had been days such as this—days spent doing wrong and unpleasant things for her father, not days spent in the arms of another woman. He had been hers more completely than she had ever known, and the hurt of that knowledge learned too late ached inside of her, for she hoped nothing more now than that she would never have to see him again.

JANSON STRODE up the steps and onto the wide front veranda of the Whitley house less than an hour later, his heavy shoes making dull, thudding noises on the wooden flooring beneath him—he had to find Elise. He had to find her and make her understand before she could say or do something that might push her father too far—and it might already be too late. If Whitley had come here directly after leaving the barn, he had been home now for over three-quarters of an hour—three-quarters of an hour in which Elise could have confronted him, could have said or done anything that might have set him off. Janson had never before believed that Whitley might actually harm his own daughter—but this time he could not be certain.

The man's temper had been at the breaking point already after Janson had stopped the beating, and then Elise had shown up. Janson had known from the look on her face that she had to be gotten out of there before she could say or do one thing too many—it had torn him apart inside to watch her run away, knowing what it was she had to think of him now after what she had walked into.

And now she had been here in the house with her father for over forty-five minutes. With her temper, with how quick she was to speak without thinking, with her pure cussedness, Janson knew she would have confronted him by now. Forty-five minutes—

He caught sight of himself in the frosted glass panes set into the wide front doors—he was dressed in a new pair of dungarees, his best Sunday shirt, and the only pair of shoes he owned. His straight, black hair, so neatly combed back and pomaded earlier, was now tousled and disheveled—he had been so careful with his appearance this morning, had taken time as never before, because he had known he would be spending the day with her. He had wanted her to notice the care he had taken, had wanted her to be totally unashamed to be seen with him on this day, had even allowed himself to dream—

But that was all gone now. After what she had seen, after what she had walked into, after what she must believe of him now—

But none of that mattered at the moment. All that mattered was that he had to find her, make sure that she was all right, and that he calm her temper and still her questioning before she could push her father too far—if it was not already too late. He knew she could never be told the truth, never be told that Gilbert Baskin had simply become a threat to her father's bootlegging operation—no, she could never be told that. He had hoped earlier that by getting her away from the barn as quickly as possible, by putting that distance between her and her father, that both tempers would have time to cool before they could confront each other. He and Franklin had been sent into town to put Gilbert on the first train out of Endicott County, to warn him one last time that to ever show his face within the County line again might mean his immediate death—as they had driven away, he had seen Whitley start for the house, an angry look on his face. Forty-five minutes ago, and anything could have happened by now. Anything.

The place seemed deserted, too quiet, neither Whitley's car nor Bill's parked in the curve of the drive before the house. There was no sound of the radio playing from within the front parlor, or of the Victrola, or even of voices—Janson pounded on the heavy wooden door until the frosted glass pane rattled in its frame, waited a moment, then pounded again. "Goddamn it—answer—" he swore aloud, clenching both fists at his sides.

One of the heavy doors swung inward almost in response to his curse, and he found himself staring down into the surprised face of Mattie Ruth Coates. He pushed past her and into the wide hallway, looking toward the staircase that rose to the floor above. "Where's Elise?"

For a moment she did not answer, staring up at him with clear disapproval in her eyes. "She's done gone—"

"Gone—gone where?"

"T' th' doin's in town, with th' family."

"An' her pa?"

"He went with 'em, made her go. She didn't much want t'—" But the remainder of her words were lost as he pushed past her again and out onto the wide veranda. "Where're you goin'?" she yelled after him from the open doorway.

"Int' town," he said, not stopping or looking back. "I got t' find Elise—"

THE GAWKY Ford rattled down Goodwin's Main Street as it neared the picnic grounds at the far end of town that morning, finally rolling to a stop beside the collection of cars, wagons, and trucks already parked there at the edge of the meadow. Elise sat staring out the car window, unmoving, her eyes set on the growing crowd of picnickers, until her door was yanked open and she looked up to find her father glowering down at her. She got out of the car quickly and moved a few steps away, wanting only to distance herself from him—but she felt a sudden rough hand on her arm, drawing her up short, turning her to face him.

"You listen to me, Elise—" he said, his tone hushed, angry, his brows lowered, his eyes dark and furious still as they stared down into her own. "You keep your mouth shut about things you don't know anything about; do you hear me?"

For a moment she did not answer, but just stared up at him, the anger and rage growing inside of her again—she had not wanted to come here in the first place, had not wanted to spend the day acting just as if she had seen nothing, just as if she had learned nothing as she now wished she had never known.

This had been his idea, his demand, when he had returned to the house—she would forget what she had seen, what she had walked into. She did not understand what had happened, he had said, or the reasons for it—but she understood enough; she understood there was something her father was involved in, Bill was involved in, even Janson was involved in, that she had been meant to know nothing about. They were doing something wrong, wrong perhaps both in the sight of God and the Law, and Gilbert Baskin had somehow gotten in their way—she knew Gilbert had left the place sometime during the months she had been away at school, sometime during the months when Janson had first come to the place; but now Gilbert was back, and they had beaten him, perhaps even meant to kill him if she had not interfered. No man alive could have deserved what they had done to him, what they had intended to do; her father, Bill, Franklin Bates, Janson—how she despised them now for what they had done, what they were capable of doing. They somehow frightened her, enraged her, for they were none of them the men she had thought them to be. None of them, not even her own father or brother. Not even Janson, who she had wanted to spend her life with—how much she had thought she loved him, and what a fool she had been. What a fool.

Her father yanked at her arm, hurting her, demanding her attention. "You just keep your mouth shut—" he said, his fingers digging into her flesh. "Do you hear me?"

Elise yanked her arm free of his grasp and took a step back to glare up at him. "Oh, I hear you all right, Daddy."

He looked around quickly, at the others getting out of the car, at the picnic baskets being unloaded, the festivities being prepared for, then he looked quickly back to her, his eyes growing only darker. "You forget what you saw, or what it is you think you saw. You don't know a goddamn thing—and I'm getting tired of your smart mouth. All you've got to worry about today is J.C. Cooper, and being nice to him. That's all you've got to worry about from now on—do you understand me?"

Elise stared up at him, realizing for the first time in her life that she did not know, or even really like, her own father. "Yeah, I understand you, Daddy," she said. "Maybe for the first time in my life, I understand you."

BY THE time Janson reached town that morning, there was already a sizeable gathering of people at the meadow, some already sitting down to picnic dinners, others only now just arriving. He had caught a ride toward town on the wagon of one of the Whitleys' sharecroppers, sitting on the back in silence, his legs dangling down, the ride seeming to him to take forever to cover the distance. The farmer had taken him to within a mile of the edge of town, and he had walked the remainder of the way, his steps determined, single-minded—he had to talk to Elise, whether she wanted to see him or not. He had to talk to her, make sure she was all right, and then make certain that she forgot forever what it was she had seen today, not for his sake, or for her father's, but for her own. She could never know about the bootlegging operation, but she had to understand enough to know that she could never confront her father again about what she had seen, never take the chance of pushing him too far—Janson had known before that William Whitley could be a dangerous man, but he had never realized how dangerous, not until today, not until he had seen that beating take place, that beating that he had known had been as much for his benefit as for Gilbert's own. It had been a message, a clear warning, that he should never let himself become a threat as well.

He made his way past a group of small boys shooting off firecrackers at the edge of the picnic grounds, past a group of men heatedly discussing politics, and several young couples walking arm-in-arm over the newly mown grass, his eyes searching the area for Elise. It seemed as if most of the County had turned out for the celebration, for the picnic, the speeches, and the dance and fireworks that would come later. There were families already sitting down to picnic baskets, elderly ladies gossiping beneath the shade of nearby trees, and young people courting away from the eyes of meddlesome mothers. Janson caught sight of Stan Whitley standing at a distance of about half-way across the meadow, J.C. Cooper nearby, and he started in their direction, knowing that Elise would be somewhere not too far distant—then he saw her, kneeling at the edge of one of the blankets her family had spread out, both she and her mother helping to unload the picnic dinner that had been brought in the many baskets surrounding her. She seemed to lift her eyes and see him at the same moment, appearing surprised at first, then flustered; then she hurriedly got to her feet and started away, toward the far side of the picnic grounds, putting an even greater distance between them.

Janson started toward her, pushing past a group of men near the edge of the meadow, stepping around picnickers, almost knocking one man off his feet in his rush to reach her—she would have to listen to him; he would give her no other choice. She would have to listen to him, and then—

And then only God knew.

ELISE DID not know where she was going, and she did not care. She only knew she had to get away, away from Janson before he could reach her, away from her father and the picnic grounds and all the people who did not know that the world had forever changed on this day. She saw the woods ahead of her and she headed in that direction, knowing somehow she would never make it to their cover before Janson could reach her side.

She felt his hand on her arm, gently but firmly drawing her up short, putting an end to her flight, and she turned to him, rage filling her as she tried to jerk free. "Let me go, goddamn you!" she demanded, struggling against him, only to have his free hand close over her other arm as well. For a moment his eyes searched her face, and she felt herself weakening, then she shoved hard against him again, determined to not lose herself to the lies she knew that lay behind those green eyes. "I said, let me go!"

"Quit fightin' me, Elise, before you hurt yourself—"

"Isn't that what you intend to do, Janson Sanders, beat me up as well?" she demanded, finally stopping her struggles only to stare up at him.

His hands fell from her arms and a hurt look came into his eyes. "You know I wouldn't never hurt you—"

"But you hurt other people, don't you? That's what you've been doing all along, isn't it, all the times you left and told me lies about where it was you were going and what you were doing—you and my father, you're involved in something you don't want anyone else to know about, something that's wrong, something that's illegal. That's it, isn't it—he's got you doing terrible things for him, hasn't he, just for the money. Just for the—"

"Leave it be, Elise—"

"Hasn't he!"

"I said leave it be! You don't unders—"

"Oh, I understand enough, and I hate you for it. You're not the man I thought you were, and I can never forgive you for that, never!"

For a moment he only stared at her. "You don't mean that."

"Don't you dare tell me what I mean!" she said, clenching her hands into fists at her sides, her entire body shaking now with fury. "You'll do anything for money, won't you? Anything—"

"But, you don't—"

"Why did Daddy have you do it? Why did he have you beat up Gilbert—you, Bill, Franklin—"

"Leave it be, Elise. He's got his reasons. It ain't my place t' say—"

"Well, maybe my father will say!" She turned and started away, back toward the center of the picnic grounds, back toward her father and her family and the picnic dinner she knew she would never be able to eat, but suddenly he had her arm again, turning her to face him, holding her still before him. When he spoke his voice was low, firm, something unreadable in his eyes.

"You listen t' me, Elise Whitley. You leave your pa alone; don't you go askin' him no questions."

She tried to jerk free, but he would not release her, his hands holding her only more firmly, his eyes never once leaving her face.

"You just stay outta this, you hear me? Don't you go messin' in things you don't know nothin' about—"

"You sound just like my father!" She spat the words at him, unable to stop herself.

"Maybe I do, but you listen t' me. You stay outta this. Don't go messin' with him; he ain't nobody t'—"

Suddenly he seemed to realize he had said too much. She stared at him, realization slowly coming. "You actually think he would—Janson, he's my father! You can't really believe he would hurt me!"

"I ain't sayin' he'd hurt you, but it's best that you forget you ever saw anythin' t'day. No matter what it is you think about me, or about anythin' else, don't go sayin' nothin' more t' him about it."

She took her arms from his grasp, and this time he released her willingly. She took a few steps away to stand with her back to him. "You really believe he would—" but her words trailed off. After a moment she spoke again. "He has you doing something illegal, doesn't he?" she asked, but he did not respond. "Damn it, answer me!" She turned back to face him. "I have the right to know! He's my father, and you're—" but she could not finish.

"He's got his reasons for what he does, Elise. Just leave it be—"

"I will not leave it be! And I don't care what his reasons are! I see you helping to beat a man half to death, and my father—what is it you're involved in?"

"I said leave it be!"

Something of the urgency in his voice cut through her. She stared at him, an awful understanding coming to her. "My father, he could turn on you like that, couldn't he?" she asked, but he would not answer. "What happened to Gilbert, it could—"

"Elise—"

"Answer me!" she demanded, her voice rising. "It could happen to you, couldn't it?"

"Your pa don't do nothin' unless he's got a reason."

"But, if he had a reason, he could hurt you, have someone else hurt you, maybe even—"

"I ain't givin' him no reason—"

But she knew. She stared at him, realizing fully what it was her father might be capable of doing. "Janson, you've got to stop whatever you're doing for him, quit it now, before he—"

But he cut her words short. "I cain't do that—"

"Why not? Is the money that—"

"Th' quickest way for me t' end up like Gilbert Baskin is for me t' quit doin' what your pa says—is that what you wanted t' hear!" he demanded, and then seemed to realize what his words had done to her. "Elise, I—"

But she turned away, her voice hushed as she spoke. "My God, what kind of man is he—"

"Elise, it ain't important. Just forget—"

"Do you really think I can forget?" she demanded, turning to him, knowing suddenly that she was going to cry. "Seeing you hurting someone, and my father—how did you ever get involved in something like this?"

"I do what he pays me t' do—"

"Even hurting people!"

"I ain't hurt nobody."

"I saw you! You were helping to—"

"An' I put a stop t' it when it went too far—" But she only stared at him. He sighed and shook his head. "That don't matter now," he said after a moment. "Th' only thing that matters is that you leave your pa be. Don't go askin' him no questions."

Elise stared at him for a moment, and then turned her eyes away, looking toward the throng of picnickers, toward people she knew she would never be able to see in the same way again. When she brought her eyes back to him she found him watching her, a look in his eyes once again that she could not understand.

"Are you all right?" he asked after a moment, his eyes never once leaving her face.

She nodded, looking away again.

"Your pa, when he came back t' th' house, he didn't—"

"No, he didn't," she answered, not letting him finish, not wanting to hear the words.

"You an' me, I don't guess you'll ever—" but his words fell silent. When she looked back at him there was pain in his eyes.

"I'll ever what?" she asked.

"After t'day, I don't guess you'll want anythin' more t' do with me again."

She could only stare up at him for a moment. "You're still my friend," she said finally, her words quiet.

"You said you hated me."

She sighed and shook her head. "I should never have said that."

"But, do you?"

"No, I couldn't hate you."

He was silent for a long moment, his green eyes moving toward the nearby picnickers, and then coming back to rest on her again. There was a longing in him she could almost sense, that she could see in his eyes, and she knew that he had not been a lie, that he had never been a lie, no matter what it was she had seen today. "Before, you said that you wanted t' spend part 'a th' day with me. You don't have t' now, not if you don't want t'—"

For a time she could only stare up at him, letting the realization of all she had learned sink into her, the realization of all that she still did not know. Then she suddenly found herself smiling, and she reached up to place a gentle hand on his cheek, knowing somehow that she would love him anyway, no matter what else it was she might learn. "Yes, I still want to spend the day with you, as soon as I can manage to get away from my family."

A slow, reluctant smile touched his lips, and he reached to place a warm hand over her own. For a moment she understood, knowing more certainly than ever before that he did love her. Then his face sobered. "Elise, you just remember what I said. You forget what you saw this mornin'. Don't say nothin' more t' your pa about it."

But she would not answer.

"I mean it, Elise, don't you go pushin' him—"

"You just be careful," was all she would say. "Just be careful—"

WILLIAM WHITLEY stood beneath the shade of a large water oak at the edge of the picnic grounds that morning, never once taking his eyes from his daughter and Janson Sanders—they looked more like bickering lovers than merely friends, he kept telling himself. They looked more like—

Somewhere inside of himself he knew that he had made a mistake. He should never have allowed the relationship to go on this long, to have become this close. He should have put a stop to it much sooner—but it was not too late even now. Elise might be making a fool of herself and William as well here in a public place with half the County watching—but it was not too late.

Elise was far too headstrong, and she could be trouble enough on her own—and now it seemed as if Janson Sanders might present a problem of himself as well. The boy had already shown a streak of defiance that day, sticking his nose in where it did not belong, trying to put a stop to what Gilbert Baskin had rightly earned for himself—and William did not like defiance, especially not out of a farmhand, and most especially not out of one he was using in the bootlegging operation. The boy was forgetting his place, and William knew that could be dangerous, considering what the boy already knew, and also considering how close he was becoming with Elise. Janson Sanders was a normal, healthy young man, and Elise was a pretty and naturally flirtatious girl, with more daydreams than she had common sense—yes, William should have put a stop to this long ago. Elise had J.C. to think about, and William had no intention of letting the half-breed Sanders make more of a problem of himself than he already was.

William folded his arms across his chest and shifted his cigar to the other side of his mouth, watching as Elise smiled up at Janson and reached up to touch his face—William's teeth clamped down hard on the cigar. That gesture said too much. There was an intimacy to it, a caring. It said too—

"Is there something wrong, Daddy?" his son Bill asked from where he stood nearby, but William's eyes never once left the young couple.

"Could be," William answered, squinting in spite of the shade of the tree beneath which they stood. "Could be you've been right about Janson Sanders all along. He might have to be taken care of before he can turn himself into a real problem." He watched them for a moment longer. "He just might have to be."

# 14

PHYLLIS ANN BENNETT lounged back against the rough bark of a pine tree in the midst of the picnic grounds that morning, ignoring the stares of the old women who sat nearby on chairs pulled beneath its shade. She bit into the large apple that was the last remnants of the picnic lunch she had shared with Bullock Calhoun before she had managed to so recently, and quite intentionally, lose track of him—Bullock would never have been her first choice in a man, with his thinning red hair and his great, sweeping mustache that made him look as if he were part of another century; but he had been the only man to have asked her to the picnic, and to the dance afterward.

And she knew whose fault that was.

The wind lifted a lock of her bobbed brown hair and blew it into her eyes, and she brushed it away absently, staring out across the picnic grounds toward where J.C. Cooper stood talking to Stan Whitley, the older boy continuously fidgeting with his eyeglasses—Elise's fiancé, or so she had been hearing. But, then again, she had always known the two of them would get together one day, in spite of all Elise's protests to the contrary. J.C.—James Calvin—she smiled to herself, the weak fool. He was the only kind of man who would ever be interested in Elise, if he could even be called a man, the only kind of man Elise would ever be able to have—if she ever had any man at all. Elise probably thought she had her future all planned—

But, then again, Elise was so seldom right about anything these days.

Too bad—Phyllis Ann thought, smiling to herself. This was the end of Elise Whitley always getting what she wanted. Elise would not be a bride this year or any other—not if it was the last thing she ever did. The very last thing.

Phyllis Ann laughed to herself, drawing peculiar stares from the old women who sat nearby. She tossed the apple aside with only the one bite taken from it, and then started across the picnic grounds, leaving the shade of the pine tree to the old women beneath it.

THE AIR in the basement of Town Hall was thick with tobacco smoke that night. People moved about the crowded room, laughing and talking in a hundred different conversations, often trying to shout over the loud jazz music that came from the Atlanta musicians on the raised platform that dominated one corner of the room. Young couples danced, while others flirted outrageously in odd corners, and still others slipped outside through the sets of large, double doors that opened out onto the area behind Town Hall, hoping for the privacy that the night, and the parked cars, might provide them.

Young flappers in straight, shapeless dresses that barely even touched their knees danced and carried on and strolled about the edges of the room, flirting with first this boy then that, teasing and laughing and then moving on. A bottle of bootleg whiskey was being passed about almost openly in one corner of the room, and corn liquor was being sold from a car parked not far outside the building. Older people sat in chairs beneath the bright lights, nodding their heads now from the lateness of the hour, the large suppers many had by now eaten, and the amounts of illegal liquor that some had already consumed. The musicians began the already-outdated Charleston, and many of the nodding heads came up, expressions showing clear disapproval—scandalous, down-turned mouths and lowered brows said as young people laughed and danced and enjoyed themselves. A flash of thigh was seen, and many a view of the tops of rolled silk stockings as couples tried to outdo each other, and pouting lips, shaken heads, and set expressions showed reaction—young people these days would come to no good ends, the faces said; all they thought about was sex and drinking and doing things they shouldn't do in parked motor cars, petting and necking and carrying on in all sorts of immoral ways. The entire generation was going straight to the devil, said the faces—straight to the devil in a handbasket.

Janson made his way through the edge of the dancing couples, his eyes scanning the room for Elise. She had kept her promise to him even after all that had happened that day, had met him behind the Methodist Church at the edge of town just as soon as she had been able to slip away from her family. They had gone for a long walk through town and the nearby countryside, then had talked for hours, sitting on the grass at the beginning of the woods near the edge of town, sharing for supper the sandwiches and apples she had thought to take from her family's picnic dinner. Several times she had brought up the subject of what she had seen earlier in the day, until finally she had seemed to realize he would tell her no more. She had at last promised that she would leave her father be, and that, for now, was enough for Janson. Still the worry was there—but the day had been so wonderful, so special, that even that worry could not ruin it. Elise was his for just this one day. Tomorrow she might go back to being Miss Whitley—but for today, for tonight, she was Elise, his Elise, and he could allow himself to dream.

All day long, since she had first met him behind the Methodist Church after the picnic, she had been treating him differently, not, it seemed, because of what she now knew, or suspected that she knew, about him and her father and Bill, but simply because he was a man, a man like any other, and a man she seemed to care about. She had talked to him, had listened to his opinions and thoughts, as she always did, just as if he were the most knowledgeable and educated man she had ever known—and she had flirted with him, flirted with him as she had not flirted since that day when she had learned that he could not read. For the first time in the months he had known her, he was allowing himself to hope, to believe that they were nothing more than a man and a woman, and that their differences did not matter—she could care about him; she could love him. When she looked up at him, when she smiled, when she touched his cheek, he told himself that it did not matter that he was a farmhand, that he did things for her father that she could never know about—it did not matter, not if she loved him. Tomorrow morning he might not be able to allow himself to believe—but tonight, for just this one night, he could dream; tonight, at least, he could believe.

They had come to the dance together, slipping in through the double doors that led into the basement from the rear of Town Hall, and had stood listening to the music for a time. They had gotten lemonade from ladies serving at a table in one corner, and then had watched the dancers, had laughed and talked—he knew what an odd sight they must make, he in his farmer's clothes, and she in her fine dress and silk stockings. There were other country people there, hired men from the various places, small farmers, sharecroppers, but they were staying mostly to themselves, dancing rarely, for the most part being tolerated, and ignored, by people such as the Whitleys. Elise had seemed not to even notice the stares being directed their way, or the whispers that seemed to pass between people she had known all her life. She laughed instead, swaying to the music, touching his hand on occasion, just as if touching him was the most natural thing to do. She had not asked him to dance with her, and he had been glad, for he had never once danced in all his life, having been taught against it in his growing up—but now he wished he knew how. Now he wished that it were proper to take her out among the other couples and hold her in his arms to slow music, as so many of the other young people were doing.

She had suddenly seemed to grow nervous, and Janson had soon realized why. Her father was standing directly across the room from them, staring at them through the haze of cigarette smoke and the laughter and dancing couples in between. Elise had excused herself for a moment, and Janson had not followed, though he had felt a trace of worry—it would not have been proper for him to follow, just in case she had excused herself in order to use the water closet, or to freshen up, as he knew ladies often did.

But that had been half an hour ago, and still she had not returned. Half an hour ago, and he had now lost track of her father as well. And he was worried.

Elise had promised that she would not question Whitley again about what she had seen, what she now suspected, but, with her temper, Janson knew she would speak before she thought if her father once brought it up. There had been no kindness whatsoever on her father's face as he had stared at them from across the room—there had been anger there, anger, and something more. Hatred?—but there was no reason for that.

A knot of anxiety tightened in Janson's stomach as he moved through the room, his eyes searching for Elise. He kept telling himself over and over again that Whitley would not have hurt her, not his own daughter—but where was she? She would not have left him on this of all nights, not after the day they had just shared, left him to not return of her own free will—something had happened. Something had happened, and he was going to kill William Whitley if he had hurt her in any way. He was going to kill William Whitley, and—

He stopped before one set of the doorways that opened out onto the area behind Town Hall, his eyes searching the room one last time for Elise—he would go back to Whitley's place if he had to, search the big house room by room until he found her, and if Whitley had hurt her—

There was a sudden touch on his arm, a hand grasping him by the shirt sleeve—there was no time for him to think, no time to react. There was time only for one startled gasp before he was pulled through the open doorway and out into the darkness behind Town Hall.

"ELISE, WHAT in the name of God—where have you been? You had me worried half t' death!" Janson said, his face a mixture of concern, surprise, and relief as he stared down at her in the sparse light that fell through the open doorways behind them.

"I didn't mean to scare you."

"Well—" His eyes moved over her for a moment, as if to assure himself that she was unhurt. "Where were you? I looked all over th' place for you."

"I saw Daddy watching us. I didn't want him to ruin the evening, so I slipped out here. I was beginning to think you would never come this way; when you did, I just grabbed your sleeve—"

"You had me worried half t' death."

"I'm sorry. I never meant for you to worry," she said, smiling at the concern on his face, and, after a moment, he smiled as well, seeming to relax. "It's nice out here, isn't it?" she asked. "Quiet, and no tobacco smoke. Just the two of us, and you can still hear the music—it's pretty, isn't it?"

His eyes never once left her face. "Yes, it is—" he said, very quietly.

She glanced back toward the open doorways. "We'd better move away from the doors; someone might see us out here—" She put her hand on his sleeve again and led him farther out into the moonlight, away from the lighted building, and into the shelter of the tall hedges blooming there thick with summer scents. Her pulse was racing—she had him alone. Not just alone, but together here in the moonlight, the rustling branches of the oaks and the pecans and the cottonwoods overhead, the scent of flowers in the air—she could have planned it no better. She would remember this night, this moment, forever, she told herself. It would be a part of her as long as she lived.

"I was hoping you'd ask me to dance earlier, when we were inside," she told him once they were away from the building, in that moment damning conventionality and lady-like behavior forever behind her.

"Your pa wouldn't 'a liked that—"

"Well, he's not here now."

He shifted uncomfortably, then smiled, an embarrassed look coming to his face. "I don't really know how."

"That doesn't matter. I can show you—" She moved into his arms easily, feeling her heart speed up at his nearness. She took his hand, guiding the other to her waist, thanking God in one breathless moment that the music was slow and romantic so that he would have to hold her. She looked up at him, preparing to say something—but all words left her as she stared at him, finding his eyes moving over her own. For a long moment she thought that he would kiss her—but he only continued to stare, his eyes holding hers for a time before bent at last, and briefly, lightly, touched his lips to hers.

When he looked down at her again she saw a touch of uncertainty in his eyes, and she realized suddenly that he was afraid she would pull away from him—but she stayed where she was, looking up at him until he released her hand to put both of his at her waist, and his lips came to hers again, touching them lightly. Then again, as she moved closer into his arms. When his lips at last left hers and he looked down at her, she started to speak, but he touched a finger to her lips, silencing her words. "No—don't talk, not yet—"

Her eyes searched his face in the moonlight, memorizing each curve, each line, making the vision of him a part of herself. His finger left her lips and trailed lightly over her cheek for a moment, then his lips came to hers again, his arms drawing her closer—I love you, she thought the words she had been about to speak. I love you, Janson Sanders.

She felt as if she could stay in his arms, feel the warmth of his body against her, for as long as she might live—I love you, she thought. I—

There was a sound, the crack of a twig, the rustle of leaves nearby. The kiss ended abruptly, and Janson released her and moved a step away. She looked at him, longing to be back in his arms, longing for his nearness, for the kiss, to continue.

"Elise—?" came a voice, and she turned to find Stan staring at her from beyond the hedges that stood between them and Town Hall, his face somehow unreadable behind the round-rimmed glasses. "Daddy sent me to find you. He says we're leaving, for you to come—"

"I'll be there in a minute," she said, brushing her hair back from her eyes self-consciously, feeling a slight blush rise to her cheeks.

"Daddy said now."

"Okay, in a minute I said." Her voice rose slightly.

Stan looked from her to Janson, then back again, his face never changing. After a moment he turned and started back toward the lights of Town Hall, leaving them alone once again in the darkness.

Elise looked up at Janson. He smiled at her, a thousand thoughts and feelings in that smile. No words needed to be spoken. They both knew. They both understood. Perhaps they always had.

He reached and gently took her hand, squeezing it briefly, then releasing it. He turned and walked away.

WILLIAM WHITLEY paced back and forth on the sidewalk before Town Hall, stopping occasionally to take the watch from his vest pocket and hold it to read the time by the light from the windows behind him—eleven p.m., and no Elise. Damn that girl, she would soon drive him to an early grave with her constant trouble, arguments, and stupidity. She did not know her own mind, and seemed lately only to delight in making him trouble—but no more; never again after this night.

He had been pleased earlier in the day when Elise and J.C. Cooper had both disappeared from the picnic grounds at near the same time, satisfied for the moment that the worries he had held about his daughter and the farmhand Janson Sanders had been unfounded—maybe the girl was at last coming to her senses. Maybe she had at last realized what a catch young Cooper was. There could be nothing wrong in the few kisses or embraces they might share, and it might be just what was needed to finally light a fire under the boy and get a ring on Elise's finger—William was not getting any younger, after all; he could not wait forever to get his hands on the cotton mill. Elise would have to hook the boy, and hook him soon, before some other girl could set her cap for him—and perhaps she had at last decided to make her move. Perhaps she had realized that her father had only her best interests at heart. Perhaps—

And then she had shown up at the dance tonight with Janson Sanders, with one of his farmhands. William Whitley's daughter and a farmhand—the damn fool girl would have the entire County gossiping about her. Elise Whitley and a farmhand—a cold anger filled William with even the thought. J.C. Cooper was off only God knew where, and Elise was here making a spectacle of herself with a dirt farmer—and, good God, the boy wasn't but half white! William had thought things could be no worse, and then Elise and the boy had both vanished again, and William's mind was now playing over a thousand images, each worse than the last. Bill or Stan had better find her, and they had better find her soon. She was going home before she could do any further damage to her reputation, or to William's good name. And, as for Janson Sanders—

Janson Sanders would never be a problem to anyone again after this night. Never.

PHYLLIS ANN quietly made her way across the closely clipped lawn toward the front veranda of her home that night, her eyes on the dark house before her. J.C. had wanted to bring her right to the door, but she had made him let her out at the end of the road, and she had walked the remainder of the way—what she needed less than anything else at this moment was a car waking her father at this hour. He had been drinking before she had left earlier, and she was in no mood to face an ugly drunk. One look at her would be all he would need—the disheveled hair, the rumpled clothes; he would know she had just bedded a man.

A man—she almost laughed aloud with the thought; no, J.C. Cooper had been no man, but he was much more one now than he had been a few hours before. He had been so easy, had left the picnic grounds with her much more readily than she had ever believed he would—but, then again, she hadn't known that he was in love with her then. That was the most ironic part of all—J.C. Cooper had been in love with her all along, had wanted her, and never Elise. It was just too bad that she had not known that until after she had let him have her—let him; but it had not really been like that. It had seemed that he would never get on with it, amidst his shy kisses and bashful fumblings. They had taken his car to a deserted spot on a back road and parked. He had been backward, shy and inexperienced, leaving Phyllis Ann to make the first move, and almost every one after that. He trembled as she touched him, and whispered her name as he lay on her; he had even finished so quickly that she had not even had time to make him pull out.

And then he had said that he loved her, that he had always loved her, and that he wanted her to be his wife—she had almost laughed in his face at the very idea. Mrs. J.C. Cooper, putting up with his bumbling touch every night—no, thank you very much. But she had left him room for hope, room for his pathetic little dream, for he was, after all, Hiram Cooper's son, and, as such, he could help her undo the damage that had been done her in the County because of her father's stupidity.

She sat down on the front steps to remove her shoes, then quietly gathered them into one hand and walked up the remaining steps to the veranda. She turned the doorknob in her hand, wincing at the squeak of the ancient hinges as she pushed the door open just enough to slip through and into the wide hallway. She breathed a sigh of relief as the door closed behind her—she had made it; it was just up the stairs now and to her room. She had—

"Goddamn slut—" a voice came from the darkness of the open parlor doorway to her right. She gasped and turned in that direction, feeling for a moment as if her heart had leapt into her throat to choke her.

There was a groan of shifted weight on leather upholstery, and then the room was flooded with light that spilled out into the hallway to wash over her. She blinked for a moment at the sudden brightness, her eyes hurting—and then she saw him, her father, sitting in an arm chair, staring out the open doorway at her.

He rose slowly to his feet, his eyes moving over her, taking in her appearance. "Goddamn slut, out rutting all night, like a bitch dog in heat—" His voice was deadly calm; he was past anger, past drunk, and she knew her heart would stop beating inside her as she stared at him—he was going to kill her this time; she knew it. He was going to—

"Who was it this time? Who've you been fucking—and how many others while you've lived under my roof: five, ten, twenty—" He began to cross the parlor rug toward her, coming out the open doorway and into the hall—she could smell the liquor on him, even over the distance between them, and she tried to move away, but her back came up against the closed front door behind her.

"You don't understand, Daddy, he—"

"Who was it!" He grabbed her as she tried to dart past him, slamming her hard back into the door. "Who was it!" His fingers dug into the flesh of her arms, bruising her, his breath hot on her face, the smell of stale alcohol filling her nostrils. He pulled her away from the door again, then slammed her hard back against it, then once more, until she heard one of the glass panes crack as her head impacted it. "Goddamn you—tell me!"

"It—it was J.C. Cooper—he—he raped me, Daddy! He raped me!"—it would work; it had always worked. Just turn him on someone else and—

"Goddamn tramp!" The slap came as a complete surprise, causing her senses to spin—it couldn't be! He didn't believe her; he didn't believe—

"He raped me, Daddy! J.C. raped—"

"Out whoring all night; come sneaking in—did you think you could fool me? Did you!?"

He wasn't hearing her—dear, sweet Jesus, he wasn't hearing her! She was about to die, and he would not hear—"It was rape! J.C. made me! He hurt—"

He slapped her again, hard, backhanded, across the face. She could taste blood from where she had bitten her lip, smell it, from where her nose had begun to bleed. "How many others? Damn you—how many others!"

"Daddy, he—"

"Slut!" He slapped her again, making her face ache. "Stupid bitch—how many have there been! How many—ruining my name all over the County, spreading your legs for just anybody—" He struck her again and again; her face hurt, her body hurt, her head hurt. She could taste blood, feel it over the lower part of her face. "Goddamn—"

Suddenly something snapped inside of her—she wanted to kill him. She could die happy then, if only she could—her hand flailed out, searching for something, for anything she could use. It would end tonight, everything would end—the abuse, the beatings, the curses, what he had done to her life, the hell she had lived in—it would all end; he would end. He would die. She brought her hands back to his face, clawing at his eyes—she knew she had to get free, even if just for a moment. Her nails dug in, bringing a scream of pain from him as he shoved her away. She hit the floor hard, knocking the breath from her body—but he was after her again, coming toward her. She scrambled through the open parlor doorway, almost falling over the rug as she made her way across the room toward the fireplace—she grabbed up a poker and turned to hold it on him, keeping it raised between them.

"Come on, you fucker!" she screamed, the rage filling her. "Come on! I'll show you what hurting is, you goddamn son-of-a-bitch!"

He stopped half way across the rug, staring at her. He breathed heavily, swaying slightly on his feet.

"Come on, you coward! You're so goddamn brave, beating me up when I can't defend myself—how about now! Come on, you cock-sucking son-of-a-bitch, how about now!"

With that he screamed with rage and lunged at her—but that was what she wanted. She brought the poker up and swung it hard, aiming for his temple, but the blow struck his jaw line instead, sending him staggering sideways, shock and disbelief in his eyes. She swung again, this time impacting his temple, then again—there was a moment of knowledge in his eyes, and then they went glassy. He stumbled and fell against a table, then crashed to the floor, pulling the table and lamp over on top of him.

She stood there for a long moment, holding the poker in her hands, swaying slightly as she stared down at him—he's dead, she told herself. He's dead; I killed him. For a moment, there was nothing, no feeling, no thought, just the fact—he's dead; I killed him. There was an awful ringing in her head; her entire body ached, and she could taste blood from her nose and where she had bitten her lip.

He's dead; I killed him.

Slowly feeling returned, relief flooding her. It was over. It was over forever.

He's dead; I killed him.

She looked down at the still form lying on the floor, blood already matting the graying brown hair on one side of his head, running down his cheek to soak the blue rug beneath him—her tormenter, her nightmare. Her father. Dead.

He's dead; I killed him.

She dropped the poker, hearing the dull clang as it struck the floor, then stood for a moment, taking deep breaths of air as she stared down at him. There was a sudden scream from the open doorway behind her, and she turned to find her mother standing there, clinging to the door frame with both her hands.

"Ethan! Oh, God, no—Ethan!" She stumbled across the room, almost falling over the hem of her long wrapper, then sank to her knees beside her husband's body, her short, bobbed hair falling into her eyes.

She began to wail, rocking slowly back and forth on her knees, her hands clasped together in her lap as if she could not bear to touch him.

Phyllis Ann stared down at her for a moment, the grief before her meaning nothing.

"It's over, Mother," she said at last, her voice very quiet. "He's dead."

Slowly Phyllis Ann Bennett began to smile—He's dead; I killed him.

# 15

JANSON STARED THROUGH the side window of William Whitley's truck that next morning, his eyes fixed on the tall, straight pines that passed alongside the road—he was uneasy, ill-at-ease, as he sat beside Franklin Bates. There was something in the man's manner, something about the look in his eyes, or the set of his jaw as he steered the truck over the rutted clay road, that made the hairs along the back of Janson's neck rise. He had been at the stills earlier, getting ready for a run of corn liquor with Tate, when he had turned to find Bates there.

"Mr. Whitley wants to see you, boy—right now," Bates had said, that peculiar look in his eyes.

Janson had gone, but not before he had exchanged one quick look with Old Tate—there had been concern there in the old man's eyes, worry. He knew, just as Janson did, that Franklin Bates was no messenger boy.

The truck turned in the drive before the Whitleys' big house, then rolled to a stop only a few feet short of the front veranda. Janson's eyes searched the tall windows for sight of Elise as he got out of the truck—the night before seemed now almost a dream to him. But it had been no dream; it had been real. He had held Elise Whitley in his arms, had kissed her—he had awakened this morning knowing she could love him, if not now, then someday. She would never have let him hold her, kiss her, as he had done, if she had not at least felt something for him, if it were not at least possible that—but, as he entered the house behind Franklin Bates that morning, she was nowhere to be seen. And last night seemed very far away.

He followed Bates through to the library, entering the imposing room just as he had on that first night he had come here those months ago. It was all still there—the books, the brocaded settees, the desks and reading lamps, just as he remembered it. William Whitley stood now across the room, his back turned to them, his hands clasped together behind him, his eyes staring out one of the tall windows at the smooth lawn and the green cotton fields beyond. Bill sat at the rolltop desk, a sheaf of papers in his hands, his eyes rising to meet those of Franklin Bates as he and Janson entered the room.

Janson heard the heavy wooden door close behind them. He could hear the ticking of the mantle clock, and, in the silence, he fancied he could hear the breathing of each of the men in the room. He waited, staring at Whitley, feeling the imposing presence of Bates where the man stood just behind him. It seemed a very long time before Whitley turned—and, when he did, Janson felt the cold knot of anxiety tighten in his stomach. He had seen that look in Whitley's eyes only one time before, had felt its presence—it was the same look he had given Gilbert Baskin just before he had ordered the man beaten.

Janson took a deep breath and prepared himself for what he knew was to come—Whitley might order him to be beaten, for whatever real or imagined sin, but the man would have no satisfaction from it. Janson would not beg for mercy as Baskin had done; he would not plead to be spared—Whitley would kill him first.

He lifted his chin and returned the man's stare. He was not afraid.

WILLIAM WHITLEY stared at Janson Sanders for a long moment before he spoke—the boy's face was unreadable, but his eyes held strength. There was no fear there, not even a hint of subservience—the boy looked at William as if he thought he were his equal. And William wanted nothing more than to kill him for it.

He had waited until this morning, had waited until he thought he could control his temper before he had the boy brought to him. But now it seemed as if the wait had been for nothing. The anger returned, the outrage, just as strong as it had been the night before, and he fought again to control it. The image of his daughter and this half-breed filled his mind—but the boy would die before William would allow that to happen. He knew now that he could never allow the relationship to continue, not in any form—William Whitley had no intention of having dark little grandchildren with one-quarter Cherokee Indian blood in their veins as well as his own, and no intention of having Elise make any greater fool of herself than she already had. He would sooner kill the boy now than ever to allow Elise near him again, even in friendship, for friendship could so very easily become so much more. It would end, or the boy would end. It was as simple as that.

"Bill, Franklin, leave us—" he said at last, his voice low and controlled, his eyes never once leaving Janson Sanders's face. Franklin moved immediately to obey, but Bill delayed. "Leave us!" The carefully held control threatened to break, and William fought again to maintain it as he heard the door at last close behind Bates and his eldest son, leaving him alone with the farmhand.

I want to kill you—William thought as he crossed the library rug toward Janson Sanders, seeing the proud, defiant look that remained on the boy's face—I want to kill you, for the feeling I see in my daughter for you, for the feelings I see in you for my daughter. I want to kill you, but I can still use you. I want to kill you—and I will, if it does not end here. The friendship is over—if I ever see you near her again, your life is ended. I will kill you with my own hands.

"You and me need to have a talk, boy," he said, trying to force his nature under control. The boy did not respond, but the green eyes never left William's face. The pride there made William want to hit him—but he clamped a tighter rein over his temper instead, clenching the cigar in his mouth only more tightly between his teeth. He knew that if he let go now he would kill the boy—but he could not afford to do that, not unless he had to. Janson Sanders was too valuable an asset to the bootlegging operation for William to allow himself to get rid of him in a fit of rage—how long it had taken William to realize that in the hours since he had first begun to see what this farmhand and his daughter were starting to feel for each other. He needed the boy to haul corn liquor across the County line for sale, and he needed him in the stilling itself. There were too few men who could be trusted, too few men who could keep their mouths shut, when the law and the revenue agents were constantly out to put a man out of business and into jail if he were caught. Janson Sanders had proven himself valuable over the past months, and he could prove himself valuable far into the future—but not at the expense of William's daughter, or of the plans he had made for her so long ago. William would not give up the Whitleys' good name, or his family's standing in the community. Elise would marry no farmhand—but neither would William give up a key man he needed in his bootlegging operation just because of the foolishness of a girl. It had taken most of the night, but William had at last found the way—after today there would be no more chance of a romance between Elise and this half-breed. No chance at all.

"Sit down, boy." He motioned to one of the settees, and, after a moment, the boy moved to sit down. He had not once spoken since entering the room, and his silence was somehow unnerving to William. The green eyes stared up at him—proud and defiant, William thought as he stood over him. "There's no other way to say this, boy, than to just come out with it," he said. "Elise came to me this morning and asked me to talk to you. I don't know what's been going on between you two, and at this point I don't want to know, but she wanted me to tell you that she wants you to stay away from her from now on." He told the fabrication easily, and watched the boy's expression change—he had hit a nerve. It was evident on the dark face; and he knew he had acted none too soon. "She's afraid you're starting to feel things for her that you shouldn't be feeling—now, you believe me, boy, I'd kill you right now if I thought you'd ever tried to take any liberties with her. I don't think you would, and, if I ever find out differently, I'll break your neck with these two hands myself, do you understand that?" He stared at the boy for a moment. "Elise is worried that you've taken a fancy to her. It's understandable if you have, boy, because she's a pretty girl, but you've got to realize, like she has, that she's a cut above you. She's grateful for what you did that night to save her from Ethan Bennett, and she feels sorry for you, but she just let it go too far. You've been taking up too much of her time, and you've been interfering between her and J.C. She's afraid you're forgetting who and what you are, and that you're starting to think you're just like the rest of us, when you're not. You've been getting too familiar with her, and too attached to her, and she's worried that you're starting to think she's feeling things that she could never feel for someone like you."

He felt a moment of inward triumph—there had been a flicker of pain in the boy's eyes. William had gotten through that wall of pride and strength, and had actually managed to hurt him.

"Elise will be getting married soon, and she thinks it would be best if you stayed away from her from now on. She's afraid people will start to talk about her, considering who and what you are, and she's right about that, so I'm telling you myself to leave her be. I'll tell you one other thing, boy; if she had taken a fancy to you as well, I'd kill you first before I'd see the two of you together. Elise is my only daughter, but I'd see her dead as well before I'd see her with the likes of you—but I don't have that to worry about, do I, boy, because she's going to marry J. C. Cooper. She's got her future to think about, so you just stay away from her." He watched the agony he fancied going on inside the boy for a moment. "You understand me, boy?"

Janson stood, surprising William, who took a step backwards. "I understan'." The boy spoke for the first time since entering the room. His voice was low, controlled, the green eyes now masked, showing nothing. But a muscle clenched in his jaw. "You through with me now?"

William stared at him. "Yeah, boy. You can go."

Janson Sanders turned and left the room, his eyes fixed straight ahead as the heavy door closed behind him. William watched him go, relief coming to him. The boy was hurt and humiliated. He would stay far away from Elise from this day on—and his pride would never allow him to speak to anyone, least of all to Elise herself, of what had happened in this room on this day. He would simply end the friendship, the relationship, before it could have the chance to go any further—and he would do it because he believed it was what she wanted. She would never know what had happened. She would be confused, even hurt; she might even try to question the boy—but Janson Sanders's pride was his undoing. In his mind, Elise wanted nothing more to do with him. In his mind, she was afraid that her reputation would be soiled by association with someone so far beneath her—as it would have been. In his mind, she felt sorry for him, and, to Janson Sanders, that would have been the worst insult of all. He would never face her with the truth of what he had been told, because his pride would never allow it. If she forced her presence on him, he would simply walk away; his pride would allow him to do nothing else. She would never know what her father had done for her, and might be so adrift after the loss of the friendship that she could even be easier to handle, more pliable to his will, as a daughter rightfully should be. He would tell her some story as well, that the boy had come to him, asked him to speak with her—she would be no more difficult to handle than Janson Sanders had been. Her own pride would never allow her to confront him either once William was through with her. Pride was the one characteristic the two of them had in common. The only one.

And, still, William had managed to salvage a man valuable in the bootlegging operation. He had no real concern that the boy might quit now, pack up and leave the place. Sanders might have taken a fancy to Elise, and that could be understandable, for she was lovely and charming and would have to be far above any other girl someone like him would ever have known. His pride might be hurt now, even his feelings—but pride and hurt feelings would mean little to the boy compared to the money William paid him. Janson Sanders had a liking for money; why, William did not know, for he still never seemed to spend any. He was willing to do whatever it took to earn a dollar. Even run a still. Even haul bootleg whiskey—and Elise could not have meant that much to him anyway.

William moved across the room to the mantlepiece, struck a match, and lit up his cigar. Martha might whine and complain later about the scent of smoke in the draperies—but, Martha be damned, this was his home, and he was master of it. He would smoke if he damned well pleased. He would do anything he damned well pleased.

JANSON SAT on the ground with his back against a tree at the edge of the clearing in the woods a short while later. He did not know why he had come here, to this place they had shared so many times, this place where they had picnicked, had laughed and talked—after he had left Whitley, he had just walked, feeling that he wanted only to escape the words the man had given him. After a time he had looked up to find himself here, and here he had stayed.

At first there had been nothing inside of him. Absolutely nothing. There was just a blankness crowding out the confusion. He sat, staring toward the pines that bordered the clearing, not thinking, not feeling—and then a thought had come: This is life without Elise; and the first wave of almost physical pain had hit him.

Until then there had always been a dream, always even the slightest hope somewhere in the back of his mind that she might learn to love him. When she had allowed the kisses, the closeness, the night before, he had even let himself believe—

But there was no belief left now. No hope. No dream that she might someday love him, might even be willing to marry him, no matter how different they might be. She was going to marry J.C. Cooper.

And she wanted nothing more to do with him.

He looked around at this place he knew so well, remembering the girl he had known, had loved, for months—how could he have been so wrong. How had he spent so much time with her, loved her so completely, and yet never known her at all. He had been her friend, had allowed her closer to him than he had allowed anyone since his parents had died—and now she thought she was too good for him, so much better than he was. She was afraid that people might talk, afraid that he felt things for her that she could never feel—when she could never know how he had felt, how he had loved her. Last night she had let him kiss her, had let him hold her in his arms, had let him believe—

But today she wanted nothing more to do with him. Today she felt sorry for him. And lacked even the courage to tell him so herself. She was no lady. She was nothing at all.

There was no reason to stay here now. No reason. He did not want to see her, could never see her, look at her, knowing what it was she felt. Knowing—

Suddenly he found himself longing for the red hills of Alabama as he had not for many months, longing to see his grandparents again, longing to see the small white house where he had grown up, and to visit his parents' graves where they rested now side-by-side in the little Holiness cemetery in Eason County. But he could not go home. Not yet. He had sworn never to go back; never—not until he had the money to buy back his land, the money to buy back his parents' dream, and his own. Something so small would mean nothing to someone like Elise Whitley—but it was all he had left now.

He got to his feet and took one last look around at the tall pines, the red earth, the blue Southern sky—so like home, and yet—

But he could never stay here. Never, not knowing now how it was she really felt. He would go some other place, somewhere where he could earn the money it would take to buy his land back. He had a strong back, two strong hands; he knew how to farm, how to run a whiskey still, and the tricks of hauling corn liquor—he would find work. It might never pay as well as running corn liquor for Whitley had, but he would at least be where he could be a man again. And he would never have to see Elise Whitley for the remainder of his life.

He cut through the woods, toward the fields thick with rows of green cotton plants, and the red clay road beyond. As he broke free of the trees he stopped for a moment to stare back at the tall, imposing structure of the Whitley house where it sat on its slight rise of ground, its wide verandas, white columns, and broad steps shining in the sunlight—rich people deserved each other, he told himself; may they all burn in hell together.

He walked across the yard to the road, going toward the barn and his small room. He tried to comfort himself with the thought of the money he would be taking with him—but it no longer seemed to matter so much. There were no dreams left inside of him for it to buy. There was nothing left, nothing but anger, nothing but a sense of betrayal, nothing but humiliation. Something within him had died that morning, and even the dream he had held for so long, had worked for, sweated for, seen his parents die for, seemed to matter little now. There seemed no reason for dreams now.

There seemed no reason for anything.

THE SHORT trip from Goodwin seemed to Elise to take forever that afternoon. She sat in the rear of the big Studebaker, staring out through the side window glass, eager for the sight of home. It had been a wasted morning, spent in town with her mother, Titus, and her brother Stan. She had not wanted to go in the first place, for there were too many other more important matters on her mind to allow her to enjoy shopping, or even trying on the latest styles—but her father had insisted. There was an important package coming in for him on the 11:40 train from Atlanta, and he wanted it picked up immediately. They could go in early, spend the morning in town, do some shopping, and have dinner at the drugstore before returning home. Elise had known that it was little like her father to insist that she and her mother go shopping, for he was usually much too tight with his money to do that—but he had said the package was important; and, besides, she had told herself, he was just trying to buy his way back into her good graces, considering what she had seen the day before, and what she had learned.

But now she was worried.

The train had come and gone. There had been no package on the 11:40 from Atlanta—and her father did not make mistakes like that.

She sat on the edge of the seat, willing Titus to drive faster. The morning was wasted, the boxes of new dresses and shoes and underthings too little payment for the time she had lost. She might have been able to see Janson already this morning if she had not gone into town, might even have been able to spend the day with him—but it was not too late now. As soon as she reached home and got her new things up to her room, she would go find him—and she would say at last the words he had stopped her from speaking the night before. She would tell him that she loved him.

Nervous butterflies were flitting about in her stomach—what would he say when she told him? What if he laughed at her—he was little more than three years her senior in age, but he seemed so much older, seemed to know so much more about life and the world and—could he really love her? She was months past her sixteenth birthday now, but, until last night, he had never before really treated her as if she were a woman, had never tried to kiss her or—but he had to know she was no child. The memory of his arms around her, the way he had kissed her, the way his body had felt against hers, had told her that he knew she was a woman. That he—

But had she been too forward? He could be so damnably old fashioned about so many things—could she have ruined everything by being too pushy, by having been the one to have done the luring out into the darkness behind Town Hall, by having been too easy to let him kiss and hold her. Her mother had always said that men really cared little for bold, flirtatious women, except for what they could get from them—for once in all her life, should she have listened to her mother? The modern thing to do nowadays was to be audacious and bold, flirtatious and daring, like Clara Bow and Zelda Fitzgerald and so many others. Women drank now days, even though liquor was illegal; they smoked and went to speakeasies and got arrested just as men did. They wore one-piece bathing suits, even if it did mean the police would get them. They wore rouge and face powder and lipstick; they danced to jazz music and wore short dresses; they bobbed their hair and drove cars and had a good time—but, damn it, Janson often seemed as if he were from another time. He probably did not even think women should have the vote, as they had since 1920, seven years before. Did he now think she was easy, just because she had let him hold her and kiss her—several times. Men never married girls who they thought were easy; her mother had said that as well. Had she managed to lose him even before she had him, by being too bold—damn it, why did he have to be so unlike anyone she had ever known, so impossible to figure out, or understand.

She had kissed plenty of boys before, a fact she would never let her mother know, or Janson—but no one else had ever made her feel as Janson had when he had kissed her. She had felt it through to her soul—that told her he did feel something for her, that he did love her, just as she had always known that he did—but had she been too forward? He had done the kissing, but she had made it obvious that she wanted to be kissed—what was he thinking this morning? Could he really love her as much as she loved him—if so, she could be married in a few months time. Mrs. Janson Sanders—oh, it would all be so wonderful. If only—

At least she would know soon. Nothing could be worse than not knowing, she told herself—but she could be so wrong; she knew that it would be so much worse if she knew that he did not love her. So much worse—but she could not think about that. She would never have the courage to tell him what she had to tell him if she did.

She sat on the edge of the seat, her hands twisting in her lap—almost home. Almost to Janson. The nervous butterflies flitted about in her stomach. Soon she would know. For better or worse, at least she would know.

THERE WAS only silence to greet Elise as she entered the tiny room off the barn half an hour later. There had been no answer to her knock at the splintery door, nothing but the overwhelming, lonely silence as a response, drawing her into the room as no greeting ever could.

The aged door hinges screeched in protest as she swung the door inward, and she stood for a moment, looking around, seeing the room clearly for the first time, as she had not those months ago when she had run here on the night her brother, Alfred, had died. Light filtering in through the small, single window, the open door behind her, and the spaces in the ill-fitting walls, threw the room's sparse furnishings into a canvas of light and shadows—such a small, shabby little room; with its rough, unpainted walls; its tin roof showing rust stains where it leaked in places; its bare dirt floor; its cheap furnishings; was where Janson lived. As her eyes moved about the room, her heart went out to him in pity—how horrible it must be to live in one small, dark little room such as this.

How cold it must be in winter, with the wind whistling in through the spaces between the rough boards in the walls, the black stove so far inadequate to heat even the small space on bitter winter nights.

Her heart suddenly ached for him, for all the things he must have had to live without all his life. She had so much, and he so little—it was so unfair. No one should have to live like this. No one should have to do without the things that made life pleasant, or even bearable. For the first time in her life, Elise Whitley had a slight vision of what it was to live without—and she did not like it. No one should have to live this way. No one. Especially not the man she loved.

Her eyes moved about the room, and a sudden, inexplicable chill moved up her spine. There was a feeling of something more than loneliness, something more than poverty, here. There was nothing lying about to tell anything of the man who lived here, no family photographs or Bible, nor even cast-off clothing waiting to be washed in the tin wash tub in the corner; nothing lying about to even show the room had an occupant. It had an air of emptiness instead. Of near desertion.

Suddenly her heart leapt within her—she knew, even before she crossed the narrow room and yanked open the drawers of the chifforobe. He was gone.

Her mind screamed out in protest—it could not be! He would not have left her, not after last night. He would not have—but the chifforobe was empty. There was nothing of his left here. Nothing. She turned and looked about the room, willing it to not be true—but it was true. Everything was gone. Janson was gone.

Her eyes fell on a small book lying in the center of the sagging cot. She moved to pick it up, and then sank down to sit on the straw tick, her knees going weak beneath her. The book—it spoke more clearly than any words ever could. He was gone. And he was never coming back.

She stared at the slender volume, the familiar binding, seeing it, and yet not seeing it. It told her clearly what he thought of her, as he himself had not been able to—Mrs. Browning's *Sonnets From the Portuguese*, the book Elise had given him, the book he had kept even when he had felt she had deliberately insulted him, now lay in her hands. He had left it. He had left the one thing she had ever given him. And he had left her.

She wanted to cry, but the tears would not come, the hurt too deep, too new—he's gone, some part of her mind kept repeating the words to her, over and over again, as if she did not know them already. He's gone, and he's never coming back.

She stared at the book in her hands, unable to grasp anything beyond that one thought—for beyond that thought was emptiness and pain. Beyond that thought was tomorrow, and next week, and next year, in a life she now knew she would have to live without Janson.

SHE STAYED there in his room for a long time, unable to make herself leave, for to leave would be to somehow accept that he was gone, that he was never coming back. At last she left the small room and made her way across the cotton fields, toward the woods, and the road that led across her father's land. There she stopped, staring down the red clay expanse to where it twisted between the pines—she knew she would never be able to find him, not even if she followed the road all the way to Goodwin, and even beyond. There was nothing she could do. Nothing. She had caused this; she knew she had. She had caused this—and she would never see him again.

The tears came at last, moving down her cheeks as she tried to wipe them away. She moved from the sunshine and to the shade at the side of the road, stopping to lean against the rough bark of a pine tree there, losing herself to the ache inside. The quiet in the shadow of the woods was almost overwhelming, only increasing the loneliness—so this was alone. She had been alone before Janson had come, but this was somehow different, this awful emptiness inside.

There was a sound in the distance, a car coming along the road, and she turned away, wiping at her tears, not wanting anyone to see her like this. After a moment she turned back, watching as the car moved past her and down the road, watching as it slowed just before leaving her sight to avoid a man walking along the roadside from the direction of Mattie Ruth and Titus Coates' house, coming in her direction—Janson.

For a moment she could only stare, not believing—Janson, not gone from here forever, at least not yet. He walked alongside the clay roadbed, his shoes slung over one shoulder, a leather-sided portmanteau in one hand. He was still here, and there was still time—

Suddenly movement came to her. She burst from the shade and cover of the trees and ran toward him—there was still time, and there was still a chance. She could make him stay; she could—

He stopped where he was, surprise, confusion, hurt, and anger all passing across his features in an instant. Her running steps slowed, and she stopped a few feet short of him, looking at him—what could she say? She had pushed herself at him and had caused this—what else could it have been? Oh, what a fool she had been last night! He had accused her before of not acting like a lady, when she had done nothing more at the time than flirt with him—she had been so stupid! So very stupid!

"You want somethin'?" he asked a last, staring at her. His words were short, angry, and for a moment she could do nothing but look at him, trying to think of something to say.

"You're leaving?" she asked, surprised that her voice sounded so calm, so natural, betraying nothing of what was going on inside of her.

"Yeah, I'm leavin'."

"Why? I mean, I—"

"Why!" The word exploded at her, filled with more anger than she had ever seen in him before. "Hell, I don't think I have t' explain anythin' t' you—"

She stared at him, feeling almost as if she had been slapped—nothing she had done could have deserved such anger, such fury as she saw now in his eyes. Nothing—

"I'll say one thing for you, you've got even more nerve 'n I ever gave you credit for, comin' here now—you couldn't let things go like they was, could you? No, you had t' go an' rub my nose in it again—"

"I never—"

But he would not let her speak, silencing her words with a quick movement of his hand. He took a step toward her, causing her to shrink away. "You know, I feel sorry for J.C. Cooper; he deserves better 'n you; anybody'd deserve better 'n you. You ain't nothin' but a spoil't, selfish, stuck-up brat of a girl—you ain't no lady, an' you ain't never gonna be no lady."

For a moment she could only stare at him, shocked beyond speech, beyond any defense of herself. She opened her mouth to speak—but the look in his eyes silenced her. Dear God, all this from her little flirting, from the few kisses they had shared, from—

"I wish you luck marryin' J.C., 'cause you're gonna need it. You're too much of a spoil't brat t' be marryin' anybody—you with your fancy ways an' fine learnin'. You didn't even have courage enough t' tell me t' my face that you think I ain't good enough for you, did you; you had t' send your pa t' do it for you—"

Your pa to—Elise stared for a moment, feeling as if all the breath had been taken from her body. Her father had—

"Janson, I—"

But he would not listen to her, turning away, seeming intent to leave her standing there at the side of the clay road. She took hold of his shirt sleeve, moving directly into his path, determined that he would have to listen to her.

"Janson, please, you've got to—"

"I ain't got t' do nothin'," he said, interrupting her words, looking at her with something very near to hatred in his eyes. "You Whitleys think you're all s' high an' mighty, but you ain't no better 'n nobody else—you know your pa even said he'd see you dead before he'd see you with th' likes of me. That ain't no kind 'a man, threatenin' his own flesh an' blood over—"

"My father said—"

"Yeah, an' that he'd kill me too before he'd see us t'gether."

For a moment she could only stare up at him, certain in that moment that—

"That's why you were leaving, because you were afraid my father would—"

"I ain't afraid 'a your pa or nobody else. I'm leavin' 'cause I don't want nothin' more t' do with you, with any 'a you, for th' rest 'a my life."

His words hit her almost like a physical blow. "You don't mean that."

"Yeah, I mean it." This time he did not turn away. He stared at her as if to make certain that she understood, and this time it was Elise who turned away. "You can go burn in hell for all I care; that's where th' lot 'a you are goin' anyway," but she could not listen to him. She felt the tears well up in her eyes and spill over, and she tried to wipe them away, refusing to allow him to see what his words had done to her. "You go on an' marry your fancy J.C. now," he said from behind her. "That's all you intended t' do in th' first place, no matter how much you played up t' me. He's got money an' a car an' all th' fancy things that are what's important t' you—"

"I'm not going to marry J.C.; I never intended to marry J.C.," she said, though she would not turn to look at him. "That's what my father wants, not me—and I never asked him to say anything to you."

There was silence behind her—she wished he would just go if that was what he intended to do. Wished he would—

"You didn't ask your pa t' talk t' me?"

"No, I didn't," she said quietly, but did not turn to look at him.

"You didn't have him tell me t' stay away from you?"

She turned to bring her eyes to him, surprised that he had said—

"My father said that I wanted you to stay away from me?"

He nodded, his eyes never leaving her own. "He said you were afraid I was feelin' things for you that I shouldn't be feelin'; that you were afraid people'd start t' talk."

"I never asked him to say anything like that; I never asked him to say anything to you at all." For a moment she could only stare at him. "That's why you were leaving, because you thought I wanted you to?"

"I couldn't stay aroun' here, knowin' how you felt, how your pa said you felt."

"That's not how I feel."

He stared at her for a long moment. "How do you feel?" he asked, and for a long time she could only look up at him.

"I thought you knew," she said, but he only stared at her. "After last night—" Her words trailed off. How could she tell him? How could she, when every time she tried—"How do you feel, about me?"

For a long moment he only stared at her. Some part of her was afraid that he would not speak, that he would not say what she needed to hear him say—but then she realized he did not need to. He reached out to briefly touch her cheek, wiping away the tears still there, then he drew her into his arms—she knew she should feel happy. She knew she should—

But all she could remember were his words—her father would see them dead before they would ever be together. Her father would see them dead.

PHYLLIS ANN Bennett sat on the front veranda of her home, rocking slowly back and forth, staring out into the yard—it was over. The sheriff had come and gone, as had the men with their somber faces who had taken her father away, and the neighbors with their curiosity and condolences—it was over. There would be no more hurt, no more hate; it was over. And she would never have to be afraid again.

She smiled. "Just defending myself," she said to the silence around her. Her father would have appreciated that; it was the same excuse he had given when he had killed Alfred Whitley. It had worked for him, and it had worked just as well for her. "Just defending myself—" Oh, yes, he would have appreciated that.

She rocked slowly back and forth, not yet willing to go back into the house, not wanting to face the pain and mourning and grief on her mother's face. Her mother had loved him—that had come as a surprise; no matter what he had done to her, to them both, Paula Bennett had loved him. She now looked at her daughter with that same mixture of fear and dread she had always looked at him with—I wonder if she loves me, too? Phyllis Ann mused. I wonder if—

J.C. loved her. He had been one of the first to arrive last night, just as soon as he had been told. He had been so pathetic, fluttering about her with his sympathy and his inane condolences. His concern had been genuine, unlike that of the mass of others who had come to do nothing more than satisfy their morbid curiosity. She could act the grieving daughter before them, but not before J.C.. The sad sympathy in his eyes had made her nervous, and so she had sent him away—but he would be back. He would always be back. He loved her, just as her mother had loved her father. No matter how many times she might send him away, he would always be back—poor, pathetic little J.C.; he was her only hope now. She smiled at the irony of that—J.C. Cooper, who she had laughed at and tormented all his life, was all that she had left. And she had gone after him only to get back at Elise.

Elise—her hands clenched into fists in her lap. Elise had it all—a spotless reputation, her family's name, respect in the community, her virgin whiteness—she had always had it all. She had never once in her life known trouble or pain. Never once—but she would.

Oh, how she would.

# 16

"WHAT ARE WE GOING TO do?" Elise asked a short time later as they sat beneath a tree at the edge of the clearing, the same clearing he had come to those hours ago when he had thought her gone to him forever. That seemed a lifetime ago now.

She sat with her legs curled beneath her, her short skirt fanned out about her knees on the grassy slope—Janson sat only a short distance away, but he could not touch her. The feelings stood now between them like a stone wall. He had never loved anyone as he loved her, and he had never loved her more completely than he did in this moment—but what could he offer her? She had faced so much in the past two days, had seen so much of her protected, little-girl world shattered—it had been there in her eyes as he had led her away from the open roadway and into the shelter of the trees. She knew her father would never let them be together, and she knew something of what he might be capable of doing in order to keep them apart. Now she was afraid, afraid perhaps for the first time in her life; afraid for both of them, and afraid of losing what it was they had at last found.

"Janson, you know you can't stay here, not after—" Her words trailed off and she sat staring at him for a time from that unbreachable, short distance away.

"I'm not gonna leave you."

"That's not what I meant. I thought—" She stared at him a moment longer, and then turned her eyes away, her cheeks coloring slightly—but Janson understood. He knew now that she would leave with him if he asked her to, but he could not ask her, at least not yet. He had nothing to give her to compare to the life she would give up to become his wife. He knew they could never be together here, for her father had made that more than clear with the lies he had told this day—William Whitley would kill him first, had threatened to kill them both, before he would allow a half-breed dirt farmer to pay court to, or marry, his daughter. Janson could not really believe Whitley would hurt his own daughter—but he could not know that for certain, and he knew, with the look in her eyes, that Elise likely feared for them both now.

He watched her for a moment, watched the light play in her red-gold hair, turning it to copper, watched the face that filled his dreams already—before he had known that she loved him, he had been prepared to leave, had wanted to go, but he could not do that now. He could never leave her behind, but he also could not ask her to go with him. There was nothing in the world he could give her, no home, no life, nothing that could make up for all that she would lose. He loved her, and he could not ask her to live the only kind of life he could give her now—a sharecropped house, a tenant shack, a rented house in a mill village; that was not the kind of life Elise Whitley should know, not the kind of life she should ever have, and it was not the kind of life he would take her to. He wanted to be with her, wanted to spend the remainder of his years as her husband, wanted to have a family with her, to live into old age at her side—but he had nothing he could give her, nothing that was worthy of someone such as Elise Whitley. He had nothing, nothing except—

"I ain't never told you about my place back in Alabama, have I?" he asked, and her eyes came back to him. Suddenly he wanted nothing more than to tell her about those red acres and that white house, about the rich cotton land, and the people who were all somehow a part of him. As he spoke, his eyes left her and settled on the pines at the edge of the clearing, and on something beyond. He told her of falling cotton prices and fire, and of the loss of the land; of his parents, and of what he had seen the night the cotton fields had burned.

"Walter Eason even had th' nerve t' come t' my place not long before I left," he said, his eyes coming back to her. "He offered me a job in th'

Mill, an' a mill house t' live in; said he could use a 'good, hardworkin' boy' like me—that's when I knew I had t' leave. I might not 'a been able t' hold ont' th' land, or t' everythin' my folks had worked s' hard for, but I wasn't gonna let it be like they had never lived. My pa swore he'd never work in that Mill again, an' he swore he'd never see me in it—I left, an' I came here, an' I been workin' an' savin' ever since. I'm gonna go back there someday, an' I'm gonna buy my land back an' I'm gonna sell my cotton wherever I have t' sell it t' hold ont' th' land—"

He moved closer to her, kneeling before her now, taking both her hands in his and squeezing them almost without thought. "Elise, it's th' best cotton land in Alabama. It's rich, an' it's red, an' it'll grow most anythin' a man takes th' time t' plant in it. A man could make a good livin' there; he could put a good roof over his wife's head, raise a family, an' send his children t' a proper school where they could learn just as good as anybody. He could save some money, put it aside for his old age—Elise, we could be real happy there. I could get electricity brought t' th' house, an' runnin' water; you could fix it up just like you want. Elise—" But suddenly he realized what he was saying, what he was asking her. He was asking Elise Whitley, with her big, fine house and her fancy clothes and her motor cars and all the money in the world, to come and live with him in that little six-room house, to leave behind everything she had and live with him in a life such as she could never understand. He was asking Elise Whitley to—

She was smiling, tears coming to her eyes, tears she did not even try to blink away. "Are you asking me to marry you, Janson Sanders?"

For a moment Janson could only stare at her, realizing how clumsy his words had been, how awkward, how without thought. He looked down to where her hands rested in his, realizing for the first time how soft they were, how white, as they rested there in his calloused palms. He lifted his eyes back to hers. "I reckon' I am," he said, watching her face.

Her smile broadened even further. "Well?"

"Well—what?" he asked, unsure.

"Well, ask me."

He released her hands, feeling more awkward in that moment than ever before in his life. He wished he had something fancy to say, something she could always remember, whether she agreed to marry him or not, but he could think of nothing. He sat back and looked at her for a moment, thinking how lovely she was, how very lovely, and how very unalike they were. "I love you. An' I'll always love you, no matter what you say t' what I'm askin' now—but there ain't nothin' I want more in this life than for you t' be my wife. I cain't give you no fancy place t' live; I cain't even give you that place back in Alabama yet, but I'm workin' t' make that real. I'd give you anythin' in this world I had, anythin'; it won't never be what you're used t'; but we'll be happy. We can have a family, an' you can fix th' house up anyway you want. I'll get electricity for you, an' runnin' water—" He stared at her for a moment, knowing she was waiting. Then he took a deep breath, resting his world on the final words. "Elise Whitley, will you marry me?"

She was crying—but a woman ought not to be crying when a man had just asked her to marry him. Then she was in his arms, her breasts pressed to his chest, her arms about his neck, and she was kissing him, crying and saying something he was not sure if he understood. He held her at arms length away, looking at her, seeing the tear-filled eyes, not sure if he should believe—

"What'd you say?" he asked, demanded, staring at her.

"I said yes—" she said, nodding her head and crying still. "I said yes—yes, I'll marry you—"

For a moment he could only stare at her, watching as she wiped the tears from her eyes—then she was in his arms and he held her, his cheek against the softness of her hair: she loved him. She loved him, and she would marry him. That was all that he needed.

After a time he moved to lean back against the tree, her head resting on his shoulder, and he marveled at how she seemed content to just be in his arms—a year or more would not really be so long, he told himself, a year or more until they could leave here, a year or more until he would have the money to buy his land back, a year or more before he could with good conscience make her his wife. He could offer her no kind of life until then, and he would take her to nothing less than the best he could offer. Until then they could be together, see each other, keep her father from finding out, plan and dream and save; he would work harder than he had ever worked in his life, put more money aside, moonshine and haul liquor and do whatever else he had to do to make their leaving a reality. He held her, thinking of all the years that lay ahead of them, of all the living they would have together. He was content, happy as he had not been in many years, simply enjoying the feel of her in his arms, the feel of her against his body—but that made a year or more seem like a very long time. "It won't be that long—" he said, as much to himself as to her.

But she was saying something altogether different. "I wish there would be time to buy a new dress, a white one of course," she said, smiling up at him, her cheeks coloring lightly. "I really wish Mama could be at the wedding, and Stan, but I know that—" then she seemed to note the look on his face as she looked up at him, and the expression in her blue eyes changed. "What's wrong?"

"Elise, we're not gonna be able t' leave anytime soon."

"But—"

"I thought you understood," he said, watching as she sat up to look at him. "It'll be at least a year, or even more, before I've got th' money for us t' be able t' leave."

"But, you can't stay here for a year or longer. Daddy knows how we feel about each other; there's no other reason he would have told you the things he told you today. He has no intention of—" She let her words trail off, but Janson understood.

"Of lettin' you marry no half-Indian dirt farmer—"

"That's not what I said."

"But, that's how he feels."

"That's not how I feel," she said, staring at him. His heritage was a subject they had never discussed. "It doesn't matter to me that—" but her words trailed off again.

"That I'm half Indian? That I'm only half white?" he asked, his eyes never leaving her. "That your children will be mixed blood?"

"I love you, and I want your children. That's what matters."

"But that's not what matters t' him—"

"And that's why you can't stay here—Janson, he said he'd kill you before he'd see us together. You can't stay here, not for a year, not for any time. We have to leave now, today or tomorrow at the latest. We can be married and go to Alabama, and we can live there where he can't—"

"Elise, we cain't do that, at least not yet."

"But, why not? Why—"

"I ain't got th' money yet. I've got a good bit saved, but it ain't enough t' buy my place back. I cain't take you t' no tenant house or no sharecropped land, that wouldn't be no kind 'a life for—"

"But that doesn't matter, not so long as we could be together."

"No, Elise."

"But—"

"No." He reached to gently touch a finger to her lips, silencing her words before they could come. "It'll only be 'til we can get th' money t' leave. We can see each other 'til then, slip aroun' t' keep your pa from finding out. I wouldn't take no chance on lettin' him hurt you, you know that—an' it may not even take a year; I'll be workin' hard as I can, savin' everythin' I can, an' we'll leave as soon as it's possible for us t' go. We'll be t'gether for th' rest 'a our lives; a year or a little more ain't gonna be s' long t' wait."

She took his hand and drew it to her heart, holding it tightly. Her blue eyes were worried, frightened. "Daddy wouldn't hurt me, I know that—but, Janson, he said he'll kill you before he lets us be together. He'll—" For a moment it seemed she could only stare at him, then she moved into his arms and he held her, feeling her press her cheek to the roughness of his workshirt where it covered his shoulder, a moment later feeling the warmth of her tears soak through the fabric there.

"Don't worry," he told her quietly, his lips against the softness of her hair. "Ain't nothin' gonna happen t' either one 'a us. Ain't nothin'—" But he could hear her father's words, somewhere in his mind—I'd see her dead as well before I'd see her with the likes of you.

I'd see her dead—

ELISE CROSSED the wide yard a few hours later that afternoon, going toward the front of the great house. Behind her, just out of sight at the edge of the woods, Janson stood watching—she knew he was there, knew that he would stay there until she left his sight, and long after. The knowledge of his presence made her feel only more secure, only more protected—not that she had any reason to fear, no matter what her father had said, for she knew that it was Janson, and not she herself, who was in danger. But his watching only confirmed his love, and it made her love him only more—Janson loved her; how she had longed to hear him say those words. But that love had only put him in danger. If her father were ever to find out—

But she could not let that happen. She would keep Janson safe, no matter the lies she had to tell. Her father had to believe, everyone had to believe, that anything they might have felt for each other had died forever this day. She could never let her feelings show, never her love or caring, for she knew it could cost Janson dearly. Her mind was still spinning from all she had learned in the past two days, all she now knew her father could be capable of—how could she have lived so blindly all her life to never have seen, to never have known, that her father could hurt someone so terribly if it suited his aims. It was still so hard to believe, to know that her father could hurt Janson, that he could even—

But she knew it could happen. Her father would never let her marry Janson—she knew that now—and he would do anything he had to do to keep them apart. William Whitley had his own ideas as to what his daughter's future would be, his own reasons, his own purposes—but Elise knew what she wanted for her life. That life would be very little as she had always thought it would be, but somehow that did not matter anymore. She would be with Janson, and she would be his wife—and she would keep him safe until the day they could leave here together, no matter what she had to do to assure that day would come. No matter.

Janson had talked to her today as he had never talked to her before, had told her things, spun her visions in words she knew now she would never forget. They had sat for hours, holding hands atop his knee, their fingers intertwined as if no one and no thing could ever pull them apart again—he had told her about Alabama, about Eason County, about the little house he would take her to someday, about his grandparents and his kin; about fields of white cotton and people he had known and how much his parents had loved each other. He had told her about the red hills and the blue sky and the tall, straight pines, until she could see it all so clearly in her mind. He wanted a large family, and he wanted to farm the land his father had farmed—and he wanted his sons, their sons, to farm it one day. He had given her so many dreams to dream, so many visions to see, and it would all be true one day, when she could at last become Janson's wife—Janson's wife, for that day she could lie, and she could deceive, and she could do it all so easily. She was her father's daughter, after all.

She walked up the wide front steps and onto the veranda. The sheriff's car was parked in the curve of the drive before the house; she knew he was probably inside now, discussing politics with her father in the front parlor. If she was very lucky, she might be able to slip into the house and up the stairs to her room before anyone could even know she was home. She did not want to see anyone just yet, least of all her father; she needed time to gather her thoughts and calm her temper before she had to face him. At the moment she still wanted nothing more than to slap his face and tell him what it was she truly thought of him and his lies—but she knew she could not do that. And, for Janson's sake, she knew she never would.

She stopped for a moment with her hand on the front doorknob, looking back toward the woods one last time. There was a slight movement there, a touch of blue among the greens and browns of the trees—Janson, watching and loving her. Somehow that knowledge gave her the strength to turn the knob and enter her father's house—never her home again, for her home was wherever Janson was. Her home was that little white house Janson had told her of, that little white house she could now see so clearly in her mind, that place where they would live together one day when they could at last leave here.

She quietly closed the door behind herself, hearing the sounds of muffled voices from just beyond the open parlor doorway to her right.

She made her way toward the stairs and started up, anxious to reach the upstairs and the safety of her room.

"Elise—"

She froze where she was for a moment, halfway up the stairs, and turned back, finding her father staring at her from where he stood just within the doorway to the front parlor. There was a set expression on his face as he looked up at her, his teeth clenched down on the unlit cigar in his mouth, and a fresh surge of anger filled her at the sight of him, and at the knowledge of what he had done to her, and to Janson. She wanted nothing more than to strike him, to tell him how much she hated him for the danger he was to Janson—but she knew she could not. He stared up at her, seeming not to notice her hands clenching into fists at her sides with the feelings that surged through her, and she hated him all the more that he did not notice.

"Come into the parlor for a minute. Sheriff Hill has something to talk to you about." He waited for her to descend the stairs before he turned and went back into the room. Elise crossed the hallway going toward the open parlor door, trying to force a control over her emotions—her feelings could never show. Never. Not toward her father. Not toward Janson—she smoothed her hands over her bob, took a deep breath, and made herself walk through the doorway and into the room.

Sheriff Hill stood from the chair he had been sitting in before the tall front windows. He looked exhausted, with dark circles under his eyes, as if he had slept little the night before. His clothes were rumpled, and there was a serious expression on his usually kind face—something's wrong, a voice inside of her said. Her eyes moved to her mother where she sat on the sofa across the room, Martha Whitley's hands fidgeting at her needlepoint. Her father stood now, silent and distant, before the fireplace. He lit his cigar, and then puffed on it heavily, his eyes settling on the sheriff through the blue haze of smoke.

"Elise—Miss Whitley—I thought it might be better that I tell you," the sheriff began, and her eyes came back to rest on him, "before some of the County gossips get a chance, considering, well—" He turned his hat in his hands, and a cold chill moved up her spine. "It's about Ethan Bennett and Phyllis Ann—"

Ethan Bennett and Phyllis Ann—she thought, then: please, God, no more.

ETHAN BENNETT was dead, and Phyllis Ann had killed him—Elise sat on the bed in her room a short while later, one leg tucked beneath her, her back against the tall, wooden headboard of the bed. She reached to take up a favorite, indestructible Roanoke doll from where it usually rested against the pillows, and held it securely in her arms as she stared at the wide expanse of white counterpane before her, trying to let the full realization sink in—Ethan Bennett was dead, and Phyllis Ann had killed him. Phyllis Ann had—

She wondered now if there had been anything she could have done weeks, or even months, before that might have prevented things from ever having gone this far. Phyllis Ann had at one time been her best friend; they had once been closer than many sisters—Phyllis Ann had even asked for her help no more than weeks ago, but Elise had refused to give it. She had known what Ethan Bennett could be capable of doing, had seen the bruises and blacked eyes, even the broken collarbone the day of Phyllis Ann's tenth birthday. But this time Ethan Bennett had beaten his daughter one time too many; this time she had taken up a fireplace poker and had ended his life—there would be no need for a trial, no need for punishment, the sheriff had said, for it had been clearly a case of self defense. Phyllis Ann's life would go on much as it had always gone on, with the one exception—she would never have to fear her father again.

Elise thought briefly about going to see her, about trying to forgive and forget all that had happened between them over these months, but she knew she could not. She felt a great deal of pity for Phyllis Ann, for all that she had gone through, and for all she was going through even now, but she could not forgive, and she could not forget—Phyllis Ann had caused Alfred's death. Elise could never forgive that.

But it was over now. Ethan Bennett was dead. He would never again be a threat to anyone. And the trial, finally scheduled for only weeks in the future, the trial where Bennett would have at last had to face a judge and jury for what he had tried to do to her, the trial she had tried so hard not to think about, would never take place. Her attacker was dead. It was over.

She sat at the supper table hours later that night, staring over the bowed heads at her father as he offered the blessing over the food, and she found herself wondering if he prayed to the same God that Ethan Bennett had prayed to. All her life he had been a leading member of the Baptist Church, a leading member of the community; she had always thought him so upstanding and good and right, and had felt herself so far superior to Phyllis Ann because she knew that he would never hurt her, would never beat her as Phyllis Ann's father had so often beaten her. He might be demanding and short tempered and single-minded, but he was still her father, and he wanted only what was best for her—how blind she had been. She should have known, should have seen so long ago, in those days when he had first begun to try to push her into a marriage with J.C., a marriage she did not want, with a man she did not love; she should have known when he had become so demanding and forceful—she hadn't even realized when she had seen what he had done to Gilbert Baskin.

But she knew now. He had hurt her just as surely as any beating could ever have hurt her. He had lied; had tried to tear her and Janson apart, and had come so horribly close to achieving that goal. He did not believe that Janson was good enough to marry his daughter—she had known that all along, but somehow she had convinced herself that it did not matter, that her love for Janson could convince him, but now she knew differently. Her father would never allow her to marry a farmhand, a small farmer, a man who was only half white, no matter how much she might love him, no matter how much she might beg and plead, for she was William Whitley's daughter, and she would never be allowed to marry someone her father thought so far beneath her. He had plans for her future, plans for her and J.C., plans that would one day net him the cotton mill he had wanted for so many years—and now Janson Sanders was standing in his way. She knew now that her father could be capable of doing anything to achieve his goals. Anything. And she knew a little of what he was capable of doing to anyone he believed stood in his way.

She no longer felt superior to anyone. She only felt afraid.

The following days were the happiest of her life, and also the most worry-filled. Her thoughts rarely strayed from Janson and the plans they had made. She thought of the little house he had told her of, the little house that would be all their own. She thought about furniture in the rooms and flowers in the yard. She thought of cooking for him, and cleaning for him, and knitting baby clothes; she thought of going to sleep beside him at night, and waking up beside him in the mornings. There would not be a lot of money—she knew that—but it did not matter. Old people might say you could not live on love alone, but she and Janson would, if they had to.

There was such little time they could be together now. Her father had taken from them the pretext of friendship, and now their moments had to be stolen in between times she had to be with her family, and times that he had work to do for her father. There was constantly the worry that someone might find out, that Janson would never be safe so long as they remained here—and, always, when he was not in her sight, there was the fear that her father might know, that anything might happen to Janson. That anything might already have.

They tried to meet each day, for whatever few minutes they might have. A kiss, a touch, a moment to be in his arms, or to look into his eyes, a moment to hear him say that he loved her, to hear him speak of the place they would go one day to be safe, one day when they would never have to be separated again. Often she would wait for hours when he could not come, and, as many times as not, he could not tell her where he had been, or what he had been doing—work for her father, he would say, and, at last, she quit asking. There was always the fear, when he was a moment late, or when there was no excuse she could find in order to meet him, that something could have happened, that he might be hurt, that—

As the weeks passed, Elise began to realize that she had taken on the most difficult task of her life. No one could know how she felt—no one, for her father might find out. She could never let her feelings show, never let anyone know that she waited now only for the day she would leave here with Janson, waited only for the day when she knew he would be safe, the day when she would at last become his wife. The days now seemed to slow almost to a standstill; it seemed as if the year, the year Janson said it would take before they would have the money to leave, would never pass. Janson was working so hard, taking on any odd work he might find, and any work her father might give him—and she would not bring herself any longer to ask what that work might be; she knew he would not tell, and she also knew that she really did not want to know. He had shown her the money he had already saved, unknotting it from an old sock he had brought from where he kept it hidden in his room, and she had begun to save as well, from the money her father gave her weekly for dresses and 'doodads and frip-frappery' as he called it—to do without a dress or a new pair of shoes or a fresh compact of rouge was little enough payment for their future together, and it would be justice enough that her father would pay for it in even that small way. She had not told Janson what she was doing. He could be so irritatingly old-fashioned about most things, that she did not think he would accept money from a woman, not even the woman he was going to marry. She would tell him once they were away from here; he could fuss all he wanted then.

The new school term would begin in a matter of only a few weeks there in the County, and she had already been enrolled in school there for the year. It had been her mother's idea, and her own, but now she wished the notion had never come up. School would take time away that she might have been able to spend with Janson—but it was too late to back out now. Her father had already agreed to her returning to school, telling her that it would at least keep her occupied and out of trouble—and J.C. would want an educated wife, she had realized, and William Whitley would see to it that J.C. Cooper would have what he wanted. The summer was drawing toward a close, and there would be a long year ahead before she and Janson could leave together—if only she could keep him safe until then. If only they could keep her father fooled. If only—

Elise sat waiting at the edge of the clearing on a hot Sunday afternoon in mid-August. She worried with the long strand of rhinestones that hung about her neck, staring unseeingly at the grass and weeds that grew thickly in a clump near where she sat with her legs curled beneath her. She had been waiting here for more than an hour now—and still there was no sign of Janson.

She had not seen him since early the morning before—there had been no more than a moment then; there was work he had to do for her father, and he was already running late. He had held her in his arms, and kissed her for a long moment, and then had looked down at her as if he were again trying to memorize her every feature—he would meet her later in the afternoon, he had told her, here in the clearing, if he finished with the work in time. If not, then he would see her the next morning, before she would have to leave for church, if she could find an excuse to get away. She had waited, afternoon and morning both, and still he had not come. Now she was worried. And frightened. Her father could have found out. Janson could be lying somewhere, hurt, bleeding, maybe even—she tried to think of any instance when she might have given even the slightest sign toward her feelings, the slightest signal that she and Janson—but she could remember nothing. She had been so careful, so very careful—if she had given her father even the smallest reason to suspect—

But she could not let herself think about that now. She caught herself chewing nervously at a thumbnail, and she made herself stop—if he was all right, then he would come to her. All she could do for now was wait. All she could do was—

The clearing was quiet, the woods silent behind her. She got up from where she sat and paced a short distance into the clearing, worry filling her—surely her father was just keeping him busy. Janson was working, earning money he could save toward their future. He was all right. He had to be all right. He had to—

There was a sound behind her, the rustle of leaves in the woods, the crack of a twig, and she turned in that direction. It had to be—Janson, just coming into sight, bowing to avoid the low limb of a young tree. He was dressed in overalls and a workshirt, his hair less than neatly combed—but he would have come straight to her from whatever work he had been doing; he would have—

She rushed into his arms, almost knocking him from his feet in her rush to touch him. "I was so afraid. I thought Daddy had—" But she never finished the thought. His mouth came to hers, sending her senses reeling and almost taking her breath away. He held her close against him, his arms tight around her. She could feel the heat of his body against hers, and she prayed that he would never let her go.

"I was hopin' you'd be here. I wasn't sure, after I couldn't come yesterday or this mornin'—" He stared down at her, holding her close against him still as his eyes moved over her face.

"I was so worried. I thought that—"

"I'm all right. Don't be worryin' about me; your pa don't know nothin' about us—"

"But, he could. If he finds out—"

"He ain't gonna find out—"

"But, if he does, he could—" But his mouth came to hers again, silencing her words. Even as her body pressed against his, and his arms tightened around her, drawing her even closer, only one thought remained in her mind—it could not go on like this forever. He was too much in danger, and each time they were together like this only increased that danger to him. Something would have to happen—something.

And she could only fear what that something might be.

THE DOWNTOWN section of Main Street in Goodwin was busy the first Saturday in September as William Whitley stood talking to Hiram Cooper. William stood on the brick-paving before Dobbins's Drugstore, one foot up on the running board of Cooper's Packard—they had been discussing politics for the past several minutes now as Hiram waited for his son, J.C., to return from the drugstore, the two men debating over the likely candidates for the Presidency now that Calvin Coolidge had announced that he did "not choose to run" for reelection. Cooper had his opinions, as did William—but presidential politics really mattered very little to William Whitley, so long as the winner in the race was a Republican, was capable of keeping prosperity at its current booming pace, and was staunchly in favor of continuing Prohibition, for, thanks to the Women's Christian Temperance Union and all the shouting preachers, the Volstead Act had made him nothing but a wealthier man.

But it was not politics or Prohibition that concerned William Whitley at the moment; it was Cooper's son, J.C., instead.

The boy had not been to call on Elise in weeks now. He had never been too attentive, but it seemed as of late that he had lost all interest in the girl. He was always elsewhere occupied, with his mind on things other than what he should be thinking of—namely that of a wife and a family and settling down as he should. And he was spending altogether too much time with Phyllis Ann Bennett.

William had been almost unable to believe his own hearing when he had been told that Hiram Cooper's son was spending so much of his days, and his evenings, at the Bennett house. The boy had never seemed the type to go sniffing around after a cheap little piece like that—and, truly, William had never thought him man enough. He had even allowed himself to wonder on occasion what kind of wedding night his daughter would have once married to the boy—but perhaps J.C. was a man after all, and perhaps that was for the best. Elise needed a strong hand to deal with her; William himself had been faced with enough trouble in the past just in keeping her in line, and had known that J.C. would never be able to handle her—but perhaps he had been wrong. That possibility made J.C. Cooper an even more attractive candidate for a son-in-law—and William was not about to allow Phyllis Ann Bennett to ruin his plans at this late date. Elise had become much less argumentative in the past few weeks, much easier to handle, and perhaps she had at last seen that her father was doing only what he knew was best for her, and for all else concerned. Now all William had to worry about was one backwards boy—and J.C. Cooper would not present a problem of himself now; William would not allow it.

"We haven't been seeing too much of J.C. lately," William said, finally broaching the subject he had intended to bring up all along. "Elise has been saying how much she misses not seeing the boy."

"I haven't seen too much of J.C. myself, lately," Hiram said, glancing toward the front of the drugstore building, as if he expected J.C. to reappear at any moment. "He's always off somewhere, busy—"

"I hear he's spending a lot of time out at the Bennett place."

For a moment Hiram Cooper's eyes came back to him, and then he looked away again—but not before William had seen in them a look he had found in his own eyes once, in the days before he had seen to it that Elise and the half-breed farmhand—

When Hiram did not speak, William continued on his own, feeling sorry for the man in a way that only one father could feel for another, and, yet, in the same moment, despising him for the weakness that would not allow him to take the situation in hand, as William himself had done. "Do you really think it's a good idea for J.C. to be seeing so much of a girl like Phyllis Ann?"

"There's not much I can do with J.C.; there's not much that anyone can do with him anymore," Hiram said, staring again toward the front of the drugstore, speaking almost as if he had forgotten William's presence. "He's changed since he's taken up with that girl, and he won't listen to me, or to anyone, about her. I'd always hoped that he and Elise would—" For a moment he fell silent. "I just don't know now. I just—"

William opened his mouth to respond, but quickly closed it as he saw J.C. walk out the front door of Dobbins's. The boy stopped on the sidewalk before the drugstore and stared at him for a moment, and then came toward the car—he even looks different, William thought. I'll be damned if he doesn't even look—

J.C. stopped at the passenger side of his father's car, looking at William across the hood of the Packard. He stared through the round lenses of his glasses, a self-assurance in his expression that William had never seen there before—I'll be damned if he's not getting under Phyllis Ann's skirts, William thought. I'll be damned if—

"Hello, Mr. Whitley," the boy said, a tone in his voice showing a maturity that even further surprised William.

"Well, hello yourself, son—I was just telling your father how much we miss not seeing you around our place anymore. Elise had been wondering why you'd quit calling on her."

"I've been busy lately, I guess."

Yeah, and I know doing what—William thought, watching as J.C. moved toward the car door in preparation of getting into the vehicle.

"Well, I hope you won't be too busy to come to dinner after church on Sunday. Elise would really like to see you."

There was an almost imperceptible change in the boy's expression, the raising of an eyebrow, the hint of amusement at one corner of his mouth. William had the clear impression that J.C. was fully aware of what he was trying to do—and that he had no intention of going along with anything that he did not want to go along with.

"Yes, I'd like to see Elise," the boy said after a moment. "I know I've been neglecting my friends lately—and Elise is certainly one of my oldest friends—" The word was stressed purposefully, that damned amusement again playing at one corner of the boy's mouth, irritating William all the more. "I'd like very much to come to dinner on Sunday—but I'll have to leave early. I promised to take Phyllis Ann for a drive Sunday afternoon." He got into the car and shut the door behind himself, then leaned across the seat to speak out the open door at his father's side. "We'll see you in church Sunday, Mr. Whitley—Phyllis Ann and I, that is—"

William took his foot from the running board of the Packard and stepped back, watching as Hiram Cooper shut the door and got the car in gear, and, after a moment, backed it out into the traffic on Main Street. He stepped up onto the sidewalk, and then turned back to find J.C. staring at him through the window as the car started away. Irritation filled William—J.C. Cooper was going to be more difficult to handle than he had ever thought it possible for him to be. William could see that clearly now—for it was a young man, and not a boy, who stared at him from the window of that car; a young man William feared he would never again be able to control.

"YOU PROMISED to spend Sunday with me!" Phyllis Ann threw herself down on the sofa in her parlor a short while later, shooting an angry look at J.C. where he stood across the room near the mantlepiece.

"And I will, most of the day, anyway."

"You can't go to dinner at her house; I won't let you!"

J.C.'s eyebrow rose, but he did not respond, making her only angrier—damn him, he was developing a habit of responding to her demands in that way, with silence, sometimes even with a smile. There was little she could do with him now, for there was little left in him of the boy she had always been able to control and second-guess; instead was this man she could increasingly seldom seem to maneuver or cajole. He still loved her—she was quite certain of that—but in the time since her father's death, he had somehow changed, had matured, become more assured and self-confident. And she hated him for it.

In the days after her father had died, there had been a hundred decisions to be made, arrangements to be taken care of, the business to consider, running the house and looking after the sharecropped farms; and it had all seemed to fall on her shoulders. Her mother had never once made a decision in all her life, and had been completely unable to cope with all that now had to be done, until even she had turned to Phyllis Ann. There had been so many pressures, so many burdens falling on her, so many people asking so many questions—and then J.C. had stepped in. He had been there all along, looking at her as if he were an adoring puppy each time she turned his way, stupidly trying to console and comfort and help, and doing a poor job of it all—and then, when she had needed someone the most, he had stepped in and had begun to make the decisions for her. He had made arrangements for the funeral, had explained and advised on matters concerning the business that had now seemed her responsibility, and had looked after the problems of the sharecroppers—the more he helped, the more she leaned on him, and the more she leaned on him, the stronger he had seemed to become. Within weeks, the air of backward, self-conscious shyness that had always seemed to be about him was seldom apparent anymore. He no longer went into fits of blushes at her look, or fidgeted nervously with his glasses whenever she was near, but instead looked her in the eye and spoke up in a voice that was rapidly taking on the tones of a self-assured man.

The first time she had thrown a tantrum with him, he had simply walked out. After days when he had not come back, she had called and apologized—she had missed him; it was as simple as that. And she needed him—that had been the hardest thing of all for her to realize; she needed J.C. Cooper, not for what she could use him for, or for the amusement and distraction he could provide, but because of who and what he was.

They were intimate—"discretely," as J.C. put it, in order to protect her reputation and her mother's sensibilities, and Phyllis Ann had begun to find herself looking forward to their times together. Somehow it felt good for him to hold her, knowing that he had seen something of her at her worst, and that he still cared. She even wondered at times if she could be falling in love with him—but she knew that could not be. How could she be in love with someone she had laughed at and ridiculed all his life.

But she was jealous now, jealous as she had never been before—and of Elise. It made her angry that she felt such jealousy, and angrier still that he seemed to see and recognize it—she wanted to slap him, to wipe that look of knowing and self-assurance from his face; to wipe that look away forever.

"Phyllis Ann, you cannot stop me from going anywhere I please to go," he said at last in a quiet voice, making her clench her hands into fists in her lap to keep from striking him.

"Yes, I can! I won't let you near me again if you go! I mean it—never again!"

"Oh?" he asked in that quiet voice, and she felt her nails cut into the flesh of her palms with the effort not to rake them across his face—she wanted to slap him, to hurt him, now even more than she ever had before. She would have been more comfortable with rage from him than this calm self-assurance.

"I mean it! I won't let you touch me again!"

"Fine, if that's the way you want it."

He turned and took up his hat from the chair where he had laid it earlier, then started for the door—but something inside of her snapped. She lunged from the sofa and struck out at him, wanting only to hurt him, but he grabbed her by the wrists instead, dropping his hat to the floor, and held her still in front of him, looking down at her with a concerned expression in his eyes.

"You goddamn son-of-a-bitch! I won't let you use me and then just throw me away!" She struggled against him, but he refused to release her, holding her gently but firmly until she finally exhausted herself. "You son-of-a-bitch! You goddamn—you—"

"I've never used you, Phyllis Ann, though God knows you've used me." There was pain in his eyes that she had never seen there before, and she wanted it to stay there, wanted him to hurt as she had hurt all her life—but the pain was soon replaced by pity, pity for himself as well as for her, and she began to struggle against him again, hating him in that moment as much as she had ever hated anyone in her life. "I love you—" he said. "God in heaven, I don't know why, but I do. If you'd only learn to ask instead of demand—" He let his words fall silent for a moment as he stared at her. "I gave my word that I'd have Sunday dinner with the Whitleys—"

"Because you want to see Elise!"

"—because the Whitleys have been friends to my family for years. Elise is a friend of mine—she was once even a friend of yours—but I'm not in love with her. I'm in love with you; the sooner you realize that, the better off we'll both be."

She yanked her wrists free from his grasp, and this time he released her without struggle. She stared up at him, her anger none the less, her hatred, her jealousy—how she despised him, hated him for making her feel this way. How she—"If you go, don't bother to come back."

But he only bent and picked up his hat, and then turned and started for the door.

"I mean it! If you go to Elise, don't come back to me!"

He went on through the door and closed it behind himself. For a moment she could only stare, not believing he had gone, not believing he had left her—and then she picked up a vase from a nearby table and flung it across the room, seeing it shatter against the door he had just gone through, and then watching as it fell in pieces to the rug beneath.

"Damn you!" she screamed into the empty room. "Damn you—and damn Elise!" She sat down heavily on the sofa again, continuing to stare at the closed door. Her anger would not leave, and neither would her hatred. Her breathing was heavy, furious.

It was a long time before she moved, before she spoke. When she did, her voice was quieter, but her words were no less filled with hatred.

"Damn you both," she said, still staring at the closed door. "Damn you both straight to hell—"

# 17

J.C. COOPER SAT IN THE front parlor of the Whitley house that following afternoon after Sunday dinner, pointedly trying to ignore the remarks William Whitley was making—but it was getting harder to ignore them, harder to ignore them, and also harder to ignore the complacent man who sat there staring at him as he made thinly veiled comments about J.C. and the life he had already chosen to have for himself.

"A young man has to be careful when it comes to thinking about his future," Whitley said for the second time, his eyes directed at J.C. and Elise where they sat only a short distance away on the parlor sofa. J.C. stared at him, not speaking—he had known this was coming, had known from the moment he had first been invited here to Sunday dinner. Whitley would never miss the opportunity to once again try to push a match between his daughter and J.C.—but it was a match J.C. was determined to have none of, a match that he would never have, no matter what it was this man wanted.

"If a man makes a mistake when he's your age, it'll haunt him the remainder of his life—you may not believe that now, but it's true, and it's the same thing I've told my own sons." Whitley patted his stomach with satisfaction, his eyes moving from J.C. to Elise, and then back again. J.C. clenched his jaw with irritation, wishing there were some way now that he could leave the room, and the house, without his leaving being the height of rudeness—but there was no way. He was stuck here, stuck here to listen to William Whitley's rude remarks and broad hints concerning J.C.'s relationship with Phyllis Ann, when the relationship was none of Whitley's business in the first place. J.C. was quite capable of handling his own affairs without interference from anyone, least of all from William Whitley—all the man wanted was to get his hands on the cotton mill anyway, J.C. told himself, and William Whitley was more than willing to sell his daughter in marriage to J.C., or to anyone else if he had to, to assure that.

But J.C. was not buying. For the first time in his life he knew exactly what it was he wanted, and he knew that he could have it. Phyllis Ann might be spoiled and bad-tempered and unpredictable, more so than he had ever dreamed possible, but still he loved her, as he had always loved her, as he always would. He might love Elise as a sister—but it was Phyllis Ann that he was in love with, often beyond reason or sanity he well knew. He had seen her faults and imperfections; he knew they were there, but he loved her still in spite of them all. Her father had done nothing all her life but teach her violence—now all J.C. wanted was to teach her love. All he ever wanted was to teach her love.

He had never been so surprised or so happy in all his life as he had been the day of the Fourth of July picnic, two months ago now, when Phyllis Ann had approached him. She had flirted and toyed with him, as no girl had ever done before in his life—and, later, as they were parked in his car in a deserted spot on a country road, they had taken each other. Even in his inexperience, he had known that he had not been the first, but that did not matter. She was loving him, letting him love her as he had dreamed of doing on so many nights when he had awakened in his bed in a cold sweat, and that was all that was important.

That had been the most wonderful day of his life, a day that he had thought would never be—but it had become the darkest day possible for her. She had returned home from their closeness only to be met by her father's drunken rage. He had beaten her, hurt her horribly, and she had at last had to kill him in order to save her own life—and, even now, J.C. wondered if it had not been his own fault. If he had only had more courage, if he had only been more of a man, he would have walked her to her door that night to ask for her hand, and, in doing so, he might have prevented everything.

But at least the violence was over for her now, the hurting, and she would never have to face such a horror again. J.C. had been at her side from the moment he had been told, offering her condolence and help, and feeling vastly inadequate to provide either—and then she had needed him. For the first time in his life, someone had really needed him, not for his father's money or the Cooper name, but for something he could offer from inside himself. There had been arrangements to be made, people to notify, and he had taken care of all that. He had handled matters concerning the business and the many sharecropped and tenanted farms, and had done his best to shield both her and her mother from the more curious and morbid side of their neighbors. From that day on he had openly courted Phyllis Ann, squiring her about publicly, using his own family's good name in order to lessen the damage done her own; and finally the talk had died down, at least to his own hearing. She had come to ask his opinion only more and more over the weeks, to seek his advice, and, the more she had leaned on him, the more he had dared to allow himself to believe that she might really love him.

And then he had met with the darker side of her nature. Over the weeks since her father's death, he had almost allowed himself to forget the girl who had laughed at him and tormented him all his life. He had almost forgotten the selfish, spiteful, mean-tempered creature with an acid tongue and a liking for hurting other people. The Phyllis Ann he knew now was nothing like that; she was soft and beautiful, and she thought well of him—and then her temper had come over some stupid incident, and words he had never thought to hear a woman say, and a viciousness and a cruelty such as he had never seen before. He had been unable to look at her, to see her, and to know how wrong he had been. And so he had walked out.

Days later, days that had been the loneliest in his life, she had called to apologize, once again the sweet, gentle girl he was in love with.

But he had never again been able to forget the Phyllis Ann he had seen that day, and again and again she had returned. There were days when he thought he could no longer live with the wild swings of her moods, days when he thought he could take no more of her viciousness, her sharp-tongued cruelty, or her self-centered, spoiled demands—but there were also days when she was soft and loving, clinging to him when they lay together, and looking at him in a way afterwards that told him that she did love him. He often still thought of ending the relationship, but he knew that he could not, and that he never would. He loved her, in spite of her very nature, or maybe because of it; he loved her—not the spiteful woman with the acid words and cruel nature, but the girl inside of her, lost and alone, a girl brought up on nothing but hatred and violence and pain. He knew that he saw something inside of her that few other people saw, a vulnerability and an innocence that had been hurt too many times to ever trust or love anyone freely again. He knew that she loved him, as much as she could love anyone. And he knew that he loved her. She had somehow given him a sense of self-worth and value, a sense of being needed. She was his lover, amazing him with a world of sensation beyond anything he had ever imagined—and she had brought something out of him that had been totally unexpected, even by himself, a strength and a self-reliance that had surprised even him, and a sense of maturity and confidence that had been lacking all his life.

Yesterday she had told him never to come back if he saw Elise today, or if he had dinner at the Whitley house—but he knew that he would go back to her. He loved Phyllis Ann, though he often wished he did not, and he intended to spend the remainder of his days with her, in spite of the opinions of people like William Whitley. Even in spite of Phyllis Ann herself if he had to.

Mrs. Whitley was fidgeting now with her knitting in a chair not far from where her husband sat. She stared at Whitley, her eyes never once leaving his face, almost as if she were trying to draw his attention and silence his words. When he lit a cigar and drew in on it heavily, she began to cough, quietly, but rather deliberately, until he silenced her with a look that would have at one time frozen J.C. in his tracks, then, almost without pausing for breath, he continued on with some portent of doom for J.C. should he continue with making a bad match.

J.C. glanced toward Elise where she sat beside him, wondering again if she felt as uncomfortable as he under her father's proddings, but he realized suddenly that she seemed to be paying little attention to anything that was being said around her. Her eyes kept wandering toward the mantle clock, as if there were some other place she ought to be. Until today she had always seemed embarrassed and ill-at-ease with her father's less than tactful matchmaking, but it seemed now as if it mattered little to her, as if something had changed, and as if something else mattered a great deal more. Her thoughts were clearly elsewhere, her mind occupied as she glanced again toward the mantle clock and unconsciously fingered the long strand of beads that hung about her neck.

"A lot of young men don't realize what an important decision it is they're making in choosing a wife," Whitley said, staring at them through the blue haze of smoke around him. His eyes moved to Elise, then back to J.C. again with meaning. "They let feelings and other things that some women can stir up in a man make the decision for them—" Mrs. Whitley's head rose sharply, but her husband seemed not to notice, or to care. "A man's got to use good, common sense in making the most important choice in his life. He's got to marry with the future in mind—but there's many a man who'll spend more thought at breeding his livestock than he will at what sort of brood he himself might sire. You'd never consider breeding just any heifer with a prize bull, or a blooded bitch with a mongrel hound, now, would you?"

Mrs. Whitley's face had drained of color, her eyes set on her husband's face as if she could not believe what she herself had heard him say. She looked quickly toward the two young people, then back to Whitley again. She cleared her throat loudly, her cheeks starting to redden, and opened her mouth as if she were about to speak, but no words came out.

J.C. tightened his hands into fists—the meaning was clear, and, at last, Whitley had gone too far. Until now J.C. had tolerated his comments, knowing them for what they were, but no more. He would ask Whitley to step outside. He would ask Whitley to step outside, and then he would—

But he caught sight of Elise at the edge of his field of vision, and then turned fully to look at her, surprised to find that, instead of embarrassment as he had expected, there was an absolute fury in her eyes. Her jaw was set, her teeth clenched tightly, her blue eyes angry as J.C. had never before seen them in his life. She looked almost as if she wanted to strike her father, almost as if she wanted to scream and yell in fury—but instead she held her control, her own hands tightening in her lap, a muscle working slightly in her jaw. She refused to allow the anger to explode as it so obviously threatened to, but, instead, only further tightened the control over herself, staring with something very near to hatred at her own father.

There was something wrong here, something very wrong, J.C. told himself, something far beyond the self-serving pushings and insulting comments that Whitley was making. J.C. had never before seen anyone in such angry control, and he felt somehow responsible for it, and for the tension that now filled the room. He knew that he had to get Elise away from her father before that control could break—and he knew that every word the man spoke now only brought that possibility closer.

"Elise, perhaps you'd like to go for a walk?" he asked, interrupting her father's words mid-sentence.

"Yes, I'd like that very much," she said, through teeth that were still almost clenched.

J.C. glanced at Whitley as he stood, seeing the obvious delight on the man's face—pompous ass, he thought, and led Elise from the room.

She seemed to relax almost the moment they left her father's sight. J.C. watched her, seeing the tension drain away as they walked from the house and out onto the front veranda. She hooked her arm through his and led him down into the yard and out across it without stopping, until they left sight of the house. They entered the woods, walking slowly arm-in-arm until they reached a clearing there, and then they stopped.

J.C. sat down on a stump, watching her as she bent to pick a wildflower. The angry, forced control was gone now, and she seemed once again the carefree girl he had known all his life, talking about mischief they had made as children. He relaxed as well, feeling the comfortable familiarity of her words. They had both changed greatly from the children who had broken the kitchen window and then lied so poorly to cover it. He was a man now, and she a woman—but still there was that comfort of experiences shared, the familiarity of a face long known. There was a feeling of kinship with her, of family, as he had felt with few other people.

"Your father doesn't give up easily," he smiled and remarked, absently adjusting his glasses with one hand as he watched her.

"No, but I wish he did." There was a sigh, a feeling of sadness and wishing about her for a moment. "I really wish he did."

"Well, he'll have to give up on me—"

"Don't you know by now that he never gives up on anything?" She smiled—rather bitterly, J.C. thought.

"He can't very well keep trying to get the two of us married once I'm married to someone else, can he?"

Her smile was immediate, genuine, and very happy for him. "You're getting married? That's wonderful!"

He grinned. "I think so."

"Phyllis Ann?" Her face became speculative.

"Yes."

"I hope you know what you're doing—"

"So do I." There was doubt, but only a bit, within him.

"You've been in love with her all along, haven't you, since we were children?" she asked, smiling again. "I think I've always known, in a way, how you felt about her."

"Yes. I don't think I can ever remember not feeling like this." For once there was acceptance of his decision and his choice. Elise might not like Phyllis Ann, and perhaps with good reason, but still she respected him enough to honor his feelings. She was genuinely happy for him, wishing him nothing but the best in the future, no matter what her feelings might be for Phyllis Ann. Her acceptance and well-wishes felt good—from everyone else he had received only arguments, resistance, and even pity. Elise was different; even after everything else, she was still his friend. "It's nice, for once not to have someone tell me that I've lost my senses," he said.

"People giving you a hard time?"

"Pretty much. I guess they can't seem to understand how I feel. I know Phyllis Ann; I know how she is, and I still love her. No one else seems to be able to see in her what I see. She's not a bad person; she's just had a rough time of it, with her father and all. I think we can be happy. I really do. She's—" There came a sound from behind him, a movement in the woods, the loud crack of a branch, cutting short his words. Elise's expression changed quickly. She was looking past him now and through the trees, her mind obviously more on what she saw there than on what he had been saying. J.C. turned and looked, thinking for a moment that he saw movement there, but unsure. "I thought I heard something—"

"I didn't hear anything—" she said, too quickly it seemed. There was a nervous pitch to her voice now, and her eyes showed a sudden preoccupation when he looked at her again. "So, when's the wedding? Have you proposed to her yet?" But her eyes moved past him again and back to the woods even as she spoke.

"Not yet, we still have some things to work out—" Once again the sound of movement came from the woods behind him. J.C. started to turn, but Elise's words caught him:

"Are you going to have a big wedding?" She was flustered. Her voice was nervous, her manner strange as she stared at him, her words rushed, showing her agitation.

"I don't know yet; it's according to what Phyllis Ann—" The crack of a twig underfoot, slight but echoing in his ears—there was someone in the pine woods behind him, someone Elise recognized and wished for him not to see. He was certain of it. It had to be—

"I know I heard something that time—" he said, rising to his feet.

"I—" She seemed suddenly at a loss for words, torn for a moment somehow between him and whoever or whatever it was there in the woods behind him.

J.C. turned and looked again through the trees, catching for a moment a glimpse of blue among the greens and browns—it looked as if someone had quickly moved behind a tree, so brief was the sight. He looked back to Elise, seeing a resignation in her eyes.

"Janson—" She called past him and toward the woods, looking in the direction of the creature he had seen for a moment. "Janson, come on out—"

J.C. stared at her for a moment, and then turned back toward the woods in time to see a man in faded overalls step from behind the trunk of a large tree. It was one of the Whitley farmhands, a man J.C. had seen about the place and in town before, but whose name he had never noted. The man was tall, with black hair and a dark complexion that seemed darkened even further still by sunburn and exposure to the weather. He stared at them for a moment, as if unsure, and then came toward them, walking past J.C. and to Elise's side. He looked down at her for a moment, and then turned again to look at J.C. with a pride such as J.C. had never before seen in any man.

Elise reached up to put her hand on the man's arm, bringing his green eyes back to her for a moment, and she smiled up at him, a look in her eyes that spoke more clearly of love than any words ever could—J.C. felt a moment of shock as he watched them; Elise was in love with a dirt farmer. He knew it before any words had to be spoken. Elise Whitley, William Whitley's daughter, was in love with one of her father's farm-hands—with a man who had sunburnt skin and calloused hands and a shirt that looked as if it had once been a guano sack; with a man who worked in the dirt and sweated in the sun, day in and day out, just to feed himself—Elise Whitley was in love with someone she should not possibly be in love with.

Then he was suddenly angry with himself. He had no right to pass judgement on Elise for how she felt; he had already had enough of people passing judgement on him for his choice in Phyllis Ann.

Elise was looking up at the dark man as J.C. watched her, her feelings written clearly on her face. "Janson, this is J.C. Cooper, the friend I've told you so much about, and, J.C., this is Janson Sanders." She looked at

J.C. for a moment, and then back to the man at her side. "This is the man I intend to marry—"

J.C. felt another brief moment of shock—Elise married to a farm-hand. Then he was over it. He held out his hand, looking into the man's pale green eyes as they came back to him.

Janson Sanders stared down at his hand for a moment, seeming somehow surprised by the gesture, then he reached out and shook it. He nodded his head, not speaking, then brought his eyes back to Elise.

She smiled reassuringly and patted his arm. "J.C. is one of the best friends I've ever had. We can trust him."

The man turned to look at him again, distrust still in his eyes. After a moment he nodded his head slightly, seeming somehow satisfied with her words.

"Trust me?" J.C. asked, looking from one to the other.

"We can't take any chance of Daddy finding out about us, J.C. You can't breathe a word of this to anyone." Elise's expression was serious. J.C. felt himself nod, which seemed to satisfy her. "Daddy's made it clear that we're to have nothing more to do with each other. He—he's gone to great lengths to keep us apart already, so we've been having to meet in secret. If he knew about us, he would—" For a moment her words fell silent. She shook her head. "We can't let anyone know how we feel about each other; Janson would never be safe if Daddy ever found out—"

"You don't think that Mr. Whitley would—"

But her words cut him short. "I don't know what he would do, and I don't want to find out—J.C., he's capable of things that I never dreamed—" Again there was silence. She looked up at Janson, and, after a moment, continued. "We're going to leave just as soon as we have the money to start a life somewhere else on. Until then, everyone has to believe that we can't even tolerate each other."

J.C. stared at her for a moment, trying to absorb all that she had said. Mr. Whitley could be obnoxious, pushy, and overbearing, but J.C. had never before considered that he might be dangerous—but, then again, men like William Whitley could be capable of doing almost anything to insure that they have what they want, and Elise seemed genuinely frightened. J.C. knew that her father would never allow her to marry a man like Janson Sanders, and that he might do almost anything to prevent that from happening—anything short of murder, and, J.C. wondered, looking at them now, if he would even stop at that. "I understand," he said at last. "I won't tell anyone about you—"

Janson put an arm around Elise and looked down at her, and it occurred to J.C. that they looked somehow right together, no matter how different they might be. Now he could well see why Elise had been so enraged at her father's remarks about keeping the blood lines pure, and he felt an even greater anger at Whitley.

"If there's anything that I can do to help, all you have to do is ask," he said, watching the dark man with his patched and faded overalls, and this girl who was long ago more sister than friend. "Anything at all—" Love more often than not had nothing to do with proper choices and good, common sense, J.C. told himself—it had everything to do with feelings and passions and pleasures beyond any right or reason. Everyone had a right to that. Everyone—whether their choice was a man who wore patched overalls and sweated in the sun—

Or if it was a girl with a bad reputation, a ruined name, and an often unpredictable nature. And J.C. Cooper would do anything to assure that.

JANSON WORKED harder during those hot fall weeks than he had ever worked before in his life, harder even than he had in those last difficult years of trying to hold onto his land. The cotton harvest had begun, the first bolls breaking open in the green fields to leave the land peppered over with white. Sharecropping families on the Whitley place and throughout the County had already begun to pick the fields they cropped on halves, and, as Janson watched them out among the rows of cotton, it only strengthened his resolve—he would never take Elise to a life such as that. She would never be one of the many farmwives out among the cotton plants; she would never see her children, children sometimes as young as three and four, picking from first light to darkness, picking until backs ached and fingers bled, ignoring school and learning and play and all that children should know, to drag long pick sacks down the rows of cotton, filling them only to empty them and return to the rows again—Elise Whitley would never know a life such as that. Their sons might pick and hoe and chop cotton—but they would do it on their own land, with their own crop, a crop they would never lose half of each year just for the use of land and mules and seed. He owed Elise that much. And his parents. And himself as well.

He picked more cotton during those hot days than did any other hand on the Whitley place, though he knew he could get by with less—running liquor for Whitley could have distinct advantages, but they were advantages he rarely made use of. He went to the fields each morning with the other hands, and picked cotton just as they did, dragging the pick sack down the rows until his shoulders ached and even his mind was tired. He took on extra farm chores whenever he could find them, and made whiskey and hauled liquor anytime Whitley had a need—always there was money he could make, money he could put away toward the day when he and Elise could at last leave here together; and work, work that could exhaust his body and his mind, and that could help the days to pass. There was so little time they could be together now, and so many hours in between when he tried so hard not to think about her, for thinking about her always made him want things he should not be wanting—but the wanting would not stop.

In the months he and Elise had been together, Janson had never once done more than hold her in his arms and kiss her, and, though she sometimes brushed against him, or pressed close when they kissed, and once had even sat on his lap for a moment, he knew she did not understand the things she made him feel and want when she was in his arms. She was a lady, and a nice girl, the girl he was going to marry—he could not ask her to give in to the things he wanted, the things he needed, even though they would not be married for perhaps a year or even longer into the future. Nice girls did not do those things until they were married, he told himself, and Elise was a nice girl. He would be her husband one day, and then he would know what it felt like to touch her and lie with her and know her as no other man would ever know her—

until then he would have to wait. He might wonder if she knew about men and women and the things that happened between them, and if she ever thought of what it would be like once they were wed—but nice girls did not think about such things, and Elise was a nice girl. And he should not be thinking about it himself, either.

Janson's body ached that Sunday afternoon from the hours he had put in in the cotton fields the day before, as he walked to where he and Elise were to meet that afternoon. He had allowed himself to sleep late that morning, the straw mattress having felt too good, and the rest too needed, to give it up too easily and venture out to church services as he knew he should have done—besides, the things he had been thinking and feeling about Elise in the past days had no place in a church. She would be sitting in the choir of the big Baptist church at the end of Main Street in town, singing her hymns, offering her praises, and that was where she belonged. He belonged in his shabby room, on his straw mattress, trying to forget the thought of her soft skin and her bright hair and—

He sat on the ground with his back against the rough bark of a pine tree, and stared across the red dirt road at the field of sharecropped cotton waiting there to be picked—work, that was what it looked like to him, hours of dragging a pick sack behind him, bending and picking until his back ached. Elise would say that it was pretty, with all the fluffs of white—that was the difference between them. He could picture her now, sitting in her church choir, looking lovely in a robe as white as the cotton. His body ached, and from more than the hours of work—and he should not be thinking those things. Elise would never understand.

There was the sound of a car coming along the road, causing him to get quickly to his feet and move back into the cover of the trees. It would be difficult to explain why he was waiting here in such a deserted spot, should anyone other than Elise find him. It was more than likely that it was her in the car coming toward him, for this was a little traveled road, but he knew it was better to be safe than to have to worry with coming up with excuses that he was not prepared to give. They had been using this spot to meet for weeks now, the road being one deep within Whitley property, and one that was rarely used, and even overgrown in places. Janson could cut across country and reach it easily, but Elise usually now came by car.

J.C. Cooper and her father had both been teaching her to drive Whitley's Model T, as had Janson over the past several weeks whenever he had the time, and she had at last become safe enough at the wheel for her father to allow her to use the car on outings. Whitley thought she used it in order to visit J.C., which was exactly what she intended that he think, but she used it instead to meet Janson. J.C. had proven himself a true friend to them both time and again over those weeks, helping in this deception and in others; and, though Janson sometimes still found himself jealous of J.C., for the time that the younger man could spend with Elise teaching her to drive the Tin Lizzie, and for the shared past they had together, he knew there was no reason for that jealousy. Elise was in love with him, and J.C. was in love with that hellcat Phyllis Ann Bennett—how that had ever happened, Janson could not understand; but, then again, he would look at himself, and at Elise—

The car came to a rolling stop a few feet from where he stood hidden among the trees. He waited—it was Whitley's Model T, but he could not see the driver as yet. After a moment the door opened, and Elise stepped out.

Janson smiled to himself, noting how the sun shone in her red-gold hair, and then he stepped out into the road. Her face brightened the moment she caught sight of him, erasing the slight worry that had been there only a second before, and then she rushed around the car and into his arms, happy, he knew, just to be with him.

"We have the entire afternoon! Everyone thinks I'm with J.C., and I'm not expected back until supper time!" she said in a rush, her arms around his neck. "I have something to show—"

But he silenced her words with a kiss before she could finish what she had been about to say. She pressed close against him, and he felt his body react, his mind somewhere lost in the scent of her hair, the softness of her skin, the feel of her against him—he shouldn't allow himself to feel these things. He shouldn't—

But they were feelings he could not stop.

IT WAS a long moment before the kiss ended, and, when it did, he buried his face in her hair, a tension evident in his body that Elise could feel in her own. She pressed her cheek against his shoulder, glad for the moment that he could not see her face—then he released her and moved a step away, making her feel a sudden distance between them that was more than the space that held them apart.

He would not meet her eyes for a long moment as she stood staring at him, but instead ran the fingers of one hand through his black hair, his eyes fixed on the ground somewhere near her feet. "You have trouble gettin' away?" he asked, his voice low and throaty as he spoke.

"No, I just told them I was going to meet J.C."

"You said you had somethin' t' show me?"

"Yes—"

He raised his eyes at last and looked at her directly, and she felt the color rise to her cheeks—he knows what I'm thinking, she told herself. He stared at her for a long moment expectantly, seeming to be waiting. She lifted her chin and met his gaze—I know what you're thinking as well, she told him silently.

He looked away again. "Well—you gonna show me?"

She turned without a word and started toward the Model T, but stopped after a moment when he did not follow, and turned back to look at him. "Well, come on."

He followed her to the car and opened the passenger side door for her—she had known he would drive now that they were together, for he seemed to prefer to now that he was no longer teaching her to drive, whether out of a lack of faith in her driving skills, or out of a desire to protect his masculine pride, she did not know or really care. There was so little time they could be together now, and so many other more important things on her mind to be concerned about.

She got into the car and waited until he slid in under the steering wheel. "Just drive straight ahead. I'll tell you when to turn—"

He did not speak, and she watched as he pulled down on the lever on the steering column and pushed the low-speed pedal, setting the Tin Lizzie in motion with a jerk. He drove in silence, barely even nodding his head as she indicated to turn onto a narrow, almost-overgrown dirt road to the left, seeming now to be lost somewhere in his own thoughts. She sat watching him for a long moment, unable to think of anything to say to bridge that silent distance between them. She felt he was pushing her away, and she felt somehow cheated—love was not supposed to put a distance between two people, she told herself, but was supposed to bring them only closer together.

The car jounced over deep ruts washed in the roadbed as she had him pull off onto a second, even narrower road, but soon came to a stop, dead-ending before a small, unpainted shack deep within the back part of her father's land. She watched Janson's face as he stared at it through the windshield, his eyes moving over the rough boards long-ago weathered to a dingy gray, the rusting tin roof, and the weed-choked yard. When his eyes came back to her she smiled and got out of the car, then crossed the overgrown yard, picking her way carefully for fear the brambles would tear her stockings, until she was standing on the sagging front porch. When she looked back, she found Janson standing beside the car staring at her.

"Come on, there's no one here," she called, then opened the door and entered the house without waiting for him.

His look of confusion changed to surprise as he reached the open doorway and stared inside at the room before him. The tiny single room of the house was spotless, its walls swept clear of cobwebs, its hearth clean of ashes, its floor swept and mopped until her back had ached and a small blister had risen on her third finger. There was a small table in the center of the room, its one short leg braced up by a narrow shim of wood, a spotless tablecloth now covering its splintery surface, and two mismatched straight chairs flanking its sides. Against the near wall was an aged and warped kitchen cabinet; across from it an old rope bed topped by a straw mattress, its tick newly washed and sun-dried, and now filled with fresh, sweet-smelling straw she had brought here herself. The quilt that covered it was old but colorful, scavenged from the attic at her father's house, its colors matched only by the bunches of wildflowers she had placed on the table and on the mantlepiece above the fireplace.

"Who lives here?" Janson asked as she took his hand and drew him into the room.

"No one. Alfred, Stan, and I used to play here as children, but I doubt anyone else has been here in years now."

"But, who—" He motioned with one hand toward the flowers and the tablecloth.

"I did. The furniture was already here; all I did was clean up a bit."

"You did?" He smiled, moving farther into the room, looking first at the table, the quilt, and then turning back to her as she came near.

"I wanted us to have a place to come to be together, where we wouldn't have to worry about someone seeing us or telling Daddy—" She put her arms around his waist and stared up at him, happier in that moment than she had been in months, just with the delight the little room had brought to his face. "No one ever comes out this way; Daddy says the land's not good enough to put in cotton, and he hasn't tenanted it out since I was a little girl—it may be on his property, but it'll be all ours when we're here. No one would ever think to look for us out here."

He reached up to brush her hair back from her eyes, and smiled down at her, the fingers of his hand trailing lightly down over her cheek. "If you'd 'a told me what you were doin', I could 'a helped."

"I just wanted to do it myself—it's suppose to be the wife's job to do the housecleaning, isn't it?"

"Wife?" he said, smiling, both his arms moving down to her waist to hold her against him.

"I am going to be your wife, aren't I?"

"You sure are." He looked at her for a long moment, then bent to brush his lips against hers before lightly touching them to her cheek.

When his lips came to hers again, she pressed closer into his arms, feeling her heart speed up as he drew her even more tightly to him, his fingers tangling in her hair after a moment to draw her head back, his lips finally leaving hers to trail over her cheek, then to her neck and down, lightly touching her skin. She clung to him, wanting, as so many times before, never to leave his arms, never to—

He released her suddenly and turned away, leaving her breathless and wanting. She reached for the back of the nearby straight chair and clung to it, staring at him as he moved a step away to stand now with his back turned almost to her, a tension between them such as she had never felt before.

"I—I'm sorry—" he said, a hoarse sound in his voice. "I—I shouldn't have—" He fell silent for a moment. "It's just that, sometimes I—" He sighed and shook his head.

"I know," she said, quietly.

"You cain't—" He turned to look at her. "You're a lady; you can't understand what I feel, what I need, what I—" He looked away again and ran his hands through his hair. "I wish we was married," he said quietly.

"So do I," she said, but he did not look at her. "It's not really very fair on you, is it? If you were in love with anyone else other than me, you could already be married, and you would still be able to work and save the money to buy your land back."

"I couldn't be in love with nobody but you," he said, bringing his eyes back to her. "I wouldn't want t' be, even if I could."

"I know."

He was silent, looking at her, his eyes saying more than any words ever could—suddenly she understood, and perhaps she had all along. Perhaps that was why she had created this place where they could be together. She stood staring at him, meeting his eyes, knowing—she wanted to be his wife. She wanted to please him and share with him and remove this distance that was forever between them. Her father could not deny them this—Janson could take her as his wife. She could be part of him today in every way but name only—and she would have his name as well, when they could at last leave here together.

She moved to stand just inches from him, looking up into his green eyes, feeling a touch of fear move through her—but that would not keep them apart. There was nothing that would keep them apart any longer. "Janson, make me your wife," she said, meeting his eyes. "Let me do for you the things a wife does for her husband—"

He opened his mouth, and she thought for a moment he would speak, but he only continued to look at her, his eyes moving over her face. She felt the color begin to rise to her cheeks and she moved into his arms, pressing her face to his shoulder, feeling his arms tighten around her. He kissed her hair, holding her against him. "You don't know what you're sayin'," he said softly, his lips in her hair.

"Yes, I do—"

"No—" he looked down at her and she lifted her head to meet his eyes. "You don't."

For a moment she could only look at him and love him all the more, knowing that he did not think she understood. "Yes, I do," she said, her eyes moving over his face. "I want to please you. I want to be part of you—"

"Part of me—" His words trailed off and he stared at her for a moment, something going on behind his eyes that she told herself she understood. "You understan' about men an' women?" he asked her quietly, his green eyes moving over her face. "You know what a man an' woman do t' please each other?"

Elise felt the color begin to rise to her cheeks again, and she moved closer into his arms, pressing her face against his shoulder so that he could not look at her. "Yes—"

She felt his lips touch her hair. "That's what you want t' happen between us?"

She pressed her face even more tightly to his shoulder. "Yes—"

His fingers gently lifted her chin, making her look at him. "You want me t' take you?—you know what that means?"

"Yes—" she said, looking into his eyes.

"Are you sure? I don't want you t' be sorry after we've—"

"I'd never be sorry for loving you."

"But—are you sure? Once we've—" but his words trailed off, his eyes searching hers, concerned that she understand, that she be sure.

"I am sure—Janson, make me your wife; make me be part of you—"

He looked at her for a moment, his fingers gently touching her cheek, his eyes holding her in a way they had never held her before. "You are part of me," he said softly. "You've always been part of me—"

A touch of fear moved through her as he gently swung her into his arms and carried her toward the bed a moment later, fear at what would happen between them, and of what he would think of her afterward—but then she was lying on the quilt and he was beside her, leaning over her, the backs of his fingers trailing lightly over her cheek as he looked down at her. "I'm gonna be part 'a your body, Elise," he said softly, looking at her. And she realized that she was trembling.

SHE LAY in his arms afterward, the soft afternoon light casting shadows on the wonder that was his body. He held her, his fingers lightly stroking her side, his eyes on her in a way that told her how much he loved her.

"I love you," he said softly, as if reading her thoughts.

"You do?"

"Yes, even more than before." He leaned closer and kissed her, his lips lingering with hers for a time before her looked at her again. "You ain't sorry it happened, are you?"

"I'd never be sorry for this. Are you?"

"No. I wanted you for s' long. I just never thought—" He let his words trail off.

"Do you think any less of me now, because we have?"

"You know better'n that," he said, a smile touching his lips. "I'd wondered if you knew about all this. I didn't know how much your ma'd told you."

"She didn't tell me much," Elise said.

"She told you enough." And Elise left it at that.

"It really doesn't make you think less of me, with us not being married yet?" she asked him again after a moment.

"Don't even think about that. You an' me are meant t' be t'gether. Married or not, it don't matter."

"But, you'll still marry me, won't you?" She propped up on an elbow to look at him.

"You proposin' t' me, Miss Whitley?" he asked, grinning up at her.

"Janson!"

He laughed, and then smiled at the hurt look that came to her face. "You know I'm gonna marry you—did you really think I wouldn't?"

"Well—"

"Ain't no way I'd give you up, especially now."

She relaxed, resting her head against his chest. He kissed her hair, and drew her even closer. She could hear his heartbeat, feel the rise and fall of his chest with his breathing.

"You're more my wife right now than any weddin' could ever make you, but I want it all legal an' proper."

"So do I—Mrs. Janson Sanders—" she said, dreaming of all the days ahead.

"Elise Sanders—"

She smiled to herself and kissed the warm skin of his chest near where her cheek rested. "Did I please you?" she asked, then felt the vibration of his laughter against her cheek. "Don't laugh at me, Janson." She looked up at him.

"I ain't laughin' at you," he smiled, reaching to stroke her hair for a moment. "Course you pleased me—couldn't you tell?"

She smiled and pressed her face to his chest again, feeling her cheeks color with the intimacy of memory. He lay stroking her hair. She was silent for a moment, thinking.

"I wasn't the first, was I?" she asked at last, not looking up at him.

She heard his sigh, felt it where her cheek rested against his chest. "Elise—" There was reluctance in his voice.

She looked up at him. "I want to know—I wasn't the first; you've been with other women, haven't you?"

There was silence, lasting only seconds, but seeming to her to stretch into forever. "Yeah—but you're th' only one that's mattered—"

In spite of her brave words, she had not wanted to know. She pressed her face to his chest again, her mind rejecting the image of anyone else ever having known him so intimately, of anyone else ever having touched him or loved him—of any other woman ever having lain beneath him, loving him, holding him as she had done, taking him as part of her body.

He seemed to sense her thoughts, gently easing her over onto her back to look down at her. She moved to cover her breasts with her hands, but he took her wrists and gently drew them away. "No—" he said, his eyes moving down to touch her as his hands had touched her before. "There ain't no place for bein' shy between us no more—" He kissed her lips lightly, then bent to touch his lips first to one breast, and then to the other. He looked down at her again, releasing her wrists and stroking her cheek with the back of one finger. "You b'long t' me now, an' I b'long t' you—it ain't never been like that with nobody else. It couldn't be—"

"Have you—since we've known each other—" She could not finish the words.

"No. I ain't wanted no other woman since th' day I met you. I knowed that you was th' woman I was meant t' be with."

"You did?"

"Yeah, I did." He kissed her and then drew her into his arms and held her. She rested her head on his shoulder, thinking—'the woman I was meant to be with.' Yes, they had been meant to be together; they had always been meant to be together. She looked down the length of his body, to the part of him she had now also taken as part of herself—she remembered the way he had held her, the things he had whispered, the feel of him inside of her; no, it could never have been the same with anyone else. He belonged to her, and to her alone. He belonged to her, and nothing else mattered.

She began to gently trace comfortable patterns on the warmth of his skin, enjoying the feel of his chest beneath her fingers—she wanted to touch him there, where she had touched him earlier, but she still hadn't the nerve. In a few days, or a week, when they were more comfortable together, she would touch him just as she wanted to touch him, with no shyness between them; she would know his body, as well as she knew her own, and he would—

Her fingers touched the healed scar at his right shoulder. She had seen it earlier, but in the heat of what he had made her body feel, she had almost forgotten. Now she traced her fingers over it, noting the jagged outline, the pink scaring different in tone from the surrounding skin. She had never in her life seen the results of a knife wound, but she imagined that it would look something like—"Janson, what happened to your shoulder?" she asked, looking up at him.

"My shoulder?"

"Yes, the scar."

"It ain't nothin'." But his jaw set even as he said the words.

"But it looks like it was. It looks almost like—" But suddenly she knew. She could see it in his eyes—her mind raced back to the night he had fought Ethan Bennett in order to protect her, and the sight of the two men struggling over the broken bottle that could so easily have ended Janson's life. But if he had been hurt this badly then, she would have known; even in the state she had been in, she would have known. And this scar seemed so much older. So much—"Janson, who stabbed you?" she demanded, concern filling her.

"It don't matter," he said. "It was a long time—"

"It does matter! It matters to me! You could have been—"

"But I'm all right, and—"

"What happened?"

"Elise—" She could tell from the tone in his voice that he had no intention of telling her.

"I have the right to know! If you had been—" But he only stared at her in silence. "After what we just—" She let her words trail off. "Who was it?" she asked after a moment, her voice quieter.

He sighed, the reluctance never leaving his face, but, after what seemed to her an eternity, he finally spoke. "It was Buddy Eason."

"Buddy Eason—one of the Easons where you come from, the family who own so much of the County, it was one of them?"

"Th' old man's gran'son."

"But, what happened? Did you get into a fight? Did you—" But she could see it in his eyes. "It was over a girl—" The words came as a statement.

"Elise—"

"Damn it, tell me! I'm not a child! You fought over some—" But suddenly she realized, looking into his eyes—if the knife had struck any lower; if the man had stabbed him again—

She shuddered and moved closer into his arms, pressing her face to his chest and holding him close against her—he could have died even before they met. She might never have known—

She shuddered again.

But he misunderstood.

"Elise, you don't understan'. There ain't no other woman that's ever mattered t' me. It ain't nowhere near th' same." She looked up at him and tried to speak, but he would not allow it, gently silencing her words, his eyes showing a concern that he make her hear, make her understand. "We b'long t' each other—an' you're my wife now, just the same as if we was married; we're one flesh, just like th' Bible says, that a man'll join unto his wife an' they'll be one flesh—"

"Janson, I know—the only thing that matters is that we're together, that we'll spend the rest of our lives together, that we'll be married ''til death do us part'—"

"No, not like that—" he said, easing her over onto her back and leaning over her, "not ''til death do us part.'" He looked down at her, something in his eyes that was such a part of her—God, she had never thought it possible to love someone so. To love someone as if he were more her than she herself was. "Dyin' won't stop th' way I feel about you; it couldn't stop it—our souls 're gonna live forever; I wouldn't want t' live forever if I couldn't be with you—"

She looked up into his green eyes, tears coming into her own. "Do you believe in heaven, Janson?" she asked him quietly after a moment.

He gently touched her cheek, his fingers trailing over her skin. "I b'lieve in us," he said simply. And she understood.

HOURS LATER that evening, Elise sat brushing her hair before the dresser in her bedroom. The room behind her, reflected in the mirror, with its huge, white-counterpaned bed, its papered walls and tall windows, now seemed a lonely, uninteresting place compared to that small, one-room house where she had learned love that day.

She smiled at her reflection, thinking that she even looked somehow different now. Her family had been blind to the change in her, their chatter floating mindlessly about her at the supper table as she had quietly replayed the events of the day in her mind—oh, what a glorious day it had been, and what a wonder it was to become a woman.

Janson's touch, the scent and feel of him, was still fresh in her mind as she ran the brush through her bobbed hair—he had kissed her body, touched her, held her in ways she had only dreamed of before. He loved her—he had whispered the words over and over again as they had held each other. She belonged to him, as she would always belong to him, and the memory of that belonging made her blush slightly even now as she smiled at her reflection—and he belonged to her in just the same way as well.

She sat the brush down and went to stretch out on the white counterpane of the bed, closing her eyes and losing herself to the memory of his touch, to the memory of the warmth of his body moving inside of her. She drew a pillow from under the counterpane and down into her arms, hugging it close, pressing her face to its sun-dried freshness, needing him, wanting him as never before. He had promised her they would be together for always.

She opened her eyes and stared at the white ceiling overhead—if only always would begin.

JANSON LAY in the darkness of his small room, watching the shadows that played over the bare, unpainted walls—he had sat and stared at Elise's window long after her light had gone out, unmindful of the cold ground on which he sat, or the slight chill in the autumn night around him. It had seemed important just to sit and watch the house where she slept, knowing she was safe and warm and protected within those walls that held him out. Just sitting and watching had made him feel closer to her—she was part of him, part in every way, as she always would be.

The door to his room creaked quietly open. Janson did not move, but just lay still on his narrow cot, watching the moonlight reflect in Elise's red-gold hair as she entered the room and closed the door quietly behind herself—somehow it seemed now that he had known all along she would come. That he had only been waiting.

He watched as she lifted the shapeless white cotton nightgown over her head and laid it aside. She brushed her bobbed hair back from her face, her body golden and perfect in the moonlight that reflected through the dingy single window of the room. She came into his arms on the narrow cot, not speaking, but just bringing her lips to his.

It seemed somehow that their bodies melted together. He could feel her thoughts, hear her heartbeat, the gentle sounds of her breathing. Her hands were touching him, bringing him to life—he could feel the warmth of her skin against his, the gentleness of her body, the giving in her, and the need. She gasped softly as their bodies joined, and she held him close, clinging to him as the pleasure came, and holding him afterward as he cried from the sheer joy of loving her.

He was home—there in her arms, he was at last home; and neither William Whitley nor the devil himself would ever take her from him. His death would be assured if her father were ever to find her here—but somehow that did not matter; there were some things in life he was willing to die for. There were some things in life any man would be willing to die for.

# 18

ELISE AWOKE SLOWLY THE next morning, feeling the warmth of Janson's body against her. She smiled to herself and stretched lazily, opening her eyes to watch him in the dim light as he slept. He looked so handsome, his features softened in sleep, making him look almost as if he were a little boy. His hair was mussed, his thick, black lashes fanned out on his cheeks, his lips slightly parted—she loved him; more than she had ever thought it possible to love anyone, she loved him.

She suddenly realized the room was too light, the edges of the single window framed in a dim pink glow. Dawn was coming, and she knew she should not be here. If someone should check her room, if someone should realize that she was gone, a search would be started, and—

She knew her father would kill Janson if he were ever to find her here in his bed. There was no doubt in her of that. If she were found here, she would easily cost Janson his life.

She gently tried to disentangle herself from his arms, only managing to wake him instead. He looked at her sleepily and smiled, reaching out to gently touch her face. "Where're you goin' s' early?" he asked softly, one leg moving possessively over hers to keep her still beside him.

"It's almost daylight. I fell asleep. I've got to get back to the house—"

She tried to sit up, but he would not allow it, gently pressing her back to the straw tick instead and moving to lean over her. He brushed her hair back from her eyes and smiled down at her. “You ain’t goin’ nowhere yet—”

“But, if Daddy—” But Janson silenced her words before she could say anything more, his lips coming to hers, his tongue beginning to explore her mouth. When his lips left hers, they traveled over her cheek and down, over her throat and to her breasts. “No, we can’t—” she protested, trying to push his hands away as they began to touch her. “If they realize I’m gone, they’ll start looking for me. Daddy’ll kill you if he finds me here.”

“Your pa ain’t gonna think t’ look for you here,” he said lightly, his lips against her skin. “You b’long t’ me, an’ I don’t aim t’ let you go just yet this mornin’.”

“But, if he catches us, he’ll kill you—”

He moved to look down at her again, leaning over her on one elbow, his right leg still over hers. He touched her cheek with the backs of his fingers, then smiled down at her. “Then hush up an’ love me back for a while, that way I’ll die happy, whether it’s a year from now, or a hundred years from now—”

She knew she should not be here, knew each moment she spent in his bed only increased the danger to him—but she could not leave. His hands and lips were insistent, and her resolve melted before the need in him, and in herself. The desire to protect him lost out for the moment to the need to possess and love him just one more time—

Afterward, she lay drowsing in his arms, warm and secure against him. She could not bear to leave him just yet, even though she knew that she must, that she had to, to make him safe.

There came a hard knock at the rickety door, shaking it in its frame. “Hey, boy—I’ve got a haul for you to make this morning!” came shouted words through the door—her father.

Elise sat up quickly, pulling the old patchwork quilt from the foot of the bed to cover her breasts, a cold knot of fear and panic gripping her heart—her father, standing just on the other side of that door. She stared at Janson, knowing that it was over—if her father opened that door, if he saw her here, she knew she would see Janson die.

WILLIAM WHITLEY stood waiting impatiently outside the door to the rough room that had been added years before to the side of the old barn. The structure had originally been appended to house sacks of fertilizer—but it was good enough to house the half-Cherokee farmhand who lived there now, William told himself. They weren't too far different anyway, he thought, farmhands and fertilizer, for they both served their purposes, and they both could be tolerated, just so long as they didn't stink the place up too much.

He pounded on the door again. "Damn it, boy! I ain't got all day!"

The door creaked open a narrow space and Janson Sanders slipped through, then closed it quickly behind himself as he stood staring at William. He was dressed in overalls and no shirt, and his hair was uncombed for the first time that William had ever noticed. The boy ran the fingers of one hand through his hair and cleared his throat. "You got some work for me t' do?" he asked.

"Ain't that what I said, boy?" William demanded, staring at him. "Why'd you take so long to answer me?" It seemed strange the boy would still be in his room at this hour. It had been daylight for some time now, and, like any other of the farmhands or sharecroppers on the place, he was accustomed to rising well before daybreak.

William looked at him more closely, noting for the first time that the overalls were wrinkled, and even showing slight stains in places—the boy might not have much, but he was undeniably proud, his clothes always clean and well-mended at the beginning of each day, even if they were old and more often than not obviously patched. It looked almost as if the boy had just gotten out of bed and grabbed the first thing he could find handy to put on. His hair was mussed, and he was obviously ill-at-ease as he shifted from one foot to the other, his eyes never once leaving William's face.

William grinned to himself, suddenly realizing—the boy had a woman in his room. All the signs were there. Janson Sanders had had a woman in his bed last night—and, by the looks of him, she was still there. "Did you have yourself a woman last night, boy?" he asked, still grinning—so, Sanders was human after all.

A muscle clenched in the boy's jaw, his eyes never once shifting from William's face—he did not smile, or even crack a bragging grin as many men would have done. Instead there was anger behind the green eyes, anger that he did not even try to conceal—you goddamn son-of-a-bitch, William thought, suddenly frowning to himself. You think you're so damned high and mighty, when you're nothing more than dirt-poor trash and a half-breed farmhand.

He took the cigar from his mouth and pointed it at the boy, a muscle clenching in his own jaw now. "As long as you're working for me, boy, you better have your ass up out of that bed before sunup every morning. I don't give a damn who you go bedding in your own time, but you're on my time now. Send your slut packing and get to work; you've got ten minutes to meet me out behind the house—" he said, then turned without another word and walked away—goddamn son-of-a-bitch, he thought. You'd think he'd just bedded one of those moving picture actresses to see how he was acting, instead of it being some stupid little farm girl or cheap back-street whore. The goddamn half-breed—

THE SOFT folds of the cotton nightgown fell about Elise's shoulders and to her feet. She brushed her hair back from her eyes, staring at the closed door, wishing that she would not have to—

The door creaked open and Janson entered the room, closing the door again quietly behind himself. He turned to look at her, and she felt her cheeks redden—she had heard every word, every thing her father had said. He had called her a slut—he had not known that it had been her to share Janson's bed last night, but that did not matter. He had still called her a slut. And now she was embarrassed, embarrassed before Janson's eyes, when yesterday, and all last night—

Her face flushed hot and she turned her eyes away. "You'd better go; he said ten minutes."

"I know—"

Her eyes touched on him again briefly, and then moved away. He stayed where he was near the door, not crossing the narrow room to come to her and take her in his arms, and that somehow made what she was feeling all the worse.

"You'd better go—"

"I will in a minute."

"But, he said—"

"I don't give a damn what he said."

Her eyes rose to meet his and she stared at him for a moment. He finally crossed the room to her, but when he touched her she pulled away and stood with her back turned toward him, her face burning. "You'd better—"

"What's wrong?" he asked, his voice concerned as he stood just behind her.

"Nothing's wrong, except that he could come back and—"

"He ain't gonna come back."

"He could, and—" She turned to look at him and her words fell silent. She stared at him for a long moment, not speaking—what was he thinking? So many times in the past months she had wondered what was on his mind, but never more than she did in this moment—what did he think of her now? Did he think the same thing her father had said? He loved her; she knew that, but—"Janson, after what we—" Again she fell silent. "Janson, do you think I'm a—that I'm—"

He stared at her, a look of surprise and understanding coming to his face even though she could not finish the words. "You know I wouldn't never think nothin' like that about you!"

"But, after what we—"

"Especially not after what we did."

"But my father—"

"He didn't have no idea it was you in here."

"But, he knew that you had been with a woman, and he said—"

"It don't matter what he said—"

"But, do you think that I'm a—"

"You know I don't!" he said quickly, cutting off her words. Again she stared at him, trying to see what he was thinking, what he was feeling.

"We're not married," she said quietly.

"That don't matter."

"But everyone says that a man won't marry a girl who'll do that with him before they're married."

"I'm gonna marry you; you know that."

"But—" She stared at him for a long moment, then turned her face away—she knew she had ruined it. She knew she had ruined everything. "You'd better go on. He'll be waiting for you," she said quietly.

"I ain't goin' nowhere, not 'til you understand somethin'," he said, and she lifted her eyes to his for a moment. When she tried to turn away again, he would not allow it, gently drawing her into his arms and holding her even as she tried to struggle away—she would not cry in front of him, and she knew she was going to. She knew—"I love you," he said, staring down at her as she felt the tears flood her eyes. "I love you, an' you ought t' know that you're my wife already; right here an' now you're my wife. I don't need no preacher to make that be, 'cause it's somethin' that's inside 'a me, part 'a me. You're more my wife right now than any weddin' could ever make you—but we're gonna have that weddin', an' we're gonna have it in a church, with a preacher, just like it's suppose t' be."

"But—"

"No," he said, shaking his head. "There ain't no 'buts' to it. You're gonna be Elise Sanders—"

"I won't be able to wear white," she said, feeling stupid and silly the moment she had said it.

He smiled, his face relaxing as he reached up to touch her damp cheek. "You can wear white if you want t'."

"But now I'm not a—" Suddenly she blushed, unable to finish, and he laughed. She looked up at him, a hurt expression coming to her face, and he smiled.

"Marryin' in white ain't just for a girl who ain't never been with a man. Just 'cause you an' me have laid t'gether don't mean you cain't get married in a white dress."

"It wouldn't seem silly?"

"No, it wouldn't seem silly."

She found herself smiling slowly and he bent to kiss her, holding her tightly to him for a moment as she pressed her face against his bare shoulder beside where one of the galluses of his overalls went up over it—she knew she had been a fool. He loved her; that was all that mattered. He loved her. "You'd better go," she said, looking up at him after a moment, still not wanting to leave his arms. "Daddy said ten minutes. It's already been longer than that."

"Yeah—" but he held her for a moment longer before releasing her. She watched as he pulled on a workshirt and then re-hooked his galluses. "You'd better stay here for a little while after I leave, an' then head back t' th' house just as soon as it's quiet out."

"I will." She walked him to the door, remembering the tone in her father's voice. "You'd better be careful around him," she warned, looking up into his green eyes as he turned toward her.

"I will be." He kissed her again, and then looked down at her for a moment, his eyes moving over her face. He gave her a gentle hug, and then he was gone.

She moved to kneel on the narrow cot, watching him through the warped panes of the small window until he left her sight. She sighed and sat back—just let him be safe, she prayed silently, over and over again. Please, just let him be safe.

She waited there until she thought it was safe out, and then left, making her way through the edge of the fields and the woods toward the house. All the while there was that one fear crowding her mind—what if someone should see her about in her nightgown at this hour; what if her father caught her, or her mother saw her as she entered the house. She finally made it to her room and closed the door behind herself, turning to lean against it for support—but still the worry was there. Janson was with her father now; if William Whitley should ever even suspect—but she could not allow that to happen. If it did, then she knew she would lose the one thing that meant the most to her—but Janson would pay the dearest price of all. He would pay with his very life.

"COME ON," Elise urged one Sunday morning a few weeks later as she led him across the white-columned veranda and in through the front doors of the big house. The place was deserted, her family gone for the day, first to church, and then to visit relatives in the next County, with Bill in Atlanta for the weekend. She had managed to beg off the family plans, pretending a headache, and now she and Janson had the day to themselves, and the house to themselves, and Janson knew she intended to make the most of it.

She smiled up at him, holding tightly to his hand as she drew him into the hallway and closed the door behind them. "Everyone's gone. Don't worry; it's safe—"

Janson looked around, filled with caution in spite all her assurances. It did not feel right to be here in the big house with her, after all the weeks and months of hiding they had been through. He knew that it did not do to play with fire—but Elise was so insistent. She had planned for days how they would have this time together; and he knew that she wanted to lie with him in her own bed for once, instead of in the old house, or on his own sagging cot, or in the barn loft, or some other such place they could find to be together—she had not had to say a word; he had known, just as he had always known. Just as he knew her.

His eyes moved from the twin crystal chandeliers of electric lights that hung there in the wide entry hallway, to the flowered paper on the walls, to the grand descent of the staircase—he was uncomfortable, ill-at-ease, here in this grand house. He knew they should not be here, and that knowledge came from more than the fact that this was her parents' home, more than the fact that Whitley's catching them together here, more than anywhere else, would probably mean his own death. It was—

"You haven't seen the entire house, have you?" she asked, watching him as he brought his eyes back to her.

"No."

"Come on, then; I'll give you the grand tour—"

She led him through the rooms, through those he had been in before, and through uncountable ones he had not, from the company parlors at the front of the house, to the dining room, and even the kitchen where Mattie Ruth had fed him that first night he had come here, that night he had tried to steal food from Elise's family—Elise did not know about that night, and he saw no reason to tell her now; that was a long time ago, a long time, and many dreams.

She smiled at his amazement over the water closets, watching him as his eyes moved over the gleaming fixtures, the white-enameled facilities and claw-footed bathtubs. There were huge bedrooms with enormous beds all for one person, and high, shadowy ceilings in every room from which hung electric lights—and everywhere there were books, shelves of them in the bedrooms and in the parlors, and even in the dining room, as well as in the library itself.

The feeling of being out of place only increased with each room she led him through. His own home back in Eason County had not even had running water or electricity, and the privy had been in the back yard a good distance from the house where it had belonged. He had never grown up in a world where homes such as this one existed—the houses he had played in as a child had more often than not had gaps in the floors and walls, and holes in the rusting tin roofs that leaked in even the slightest rains. He had known kin where eight children had slept in one bed, and where mothers had carried water from wells several hundred yards from the house. He had seen families where twelve had lived in the cramped two rooms of a sharecropper's shack, where children shivered in the cold that seeped in around doors and blew in through cracks in walls, children who went to school hungry, who had no coats, and only the most ragged clothes to wear, for the simple reason that their parents could do no better. And he wondered how such a world could exist in the same land as this one.

He looked around with amazement as Elise led him through the door and into her own bedroom. His eyes moved from the huge, white-counterpaned bed, to the walls papered with tiny pink and red rosebuds, to the tall windows hung with heavy lace curtains. The furniture was a rich mahogany, with chairs and a settee upholstered in deep rose velvet; there was a wide shelf of books against one wall, and a tall chiffonier against another, and the wooden floor was waxed and shining, then covered almost entirely by a rose-colored rug—why would anyone tend a floor so carefully, he wondered to himself as he stared down at the rug at his feet, only just to cover it up.

He looked at Elise and wished they had never come here. Never before had he seen so clearly the differences between them. The Whitleys were rich folks, the same kind of people who drank in the speakeasies he delivered liquor to, who drove motor cars at speeds beyond all safety and reason, and who had parties to all hours of the night—while his own people lived in sharecropped shacks, barely scratching out a living from another man's land year after year, and going into debt to the nearby country stores just to survive. He looked at Elise as she stood there in her expensive dress and her high-heeled shoes and her silk stockings with the seams so straight in back—how very different they were; he in his overalls and workshirt and bare feet, and the woman who would be his wife. He was so out of place in this pretty room with its high shadowy ceiling, its electric light fixtures, its papered walls and huge feather bed. He did not belong in a place such as this, would never belong in a place such as this—but Elise Whitley did.

She was in his arms, her mouth pressing his, before he could speak—he closed his eyes, trying to give in to the desire in her, the feeling of her body pressing against his. She wanted him; she wanted him here on this big feather bed. She wanted him here in this room that was a part of her life he could never know.

They sank down into the feather tick, her hands touching him in places she now knew so well—but still his mind would not stop working. What could he ever give her that would make up for all she would lose the day she left here to become his wife? They were so different, too different—what kind of life could they ever know together? He was the son of a man who had been a sharecropper and a mill hand and a small farmer burned out and killed for refusing to be something less than he was; and she was William Whitley's daughter, a girl who had everything she had wanted all her life, a girl who could never hope to understand the world he had come from, the world he would be asking her to live in with him—what kind of life could they ever know together?

Less than a hundred years before, the Whitleys had been a wealthy, slave-owning family, one of the largest cotton planters in the area, and were even now one of the wealthiest families in all of Endicott County—while his own people, his mother's people, had lived in the wilderness of north Georgia at that same time, content in their lives and in their own ways, until men very much like the Whitleys, men with a greed for land and money, and an insatiable appetite for both, had driven them out. Nell Sanders's people had been driven toward the west at gunpoint, herded like cattle through weather such as they had never known before, barefoot, poorly clothed, sick, dying—all so that men like the Whitleys could take the land that had been a home to them, and to so many others like them, for centuries.

Now Elise's family, and other families like them, had the money, and the land had grown up in cotton fields and towns and cities and mill villages, and his mother's people would never be the same—for there where four thousand silent, unmarked graves along the path of that forced march, more than four thousand graves of the men, women, and children of Cherokee blood who had died along what had become known as the Trail of Tears, and they would never be forgotten.

Janson's own great-great grandmother lay somewhere along that Trail, alongside children who had never lived to see adulthood—how many nights he had sat at his mother's feet as a boy, hearing stories that had come from her father, and her father's father before him, of that time when Janson's great-grandfather had seen so many marched away, and of the way of life that had existed before it. Nell Sanders's people had been left with nothing, as had his father's people when they had come from Ireland in the time of the Potato Famine. Theirs was a people accustomed to struggle and to fight, his mother's people and his father's both, and the hard way of life was a life they well knew, a life they had always known.

But Elise's people knew nothing of a life such as that. They had money; they had land that no one could ever take from them; they had fine ways and fancy manners and book learning—he had none of that. He was nothing like the man Elise had been raised to marry. He did not have a big fine house with electric lights and running water and enameled bathtubs; he did not have the money and fine learning, the motor cars and fancy ways—he was a dirt farmer, a hired hand, and even a moonshiner. He had skin dark from his ancestry, and darkened even further still by years of hard work in the sun. He wore patched overalls and a faded workshirt; his hands were rough and calloused, and there was dirt underneath his fingernails that it seemed no amount of cleaning could ever remove—these were not the hands meant to touch a fine, educated lady who read books and wore expensive clothes and who had a telephone right in her own house. And perhaps these were not the hands meant to touch Elise Whitley.

He rolled away from her on the bed and sat up, his back to her. He ran the fingers of one hand through his hair and sighed, not turning to look at her.

"What's wrong?" she asked, her fingers reaching to touch his back through his overalls and workshirt.

"I shouldn't 'a come here. I don't b'long in a place like this." He got up from the bed and crossed the room, stopping to stare out one of the windows at the smooth lawn, the road, and the cotton fields and pine woods beyond. "I jus' don't b'long here—"

"Why not?"

"I jus' don't. This ain't no place for somebody like me. I shouldn't never 'a come here in th' first place."

"You came because I asked you to."

"Why?" He turned to look at her. "Why'd you want me t' come up here with you? Ain't th' old house or th' cot in my room good enough anymore?"

"You know they are." She propped up on an elbow to stare at him. "We've been together in both those places lots of times."

"Then why not t'day? Why'd we have t' come up here?"

"Why can't we be together here as well; there's no one else in the house."

He looked at her for a moment—she could never understand. She belonged anywhere she wished to be, and, no matter how grand the surroundings, she would never be out of place. "I jus' don't b'long in a place like this."

"Why not?"

"I jus' don't!" He raised his voice, then was immediately sorry. He turned away, toward the window. "I jus' don't b'long here," he said more quietly—damn her, she could never understand; and damn her for being so lovely and so caring. He stared out the window, wishing that he had never stepped foot into this house today.

He heard her get up from the bed and cross the room toward him, then felt her gentle hand on his back. "Janson, tell me what's wrong—"

He lowered his head and shook it slowly back and forth. She could never understand; no matter what it was he said to her, she would never be able to know what it was he felt. It was not a matter of thoughts or words—it was what he was, deep inside himself; and it was something she could never know because of the life she had led.

"Janson, please talk to me. Tell me what I've done wrong—"

The sound of her voice cut right through him, but he could not turn to look at her—God, how much he loved her, but they were so different, so very—

"You ain't done nothin' wrong."

"Then, what is it?"

Why couldn't they have been more alike? Why couldn't she have been the daughter of some small farmer or sharecropper or mill hand; or he the son of some businessman or big cotton planter, someone who could give her the kind of life she deserved to have. He had never once been ashamed of the man he was, and he was not ashamed now—he only wanted to give her all that she deserved, all that she had always had, and he knew that he could never do that.

"I love you—please, tell me," she said softly from behind him, her voice almost pleading.

He turned to look at her, a stab of pain going through him as he met her blue eyes. "Why do you love me—me, out of everybody else you ever met?" he asked her. "Why wasn't it somebody more like you, somebody more like—"

She stared at him, and his words fell silent. "I don't know why I love you—why do you love me?" she asked, her eyes never leaving his.

"It ain't th' same thing."

"Why not? Did you have more choice in the matter than I did? Love's not something you choose, Janson; it's something that's just there—"

"But, why me?"

"Why not you?"

"You don't understan'!" He turned away, becoming angry with himself, and with her.

"Oh, yes, I do, and I can't believe you're asking me a question like that." When he turned to look at her, he found her eyes almost angry. "I love you; isn't that enough? I love you because of who you are—"

"Yeah, a hand that works your pa's place, as different as night is from day from you." His tone was sarcastic, and he turned his eyes away again, unable to meet the directness of her gaze.

"It didn't matter who or what you were—or didn't you mean what you yourself said, that you knew I was the one you were meant to be with almost from the day you met me?"

That was not fair. She was using his own words against him. He could not help how he felt about her—but she had been raised for a life so far different from the one he could give her. She had never been meant to be the wife of a small farmer, to have to worry about money for the remainder of her life, to have to do without all the fine, beautiful things she deserved—and somehow he was afraid she would grow to hate him one day for the choice she had made those months ago when she had agreed to become his wife, for that choice would one day take her away from all that she had ever known.

She seemed to be waiting for a response, and, when she did not get one, she sighed and shook her head. "I don't know why I love you, any more than I know why you're who you are, or why I'm who I am. I could have fallen in love with someone from town or from the next County—but, whoever it was, it would have been you." She finally managed to turn him to face her, and she stood staring up at him for a moment, her hands on his arms. "It could never have been anyone else but you, because you're somehow the other part of me—isn't that what your parents taught you, what you taught me? I don't care how different we are; you're still as much me as I am, what completes me and makes me whole, and I couldn't live if I didn't have you—" She reached up to touch his face, her blue eyes filled with caring. "I couldn't help but to love you. I wouldn't want not to love you, even if I could; it's as much a part of me as thinking or breathing is—"

"I'll never be able to give you all this—" With one hand he indicated the room, and, with it, the house.

"I don't want all this. All I want is you, you and the place we'll have in Alabama."

"But it won't never be like this; we won't ever have a lot of money—"

"We'll be together; that's all that's important."

"We're s' different," he said, looking at her.

"That doesn't matter."

"But it could matter t' you, someday."

"No—" She placed her fingers over his lips, silencing his words. He searched her eyes. "When we're together, when we're touching and you're inside of me, there are no differences. We love each other, and we're one person." Her eyes moved over his. "We'll be together forever; that's all that's important."

"Even if—"

"Sh-h—" She moved into his arms, pressing her body against his, feeling warm and soft and so close. "Just love me, Janson; that's all that matters. Just love me—"

They sank down onto the feather tick again, her hands touching him in ways that awakened the need—but, even as their bodies joined, his mind still refused to release the worry. Would she ever be able to live the way he was asking her to live? And, if she could not—

THERE WAS the crackling of dry leaves beneath her feet that Saturday morning in the autumn of 1927, the sounds of migrating birds in the trees overhead. Elise moved quietly along an unmarked path in the woods, trying to keep Janson just within sight ahead of her. Briers and underbrush tore at her silk stockings, and a branch snagged her sweater, sending a chill gust of autumn air against her bare skin before she could again free the knitted material. She hurried to narrow the gap between them, careful of any sound she might make—if she should lose sight of him here in the woods, she knew that she might wander for hours, even for days, before anyone found her. They were not too far from the largest of her father's cotton fields, and still somewhere on Whitley property, but she knew she would never be able to find her way back along the unmarked path Janson traveled, not even well enough to find her way out of the woods and back to the house again.

She tried to move as quietly as possible, carefully picking out each step, cringing at the sound of each twig that cracked beneath her feet—why had she not worn more sensible shoes; why these high heels when she had known all along what it was she had intended to do this morning? But at least she would soon know what it was she had come to find out. At last Janson would hide nothing from her any longer—before this day was over she would know what it was he did for her father; today she would know where it was he went, what it was he did, when he left her to do things he would not speak to her of later. Today, at last, she would know everything.

She had the right to know, she reasoned to herself, carefully keeping him in sight. There was no reason for secrets between them, not as close as they had become. She was his lover, and she would be his wife—she was prepared for the truth, no matter what that truth might be, she told herself, just as she had been prepared for it for months now. She was coming to understand what kind of man her father was, and she knew that whatever he and Janson were doing was most probably illegal—but it was the one thing that Janson kept from her, and the one thing that still held them apart. She had a right to know, and she was ready for what she would find—and, after this day, Janson would never hide anything from her again.

He seemed almost to sense that someone was following him, for he stopped suddenly and turned back, causing Elise to step behind a tree quickly to keep from being seen. His eyes moved through the woods for a moment, searching for the source of some slight movement or sound he had detected. After a moment he moved on, and Elise breathed a sigh of relief, doubling her efforts to be quiet as she stepped from behind the tree and made to follow him again. If he had caught her—

But she would not worry about that now. He would be furious once he discovered what she had done, but that could not be helped. He would forgive her, just as she would forgive him once she knew what it was he was hiding. There was no doubt in her mind of that.

He slowed his pace, and she felt a sense of relief—at least she would not lose him here in the woods before she could even make her discovery. He seemed to know exactly where he was going, making his way along some path he knew—toward what, she wondered again, thinking over the possibilities. She knew it was probably illegal, this thing that her father had Janson involved in, and, if not illegal, it was at least something her father would not want everyone in the County to know he was doing. She had been convinced for days now that it had something to do with gambling, for her father was extremely fond of his poker, even though he might loudly condemn card playing to the deacons in church on Sundays. If not gambling, then it had to be the sharecroppers and tenant farmers on the place, for her father had cursed often enough about the men who he always swore never got enough work out of their families or out of the land—maybe he was using Janson to keep them in line, forcing higher rents from them, or a larger percentage of their crops each year. Perhaps it was underhanded business dealings, money her father was earning from some source he would never openly admit—whatever it was, it had to be shady, if not downright against the law; and he was using Janson to do it. She had wondered about it for so long, worried about it—but today she would know. Today, at last, she would know.

There was a peculiar odor in the woods around her, stale, as if it had been hanging there in the leaves for days. She lost sight of Janson for a moment, and panic gripped her, then she caught a glimpse of the blue of his overalls through the leaves, and she moved to shorten the distance between them—surely it could not be much farther. She had been following him for such a time already. Surely—

He seemed to break into a narrow clearing ahead, and then to pause. There was no sound of movement ahead of her now, no rustling of leaves or cracking of twigs coming to her over the distance. There was one more brief glimpse of blue, and then it was gone. Elise moved ahead cautiously, her eyes searching the woods for any sight of him. An eerie feeling moved up her spine, as if someone were watching her—but she could see no one. Her own heartbeat was loud in her ears now, the break of a small tree limb at her side as resonant as a gunshot—what if she had lost him? What if there were someone else about—what sort of person, on what sort of shady dealings, might be moving about here in the depths of the woods on a Saturday morning? She pulled her sweater closer about herself, suddenly chilled, and moved quietly ahead, her eyes searching for any movement, her ears straining for even the slightest sound. She came to the edge of the narrow clearing and stopped, seeing hidden in the woods at the other side what it was she had come to find.

She stared in disbelief at what lay before her, knowing suddenly that this was where Janson had come, what he had been doing, all the times he had left her. She had never once seen a whiskey still in her life, but she knew what it was that lay in the edge of those woods as she slowly crossed the clearing; she had heard the descriptions, had grown up with the folklore—the reddish copper, the furnaces, the barrels, the tubes and pipes; it could be nothing else. Her eyes moved from the copper boilers, to the rough rock of the furnaces beneath, to the glass jars and sacks of sugar lying nearby under a crude shelter there alongside a stream—whiskey stills, moonshine stills, and Janson had to be the one operating them. Janson, and her father.

She stared for a moment, unwilling to comprehend—liquor, but all liquor was illegal, the making and selling and transporting of it, because of the Volstead Act and the Prohibition laws. She had known that what her father and Janson were doing was probably illegal, and she had somehow accepted that—but not liquor, not when she knew so many people whose lives had been affected by it; Ethan Bennett, Phyllis Ann, even Alfred—and this was even so much worse. Moonshine, the poisonous corn liquor that could kill or cripple or blind—and her father, and the man she loved, the man she was going to marry, were the ones who were making it, selling it, doing only God knew how much harm to who knew how many people.

Her eyes came to rest on Janson where he stood near one of the stills, staring at her. His arms were folded across his chest, his jaw set, a terrible anger in his green eyes—for a moment she could only stare at him, letting her discovery, and the look in his eyes, slowly sink into her. She no longer knew what she had expected to find when she had begun to follow him from their meeting place earlier in the day, but this had not been it. This had never been—

"You had t' see; you had t' know what I was doin'—well, go on now an' look!" His voice was filled with fury, his face with more anger than she had ever before seen in any human being in all her life. "You cain't leave nothin' alone, can you? No, you had t' go followin' me—did you really think I didn't know there was somebody behind me in th' woods back there? Did you think I didn't know it was you? A man don't make it too long runnin' liquor if he's stupid!"

For a moment, she could only stare at him. "You knew I was—"

"You're damn right I knowed it!"

"And you let me—"

"Yeah, I let you!" he yelled, interrupting her words. "You wanted t' see s' bad—well, go on an' look! You wouldn't listen t' me when I was tryin' t' tell you what was best for you—"

Suddenly anger exploded within her. "Best for me!" She shouted the words at him, enraged. "How dare you try to tell me or anyone else what's best when you're poisoning people at the same time with this stuff!"

"I ain't poisonin' nobody! We ain't made nothin' but good corn liquor—"

"'Good corn liquor'—you call this poison good! You know what it does; it can kill or blind—and it's against the law!"

"God damn Prohibition!—a man's got th' right t' make a livin'!"

"Is money that important to you? More important than the lives of the people who drink this stuff?"

"I done told you that we don't make no bad liquor—an', yeah, money's important t' me. It's how you an' me are gonna be able t' leave here an' get married, ain't it?"

"I won't have our lives built on this kind of money!"

"What do you think's payin' for that big, fancy house 'a yours now, an' all that schoolin' you got, an' all them pretty clothes?"

She stared at him for a moment, realization slowly coming to her—this had not just recently begun; this had been going on for years, perhaps even for her entire life. Her father's money, or at least much of it, had come from this source, from the making and selling of bootleg liquor. From moonshine. Janson was right—the house, all her things, her entire way of life, had been built on the profits of these stills, or on other stills like them. Janson was right—but that did not make the realization any easier.

He seemed to sense what he had done to her, the confusion, the inner turmoil that his words had caused. His expression softened, and he moved toward her. "I'm sorry, Elise. I shouldn't never 'a let you find out this way. I should 'a stopped you in th' woods as soon as I knowed you was there, an' made you go back—"

"Made me go back!" She pulled away just before he could touch her, and stood staring up at him, her anger, both at her father for having kept this from her all her life, and at Janson for defending what he had been doing, now turning on him alone. "Why—so you could hide it from me even longer? So you could go on poisoning people and I couldn't say a—"

"Damn it, woman—do you really think I'd be poisonin' people!" he shouted at her, angry again. "Well, do you! Do you really think I'd be makin' liquor that could hurt folks! Th' most this stuff'll do is give somebody a headache if he drinks too much of it, but it ain't gonna do no more harm'n that!" He stared at her for a moment, breathing heavily, his eyes angry. "You know me better'n anybody else aroun' here—do you think I'd be poisonin' folks?" he demanded, staring at her. "Goddamn it, woman, answer me!—would I be poisonin' folks!"

She stared at him, remembering the man who had held and touched her so gently, who always whispered her name as their bodies were joined—the same man who made moonshine whiskey in illegal stills. "No—" she said after a moment, "not on purpose, but—"

"There ain't no 'buts' to it. Your pa turns out good liquor; there ain't no busthead ever left this place—"

Your pa—his words echoed in her ears. She had lived off the profits of bootleg liquor, of moonshine, even as she had sat in the Baptist choir and heard her father condemn 'the demon rum' to the church deacons. Moonshine, the liquor made by backwoods people and white trash—and by her father and Janson. How self-righteously she had pitied those whose lives had been torn apart by alcohol, while all the time she herself had been living off of—

"Liquor is wrong; you know that. Why else would they have made it illegal."

"Bein' legal or not don't matter. Folks are gonna drink anyway if they want t'—an' makin' a life for us ain't wrong, is it? Runnin' these stills is how I'm gonna do that."

"We can't build our future on the destruction of other people's lives!"

"Damn it, Elise—I ain't destroyin' nobody's life! All I'm doin' is runnin' good corn liquor an' haulin' it out t' th' speakeasies an' t' th' sellers in Buntain—what's s' wrong with that? You knowed that I was doin' somethin' for your pa that I couldn't tell you about—would you rather I'd 'a been hurtin' folks or cheatin' people than runnin' liquor? A man's got t' make a livin', an' this is as good a way as any, an' it's better'n most. This way I'm makin' more money, an' savin' more money, than I'd ever be able t' do if I was doin' somethin' else."

She stared at him for a moment, too confused to speak. All her life had been built on a lie, on many lies—but she had never known. She felt like such a hypocrite, having lived on the profits of liquor all these years, while at the same time living with such self-righteous blindness toward so many things that were now becoming so horribly clear—but she had never known. She had never—

Janson was staring at her, his green eyes moving over her face. "You said you wanted us t' be t'gether, t' be able t' leave here an' get married an' have a place 'a our own," he said, more quietly. "I'm doin' what I feel

I got t' do for us t' be able t' have that. If you love me, it don't seem t' me that it ought t' matter what it is I got t' do. If it does matter—"

He left the words hanging, unfinished, in the air between them. She could feel their weight almost as if they were a physical presence. She looked at him, seeing in him the man she loved, and also seeing in him a man who operated illegal liquor stills for a profit. 'If it does matter'—he had said, but it didn't matter; nothing could really matter but him and the life that he was trying to provide for them both. No sense of betrayal by her father, no injured dignity over having discovered something so unexpected, no sense of right or wrong or legalities or memories from the past was more important than the love she felt for him, and the life they would have together.

"You got t' decide, Elise. If you want us t' be t'gether, then you'll let me do what I feel like I got t' do for us t' be able t' leave here b'fore too much longer. It don't seem t' me that what that is ought t' matter too much, not so long as you feel th' same way about me as I feel about you—"

Suddenly she was in his arms, pressing her body against his, holding him tightly. "It doesn't matter; nothing matters but us, that we can be together. Nothing—"

He covered her mouth with his, crushing her against him, his relief at her words evident in the tightness of his arms around her. She could feel his body respond to her nearness, feel the desire awakening in him.

"Not here—" he said against her hair, holding her as if he could never let her go. "Not here; it's not safe. Go t' th' old house; I'll show you th' way out a' th' woods t' a path that'll take you right to it. Wait for me there. I'll be on soon as I can—"

It was not until she was away from the stills, away from Janson and the place that had stolen so much of his time from her, making her way along the path that he had shown her, that she realized—Janson could be in even so much more danger than she had ever known before, not only from her father, but also from the men her father sent him to do business with, men very much like that Al Capone and all the gangsters she had heard so much about on the radio, men who trafficked in bootleg liquor, and who openly violated the Prohibition laws—men who would think nothing of killing Janson if he even once got in their way.

A shiver ran up her spine and she pulled her sweater tighter about her shoulders, stopping for a moment to offer a prayer that he would remain safe. Then she went on toward the old house to wait for him, knowing that she would never again know another easy day until they were away from here and safely married—and knowing that, if something did happen to him, it would all be her own fault. He was doing it all for their future, he had told her—

She could only pray that future would be.

ELISE SAT staring at her reflection in the oval-shaped mirror above her dresser that October morning in 1927, the huge house silent around her, her mind somewhere lost in thoughts she had been considering over the past days. She reached and took up the ivory-handled hairbrush from the dresser top before her, and started to run it through her bobbed hair, but stopped short, staring into her own eyes—"I'm going to have a baby—" she said softly, staring at herself, feeling a thrill of both excitement and fear pass through her. No matter how many times she told herself, the thought was still so new she could hardly comprehend it—there was a baby inside of her. She was going to have Janson's baby.

They had never once discussed the possibility that she might become pregnant, though she had known they had taken the chance in taking each other. Janson often talked about the children they would have, the family they would make together, and of the home and land he would provide for them—surely he had to have thought of the possibility of a baby from all the times they had been together. He wanted to have a family, children with her—he would be happy when he found out, she told herself, excited and nervous just as she was, though they would now have to leave so much sooner than he had planned. They would have to be married and away from here before her condition could become obvious, and before anyone could find out—her father would kill Janson immediately if he knew; there was no doubt in her mind of that. There would not be enough money to buy Janson's land back right away, as he had hoped there would be, but that could not be helped now. They would find a place to live, and Janson could work, and they would have it soon enough—and they would have their baby, and other children in the years to come, and they would be so happy, together, at peace—and it would all begin so soon, she told herself, just as soon as they could leave here together. So soon.

She sat the brush down and took a deep breath, still staring at herself in the mirror as she told herself again that she was going to be a mother, and Janson a father, in only the matter of a number of months—she would find just the perfect way to tell him, and then they would begin to make plans for their departure and marriage. In a few days, or weeks at the most, she would be Elise Sanders—nothing could ruin their plans now. Nothing could spoil her happiness. God could never be that cruel. And, so she prayed, neither could William Whitley.

"I'VE GOT to talk to you—" Elise said a few hours later that morning, smiling up at Janson and looking happier than he had ever before seen her in the months they had been together. They stood at the edge of the clearing in the woods, their old meeting place, where she had asked him to meet her this morning—somehow he could not stop looking at her, touching her, feeling almost as if he had not seen her in weeks, though they had been together only the day before.

"Then talk," he prompted, pulling her to him, then covering her mouth with his before she could say a word.

She giggled after a moment and tried to hold him at arms-length away. "I'm serious!"

"So am I—" he said, smiling and once again trying to pull her closer even as she playfully tried to fend him away.

"No—I mean it!" she laughed, pushing at his shoulders. "We've got to talk."

"Okay, talk." He gave her an exasperated look at last, and then contented himself for the moment with his hands at her waist. "You can be th' damndest woman sometimes for talkin'."

She laughed at his words, and then stretched up to kiss his cheek, affectionately looping her arms loosely about his neck.

"S' what's s' important that you got t' talk t' me about?" he asked, reaching up to gently brush her hair back from her eyes—she looked so pretty this morning that he could refuse her nothing, not even talking when he wanted to touch and love instead. "I don't have much time. I got t' go int' Goodwin t' pick up some stuff for your pa in a little while."

She stared up at him for a moment, seeming to be considering something. "No—not like this," she said, moving her fingers down to play at the buttons on his shirt. "When will you be back?"

"Couple 'a hours, I guess."

"Then meet me at the old house after supper. I'll tell my folks I'm going to see J. C.."

Janson shrugged—women could be the damndest things for changing their minds as well. "If that's what you want," he said.

"It is." She looked up at him for a moment, and then threw her arms around his neck again, holding him close. "Oh—I love you so much!" she said, pressing against him.

He laughed, holding her even tighter. "An' I love you—" He smiled—he had never seen her like this before, so warm and happy in his arms, seeming so content and so much a part of him. "You sure you don't want t' talk t' me now?" he asked, enjoying the feel of her against him.

"No—" she smiled, her eyes moving over his face, more beautiful than she had ever before been in the months he had known her. "It can wait," she said. "After all, you and I will have a long time to be together."

"Forever—" he smiled.

"Forever," she answered, and then drew his lips to hers, saying more with the kiss than any words could ever tell him.

WILLIAM WHITLEY stood just out of sight within the cover of the trees at the edge of the clearing, his jaw clenched, his hands tightened into fists at his sides—never before in his life had he truly known what hatred was, but he did now; he did as he watched his daughter in the arms of the half-breed farmhand, Janson Sanders. He had thought nothing more than to take a short cut through the woods from one of his tenant houses this morning, when he had heard Elise's voice, and then had happened on this scene—a black rage enveloped William; she had been lying to him as she had kept this relationship hidden away in dark corners—how long had it been going on now? How far had it gone? If that dirty half-breed had—but, no, Elise would never have given herself to someone so far beneath her. She was William Whitley's daughter, and she had been raised for something so much better. She had been raised for—

William had thought he had killed the relationship, had thought he had killed whatever had begun to grow between them—but she had lied to him, Elise and the half-breed both. William had known all along that the boy would present a problem of himself one day, for he was too proud, too damned sure he was just as good as anyone else, when he was nothing more than red-Indian, dirt-farming trash—and now William knew just exactly what the boy had in mind, perhaps what he had had in mind from the first day he had come to the place. Janson Sanders wanted to get his hands on William's money, and he wanted to get under Elise's skirts in the process. He had probably been promising her his undying devotion at the same time he had been whoring on the side—after all William had found him one morning with some whore still in his room. What a damned little fool Elise had proven herself to be. What a damned little—

William stared, clenching his fists even more tightly at his sides until the tendons stood out on the backs of his hands in stark relief, his eyes on his daughter as she put her arms around the half-breed's neck and drew his lips toward hers—a killing rage filled William at the sight. He was certain of only two things in that moment—Elise would pay for the lies and deceptions she had been carrying on all these months, and this relationship would end, once and for all. There was no doubt of that. Janson Sanders was a dead man.

# 19

IT SEEMED ALMOST THAT Elise danced up the front steps to the veranda, and in through the front door of the house that half hour later, humming some familiar bit of jazz music to herself. William stood waiting for her just inside the doorway to the front parlor, his eyes on her as she closed the door and turned to smile at him.

"Where have you been?" he demanded, trying to force a control over the urge within him to immediately wipe the smile from her face—he would give her one last hope, one last chance to confess the relationship she had been hiding all these months—and, God help her, she had better make that confession.

"I just went for a walk," she said, the smile never changing, taunting him all the more with the lies that lay behind it.

He walked toward her, clenching his hands into fists at his sides, his voice rising in tone with the rage he fought to control. "I asked you, where have you been?"

Her expression changed, the smile weakening, becoming almost forced. "I just went for a walk. I—"

The rage snapped within him. He slapped her hard, then stood staring at the shocked look that came to her eyes. "Damn you! Tell me the truth!"

Her hand went to her cheek, covering the reddening mark his blow had left. Her eyes were large and horrified, filling now with tears—but there was no pity left within him. "Daddy, I—"

"Don't you dare lie to me!"

Martha entered the hallway from the parlor behind him, her voice frightened and worried as she reached to try to take his arm—but he would have expected nothing less from her. She had accepted the discovery of Elise's lies, and the relationship the lies had covered for, without comment—but that was what was wrong with Elise now, Martha's constant coddling, and that coddling would stop now. "William, please don't—"

He turned on her, holding his fist just inches from her face. "You shut your goddamn mouth and stay out of this!" he shouted at her, and then turned back to Elise. "Don't you even try to lie to me again! I saw you with that boy today! I saw you with that half red-Indian trash's hands on you!"

A look of terror that she could not conceal came to the girl's eyes. For a moment she seemed almost to fight to control her emotions before she could speak, and then her voice came, weak, but almost determined, to him. "Daddy, I don't know what you think you saw, but—"

He raised his fist and almost struck her again, but instead watched her shrink away, toward her mother as Martha moved around him and to her side. "Don't you dare lie to me! I saw you, goddamn it! How long has this been going on? If he's put his hands on you I'll—"

"Daddy, please, you don't understand—" Her voice was pleading as it cut into his. "It wasn't—"

"Shut up!" he screamed at her, frightening her into silence. The huge rooms of the old house echoed his voice back to him over and over again as he stared at her, his anger only increasing as he watched Martha put her arms around the girl and draw her closer. "It's over," he said, forcing the words through barely parted teeth. "He's only been using you, and you're too damned stupid to see it—but I'm no fool. I know what he's after, and he's not going to—"

"But, it's not—"

"You've been taking me for a fool all these months, you and him both—but you won't again. You're never going to see that dirty half-breed again even if I have to—"

"No, you can't—" Her eyes were filled with fear, with more horror than he had ever before seen there in all her life. "You don't understand. I—I love him, and he loves—"

"Love—" William almost laughed at the word, at the notion of his daughter in love with the dirty, dirt-farming trash, and even at the sincerity and fear in her eyes—but he could not laugh, for anger filled him instead, anger and disgust at the lies and the stupidity of a sixteen-year-old girl who had no notion of the trouble she could cause. "You don't even know what love is—and he doesn't give a damn about you," he said cruelly. "All he cares about is getting his hands on my money, and getting under your skirts in the—"

"William!" Martha's eyes were shocked, as was her voice, but he ignored her, staring instead at Elise. He started to speak, but her voice cut him short.

"He does love me! We're going to be married! We—"

"I'd kill you both before I'd see you married to that goddamn half-breed!" he shouted at her, almost striking her again. "You won't see him again, not even if I have to kill him with my—"

"No!" she screamed, grabbing at his arm and pulling at him, the tears beginning to stream down her cheeks now. "You can't hurt him; you won't! Please—you can't—"

William stared at her, seeing suddenly in her fear her very weakness. She might be just as stubborn and willful as he—but she had given him a tool now to use against her, a tool that would assure the destruction of the relationship more assuredly than anything else ever could. That tool would be her very love itself.

He pushed her hands away deliberately, and stood staring at her, feeling nothing more for her in that moment than disgust, anger and outrage. "Janson Sanders is dead for crossing me—" he said, staring at her—yes, he would love to see Sanders dead, love to see him dead and bloody and buried where he could never cause trouble again. But there were better ways to handle such matters. Dying hurt only once—but there were ways to make a man hurt for so much longer, ways to make him wish that he were dead a thousand times over in every day that he lived and walked and breathed.

"William, you can't—" There was horror in Martha's voice, but he did not even look at her. He stared at Elise instead, watching the fear in her eyes, fear that grew with each moment that passed.

"Daddy—oh, please, God—no—you can't—" The tears streamed down her cheeks unchecked as she shook her head back and forth. She stepped out of her mother's arms, her eyes never leaving his, her nails digging into the palms of her hands until he knew they were cutting into the flesh—but still he would not speak. "Please—I—I'll do anything you say—please, just don't hurt him. I'll never see him again—please—"

He stared at her, feeling a sense of satisfaction at the words he had known she would speak—she would learn, just as would any other man or woman on this earth, that he was not a man to cross. He would have loyalty and obedience from a daughter, just as he would have it from any other of his people—and she would learn that lesson, and she would learn it well, before this day was over. She would destroy Janson Sanders with the very love she professed to hold for him, destroy him and drive him so far away from her that he would never come back again. If the boy cared anything for her at all, it would be the best way to hurt him, the best way to make sure he never healed—and, if he cared nothing, then William would be rid of him anyway, and would have taught him in the process that the Whitleys were no fools, even though Elise had made a good show of herself as one. Either way, the relationship would be over, the boy gone, and Elise would be back under William's control—and she would never again forget that her foolhardy passions had served only to destroy the man she had thought she loved.

"You'll do what I say?" he asked her, his voice a deadly calm now.

"Yes, anything—" she said, her voice seeming to seize upon the chance. "Anything—if you won't hurt him. Just, please, promise you won't—"

He stared at her for a moment, knowing that he had won, inwardly celebrating the triumph even as he sealed Janson Sanders's fate. "You're going to tell him that you never loved him, that you've only been amusing yourself with him, and that you're tired of the game—and you're going to tell him to leave, that you never want to see his face again as long as you live—"

Her eyes had become more disbelieving with each word. "He'll never believe I don't love him, that I never loved him! He'll know I'm—"

"You'll convince him."

"But, I can't! He knows how I feel about him!"

"Then you'll see him die!" He shouted the words at her, and then stood looking at the horrified expression that came to her face, knowing truly in that moment how completely he had won. "You'll tell him you never cared for him, that you were only trifling with him, and that you're tired of it now, and of him—" He watched her eyes for a moment, seeing the desperation there. "And don't think you can run off with him. I'll find you wherever you go, and, when I do, I'll take the pleasure of killing him with my own hands—" He waited for a moment, allowing the full impact of his words to sink into her. "If you want to be responsible for his death, then just try leaving with him, or try even once not doing just exactly as I say. You're going to drive that boy away from you for good. Anything else, and his blood's on your hands."

She stared at him for a long moment, a hell going on behind her blue eyes. Her tears had stopped now, and he saw a set, pained, but horribly resigned look settle about the corners of her mouth.

"Are you going to do what I say?" he asked her. "Or are you going to watch him die?"

Her expression did not change. There was no longer any of the innocence of youth in her eyes, only a cold, stark resignation to a reality she could not deny. "I'll do what you say," she answered, her voice flat, drained of emotion. "I don't have any choice."

She turned, glancing briefly at her mother, and then started toward the staircase. After a few steps, she stopped and turned back to look at him again. "I hope you know I'll always hate you for this," she said. She stared at him for a moment longer, then turned, and, without another word, she mounted the first step.

THE SINGLE room of the old house seemed chilly that evening in spite of the fire Elise had lit in the fireplace. She stood staring down into the flames, going over in her mind the thousand things that must never seem amiss tonight—the gathering darkness outside would help to hide the smoke from the chimney, the dark cloth over the windows concealing the light from within, just as it had done on so many other late evenings when she and Janson had met here to be alone together. There would be nothing to alert him that anything was different this time, nothing to tell him that their relationship had been discovered, and that it would end, that it must end, for his sake this night.

She had sat in her room for hours before coming here, trying to think of some way, of any way, she and Janson might still be able to leave here and be married—but there was no way. Her father would find them, and at that time she would see Janson die—". . . his blood's on your hands," her father had said, and that would be true, months from now, even years from now, once her father found them. She would have to drive Janson away from her, drive him away so far and so completely that her father could never find him—there was no other choice. She would have to drive him away, and then she would have to wait—for it would be only a matter of months before her condition would become known, and before William Whitley would discover that Janson had gotten her with child. Then her father's anger would turn on her—for ruining her name, for ruining his, for getting herself into this predicament, for saddling him with a child he would have to deal with, a child with one-quarter Cherokee blood in addition to his own. She would be spirited off somewhere to await the birth of the baby, and then she would return to Endicott County alone, for she knew her father would never allow her to keep and raise the child herself—the scandal could ruin the family name forever, and William Whitley would never allow that; but he would make sure the baby was given a good home, a good family, and that was all she could hope for now. Janson would be safe, and the baby would be safe, and she would be alone—but she could not think about that now; if she did she would lose her resolve, and she knew she had to keep her mind clear and her courage up to tell Janson what she would have to tell him this night.

She pulled one of the old straight chairs toward the fireplace and sat down, continuing to stare into the flames. The fire had already been laid before she had arrived, waiting only for the touch of a match to the kindling to start its blaze, and the sight of the burning logs made her heart ache all the worse—Janson must have stopped here before going into Goodwin earlier, taking the time to lay the fire so she would not have to be cold, and that knowledge of what he had done made what she knew she now had to do hurt all the worse. She pulled her sweater tighter about herself, hugging her arms for warmth, but the chill seemed to be coming from within her now just as much as from without, and she found herself wondering if she would ever be able to feel warm again.

She had arrived here early tonight, hoping for time to prepare herself and her mind before Janson could arrive. Her father had allowed her to leave the house without protest, sure of himself and his power over her, making her hate him all the more simply for that assurance—she had carefully chosen this position before the fireplace, hoping that the shadows it cast, plus those thrown by the kerosene lamp on the table behind her, would help to hide the bruise on her face. She knew she would have to remain at least partially turned from Janson as they spoke, making sure he would never see the left side of her face, or he would know immediately they had been discovered, and that her words were not her own.

She took a deep breath and tried to calm the pounding of her heart, rehearsing in her mind the things she knew she must say—oh, how different these words would be from the ones she had intended to give him this night.

The sound of his footsteps came up the narrow board steps and across the rickety front porch, and the door opened behind her, sending a chill gust of wind into the room for a moment. She did not turn, and did not have to, sensing his presence as he entered the room and closed the door quietly behind himself.

"What're you sittin' there s' still for?" he asked, his tone light, a smile in his voice that she could hear, sending an even further stab of pain through her. "You wanted t' see me bad enough earlier."

The sound of his voice cut right through her, bringing a lump to her throat. She swallowed it back and glanced quickly at him, and then away again—she had to look at him one last time while he still belonged to her, take one last memory that would remain in the years ahead.

"I have to talk to you," she said, her voice sounding so terribly flat and lifeless in the room—is that me? she wondered. It sounded so cold, so absolutely dead of feeling—is that really—

"Yeah, I remember." The smile was still in his voice, his words holding added meaning, and her heart pained at the memory of having made this date to meet him, of how he had wanted to touch and hold her when she had needed to talk, and of the reasons she had wanted to speak to him in the first place—oh, how would she ever be able to do this? How would—

"You wanted t' talk, s' go on an' talk," he said, shrugging out of his coat and tossing it across the edge of the table, and then starting across the room toward her—he was going to take her in his arms; she knew it. He was going to—

"I think we've made a mistake—" she said, rising from her chair and moving toward the fireplace, not looking back. Her words were rushed, determined to keep a distance between them—if he touched her, she knew she would fall apart. She knew—

He stopped where he was halfway across the room and stared at her. She could feel his eyes, feel them touching her, though she did not turn to look at him. "A mistake?"

"Yes—that is, I've made a mistake."

He did not speak, and she knew that he was waiting.

"I should never have let it go this far; I realize that now, but, well, I can't change what already has been," she said, staring at some spot above the mantlepiece before her, not daring to look at him, for she knew she could never speak the words if she had to look into his face.

"Let what go this far?"

"The two of us—I've just come to realize that what has been happening between us is nothing more than a mistake. We have nothing in common, nothing we could ever hope to build any kind of life on. If I've led you on in any way, I'm sorry, but—"

"Quit foolin', Elise. I don't like this," he said, a note of warning in his voice.

"I'm not 'fooling'; I'm absolutely serious. After tonight, I don't want you ever to try to see me again or get in touch with me for any reason." She tried to make her words sound firm, but knew somehow that she failed miserably. There was a terrible ache inside of her as she finally turned her eyes toward him, a loneliness for the love she was at that moment destroying—but it was too late, and she knew she had no choice in the matter anyway. She had to do this—she had to, to make him safe.

"Stop it, Elise—"

"I mean what I'm saying. Don't ever—"

"Stop it! You cain't tell me you don't love me." He came closer, stopping before the fireplace to stare down at her as she turned her eyes away again, and she thanked God in heaven that he had chosen to stand on the side away from the bruise on her face. From the corner of her eye she watched the firelight playing off his features, off the high cheekbones and the firm jaw, and a pain went through her again.

"I do not love you, and I never have. It was nothing more than a silly infatuation—and it's over now—" Each word seemed to drive a dagger into her heart. She refused to look at him again, but stood staring down at the logs burning in the fireplace.

"That's a lie," he said, his voice rising in tone. "I don't know why you're doin' this, but I don't like it. You cain't make me believe you don't love me. You even let me lay with you—"

She clenched her hands into fists at her sides—she knew there was only one way, only one thing that would push him far enough away to make him safe. She took a deep breath, and then steeled herself for what she knew she had to do. "Love you—" she said, the bitterness in her voice genuine, but directed at life, and never at him. "Don't be absurd. How could I love you?"

Silence lay between them for a long moment—please say something, she begged inside. Please—"You don't mean that," he said quietly.

"Do you really think I could love someone like you?" she asked, raising her chin and glancing at him for a moment, and then away again.

"Like me?"

Goodbye Janson—she told him silently. "You're nothing but a dirty, sweating farmhand—do you really think I could love someone like you?"

He stared at her for a long moment, not speaking. "I don't believe you," he said at last. "Somethin' has happened, an' I want t' know what it is." His words were clear and determined, his voice strong—he did not believe, would never believe, that everything between them had been nothing but a lie.

Dear God, don't make me do this! Don't make me have to completely destroy him just to make him safe! Please, make him believe me! Make him believe—

"The only thing that has happened is that I've gotten tired of this game," she said, trying to keep the shaking from her voice. "It's over. You'll just have to understand—"

"'Understan'—hell! You're gonna tell me what's happened! Somebody's found out about us, ain't they?" She could feel the rage building within him—not at her, but at whoever, or whatever, was doing this to them.

"No one's found out!" She raised her voice in agitation, her words sounding an anger she did not feel.

"You're gonna tell me th' truth, an' you're gonna tell me right now," he demanded, his tone leaving no room for disobedience.

There was no choice, no alternative left. She knew what she had to do. She knew—

"How do you think I could love you—you dirty, ignorant, half-savage dirt farmer—" The words tore her heart in half. "You make me laugh." That was it. It would be over. He would be safe.

There was nothing but silence in the room for a long moment. She felt almost as if she would scream if he would not speak, if he would not at least curse her or damn her soul to hell forever. When he did speak, she wished that it were a curse, wished that it were anything other than the soft, gentle voice that came to her, a voice filled now with nothing but love and concern.

"What's happened? Who's found out about us? Is it your pa?"

He reached to place a gentle hand on her back, and she leapt away from him almost as if she had been scalded. "D—don't you touch me!"

She screamed the words at him, then quickly turned away again before he could catch sight of the bruise on her face—if he touched her again, she knew she would fall apart. She knew—"Don't you ever touch me again!" She groped desperately within her mind for something, for anything, to scream at him that might make him hate her as he must. "You—you disgust me, you dirty half-breed—"

"Stop it!" he yelled, reaching for her again, determined to turn her to face him even as she tried to push his hands away. "I know somebody's makin' you do this, so just stop it! I know you love me! There ain't nothin' in this world that'll make me believe you don't! I can feel it!"

"Let me go!" she screamed at him, slapping him hard once across the face as she tried to struggle away. "I don't love you! I never loved you!"

"You do! You know you do! I remember all th' times we laid t'gether, th' way you touched me—you cain't tell me you don't love me! I know you do. I feel it." He struggled with her, trying to turn her to face him. "Somethin's happened. I know it has. Your pa knows, don't he? He's makin' you do this. He—"

He finally managed to grasp her shoulders and turn her toward him. An awful look of comprehension came to his face as he saw the bruise darkening her cheek. Her hand flew up to cover it, but it had not been quickly enough.

"Your pa—" His green eyes showed shock, concern, and a growing rage within them. "He's found out about us. He did this to you; he made you say all these things—"

"No! You're wrong! He doesn't—"

He reached to gently pry her hand from her face. "Oh, my God—what's he done t' you?"

"No, it wasn't—I bumped it. It wasn't—"

"Don't lie t' me. It was your pa, wasn't it?"

"No—" She stared up into his eyes. "It wasn't—I don't love you. I—I never have. I—"

"Yes, you do, an' I know you do. Just like I love you—" He looked into her eyes in the flickering light for a moment, then repeated, drawing her closer against him. "I love you."

The ache welled up inside of her—he was assuring his own death with those words. Her father would never let him live now. Never—

She opened her mouth to deny her feelings, to tell him that she hated him—anything that would take him from her forever, anything that would make him safe. But she could not speak. She stared up into his green eyes, feeling herself quietly fall apart inside. There was nothing left, no strength, no energy—only a horrible ache within her. She struggled hard to maintain control, but failed. The tears came, and she could not stop them.

He held her, gently stroking her back, his lips in her hair, speaking soft, soothing words to her as she cried—he would never leave her, never. No matter what her father might do to him, no matter what hells they might have to face to be together. He would always love her, always be with her, always—

The words of love and promise terrified her even as they should have comforted. He loved her and would never leave her—and those words did nothing more than to assure his death at the hands of her father.

"No—you've got to leave! You can't stay here! Daddy'll kill you! He said he would; he'll kill you!" She held him at arms length away, looking up at him, the tears still streaming from her eyes and down her cheeks.

"I ain't goin' nowhere, at least not without you—"

"But we can't! We—"

"We knowed we'd be leavin' one day; we'll just be goin' sooner than we expected. I may not have enough yet t' buy my place back, but it might be enough t' put down on it, an' we can take a mortgage for th' rest. It may be hard goin' th' first few years, but—"

"No!" She screamed the word at him, silencing him immediately. "He said he'll kill you if we try to leave together! He can find us anywhere we go, especially if we go back to Eason County! I can't be responsible for—"

"I don't care what he says, Elise. I ain't goin' nowhere without you."

"But—"

"No," he said, touching a finger to her lips, and then moving it to gently touch the bruise on her face. "Ain't neither one of us can stay here now, not after what he's done t' you. I ain't leavin' you. We'll go, but we'll go t'gether."

"But, he said I'd see you die once he finds us. He said he'd see us both dead before he'd let me marry you. I can't let—"

"There ain't no lettin' to it, Elise. I ain't leavin' you, not now, an' not ever."

"But, if he finds us—"

"No—" he said, his green eyes moving over hers, his fingers still lightly touching the bruise at her cheek. "I ain't gonna leave you. There ain't much in this world I can promise you, but I will promise you that. I won't never leave you. Never—"

He drew her closer into his arms and held her against him, repeating the words, even as she began to cry anew. "I won't never leave you. Never—"

But all she could hear was her father's voice, and his words, time and again, drowning out Janson's own: "I'll find you wherever you go, and, when I do . . . his blood's on your hands."

His blood's on your—

THERE WAS nothing but a complete, dead exhaustion as Elise reached home that night. She was altogether drained of feeling and emotion after the past hours—Janson would not leave, no matter how she had begged and pleaded for him to protect himself. He would not leave her, not give her up—they would leave together, just as soon as she could slip away from the house undetected. They would have their life together, just as they had dreamed, just as they had planned, no matter what it was he might have to risk to allow that to be. She had not told him about the baby, and she knew she could not, not until they were safely away from here. There was enough for him to worry about already, with her safety now as well as his own to think of, for her to add that extra burden as well. He had not even liked the idea of her having to return to the house tonight to face her father, worried about what might happen to her should she rouse his anger again, but there had been little choice. Her father would be waiting for her, waiting to make sure she had done exactly as she had been told—she had to go home, had to wait those hours, those days, until they could leave here safely. Janson would meet her then, once she could slip away undetected, and they would leave together, with hopefully enough time to be out of the County before she could be missed. Until that day, she could only pray that her father would believe his plans had worked so that he would not be watching her all the more closely—that would make communicating with Janson in the meantime all the more difficult, and it would make leaving nothing less than dangerous for them both.

She walked across the front veranda and entered the house, closing the heavy wooden door behind herself, then turning to find her father staring at her from the open parlor doorway to her right, her mother only slightly behind him, the older woman's face worried, concerned—he had been waiting for her, waiting just as she had known he would wait, waiting to make sure she had destroyed herself, and Janson, just as he had intended she would. She felt a fresh surge of anger and hatred as she stared at him, anger and hatred that she did not even try to conceal.

"Did you do it?" he demanded, taking the cigar from his mouth and looking at her in much the same way he looked at his house or his automobiles or his horses, or at anything else he fancied he owned.

"I did it," she said, her feelings for him apparent in her voice.

"Well?" he prompted, his eyes never leaving her.

"He's gone, if that's what you wanted to know." She stared at him for a moment longer, angered even more by the smug and satisfied look that came to his face. "And may you rot in hell for it," she said, seething with anger, then she turned and started toward the staircase, never once looking back.

MARTHA WHITLEY stood at the bottom of the stairs a moment later, watching her daughter ascend into the darkness above. There was a sense of surprise and sudden awareness in her now as she watched Elise disappear from sight, awareness as she had never known before.

She turned and looked at William, finding a look of self-satisfaction on his face—yes, he thought he had won, thought he had defeated the feelings his daughter and Janson Sanders had been hiding for so long. But, oh, how wrong William was. It had been written plainly on Elise's face only a moment before—love, anger, defiance; if only William were not so blind to anything other than himself—but perhaps it was best that he was blind. Perhaps that was the only hope Elise and the boy had left.

Janson Sanders was not remotely what Martha would have chosen for her daughter. He was a decent-enough young man, well-mannered, hardworking, sober, religious in his own way—but he had no home, no money, no social standing, no prospects in the future of ever becoming anything more than what he was now. He was a dirt farmer, a hired hand, and was so far beneath Elise that she should never have given him a second thought—and, for heaven's sake, Martha could never forget that he was only half white. Elise could have made no worse choice if she had planned it, though Martha could not believe the boy capable of a deliberate plan of using Elise just to further his own aims, as William thought. They had simply allowed themselves to be carried away in their fancies, their dreams, for, as Martha well knew, to a sixteen-year-old girl, dreams could quite often be more real than life.

When William had told her of his discovery, of what he had seen in the woods earlier in the day, Martha had been surprised, shocked, and more than a little dismayed—Elise, and the half-Indian farmhand, it was almost more than she could believe. But William had seen, and he knew, and then Elise had confessed—they had planned to run away together, had planned even to be married, and only the grace of God had allowed William to find them out before it had been too late.

But what William had done then had been unforgivable. He had struck Elise, struck her when he had never before struck any of the children. He had threatened Janson Sanders's life, and then had forced Elise to tell the boy the cruelest of lies in order to end the relationship. Martha had pleaded with William, had tried to reason with him, had tried again and again to convince him there were better ways to end the romance, ways not so cruel to Elise or to the boy, but he had refused to listen, cursing her as he had never before cursed her in the twenty-seven years of their marriage. And now he had perhaps sealed all their fates.

There was nothing Martha could do now, nothing to put to a stop what William had set in motion, and nothing to change the decision she had seen in her daughter's eyes. Elise was not yet a woman, but she was also no longer a child—Martha had never before seen that so clearly as she had tonight. It had not been the face of a heartsick child that her daughter had worn, but the face of a young woman instead, a young woman angry at the injustice she believed done her, and determined to protect the young man she thought she loved, no matter the cost to herself. There was nothing Martha could do to stop that now, nothing, for, though she feared her daughter had made the wrong decision tonight, a decision she might live long to regret, she feared even more what William might do should he find out his threats had not worked.

She looked back up the stairs toward where her daughter had gone, sad for her little girl who was no more, and sadder still for the young woman who had taken her place. She knew Elise would not have an easy time ahead, especially not if she had chosen still to be wife to her farmhand, for Martha well knew that Elise would never again know another easy day in her life if she wed Janson Sanders.

But she could not tell her daughter that. She could not tell her daughter anything. She herself well knew there was no way the girl would listen. There were too many memories inside her of another sixteen-year-old girl who had chosen against her own parents' wishes, a sixteen-year-old girl she herself had been all those years ago. She had taken William then, had taken him in defiance of her family and her friends and everyone else she had known. Sixteen-year-old girls rarely listened to reason; they listened to their hearts instead.

Martha Whitley turned away from the staircase, her mind suddenly filled with thoughts and memories and with more pity than she had ever known before.

It was a long time before she realized who that pity was for.

IT HAD begun to rain, a cold, insistent drizzle that soon built into a steady downpour. Janson was soaked through to the skin by the time he reached Mattie Ruth and Titus Coates's house that night. He walked up the slanting front steps to the old porch, pounded on the front door, and then waited, trying to pull his sopping coat tighter about himself.

After a long moment, the door swung inward and Titus stood peering out at him, a kerosene lamp held high over his head to try to better see the unexpected visitor. The old man was dressed in a faded nightshirt alone, his bony legs peaking from beneath it, with Mattie Ruth just behind him in a heavy cotton nightgown that brushed the floor, her hair hanging in two thick, gray braids down over her shoulders.

"Janson—that you, boy?" Titus asked, squinting into the darkness that lay beyond the edge of the lamplight. "What're you doin' out this time 'a night?"

But Mattie Ruth pushed her husband aside before Janson could answer him. "Titus, cain' you see th' boy's clean soaked through?" She moved up to view Janson better, taking the lamp from her husband's hand. "Lor', boy, what're you doin' out on a night like this? You'll ke'ch your death—well, com'on in out 'a th' cold an' th' wet," she said, stepping back for him to enter.

But Janson shook his head. "I don't want t' drip all over your clean floor, Mattie Ruth. I just wanted t' know if it'd be all right for me t' sleep in your barn t'night. I didn't want you thinkin' I was some kind 'a thief or no-good, puttin' myself up without askin'." He could not help but to smile to himself, watching her own eyes light with the same memory that came to him—that seemed a long time ago now, that night she had caught him in the storeroom off the Whitley's kitchen, that first night when he had tried to steal food to eat. That had been before he had met Elise, before he had met any of the Whitleys, before he had—

But he shook the memory away, watching Mattie Ruth smile and shake her head good-naturedly—at least she was not armed with a cast-iron skillet this time. "Lor', boy, don't you think I know by now that you ain' a thief or a no-good—but what do you need t' be sleepin' in th' barn for? You in some kind 'a trouble?"

"Not exactly trouble, at least not yet—"

"You an' Mist' Whitley have words?" Titus asked, staring at him from just beyond Mattie Ruth.

"Not exactly words—but you ought t' know that Whitley's said he'd kill me if he ever saw me again—" It would not be fair to involve them without their knowledge that Whitley's anger would extend to them as well should it ever be found out that they had given him shelter. It was not fair to involve them in this at all, but he had little choice. He could not stay in his room any longer, for Whitley had to believe he had left the place for good, and the old house might not be safe, for Elise might easily have been followed there tonight. Mattie Ruth and Titus's barn was the only alternative. He knew that it was dangerous to stay anywhere on Whitley land now, especially so close to the big house itself, but he could not leave. He had to remain close-by in case Elise should need him. She was still there in the house with her father—if she should make one slip, if she should give herself away, then Whitley might hurt her again. There was no way Janson could leave Whitley land, not yet, or ever, until she was safe with him; no way he could leave, no matter the risk he was taking. Her safety meant more than did his own anyway.

"Mist' Whitley said he'd kill you?" Mattie Ruth stared up at him for a long moment. "Lor', boy, what've you done?"

"I fell in love with his daughter," Janson answered simply.

She and Titus both stared up at him, neither speaking.

"An', I'm gonna marry Elise, that is if he lets me live long enough t' do it."

Neither spoke, and for a long moment Janson could not tell what they were thinking. He watched their faces for a moment, faces shrouded in dim yellow light and deep shadows cast by the kerosene lamp in Mattie Ruth's hand, and it struck him how strange it must sound to them that he was going to marry Elise Whitley, a girl who had everything in the world, when he had come to their door tonight in bare feet and patched overalls, his wet coat tattered and frayed, his only pair of shoes slung over his left shoulder, and everything he owned existing in the battered portmanteau in his hand—but then the feeling was gone, for he knew somehow that he and Elise had taken the last step somewhere in this day, and that there was no going back now.

"You an' Miss Elise?" Titus asked at last, his face still cloaked in that unreadable light and darkness.

"Yeah."

"An', he foun' out about you, what you're plannin'?"

"Yeah—he told Elise she wasn't t' have nothin' more t' do with me, that she was t' break off with me for good, or he'd kill me. She tried, but—well, I wouldn't believe her. We're gonna leave t'gether as soon as we can, an' we're gonna get married an' go someplace where he cain't never bother us again. But, he's gonna be watchin' her close; it may be a while before she can get away without him knowin' an stoppin' her."

"An' you need some place t' stay 'til then?"

"It wouldn't be more than a few days, or a week at th' most. I'd be careful that don't nobody see me—but you got t' know that Whitley'd be madder'n th' devil if he found out you were hidin' me. He could throw you off th' place, an' I don't know what else—"

Titus looked toward Mattie Ruth, and Janson did as well, waiting for her to speak. He knew the decision lay in her hands, just as his life, and perhaps Elise's as well, lay in her hands at the moment—but he would never blame her if she should turn him away. Her home, the home she had lived in for most of her married life, the home where she had borne and raised two sons, both now dead, could be lost if they gave him shelter and were ever found out. Their livelihoods rested with William Whitley, and Janson knew their loyalty should rest with him as well.

After a long moment, Mattie Ruth nodded her head, her decision made, and Janson put his fate in her hands. "You stay here long as you need t', boy," she said, moving out onto the porch to hold the lamp higher as she stared up at him. "There ain' no better husban' Miss Elise could fin' for herself than you. You got t' love her a lot t' be willin' t' take on Mist' Whitley t' have her. We'll do anythin' we can t' help you, boy; all you got t' do is ask—"

JANSON LAY on a bed of hay in the barn a short time later, shivering beneath a damp quilt Mattie Ruth had given him. He could hear the sound of the rain outside, falling steadily on the tin roof, dripping through and into a rusting tin can nearby, the sound slowly turning from a sharp pinging into a dull plop as the can filled.

He twisted uncomfortably under the quilt, pulling the portmanteau closer and trying to use it as a pillow. Inside the worn old leather case was everything he owned in the world, and more. Inside it were the dreams of a lifetime, and the future he and Elise would share together; inside it was the money he had saved over the months of working on the Whitley place, the money that would help him to buy back his parents' dream and his own, the money that would buy the home and land he had promised Elise they would have. It was not as much as he had hoped to have before they left here, but it was still more money than he had ever before owned at one time in all his life. There would not be enough to buy his land outright, but they would make do; he might have sworn never to use credit again, never to have another mortgage against the home and land he had lost before, but he would do it now to give Elise all he had promised her. There would be hard years ahead, but they would survive them. They had survived hell already just to be together.

He shifted uncomfortably, unable to sleep, the sound of the rain grating on his nerves. He was worried about Elise, worried about her, as he would remain worried until they were far away from this place. For the first time in these months he knew with a certainty that she might not really be safe there in the house with her own father. He had never before believed the man capable of deliberately hurting his own daughter, no matter his threats, and no matter what else he knew William Whitley might be capable of doing—but Whitley had hurt Elise today, and Janson knew he might very well hurt her again. He now held no doubt that William Whitley could be capable of doing anything, and to anyone, if it suited his purposes.

The memory of Elise's bruised face haunted him still as he lay staring into the darkness. He knew the bruises she had suffered over the past hours had gone much more than skin deep, and for that he could have very easily killed her father. The man had forced her to deny the love she felt, had forced her to face Janson and say things to him that neither she nor Janson would soon forget, things that had been meant only to drive them apart, and things that had scarred her in a way that might never heal. Janson had known from the moment she had spoken the words that they had been nothing more than a lie, just as he had known that it had been Whitley behind the lies from the moment they had been spoken—Elise loved him; that was the one thing in life that Janson would never doubt again, the one thing he would always be certain of. Elise Whitley loved him.

Janson pulled the damp quilt closer about himself, trying to shut out the cold and the damp and the sound of the rain. It would be a long night ahead, a long night of lying awake listening to the rain on the rusting tin roof, a long night of worrying his mind and his heart over Elise—only a few more days, he promised himself silently. Only a few more days, and we'll leave together. Only a few more days, and—God help me—William Whitley will never hurt her again.

ELISE SLIPPED quietly from the side door of the Baptist Church there in Goodwin that following Saturday morning. She stopped on the steps that descended into the churchyard, listening to the sound of the choir practice from within the building behind her, her eyes moving over the area around the church to make sure she was not being observed before she moved on. Once she was satisfied that no one had noted her departure from the practice, she quietly slipped down the remaining steps and made her way across the near-empty parking area toward the old graveyard that lay to one side of the church. She stopped again no more than a moment later, one hand on the black-painted iron gate, looking about to assure herself again that she was alone, then she entered the graveyard and turned to close the gate again quietly behind herself.

The cemetery stood silent before her as she turned back, the sounds of the Baptist hymn left far behind her now. She stared at the rows of silent gravestones that lay ahead of her, shivering involuntarily and pulling her sweater more tightly about herself—why, she wondered, after the days of fear and constant worrying, unable to see Janson because of the danger he had put himself in just for her and the love they shared;

why, after the days of being constantly watched and observed, had they chosen this of all places to spend the few moments away from the watching eyes of her father and her family?

She forced herself to walk forward, making her way through the gravestones, going deeper into the old cemetery, away from Main Street, her fear for Janson gnawing at her as it had been for days now. The quiet of the old graveyard seemed to seep into her as she walked, the very finality of it, and she stared around her, realizing for the first time in her life how very uncompromising the end of life could be. Her father's words kept rising to her mind—" . . . just try leaving with him . . . and his blood's on your hands."

". . . just try leaving with . . ."

She felt a light touch on her shoulder, and for a moment she felt a sudden and irrational fear that one of the spirits of the dead had risen up to meet her. She jumped, startled, and turned to find Janson behind her, smiling at the very real fear in her eyes.

Suddenly she was in his arms, warm and safe from all the things that had haunted her mind in the last days.

"I've been waitin'—" His words were warm against her ear, his arms tight about her, as if he would never let her go.

"I didn't know if I'd be able to get away, if it would be safe." She stared up at him. "No one saw you, did they? Oh, it's so dangerous for you to be here. Someone could come. Someone could—"

But he silenced her fears with gentle lips on hers, pressing her body tightly to his. For a moment, she was lost in the warmth and nearness of him, worlds away from the fears and worries that now filled her days. When the kiss ended, she was breathless, staring up at him with eyes that searched his own. He looked tired, though he had put on a good face for her. He was clean shaven, in clean dungarees and a workshirt, his hair neatly combed back, as if there were nothing wrong, just as if he were not hiding out even now for his very life—but she knew differently, as did he. She could see it in his eyes, in the set of his jaw. He knew the danger being here with her placed him in. He was making a good show of trying to ignore it, as if it were nothing, but they both knew the truth.

She held him at arms-length away, staring up at him, assuring herself that, at least for the moment, he was safe. "Mattie Ruth said you had been staying with her, out in her barn—oh, I've been going out of my mind worrying about you, wondering if you were safe, if you were warm and dry—" What an answer to her prayers Mattie Ruth had been, coming to her the day after she and Janson had last parted, telling her she knew about the relationship, and that Janson was safe at her home, and that he would remain there until the day she and Janson would be able to leave together. Mattie Ruth had brought her messages from Janson each day since, telling her that he loved her, and that he was safe, and asking her to meet him here in the church cemetery if she could leave choir practice without her father knowing. Those messages had given Elise the little peace of mind she had known in the past days.

"I'm all right," Janson said, smiling and touching her cheek for a moment.

"Are you eating? Is it dry? Have you been able to keep warm—it was so cold last—"

"I'm all right," he said again, clearly not wanting to discuss the subject, and she felt a stab of pain go through her at the knowledge of what conditions that loving her might be forcing him to live under. "How've things been at your place? If your pa's hurt you again, I'll—"

"It's okay," she said, cutting his words off. There had been enough threats of death already in the past few days; she did not want to hear any more. "Daddy's been leaving me alone. He believes it all worked, that you're gone. But he's watching me still. Either he or Bill or Franklin have been with me almost constantly since that night—"

She shuddered even now at the memory of Bill's reaction to her father's discovery. He had gone into a violent rage, threatening to hunt Janson down and kill him even then. Elise had never seen her brother like that before, had never dreamed to see anyone like that, and it had terrified her. It had been nothing less than her father's physical restraint that had stopped him—Janson Sanders was long gone, William Whitley had said, and was not worth the time or the trouble it would take to end his life. Bill had not been easily stopped, screaming violent obscenities at both her, her father, and her mother, until the rage had at last cooled—but still, even now, he looked at Elise in a way that made her uneasy, looked at her in a way that made her wonder if he did not know, or at least suspect, that Janson was still somewhere nearby, still somewhere within Endicott County. Somehow she was now almost as frightened of him as she was of her father, frightened for Janson's sake, and for her own, and for what she knew they might both be capable of doing should they ever see Janson again.

"I guess they thought it was safe enough to leave me at choir practice, or maybe Daddy finally believes that you're gone, but he drove me this morning, and he'll be picking me up in a little while. I—"

There was the sound of a car coming along the side road beside the cemetery, going toward Main Street, frightening her into silence. They moved quickly out of sight behind a monument, then stood looking at each other, both praying they had reacted quickly enough to not have been seen. Elise realized suddenly that she was holding her breath, filled with worry that it had been her father or Bill, and that they might have been seen before they had moved into cover. She forced herself to exhale slowly, listening as the car seemed to slow for a moment, and then pick up speed and drive on past. She looked up at Janson, finding the same worry there in his green eyes.

When the sound of the car had at last died away, he bent to gently kiss her and brush her hair back from her eyes. "You know, it's been drivin' me crazy these last days, worryin' about you," he said, "not bein' able t' see you." His eyes were warm on her, filled again with nothing but love and concern.

"I know. It's driving me crazy, too—"

"Here, I want you t' hold ont' this," he said, reaching into a pocket of his coat to pull out a handkerchief he had knotted something into. He put it into her hands, then closed her fingers tightly around it, holding both her hands in his. "It's part 'a th' money I been savin'—if your pa tries t' hurt you again, or if we get separated somehow in leavin', this is enough money t' get you t' Eason County an' t' make sure you're okay—"

"But—" She felt a superstitious fear rising within her, compelling her to whisper a secret prayer to counteract his words.

"No—just in case you need it—t'morrow, while everybody's in church, do you think you can slip out an' meet me here?"

"I guess so."

"Well, try if you can. I'll be waitin' here for you; bring only what you have t', an' we'll leave."

Tomorrow—tomorrow they would leave together, she told herself. Only one more day, one more night, and they would never have to be separated again—only one more day, and she would leave here forever.

There was a sudden, unexpected touch of homesickness to the thought. Once she left here, she would never be able to come back again, never be able to see her mother or Stan, never be able to see the house or this place she had grown up a part of—never be able to come home again. For a moment, she felt a sadness and a sense of loss she had never expected to feel. She looked up into Janson's green eyes, knowing she could never have both him and the security of the home and family she had always known. There had to be a choice—and she knew that choice had already been made.

"I'll meet you tomorrow," she said, staring up at him, knowing in that moment those words would change her life forever.

PHYLLIS ANN Bennett eased the LaSalle forward, craning her neck, trying to see—damn them for moving behind the monument! If only she could manage to get a little closer without them hearing the car—

Yes! Yes—she had been right! It was Elise and that damned farmhand! Elise Whitley in the arms of a dirty, sweaty, sunburned trash farmhand! Oh, it was almost too good to be true! Elise and that half red-Indian trash!

She had thought it had been them she had seen in the graveyard the first time she had driven by a few minutes before, but they had moved out of sight before she could be certain. She had gone into town and circled around to come back, creeping along so as not to warn them before she could bet a better look. Oh—she could almost laugh and dance with the discovery!

How she hated Elise Whitley, with a passion she had felt toward few things in her life. Elise had been somewhere behind all her troubles and problems, and now, when it had at last seemed as if her life was straightening out, as if J.C. would propose at any moment, then Elise had ruined that as well. Elise had lured him away, getting him to divide his time and his attentions between the two of them. She was stealing him away, stealing him away deliberately—and Phyllis Ann knew she was doing it out of nothing more than sheer spite.

Well, we'll see who has the upper hand now, won't we? Phyllis Ann thought, smiling to herself. She knew Elise did not really want J.C., that she had never wanted him, and that she was apparently even carrying on with this trash farmhand now—she never did have any taste, Phyllis Ann thought, except in J.C. of course.

Phyllis Ann hated the red-Indian almost as much as she hated Elise herself. He had dared to threaten her once, had dared even to stop her from giving Elise what she had so richly earned for her disloyalty—they were probably carrying on even then, she told herself. Well, they deserved each other, Elise and her red-trash farmhand—and, oh, they deserved so much more!

We'll see who has the last laugh, Miss Whitley! Phyllis Ann told herself, thinking delicious thoughts of the trouble she could stir with this bit of information. Oh, such delicious thoughts indeed.

She slowly turned the LaSalle around in the road and drove toward town again, laughing quietly to herself all the while. Elise Whitley carrying on with that piece of red-Indian trash—William Whitley would not be pleased to hear of this. Oh, he would not be pleased at all.

# 20

THE SINGING OF THE BAPtist congregation floated faintly over the distance to the church cemetery that next morning. Janson leaned against a tree there in the depths of the graveyard, waiting for Elise, just as he had been waiting for a time already. He fancied that he could almost hear her voice above the others as he listened, pure and clear, and singing, it seemed, only for him. She would be waiting now for the choir to finish their hymns and be dismissed to the congregation, biding her time until she would be able to slip away to meet him. The day had finally come, the first day of the life they would have together.

But instead of relief and peace as he had expected to feel now, there was a growing tension building in the pit of his stomach. Nothing in life had ever come easy to him. He had always had to fight and struggle his way through each day, from that very first moment he had been born the son of Henry and Nell Sanders, with skin darker than that of his neighbors in Eason County, and a pride unwilling to accept anything less than what his soul demanded. In the twenty years since that birth, he had well learned the meaning of poverty and loss, of hard work and doing without. He knew the struggle to hold onto a dream by its bare, tattered remnants; he knew the feeling of cold and hunger, of worry over where the next meal would come from, and of working until he felt he would drop—but now it seemed all his dreams were finally within sight. The money he had saved from his wages and the moonshining, except for the part he had given Elise, was safely stored away in the portmanteau at his feet, and Elise would be meeting him here within minutes so they could leave together. She would soon be his wife, and they would be back home in Alabama. The land would be his again, even if there would have to be a mortgage. Elise would have the home he had promised her, the best life he could give. It was all within reach finally—it seemed. And that worried him.

He and Elise had known their troubles in getting together. They had fought and struggled, often against each other, in learning to love and in deciding to leave. Now it seemed as if all the troubles were behind them—it seemed.

Some instinct deep within him, something very closely akin to self-preservation, would not allow him to relax. Something kept warning that this was coming all too easily now, that there would still be a struggle ahead to make Elise his wife. He was willing to fight for their life together if he had to; he just prayed it would not come to that. Elise had been through so much already—please, God, no more.

He was on edge, watching, nervous, and, as the minutes passed, the worry only increased—where was she? What was taking so long? Why had she not come to meet him yet? He looked up at the sky, judging the time from the position of the sun through the trees. The minutes were slipping away from them. They would need time to be gone from here before church services could break up, before Elise could be missed. They would need time to—

There was no sound coming from within the church now, nothing coming to his ears but the slight nicker of horses in the pasture beyond the cemetery, and the distant sound of a truck rattling by along Main Street. He looked back up at the sky—she would have to come soon or the opportunity would be gone. She would have to—

ELISE SLIPPED into the back hallway of the church and closed the door quietly behind herself. She leaned back against it, trying to calm the beating of her heart and slow her hurried breathing. It had seemed as if she would never be able to get away. Janson would be worried about her by now, but it could not have been helped. Her father and Bill had both seemed to be watching her even more closely today than in the past days, and Franklin Bates had been near since early that morning. There had been something about the look in their eyes that had frightened her, something that had set her on guard—had they found out? Had she somehow given both herself and Janson away? Were they only waiting now for her to make her move so they could follow her to Janson, so they could do what they had threatened to do? She had kept reassuring herself all morning that there was no way they could know, no way they could have found out—but still there was that look in their eyes. Still there was that look.

When she had suddenly found herself unwatched in the midst of the services, her father and brother both involved in passing collection plates through the congregation, and Franklin Bates nowhere within sight, she had taken the opportunity to slip away, breathing a sigh of relief—if they had suspected her plans, they would never have left her unobserved even for that moment. Janson was still safe—thank God, he was still safe.

This is it, she told herself silently. I'm leaving.

She paused for a moment there in the back hallway, letting the thought sink into her. She wished there could have been some way she could have said goodbye to her mother and to Stan, but she knew there was no safe way she could have done so. She would write to them once she and Janson were safely away from here, sending the letter in care of Mattie Ruth and Titus so that her father would never have to know, and would explain why she had to leave, and why she had been unable to tell them. She would miss them both horribly; she knew that, but she also knew she had to be with Janson. They would understand; they would have to.

Janson—the thought spurred her to movement. She was being foolhardy to stand here in the rear hallway of the church. Each moment she wasted now only served to put them both in greater jeopardy, each was nothing but a moment lost to them—and suddenly moments seemed so very precious to her.

She slipped out the side door of the church, a chill wind hitting her as she stepped out into the autumn air, and made her way across the parking area to the old Tin Lizzie, to retrieve the small valise she had hidden there the night before. In it were the few things she would be taking on to her new life with Janson—a family photograph, a book of poetry, her Bible, what clothing she could carry, the ribbons and small mementos Janson had given her over the months, as well as the money he had given her the day before, and the little money she had managed to save from her clothing allowance, money she had still told Janson nothing about. At first it had seemed so hard to choose among all her possessions as she had packed the small bag, among all the personal items grown fond and favorite over the years. There was so little she could take, and so much that would have to be left behind her forever, that the choices had seemed impossible—but, in looking around her room, she had suddenly realized that the things around her, things so important and vital only months before, mattered little to her now. It was as if they belonged to someone else, a girl she remembered but who she no longer knew. The things now packed within the small bag had been easily enough chosen then, things for their future, and not of the past.

She took the valise from its hiding place and quietly closed the door of the Model T, then made her way across the remainder of the parking area toward the cemetery. There was a nervous worry growing within her, a feeling that there was something wrong, though she could not pinpoint the source of the worry, no matter how hard she searched her mind—but it was there, nagging at the back of her thoughts, making her fret even more for Janson's safety.

She sped up her pace, wincing at the slight squeal the aged hinges of the iron gate gave when she opened it. She moved on into the graveyard, the nagging worry sitting like a lump near her heart—there was something wrong, some part of her mind kept telling her, something very wrong; she could feel it.

She unconsciously brought one hand to her stomach, comforting herself with the presence of the child that grew within her, Janson's child, their child. "I'll be all right," she told the baby aloud, reassuring herself with the words. "Nothing can go wrong now—it'll be all right."

She suddenly froze, thinking for a moment she had heard the slight squeal of the gate hinges at a distance behind her. She turned back, listening, every nerve within her straining for any sound that might mean she had been followed from the church. She held her breath, her eyes searching the graveyard. The gate was hidden from view by trees and tall monuments that stood in the way, but she dared not move to get a better look. She listened, praying to hear no sound that would tell her she had given Janson away. If they found him now—

She refused the memory, but it came anyway—". . . you'll see him die . . . his blood's on your hands . . ."

*His blood's on your—*

If she had brought someone to Janson now—but, no, that could not happen. It was a thought too horrible for words, for feeling. She moved quietly to a position where she could see the gate. It was closed, undisturbed. All seemed still. There was no sound to be heard within the graveyard now, no movement to give reason to believe she might have been discovered, that she might have been followed. Her eyes searched the entire area again—there was nothing to account for the cold lump of fear that sat next to her heart. There was nothing—

It's just my imagination, she told herself. It has to be—only my imagination. Her eyes continued to scan the area warily, then she at last moved on, using even more caution than before.

Something—she stopped once again and turned back. It had not been sight or sound, just a feeling, something wrong.

She stood for a long moment, reassuring herself that her mind was only playing tricks on her, then turned and made her way over the remaining distance to where she and Janson were to meet.

He was there, sitting low on his haunches behind a tree. He smiled at the sight of her, relief coming to his face to push aside the worry and fear that had been there only a moment before. He was risking so much—risking so much, only because he loved her.

He rose and came to her, taking her into his arms and holding her tightly to him, as if his very life depended on her nearness. "I was gettin' worried, afraid somethin' had happened t' you," he said, looking down at her for a moment, his fingers touching her face, then his mouth found hers, taking her breath away. "Are you all right?" he asked a moment later, love and concern in his eyes as they held hers.

"Yes, I'm fine now." She smiled at the happy look on his face. "I was beginning to think I'd never be able to get away, though. I was so afraid someone would follow me to you, so afraid I'd get you hurt or—" She left the sentence hanging there in the air between them, as clearly understood as if she had given voice to the words she could not speak. "We can leave now," she said, smiling up at him, happiness and relief filling her and almost making her giddy.

"Yeah, we can—"

There was a definite sound this time, from very close by. The smile vanished from Janson's face in an instant, and Elise felt a cold stab of fear go through her as her hands tightened almost convulsively on the sleeves of his coat. There was movement at the corner of her eye, and she turned her head quickly in that direction, feeling for a moment as if her heart would stop beating within her—

Her father, standing just yards away, was staring at her, something far beyond anger in his eyes. Her father—

"Oh, dear God, no—" she heard herself saying, her knees going weak beneath her. "Oh, dear God, no—"

THERE WAS hatred on William Whitley's face, hatred and anger and rage beyond anything Elise had ever known before. She stared at him, unable to take her eyes away, unable to speak or to move or to run, until she saw her brother Bill, Franklin Bates, and a farmhand from her father's place move into position around them, and she knew there was no means of escape.

Janson held to her arms, supporting her, even as the muscles in his forearms tensed beneath her hands—she knew this was the end. She knew this was—

"You knew better than to lie to me again," her father was saying, staring at her, his voice cold, flat, unemotional, as if there were nothing left within him of the man she had known all her life.

"Daddy, please, you don't unders—"

"I told you what would happen. I told you—"

"Please, you can't—" She could not breathe, the muscles in her chest constricting, blocking out the air, the words filling her mind—I'll find you wherever you go, and, when I do . . . his blood's on your hands. His bloods on your—"Daddy, please—"

"You never listen. You never—"

She was crying now; she could feel it, could taste the tears, could—"Please—"

"Leave us be, Whitley," Janson said from beside her, his body tense, ready for what they both knew would happen. "We ain't done nothin' t' you. Just let us go on in peace—"

"There's not going to be any peace for you, boy, ever again," her father said, staring at him. "Ever again—"

There was a quick movement of his head, and Bill, Franklin Bates, and the farmhand began to move toward them—Elise shrank against Janson, trying to stay between him and the three men, but a rough hand grasped her wrist, and arms encircled her waist, dragging her away. She began to kick and struggle, fighting against Bill, but he would not release her, holding her still, hurting her it seemed deliberately as she watched Franklin Bates and the farmhand descend on Janson. Janson sent the hand to the ground almost immediately, and Franklin stumbling backwards for a moment before the two men could lay hold on him. He almost freed himself again, screaming words she could not understand as he tried to reach her, fighting as if he would die before he would let them be held apart—until her father's fist, backed by anger and outrage, at last weakened his struggles.

The blows landed on his face, bloodying his nose and splitting his lip, in his midriff, along his jaw—her father delivered the beating himself, until the blood covered his fists, but still he would not stop. Elise collapsed against her brother, her legs finally giving way beneath her, tears streaming down her cheeks—but still the beating continued, only the pressure of Bill's confining arms keeping her from sinking to the ground as he forced her to watch her father slowly killing Janson.

Janson's head snapped back with a blow, blood covering the entire lower half of his face now, the collar of his shirt, even the bib of his overalls soaked with blood. The two men released him and he collapsed to the ground, to lie there bleeding and unconscious. Elise tried to pull free to go to him, but Bill refused to release her, roughly resisting her struggles—he was hurting her, but she did not care. She did not care about anything anymore.

She could hear someone pleading, and she realized suddenly that it was her own voice, her words almost incoherent. She begged—for Janson's life, to be allowed to go to him, for her father to take her life instead—she did not know. Her words seemed independent of her mind now, of her thoughts, somehow functioning free of her will. She was aware of the men around her, the men who had helped her father hurt Janson, aware that her brother held her away from the man she loved, aware that her father stood looking down at the blood on his hands—Janson's blood—but her mind was somehow too filled with horror to register any clear thought, any clear meaning. She could not take her eyes from Janson, from the man who lay hurt, unconscious, bleeding, maybe dying, on the ground at her father's feet, his only crime having been to love her.

She was suddenly aware of her father's stare on her, of the hatred and rage still within him, and she lifted her eyes to meet his, finding them somehow cold and unfeeling and something less than human.

"What kind of man are you?" she asked, the words a harsh, choked whisper in the quiet that now filled the graveyard. "He didn't do anything to you. He didn't do anything but love me. He didn't—"

"I told you," he said, his eyes on her, and she understood with an awful finality what she had known all along.

She began to scream, to struggle anew as her brother lifted her off her feet to drag her away. I told you—the words echoed in her ears over and over again. I told you—

ELISE SAT on the bright rug that covered the floor at the foot of her bed sometime later that day, her eyes staring straight ahead, transfixed, unseeing. Her mind seemed a blessed nothing at the moment. She could not allow herself to think, for horror and reality came together with thought, but she could not stop herself from feeling—fear, guilt, horror, love, grief; they filled her now to the point there was no room left for anything else. She could still see Janson there in her mind, lying on the ground in the cemetery, bleeding, unconscious—the picture would not leave her, and she could not want it to. It might very well be the last image she would ever hold of him.

Bill had brought her here to the house, dragging her away from the graveyard, silencing her screams with a cold, hard slap that had knocked her unconscious before her cries could bring help from the church. She had awakened here in her room later, horrified at the time that had passed, and at what might already have happened. She had screamed and pounded on the locked door, clawing at it until her hands hurt and her fingers bled, but no one had come to help her. She had tested the trellis outside her window again and again, desperate to find any means of escape—but the trellis had shaken beneath her testing hands, and she had known it would never support her weight. If she should try to climb down, and it should fall or break, she knew her baby would never survive the fall to the ground below. She was not worried for her own life now, for she would have gladly taken death in that moment if Janson was gone, but she could not risk the child they had made. If Janson were dead, the baby was the only part of him left to her, a part she could never bear to lose.

She had paced, from wall to wall, from corner to corner, from window to door, again and again—but there was no escape, nothing, nothing she could do. At last she had collapsed to the floor at the foot of the bed, her mind sinking into that blessed nothing, her feelings overwhelming her and crushing her beneath them, her eyes staring straight ahead, transfixed, unseeing—

I told you—echoed somewhere in the back of her mind. And, from somewhere in her memory—his blood's on your hands. His blood's on your—

IT'S OVER—William Whitley thought as he stood staring down at the still form of Janson Sanders where it lay in the back of the truckbed, the blood now long-ago dried on the dark face—it's over. He stood behind the old barn on his property, Franklin Bates beside him, his son Bill approaching from the Packard nearby—it's over.

He stared down at this man who had caused so much trouble, so much anger—never before in his life had he hated any man as he had hated this one, never before had he wanted to take any man's life as he had wanted to take this life—but he had been unable to do so. Sometime during the beating, sometime in the midst of Elise's screams, the smell of the blood, and the utter helplessness of this boy now at his mercy, something had changed within him. The hatred was still there, no less powerful than before, but cold and unimpassioned now, no longer fueled with the rage or the need for blood and revenge that had fed it before. He had wanted to kill this man, had wanted to kill him more than he had ever wanted anything in his life, but he could not do it, and that inability to administer what he knew the man had earned, combined with his surprise at a part of himself he had now seen, a part capable of nothing less than blind fury, now fueled a new anger—but the anger was not directed at this man. Elise—she had always thought she could have her own way, no matter the consequences. He had warned her time and again, had told her what would happen, but she had not listened; she would never listen. She had brought this on herself, on the boy now lying unconscious in the truckbed, on them all—why would she never learn. Why, when it had been all for her own good anyway—but she never listened. And now she had caused this, caused this by her selfishness and her spoiled ways—it had been all her own doing. Nothing but her own doing.

God damn her—why could she never learn. If it had not been for Phyllis Ann Bennett having thrown it in his face in town that she had seen Elise with a farmhand, Elise could have been anywhere by now, gone to him for good—William Whitley's daughter living out her life as the wife of a dirt-poor farmer, spending her nights with that half-breed's hands on her, breeding little dark children with Cherokee blood—it would never happen. Never.

William sighed, continuing to stare down at the still body. It was over. The boy would never dare to come back after this. William would have him taken out of the County and left by the side of some deserted country road somewhere. Elise would be without her farmhand—and she would think twice before ever lying to William again.

Damn her—at least this time she would learn! At least this time!

He could not look at the boy anymore. It reminded him too much of what he had almost done, what he could be capable of doing.

"Franklin, get him out of here. Take him across the County line and dump him someplace away from a town, where he'll have to do some walking to find help. That'll give him time to think before he goes doing any talking."

Franklin nodded, not speaking, and moved toward the front of the truck.

"I'll go with him, Daddy," Bill said, a note of eagerness to his voice that William did not like. He looked toward his eldest son, finding a look of almost studied unconcern on his face.

William shrugged inwardly—what did it matter anyway—and nodded his head. If Bill wanted to waste his time, then it was none of William's concern. He had enough concerns already to think about without taking on others. The boy might no longer be a problem, but there was still Elise to be dealt with. Her recent interest in J.C. Cooper would have been nothing but a ruse to cover this relationship, and it was William's bet that young Cooper's attentiveness to her had been nothing but a quiet conspiracy between the two to aid in the deception. It was likely that Elise had at last once and forever ruined all chances at a union of the Whitley and Cooper families. William would have to find another way of getting his hands on a share of the mill; Elise had left him with little other choice. Damn her, she had only made it more difficult, but not impossible. He would have to tell her the boy was alive, but gone from her forever now just as certainly as if he were dead—but that could wait until tomorrow. Tonight he wanted only rest, time to gather his thoughts before facing the look in her eyes, the hatred, the distrust—she would get over it, he assured himself. She would have to.

He turned and started toward the Model T parked nearby, but was stopped short by a note he heard in his son's voice, something he could not quite identify, but that he did not like.

"Come on, Franklin, let's get rid of this son-of-a-bitch," Bill said, getting into the passenger side of the truck and slamming the door behind himself.

William stood for a long moment staring after the truck as it drove down the dirt road and away from the barn. There had been something in Bill's voice. Something—

He turned and started toward the Tin Lizzie again, wondering why a sudden, cold chill had moved up his spine.

THE TRUCK rattled and swayed beneath the two men as they drove down a rutted, little-traveled country road a short time later. Franklin Bates divided his attention between the driving, and the man who sat beside him, watching Bill Whitley closely while making certain he gave no sign that he was doing so—there was a streak of bad in the man, a streak of meanness, a tendency to take pleasure in doing things that even Franklin often found distasteful. There was something wrong about Bill Whitley, something less than human, something that made Franklin wary whenever the man was near.

"Stop the truck," Bill said suddenly from beside him, leaning forward and staring through the windshield toward something Franklin could not see.

Franklin stopped the truck and shut the motor off, turning toward Bill—but the man was already out of the machine, seeming to have forgotten his presence for the moment as he went to stare down at the unconscious man lying in the truckbed. Bill did not speak, but just continued to stare, something going on behind his eyes—Franklin could feel it, could see it in the cold set of his jaw, in the slight twitch of a muscle at the corner of his mouth. Bill moved to the rear of the truck and stepped up into the truckbed, then bent to examine something, causing Franklin to move quickly to get out of the vehicle—he did not like the idea of having Bill Whitley at his back, out of his field of vision, for even a moment.

Franklin stepped out onto the cracked clay surface of the roadbed, hearing dirt and loose rocks crunch beneath his heavy boots—it was a deserted place Bill Whitley had chosen to stop, still well within the County line, and, unless Franklin was badly mistaken, still on Whitley property. There was a fire-blackened chimney to one side of the road, the only evidence remaining of the sharecropper's shack that had once stood there, its once bare-swept yard now grown high and choked with weeds and brambles. Remnants of an old barn stood nearby, its roof long-ago fallen in and decayed to nothing. November-browned remains of cornfields stretched away from the barn to either side of the road, encroaching even upon where the house had once stood, the entire area seeming now to stand rotting in the chill air.

Bill Whitley was kneeling beside Janson Sanders, going through the old, battered leather case the man had with him when they had found him in the Baptist graveyard ready to run off with Elise Whitley—damned stupid, Franklin thought, for the man to be fooling around with Whitley's daughter, planning on running off with the girl, when he had to know what kind of man William Whitley was. No woman was worth the hell a man would be taking on to make an enemy of Whitley—and perhaps Janson Sanders had taken on so much more.

Bill rummaged through the portmanteau, examining its contents, carelessly shoving aside the few possessions the man owned. Suddenly there was the clink of coins, a flash of silver and green, as Bill Whitley unknotted an old sock he had found among the other things and emptied its contents into the palm of one hand. He whistled appreciatively under his breath, counting out the money, saying almost below the level of hearing: "I wonder who the son-of-a-bitch stole this from."

He counted the money again, then quickly shoved it into one pocket of his coat, bringing his eyes to Franklin. He did not speak, but the look in his eyes carried clear meaning—no word was ever to be spoken of this. Bill hurriedly shoved the work clothes back into the portmanteau and slammed it shut. Straightening up in the truckbed, he slung it as far away from the truck as he could.

The leather case came to rest at the edge of the dead corn field across the road, springing open to spill its contents out over the ground, but Bill seemed not to have noticed or to care. When Franklin looked back to him, he found the man staring down at Sanders again with that queer look in his eyes. Bill knelt and began to manhandle Sanders up and half-over the side of the truck box, leaving him hanging there for a moment before giving him a shove with one foot and sending him down onto the hard-packed clay surface of the roadbed—so, he's still alive, Franklin thought, hearing a muffled groan from the unconscious man as his body impacted the hard ground. He looked up again as Bill Whitley jumped down to stand beside him.

"Bring him—" Bill said, then turned and strode away toward where the burned-out sharecropper shack had once stood.

After a moment, Franklin knelt and lifted Sanders into his arms, then stood with his burden to follow Bill Whitley. He realized suddenly that he was carrying the unconscious man with an unnecessary gentleness toward his injuries, but he did not stop. Somehow he knew this could very well be the last kindness the man would ever know in this life. Somehow, he knew.

Bill Whitley was throwing aside the plank coverings to an old well when Franklin reached him and laid Janson Sanders on the ground nearby. The wooden curb to the well was long gone now, or, more likely, burned in the fire that had destroyed the house. Bill uncovered the dank, gaping hole, then stood staring down it, as if relishing the moment before proceeding on to what Franklin already knew was inevitable.

"Dump him in," Bill said at last, not looking up.

Franklin stood staring at him for a moment, not moving. He had no idea why Bill Whitley wanted this man dead, or why he was going against his father's orders, and it really did not matter to him. He had killed before, not at the behest of the Whitleys, but for other, even harder men he had worked for in the past, as well as for his own reasons and purposes when he had found it necessary. Killing did not bother him—but somehow this went against the grain. Ending a man's life was a simple process, and it could be easily and cleanly done—but to throw a living and badly injured man down a well to die of his injuries, or to drown him in the darkness of the water below, went beyond killing.

"Dump him in!" Bill's voice rose, tinged with impatience, and Franklin's eyes moved back to the man lying on the ground, to the blood caked and dried now on the battered face, and the torn and blood-stained clothes. Never once had he failed at a job, and he would not do so now—but he could show mercy. He would send Sanders down the well, but he would end the man's life first, quickly and mercifully, before doing so, and Bill Whitley would never even have to know.

But he had hesitated too long. Bill's patience had grown thin. He gave an annoyed sound and shoved at the unconscious man with his foot, and then again, finally sending Janson Sanders over the edge and down into the darkness below.

Franklin Bates stared at Bill Whitley for a long moment, seeing the look of satisfaction that came to the man's face as he peered into the well. "That's one son-of-a-bitch who'll never cause trouble again," Bill said, seeming to have forgotten his irritation at Franklin's delay. Bill continued to stare down into the darkness for a long time, and then looked up at Franklin.

"We can't go back too soon. Cover the well over and we'll go into town for a drink, maybe even find a little female company for a while." He started back toward the truck, leaving Franklin Bates standing alone there in the chill air.

Franklin looked down the open well for a moment—there was nothing anyone could do for Janson Sanders now. His fate had been sealed from the moment he had decided to run away with Elise Whitley, perhaps even from the first moment he had stepped foot on Whitley land, and perhaps it was right that he rested now on Whitley property, near Elise Whitley in death, as he had not been able to be in life.

Franklin bent and began to cover the well again with the planks Bill had thrown aside, then stood to stare back toward the truck and toward Bill Whitley who stood impatiently at its side—it was not safe to let a man like Bill live, a man who took such pleasure in killing, a man who killed with such cruelty and ease. Franklin knew he would kill Bill

Whitley one day, with no more mercy than the man had shown today, if the chance ever came.

Franklin looked back to the covered well one last time, to the place that had become Janson Sanders's grave—somehow he knew that chance would come. Somehow, he knew.

# 21

THERE WAS NOTHING BUT darkness and moisture, a deep, dank pit without sound, sight, or feeling. Confusion and disorientation floated around Janson, touching him briefly, only to move away into the darkness and back again.

Sensation came slowly, the feel of wetness, the scents of earth and moisture, the comforting darkness. There was no thought, only sensation, confusion, and wonder as he struggled to climb above the layers of fog that crowded his mind. He reached above to consciousness only to feel the crushing impact of pain take hold of him and plunge him back down into the fog again, a fog now laced with an inescapable pain.

He fought his way back above, struggling to breathe in spite of the burning that filled his side. The air was stagnant, filled with the scents of earth and moisture, of decay and disuse. His hands went out, contacting the damp clay walls around him, and fear joined the confused mass of emotions already within him.

He looked up, seeing far above him where rays of light slanted into the pit through gaps in a covering. His hands moved over the walls and down into the rising mire around him. Realization came of where he was and why he had been put here, and, with that realization, a fear stronger than any he had ever known before—he was going to die, and this would be his grave—but the fear was not for himself; it was for Elise instead. If they had done this to him, they could have done anything to her. William Whitley might be her father, but, to have done this, he had to be a madman, a madman capable of doing anything.

Janson tried to struggle to his knees, only to be plunged back into the fog again. For a moment the world was dark and he fought his way back to consciousness—Elise, the thought of her stayed in the forefront of the confused mass of thoughts, feelings, and pain within him. She needed him—Elise needed him—was the only clear meaning he could hold to.

He pushed himself to his knees in the rising muck, forcing himself to breathe through the pain that now filled his side. Almost unconsciously his hands sought the sides of this prison, searching for hold, for escape. His hand dug into a slippery foothold carved shallowly into the well side, his foot moving up, pushing, trying to compensate for an arm now almost useless at his side.

The world swam with pain around him, his hands slipping in the damp clay, and he started to lose hold, but caught, a burning sensation stabbing through his right side as it impacted the wall. He gasped as the pain shot through him, trying to force himself to breathe, his eyes moving to the light above—then darkness started to come, but from within him, and he started to slide, his hands losing hold again, his body slipping downwards—

There was one last clear thought of Elise, and then he knew nothing but darkness.

ELISE LAY curled on her side on the floor at the foot of her bed, somewhere lost in dreams that brought no peace. She had sought sleep as a release from what she knew she could never face in her mind—but sleep this day had brought little comfort. She had closed her eyes knowing Janson might be dead, and that knowledge had only followed her over the threshold of sleep to haunt her dreams.

At first, there had been nothing but the comforting void she had sought, a place where she did not have to think or feel, but soon images and pictures had invaded its sanctity. She was looking for Janson, seeing him at a distance, but never able to reach or to touch him. The baby was there, now born, but taken from her without her ever having been allowed to see or touch her own child—gone, both gone from her forever, and she was alone, so very alone.

The horror of a reality-to-be invaded her dreams, and she fought to escape it, to run to some place far away where she could mourn her loss alone, but everywhere she turned there were faces. Her father, Bill, Franklin Bates, the farmhand—they mocked her with their presence. "I told you . . . his blood's on your hands."

—his blood's on your hands—on your hands—your hands—

She pressed her hands over her ears, trying to shut out the words, but still they came, this time from within her mind—his blood's on your hands—your hands—your hands—

Then a voice, warm and gentle, touched her above the ringing torment in her ears: "Elise—" and she looked up into green eyes and a gentle smile—Janson, alive, holding her in his arms on the sagging rope bed in the old house, the warmth of his body against her; and the haunting, horrible knowledge of death and blame became a distant memory under the feel of his nearness and his love.

"We b'long t' each other—" he was saying, his body close against hers, "an' you're my wife now, just the same as if we was married," he said, touching her in the gentle ways he always touched her when they were together, "we're one flesh, just like th' Bible says . . . not ''til death do us part.' Dyin' won't stop th' way I feel about you; it couldn't stop it—"

Dyin' won't stop—

Elise came awake slowly, fighting desperately to hold the remnants of the dream to herself—she could not leave him behind there in that hazy land inside her mind. She could not—

But there was no choice. Finding herself lying on the rose-colored rug at the foot of her bed, she cried—wanting Janson, needing Janson, as never before in her life. The memories of that day she had spent in his arms, having once invaded her dreams, would not leave her now—"We b'long t' each other . . . we're one flesh . . . Not ''til death do us part.' Dyin' won't stop th' way I feel about you; it couldn't stop it . . ."

" . . . we're one flesh . . ."

The thought stuck in her mind, the meaning—if they were really one person, then how could she continue to live if he did not. How could she breathe, and think—how could she live day after day in a world where

Janson was no more. He had said his own mother had died of grief after his father was gone—how could she live if Janson was no more. How could she—

But her father had taken that from her as well, had let her live, even as he had taken Janson from her—but what if Janson had still been alive when she had been dragged from the graveyard. He could be somewhere hurt, bleeding, dying even now—

She had to find him. She had to go to him and be with him. Perhaps her father had not been able to kill him. Perhaps—

Janson could still be alive. Janson could be—

She sat up, brushing the hair back from her wet face, certain in that moment that she would somehow know inside herself if he were really dead. He had been badly beaten; she had witnessed that herself, but she could find him and take care of him. She could—

Janson could be alive—

She got up from the floor and stood staring around herself, unsure as to what to do—Janson could be alive. She had to find him. She had to—

MARTHA WHITLEY stood on the dimly lit second floor landing of her home that night, carefully balancing a supper tray in her hands. She listened for a moment, almost holding her breath, making sure there was no sound of movement anywhere within the huge old house. Once satisfied, she moved down the hallway, stopping for a moment outside the door to the bedroom she shared with William, listening to the monotonous sounds of his snores—thank God he had retired early tonight, she thought, moving across the hallway to the door to her daughter's room.

William had forbidden Elise a supper tray, after the one that had been taken her earlier in the day had been left untouched—Elise would learn a lesson, he had shouted, and she would learn it today. "This is the last one of her tantrums I'm going to put up with—just look at what she's caused!" he had shouted, pacing back and forth in the lower hallway. "I warned her, didn't I? I told her what would happen—but she wouldn't listen to me; she never listens! Well, this is the last time! She's going to learn she's nothing unless I say she is—and she's going to learn it now!"

Never before this day had Martha truly known what fear was—but she knew now. The man who had beaten that poor boy before Elise's eyes, and then had caused her to be dragged away, hysterical with fear, thinking the boy would die for her choice to run away with him, was not the William she knew. He had said that he had never intended to do anything more than frighten the boy and teach Elise a lesson in respect—but Martha knew differently. She knew he had intended to kill Janson Sanders, but that he had somehow been unable to do so—and she could only thank God in heaven that he had not been able to commit that murder, for it showed her there was still at least something of the man she had married left within him.

Never in all her life had Martha dreamed to know a hell such as the one she had lived through today—the sound of Elise's screams, the girl's pounding at the locked door to her room, her voice pleading only for Janson Sanders's life to be spared, and to be allowed to leave with him in peace—but first Bill, and then William, had physically restrained Martha from going to her daughter. Elise had to be taught a lesson, they had said; she had to learn, once and for all, and she would learn today.

The screams and pounding had been horrible, but the silence that had followed had been only worse, a deathly, eerie silence that seemed to fill the house until there was no room left for anything else. Elise had been sitting on the floor at the foot of her bed, staring, unresponsive, when William had allowed the dinner tray to be taken her, and had been in the same position hours later when the untouched tray had been removed—"She can sleep hungry for that!" he had shouted, and had kept a locked door between them for the remainder of the day, not allowing Elise a tray at supper time, or even allowing Martha in to check on her—but now William was asleep, and Martha would do what she had to do. There might be hell to pay tomorrow, but at least she would know that Elise was all right. At least, for now, she would know.

She fumbled with the huge ring of keys, balancing the tray in one hand as she tried to keep the numerous keys from making noise as she searched for the right one. She fumbled with the lock, trying first one key and then another—it was William's key ring; he had left it in plain sight on the bedside table, just as he left it every night, never once believing she would go against him. But William would learn something about his wife this night, just as she had learned so much about him.

She counted through the keys again nervously, knowing she had tried some of them several times already, and others not at all, and not knowing anymore which was which. A part of her feared what she might find on the other side of that door once she opened it, what state her daughter might have reached in her pain and grief—Elise believed the boy would die for what they had done today, that his life would be forfeit for her choice to run away with him. William—damn his soul to hell—had let Elise believe through this entire day that Janson Sanders was dead, that she had been the cause of his death, even as Martha had begged him to allow her to tell the girl the truth, to spare her at least that one ultimate horror.

But Elise would know the truth now. It was the one thing Martha could do for her daughter. And it might be the one thing that mattered the most.

She fumbled with a key again, inserting it in the lock, thinking that she had tried it several times before—but this time it turned, sliding the bolt back into the wood of the door. Martha glanced down the hallway again, then quietly pushed the door open, steeling herself for what she knew she might find on the other side of—

The door was yanked from her hand, the supper tray almost crashing to the floor as Elise tried to rush past her and into the hallway. Martha grabbed for her sleeve, trying to balance the tray in one hand as she also tried to stop the girl's escape.

"Stop it!" The words were a shouted whisper, meant to still the girl before the struggle could wake William. "Stop it! It's only me! Stop it!"

She shook Elise soundly with one hand, almost upsetting the tray again—if William should hear—

"Stop it, Elise! I mean it—stop it!"

The girl at last seemed to realize her mother was alone, halting her struggles with one last desperate look down the hallway toward the staircase that could led her to the first floor. Martha kept a secure hold on the sleeve of her daughter's sweater, listening, making certain for the moment that William had not been disturbed.

"Help me with the tray," she whispered after a moment. "We've got to get out of this hallway before—"

"You've got to help me get out of here. I've got to find—"

Martha silenced her with a quick motion. "For now we have to get out of this hallway, in case the noise woke—"

She did not need further words. Elise took the tray from her hands and reluctantly turned back into her own room, turning desperate eyes again toward the door as Martha closed it behind them. "Janson's alive, isn't he?" she asked, her voice no less desperate as she sat the tray down on the dresser top and came toward her mother. "He's alive; Daddy couldn't do it, could he? He's alive—"

"Sh—your father—" Martha warned, raising a hand to her lips, trying again to listen to make sure they had not been overheard.

"But, he's alive! I know he is; I can feel it—"

"Yes, he's alive—"

"Oh, thank God—" Elise said, relief flooding her features as she turned away. "I knew he was. I knew—"

Martha stared at her for a moment, wanting to go to her, waiting to take her into her arms and hold and comfort her as she had done when she had been a child, but unable to. She did not know what to say to Elise, and knew somehow that she would never know what to say to her again—how did a woman talk with a daughter who was now almost a woman herself?

"Where is he? Where did they take him?" the girl asked, turning again to look at her, causing a stab of pain to go through Martha at the memory of the child she had once known.

"I don't know where he is, just that William had him taken out of the County—"

"Was he all right? Did you see him? You've got to help me get out of here. I've got to find him. Daddy beat him so bad; someone has to look after him. I've got to get out of here and take care of him. I caused all this—"

"No, you haven't caused anything. Your father did—and you can't find him; you don't even know where to begin to look."

"But I can't just sit here while Janson's only God knows where, hurt, bleeding—I've got to do something. I've got to—"

"You can't do anything, not now—"

Elise stared at her for a moment, clenching her hands helplessly into fists at her sides, and then she turned away—but not before Martha had seen the look of pain that had passed across her features. It had been genuine and deep and very real, and tearing the girl apart—damn William, he had done this. Martha could not want her daughter to be the wife of a penniless farmhand anymore than William could want it, but she would rather have had that than the hurt she saw within Elise at this moment. There were no words she could offer, nothing she could do or say that would lessen the hurt or worry that was eating away at the girl. William had beaten the man Elise loved, had beaten him and had forced her to watch, and then had caused her to be forcibly dragged away, believing the boy would die for her choice to run away with him. There were no words that could excuse that, and there were no words that could lessen the torment she saw within her daughter at this moment.

"He looked so hurt—" Elise was saying quietly, turned away from her mother, "lying there on the ground, bleeding—I wanted to go to him, but they wouldn't let me—" Then she repeated the words again, almost to herself. "They wouldn't let—"

"I know—" Martha said, interrupting her, as if silencing the words would somehow undo all that had been done this day. She went to Elise and put her arms around her, as if she were still that small child Martha could remember so well. "He'll be all right. He's young, and he's strong; he'll be fine—" The words sounded empty as she voiced them, but somehow they, or possibly her mother's very presence, seemed to soothe the girl. Martha led her to the bed and they sat down at its edge, Martha taking the girl's hand in her own to pat it.

"He has to be all right; he has to be. I couldn't stand it if—" Elise turned her face away, biting at her lower lip for a moment as her mother watched her. "It's just that, I love him so much. So—"

"I know you do." Yes—she knew. Elise was in love with Janson Sanders, very deeply in love. Martha looked at her daughter for a moment. "You were going to run away with him, weren't you?" she asked.

"Yes—" Elise said, bringing her eyes back to her mother, eyes that were suddenly bright with tears at their edges. "We were going to leave and be married, and go some place where Daddy could never find us again—"

"Maybe it's better that it happened this way. What kind of life could that have been for you, married to a man without a cent to your names, barely scraping by for the remainder of your lives, raising children without any real hope of any kind of future for them—and he's only half white, Elise, do you realize what it would have been like married to a colored—"

But there was a sudden anger behind the girl's blue eyes. She withdrew her hand from her mother's, then clenched both fists in her lap. "Do you think it matters to me that Janson has Indian blood, that he's only half white? He's good and he's decent and he loves me—and we would have a good life. He's been working so hard, saving every cent he makes, so that we can buy back the land he lost after his parents died. We'd have our own home; we'd never be rich, but we'd have enough and we'd be together, and we'd be where no one could ever hurt him again or try to tear us apart—and I hope all our children look like him; I hope they all show their Cherokee heritage, because Janson's so proud of his. We'll have a good life together; we will—"

Martha stared at her for a long moment—I hope . . . our children look like him . . . We'll have a good life . . .

Surely Elise could not believe the boy would be back for her after the beating William had given him today. Surely—

"I just hope he'll be careful—" Elise said, her eyes seeming for a moment to be focused on something far beyond this room.

"You can't really believe he'll come back for you now, not after—"

Elise looked at her again, her eyes holding an absolute assurance within them. "I know he will," she said. "He'll come back. Nothing

Daddy ever does, short of killing him, would ever stop him." For a moment she looked away again, her eyes seeming distant, looking at things Martha could not see—"And even that wouldn't keep us apart, not forever," she said more quietly, almost to herself.

Martha stared at her, for a moment believing her daughter had lost her reasoning in the hell she had lived through today. "Elise, Janson would be a fool to come back for you now, and, if anything in this world, Janson Sanders is no fool. William may not have killed him this time, but he could very well do it the next."

"I know that, and so does Janson—but that won't stop him. Nothing will. Nothing—"

Martha looked at her for a moment, seeing the calm belief in her eyes, hearing it in her voice—Elise knew her heart, and perhaps she knew Janson Sanders better than anyone else could. If William had not found them out, Elise could very well have been a married woman by now—her daughter, married to a half-Indian farmhand who hadn't a penny to his name. Elise, married to a dirt farmer, a boy who was only half white—it still did not sit well.

But, as she looked at her daughter, there was something in Elise's eyes there was no way around, something that no number of beatings or violent, enforced separations would ever break. Elise was in love with Janson Sanders, and perhaps he was truly in love with her. If that were true, the trouble they had already faced would be nothing compared to the hell they would yet have to fight if they were to be together—that is, if Janson Sanders were really enough of a fool to return for her.

"Your father has no intention of ever letting you marry him. If he comes back—"

"I know—" Elise said, cutting off her words, refusing to hear them. "But, he will come back for me. And, when he does, I'm going with him."

There—the words had been said. If Janson Sanders came back, Elise would leave with him. There was no question in the girl's eyes, no doubt.

"Are you certain you want to do this, to go with him if he does return for you? You can't know the kind of life, all you would be giving up—"

"I do know. I know that once we leave here, I'll never be able to come back again, and that I may never see you or Stan again for the rest of my life—but it's what I have to do. I have to be with Janson, and we can't be together here. We have to go someplace where Janson can be safe from Daddy, someplace where Daddy can never hurt him again. It's what I have to do."

Martha looked at her for a long moment. Suddenly it seemed she was already so very far away.

"You're really certain that he'll be back for you?" she asked, quietly.

"I know he will be."

"And, when he does—"

"I'm going with him. I have to," she said.

Martha looked at her. Knowing. Understanding. Suddenly there were tears in her eyes and Elise's arms were around her, her wet cheek pressed to Martha's own. "I'll miss you. I don't know what I'll do without you here—"

"I know—" Elise said, looking up at her again, her eyes bright with tears as Martha reached to pat her wet cheek.

"You're all grown up now; I just don't know when it happened. I keep remembering my little girl—but you're almost a woman now. It's hard to believe you're almost seventeen, when it just seems like yesterday that I held you in my arms for the first time—you'll know what I mean one day, when you're a mother yourself. It's a feeling you never forget, knowing that little person needs you so completely—"

Elise's eyes left her mother's for just a moment, the expression in them something Martha had never seen there before. "I know—" she said quietly—and suddenly Martha understood.

Elise was pregnant. There was no doubt in Martha's mind in that moment. The expression on her daughter's face was the same she had seen on her own reflection the first time she had known she was with child—but it could not be! Elise was only a baby herself, not even seventeen yet, only a child—what could she know of a man's needs, or the physical intimacies between a man and woman. Martha had never been able to even bring herself to tell Elise of the intimacies of marriage, had wondered how she would ever be able to tell her—it could not be!

The mother within Martha screamed out in protest—but the woman knew. Elise had been ready to run away with Janson Sanders today, ready to run away with him to be his wife, and it was likely they would have been married months earlier if it had been possible. They had been kept from becoming man and wife out of a fear of William, a fear at knowing what he might do to keep them apart, a fear of what he had almost done this day—it was likely that, having been denied a legal marriage, they might have begun to share the intimacies of marriage anyway. Elise could very well be pregnant, and, if she were—dear, God, it could only make matters worse.

Martha stared at her daughter, almost afraid to ask the question, afraid to hear the words that would confirm what she already knew to be true. "Elise, I know you love Janson, and I know you and he have wanted to be married," she said, reluctantly. "Sometimes things happen that we never thought would happen, things that shouldn't happen between a man and a woman who aren't—" Why couldn't she think of the right words; why was she saying this all wrong. "Elise—have you and Janson become closer than you should have? Have you done things—" Why couldn't she think of what to say, what to ask. "Elise, are you going to have a baby?"

Elise looked at her mother for a long moment, a moment that Martha thought would never end. When she spoke at last, there was no shame in her voice, only a pride and a dignity in her manner that for a moment reminded Martha so very much of Janson Sanders. "The only way that Janson and I are not married is in name only," she answered quietly. "And, yes, we are going to have a baby."

For a moment, Martha could only stare, feeling as if all the breath had been taken from her body. Then breath and feeling seemed to return at the same moment, along with words she could not stop. "That's why you were leaving today, why you had to be married so soon! Because he—"

"No, we were leaving because it's not safe for Janson if we stay here; he doesn't even know about the baby yet."

"Doesn't know!—but you've got to tell him! You've got to be married right away! If your father finds out—" Dear God, if William found out,

Janson Sanders would not even live long enough to marry Elise. He was already threatening to kill the boy on sight if he should ever return, and was planning on sending Elise away to school again just as soon as arrangements could be made, to put her in a place where Janson Sanders would never reach her—if he found out now that Elise was with child—

Oh, how Martha wished she had never laid eyes on Janson Sanders! He had come into their lives, had turned everything upside down, and now he would come back to take her daughter away forever. And, if he did not come back—she could not allow herself to think about that, of Elise being sent far away to have her baby, of a quiet arrangement for someone else to take the child in. Elise could never give birth in Endicott County, and she would never be able to keep the child—no, William would never allow—

Elise was talking, and Martha tried to drag her attention back, to somehow hear what her daughter was saying.

"You've got to find out where it is they've taken him, and how badly he was hurt. And you've got to help me get out of here so that I can find him—"

Martha looked at her for a long moment—Elise, a mother; dear God, where had the years gone. "You really love him, don't you?" she asked quietly. "You'd still marry him, even if it weren't for the baby?"

"Yes, I would."

She nodded. There was nothing else she could do. Then she sighed, the sound coming from deep within her. "I'll help you, as much as I can," she said, knowing the words would take her daughter from her forever, just as they would drive a wedge between herself and William, a wedge that might never be removed. "But, for right now, you've got to eat something." She got up from the bed to take the tray from the dresser top where Elise had sat it earlier. "It's cold by now, but—"

"I don't think I could eat anything. I'm not hungry, and—"

"There's nothing we can do tonight. You've got to eat and get some rest. I'll see what I can find out tomorrow."

"But we've got to find him before he can come back. Daddy might—"

"I know—" She did not have to hear the words. She knew William might very well kill Janson Sanders on sight this time, without even knowing that the man had gotten his daughter with child. "But we'll worry about that tomorrow. For now, you just think about eating—" She placed the tray over the girl's lap, then raised a hand to silence the protest she could see coming from her lips. "No—you've got to think of yourself and the baby tonight. You've got to eat and get some rest; tomorrow we'll worry about finding out where Janson is—you want to give him a healthy baby, don't you?" she asked, seeing a touch of William's stubbornness within the girl. "Now, eat."

Elise obeyed, unfolding the linen napkin and uncovering the plate of ham, buttered potatoes, snap beans, and biscuits, long grown cold now, and beginning to eat—but Martha knew it was more for the sake of her child that she did so, than for herself. She watched the girl, feeling suddenly so very old, so very tired. All she could remember was a little girl with long, reddish-gold braids and big blue eyes that had forever held the wonder of the world—but here sat this young woman before her now, her own daughter, a woman with child. There was such an absolute faith in Elise's eyes, such a belief in Janson Sanders, and Martha could only pray, for all their sakes, that her faith was not misplaced. Elise said he would be back for her, and Martha suddenly found herself praying to God that she was right, even though she knew it would mean she might never see her daughter again through the remainder of her days.

She crossed the room to stare out the dark windows at the rain that had slowly begun to fall outside, her mind on the young man out somewhere in that darkness. Janson Sanders had already faced death once to be with Elise, knowing fully well what William had threatened to do should they ever try to leave here together, and Martha found herself praying that he would not be afraid to face death again. If he did not come back for Elise, then the girl's life would be forever ruined. If he did, it would be forever changed, but it would be the life Elise had chosen for herself long before this day, a choice they would all have to live with now—that is, if Janson Sanders could only survive long enough to make her his wife. William had almost beaten the boy to death this time, and Martha knew there would be no almost the next time. If William saw Jansen Sanders again, he would likely kill him on sight.

A COLD, steady rain had begun to fall that night, drowning the windshield before Stan Whitley, and thoroughly dampening the inside of the car. Stan knew he was in trouble already. His father had allowed him to drive the Model T on the condition that he be home by supper—but supper time had long passed now, and Stan knew there would be hell to pay when he reached home. He had gone directly to a friend's house for dinner after church that morning, and had not arrived at his own home until well into mid-afternoon—when he had asked to use the Model T to take Sarah Pate for a drive, he had never expected that his father would give in, much less that he would give in without a moment's hesitation. Stan had never been allowed to drive an automobile alone before—he had felt so grown up, so trusted, as he had driven away in the Model T—but it would probably be the last time as well, he kept telling himself, for he should have been home hours ago now.

He turned the Ford off on a narrow, little-traveled road that cut off from the main one. He had been down it only a few times in the past, but knew it was a shortcut home—he was in enough trouble already; getting home now as quickly as possible was the only hope he had left. He took out his handkerchief and wiped at the foggy windshield for the hundredth time, straining his eyes through his spectacles, trying to see the muddy road before the car—why could the thing not have a wiper to knock the rain from the windshield as some other automobiles had. He had never driven at night before, and was amazed at how very little the dim headlamps of the Ford aided in picking out the road ahead. With the darkness and the rain, he was certain at any moment that he was going to end up in one of the ditches alongside the road—his father would wear a belt out on him for that, he told himself, for William Whitley had threatened it often enough. His father would—

For a moment, through the rain and the darkness and the fogged windshield, he thought he saw something lying in the road ahead, something dimly illuminated by the headlamps of the Model T—a pile of rags, a sack of seed or guano that had fallen from the back of some passing truck, but, as he drew nearer, the pile of rags took on shape and began to look almost like a man lying there in the muddy road. Stan stopped the car and sat staring through the rain-soaked front glass, his heart in his throat—could it really be a man lying there in the rain, maybe hurt, maybe even dead—but there was no reason for anybody to be out here in the first place. There was nothing nearby but the remains of a burned-out old house and several fields of dried-up corn stalks—why had he ever taken this shortcut anyway? Why had he had to find this pile of rags that looked like a man, and why couldn't he now just turn the Model T around and forget that he had ever come down this road—but, somehow, he could not. He opened the car door instead, and slowly got out, never once taking his eyes from the form lying there in the road.

The rain pelted him, running down his glasses and getting into his eyes. He left the door open and walked around it, making his way toward the rags—it was a man, and in that moment Stan did not know if it would frighten him more should the man move, or should he continue to lie there as if he were dead.

"Please, don't be dead," he heard himself say aloud, feeling his knees begin to shake beneath him—but he knew he would scream and run if the man should move in even the slightest to prove to him that he still lived.

But the man did not move, and, as Stan drew closer, he feared that he was about to discover a lifeless body—please don't be anybody I know, he prayed silently as he reached the man's side. He knelt slowly and reached to roll him over, finding his hands to be shaking horribly as he took hold of the man's sleeve—don't be anybody I know.

The man seemed so very heavy, and so without life as Stan rolled him over onto his back in the muddy road. The rain fell in the man's face, washing away streaks of mud and dried blood there—it was Janson Sanders.

Stan stumbled back, almost falling—it couldn't be. Janson had left days before, had run off with no warning. Stan's father had told him—

Stan had been hurt, angry; Janson had been his friend, but he had left without telling him, without telling anyone, and without saying goodbye—but here he lay, and, dear God in heaven, he looked as if he were dead.

Stan tried to move backwards, away from the man lying there in the road. He slipped and almost fell, but managed to stay on his feet—he had to get help. He had to—

Fear filled him, and panic. He turned and ran, stumbling toward the car, and got in, slamming the door behind himself. He backed the Ford up, then shoved his foot down on the low-speed pedal and felt the Tin Lizzie jerk beneath him. It sputtered and coughed, almost died, then lunged forward. His hands shaking on the steering wheel, he made a wide, sweeping turn in the road, mindless of the ditch that was looming before the dim headlamps—he had to find help. Janson was lying there in the road, so still, so lifeless—and he looked so very dead.

Daddy—Daddy would know what to do. Stan would get his father. He would go home and get his father and—

But Bill would be closer, at Louise Diller's house, as he was every Sunday night. Stan would go get his brother. Bill would know what to do; he would help Janson—oh, why had Stan not at least checked to see if he was still alive! Why had he been so afraid that he had just driven away—but he could not go back now. He had to find help. He had to—

He came to the main road and made the turn back toward town, not slowing enough and almost losing control of the car as it slid in the mud. He gripped the steering wheel hard in his shaking hands, damning the rain, damning the inefficiency of the headlamps—he had to get to Bill. His brother would help Janson, if Janson were still alive to be helped. If Janson were—

Headlamps were coming toward him in the rain. He could see a shape looming behind them through the drenched, fogged windshield—but the road ahead seemed too narrow. He would never make it. He would never—

He jerked the wheel to the right, fearing collision with the oncoming lights, and suddenly found himself off the road and out of control. The car jerked and bounced over the rough terrain, throwing him against the door and knocking his glasses from his face. He slammed his foot down hard on the brake pedal, closing his eyes and praying, feeling the wheel jerk in his hands.

The car finally came to a sliding stop, his heart pounding in his chest so hard that he could hear it. He opened his eyes and forced himself to breathe, the roaring in his ears so loud that he could barely hear the rain—but he was alive. He was—

He was shaking so badly that he could hardly open the door—but the Tin Lizzie was useless now. One wheel in a narrow, muddy ditch, it sat with its rear end in the air. He got out, reaching back to find his glasses as he clung to the door for the support that his shaking knees could not give him, then he turned to stare at the useless machinery, tears at his own impotence choking him—Janson was back there, lying in the middle of the muddy road. He had to have help. He had to—

A shape was coming toward him in the darkness, a man from the vehicle he had thought he would hit, a vehicle now parked unharmed at the side of the road—a man, someone, anyone who could help him—please be Bill or Daddy or someone I know, he prayed, still clinging to the door. Please be—

Titus Coates peered at him from beneath the brim of a rain-soaked hat as he came nearer. "You okay, Mist' Stan?" he shouted over the sound of the rain and the roaring in Stan's ears. "You need some he'p gettin' out 'a th' mud?"

Thank you, God—thank you, Stan thought in a rush, relief filling him. He grabbed hold of Titus's coat sleeve, still shaking almost too badly to stand. "You've got to come—Janson, on the road back there, hurt, maybe dead, I don't know—"

He realized his words made little sense, but somehow Titus seemed to understand. "Com' on, boy. You show me—" His fingers closed over Stan's arm, his grip almost vise-like. "Leave th' car. I'll pull it out later. Com' on—"

Stan stumbled along behind him, being held up by the strong hand on his arm. They reached the road and got into the truck Titus had been driving. “Where, boy?” the old man demanded, looking at him.

No one but his father had ever called him boy in his life, or talked to him in the tone this man was now using—but Stan found that he did not mind. Some remote part of him said that Titus should not speak to him so, for he had always been taught that he was the older man’s better, the son of his employer, and Titus had never before addressed him as anything other than “Mist’ Stan”—but suddenly none of that mattered. This man was going to help him. This man was going to help Janson—if only Janson was still alive.

He’s got to be alive; he’s got to be—Stan thought, clenching his fists on his knees as the truck bounced over the muddy, rutted road. He was shaking from the chill, shaking from the wetness, shaking from tension as they sped past ditches running in muddy, red streams. Oh—why didn’t I check to see if he was still breathing! Why didn’t I at least—

Stan pointed out the road he had been on, and Titus made the turn, the truck sliding in the mud for a brief second before grabbing for traction and going on.

“Up there! Just ahead—” Stan leaned forward, straining to look through the fogged glass before him, squinting his eyes to see through his spectacles. “There! See—right there!”

The truck came to a quick stop, almost throwing him into the floorboard. Titus was already out, running toward the man lying there in the mud and the rain. Stan opened the door, almost afraid to go to Janson, to see if he still lived, but unable to stop himself. He reached Titus’s side, to find him cradling the younger man in his arms.

“What they done t’ ya’, boy?” Titus was saying, and Stan realized suddenly that the older man was crying, tears now rolling down his cheeks to mingle with the rain. “Oh, Lordy, what they done t’ ya’—”

Stan stared at him for a moment, at last finding his own voice. “Is he alive?” he asked, his voice almost a whisper. Titus looked up at him, the old man’s eyes filled with tears—but Stan’s answer came from elsewhere.

Above the sound of the rain and the drone of the truck’s engine, came the sound of Janson Sanders’s voice, his words barely audible, but clear.

He was calling Stan’s sister’s name.

FOR A moment, it seemed to Janson that he was still in the well. There was pain—everywhere there was pain, around him, inside of him, the only real thing in a world of sights and shadows that floated dreamlike around him, a world he could not touch or feel.

Scenes and pictures changed in his mind—Elise, beautiful Elise, smiling and so happy, his forever—but they took her away; away, and she had been crying.

He could feel hands on him, lifting him, and he started to struggle—his body hurt, and he thought they were going to throw him in the well. He would be dead, and Elise would be at their mercy—but they had no mercy.

A darkness came, washing in on the heels of the pain, and he floated away, then fought to come back—Elise, he was supposed to take care of Elise, to protect her. If he died, then who would look after—

Time seemed to flow in and out. The first time he had ever seen Elise, the first time they had kissed, the day he had known she loved him, the first time they ever lay together—he could see it all, feel it all, for it only to touch him and then float away again. His body was being moved, and he thought for a moment this was death—but this was not death, for with death there would be no more pain. The pain said he was alive. The pain said—

Fingers prodded his side, hands touching the bruises, and the pain—so much pain. The world floated in and out, sights and sounds and people around him—but none of them Elise. None of them—

He had to see—

They could kill him then, if only they wouldn't hurt—

If only—

Elise—

STAN STOOD out of the way in one corner of the small kitchen in the Coates' house some time later that night, just beyond the circle of yellow light cast by the kerosene lamp on the kitchen table. Janson lay nearby on a straw-stuffed mattress, feverish and mumbling, still not fully conscious—his face was beaten and bruised, as was his body. The clothes

Mattie Ruth and Titus had cut away from him had been torn and muddy, covered with dried and drying blood—someone had tried to kill Janson Sanders; someone had attempted to beat him to death, and then had left him to die there in the muddy road. Stan had never before seen anyone so badly hurt, so badly beaten, as the young man who lay twisting beneath the quilts, fighting the hands that tried to tend him.

There had been hushed, hurried words between Titus Coates and his wife, and a look of horror on Mattie Ruth's face as they had carried Janson in and laid him on the iron bedstead that stood in one corner of the narrow kitchen. Stan had been too frightened to leave, and too frightened to stay, so he just stood as if frozen, watching Mattie Ruth tend to Janson, feeling as if they did not truly trust or want him here. A thousand confused thoughts raced through his mind as Janson's words became clear enough again for a moment to understand what he was saying—he was calling for Elise again, as he had been doing all along, calling for Stan's sister.

But they had never been more than friends, Stan kept telling himself. Janson was one of the farmhands, and Elise was a Whitley—but hadn't Stan himself wondered, the night he had walked up on them behind Town Hall after the Independence Day dance, if they had not been kissing? But that was impossible. They had only been friends, and even that had ended long ago—but still Janson continued to call for Elise, to beg for her, over and over as Stan stared.

A frown wrinkled Titus's forehead, his face worried. "You need t' let me go git th' doct'r for him," he said quietly, staring at his wife across the width of the narrow bed.

"Ain' nothin' a doct'r can do for him that I cain't—'sides, you know th' doct'r's Mist' Whitley's cousin—" She said no more than that, but somehow Stan felt the words carried ominous meaning—surely she did not believe his father would not want Janson seen to. His father had always seemed to like Janson. Surely—

Janson moaned, trying to move away from Mattie Ruth's hands as they again prodded his bruised side. He twisted beneath the knotted and damp covers, his voice rising slightly, his head tossing on the pillow.

"Elise—please—don't let him hurt Elise. Please—"

His words were pleading, and somehow pitiful, Stan thought as he stared at him—why would he beg so for Elise? What would make him think that someone would want to hurt her? No one would hurt Elise. No one.

Janson's voice quietened back to mumblings again, but still Stan could hear his sister's name among other words he could not understand. He could not take his eyes from the man who lay there so badly beaten and hurt before him. Janson had been his friend almost from the first moment they had met, and Stan had been hurt and confused when his father had told him days before that Janson had picked up and left with no warning—but now here Janson was, badly hurt, maybe dying—and he was begging for Stan's sister with almost every breath. Stan felt as if he had stepped into a nightmare with no end, and all he wanted now was to get out—but, still, no matter how hard he tried, he could not make himself move.

Janson twisted fitfully, his face drenched with sweat even in the chill room, for a moment almost rising from the bed, his voice growing louder. "Elise—please—got t'—Elise—"

Stan stepped back in surprise at the feeling and need behind the words. He looked up to find Mattie Ruth staring at him, something very near to accusation in her eyes.

"You see what th' Whitleys 'a done t' him?" she asked quietly, her eyes never leaving Stan's face. "He ain' never done nothin' t' hurt nobody. All he done was fall in love with your sister—an' look what it's got him." Her words were angry, surprising Stan with their feeling, and their meaning.

Janson, in love with—"I—I didn't know. I—" he stuttered out.

"There's lots 'a things you don't know—like maybe that it was your daddy done this t' him—"

"Mattie Ruth, don't—" Titus moved around the bed toward her, laying a hand on her arm, trying to silence her words, turning a look to the boy—but she only shrugged him away.

"It's time he knew. It's time he knew a lot 'a things, like how his daddy said he'd kill Janson if he ever caught him anywhere near his precious daughter again—an' he's just about done it."

"D—daddy? You don't really think Daddy beat him like—"

"Or had it done, more likely, an' then left him for dead," she said, staring at him, no mercy for any of the Whitleys there in her eyes.

"Oh, my God—" Stan said, his eyes going back to the young man on the bed. "You can't believe—"

"Mattie Ruth—" Titus began once again, but she did not even look his way.

"It's you that better believe. Him an' your sister was runnin' off t'gether t' be married—but I guess your daddy foun' out first, an' it's jus' about cost Janson his life." She turned her eyes back to the restless form—"An' it may yet—"

Janson and Elise. His father—his father trying to kill Janson—it could not be true. None of it could be true.

Janson was pleading for Elise again, twisting beneath the quilt, his bruised face bathed in sweat. Stan stepped back, hearing the pleading words, somehow frightened—this was all a nightmare, a horrible nightmare. A—

Suddenly Mattie Ruth crossed the distance between them, taking him by the shoulders, holding him before her as she stared down at him, her jaw clenched, her eyes angry. "That boy might die t'night, but he ain't gonna die without seein' your sister. You go git her—"

"No, Mattie Ruth, you cain't!" Titus said, stepping toward her. "You'll be 'dangerin' her too!"

She glanced at her husband for a moment, and then back to Stan, her eyes no less determined as her fingers dug into the boy's shoulders. "I done all I kin do for him. Th' rest is with th' Lord, an' with Miss Elise. We can do th' prayin', but you're th' onliest one that can git t' your sister t'night—bring her back here, right now—"

Stan could only stare at her, unable to move.

"You git her, right now!" Mattie Ruth's voice rose, and she released him with a slight shove toward the doorway.

Stan stumbled, almost falling, but recovered himself. He stared at her for a moment longer, then turned and ran toward the door and out into the rain. He heard Titus come out onto the narrow rear porch of the house and call something after him, but he did not stop or even look back. He ran on down the muddy road, not slowing his pace even after he was out of sight of the house.

His mind was reeling—Elise to run away with Janson Sanders; his father trying to kill Janson, beating him and leaving him for dead where he thought no one would ever find him—no, it could not be true! None of it could be true! Mattie Ruth had gone mad; she had lost all reason. She was nothing less than mad.

Stan continued to run, his heart pounding in his narrow chest so hard that he thought it would burst through the skin. It was all an awful, horrible lie, a lie he would not believe. His father would tell him the truth. His father would see to it that Janson was taken to a hospital and away from those mad people in that house. His father would make everything right again, just as he had done all Stan's life. His father would.

His father would—

# 22

STAN WHITLEY STOOD BEfore his parents' closed bedroom door a short while later, one hand on the doorknob—he had been standing there for quite some minutes now, but somehow he could not make himself knock at the door, or turn the knob and enter. He leaned his cheek against the cool, painted wood, hearing the echoes in his mind of Janson Sanders's voice, of the pain, and of his begging for Elise—but, it couldn't be true. Elise would not run away with a farmhand, not even with Janson. When she married, she would marry someone fine and educated and wealthy, as J.C. Cooper was. She would not marry a dirt farmer who worked someone else's land for a living—not even Janson.

Janson Sanders had been much more than a friend to Stan from that first day those months ago when Janson had asked for help in making a telephone call; he had been the older brother neither Bill nor Alfred had ever allowed themselves to be. From that first day, Janson had always been there for Stan, had always listened, had always seemed to care, and had always been a person Stan could look up to for the things he knew and did—but Janson and Elise? Though Stan liked Janson, respected him even as he did not respect his own brother Bill, he could not imagine his sister married to, or even in love with, a farmhand, not even with—

But, even to Stan, Janson had always been much more than a farmhand, and, once Stan allowed himself to forget what the man was, he could very easily see his sister with a man such as Janson Sanders. Elise could love someone like that, and she could decide to run away with him—could it really be true? Could it really be—

No!—Stan told himself, tightening his grip on the doorknob. He could not allow himself to believe Elise would run away with Janson, for that would make it easier to believe the rest could be true as well, that his father had threatened to kill Janson, that he had beaten Stan's friend so horribly, and then had left him for dead in that lonely, deserted place. No, it was not true! None of it was true! His father was a good man! His father would make everything all right again! He would get Janson to a doctor and safely away from Mattie Ruth and Titus and the lies in that house. He would—

Stan twisted the doorknob in his hand and started to push at the door, but stopped. In his mind he could hear Janson's voice again, echoing in his ears—the pain, the need and feeling behind the few intelligible words Janson had said as he lapsed in and out of consciousness. Janson had called for Elise, had begged for her with feeling beyond all words or understanding. Whether anything else in the world was truth or lie, there was one thing Stan could not doubt, and that was that Janson Sanders cared for his sister. The feeling had been there in the sound of his voice, in the words, and the hurt and need behind them. Janson cared for Elise—but the rest could not be true! His father was not some horrible monster, capable of having a man almost beaten to death. This was all some awful nightmare, a lie too terrible to be real in the daylight—but his father would know what to do. His father would make everything all right again. His father would—

Stan stared down at the hand resting on the doorknob, wanting nothing more in the world than to push open that door and rush in to wake his father, to cry out the whole, terrible story, and have his father say that it was all a lie, that nothing so horrible could ever be real—but somehow he found he could not. He could do nothing but stand there shivering in his wet clothes, wanting to wake from this nightmare, wanting to forget that anything of this awful night had ever happened—but knowing he would never forget.

He slowly released his grip on the knob, allowing it to return to its normal position, and then took a step back to stand staring at the door for a long moment. Somehow it seemed as if he had closed a part of himself away behind that door he could not open. Somehow it seemed that little Stanny, everyone's baby brother, was once and forever locked away there, and that the young man who stood now staring at that closed door was someone quite different, someone who did not need his daddy to chase away bad dreams anymore.

Janson was his friend, and he was hurt. Janson needed him—but apparently he needed Elise even more. Stan could little doubt that Janson held feelings for his sister, and Elise was the only person who could tell him if she loved Janson as well, and if she had really intended to run away with him—and she was the only one who could say if the rest was true, if his father were really the kind of man Mattie Ruth had said he was, if he was really capable of doing the kinds of things that—

It was the one truth Stan did not know if he would be able to handle, and it was the one truth he knew he had to have.

He turned and stared at Elise's closed bedroom door, then slowly made his way across the wide hallway.

LITTLE MORE than an hour later, Martha Whitley stood at the foot of the bed where Janson Sanders lay in the kerosene-lighted kitchen of the Coates' small house. She leaned against the iron footboard, her hands crossed on its cool, painted surface, as she watched her daughter with the young man who had changed all their lives forever.

Elise sat at the side of the bed, holding one of Janson's hands in her lap, her fingers securely intertwined with his, as if to assure herself that no one and no thing would ever tear him from her again. She had been sitting there for almost an hour now, never once taking her eyes from his battered face, just quietly watching him as he slept.

Martha knew they would have to leave soon, to return to the house before William could discover they were missing. If he should wake to find his wife, his daughter, and his youngest son were no longer there—but she could not afford to think about that now. She had known the risks they were taking when she had left the house with Elise and Stan—but there had been no stopping Elise when her brother had told her where Janson was and how badly he had been hurt. She would have fought them all if she had found it necessary, in order to go to him—and so Martha had come, knowing that somehow during this day, somehow in going to her daughter's room earlier against William's orders, and in the discoveries she had made there, she had joined in Elise and Janson's struggle to be together, and she knew now that she would be in that struggle to the end, whatever that end might be.

As she stood watching Elise and Janson, she found herself wanting to hate this young man who had forever changed the world for them all. He had come into their lives it seemed only to turn everything upside down. He had made her daughter pregnant, and had caused a rift in her family that might never heal; he had shown her a side of her husband she did not like, and now he would take Elise away forever—but somehow she found that she could not hate him as she watched Elise brush the black hair back from his forehead and bend to gently kiss his bruised lips. Martha wanted to hate him, but she could not. Her daughter loved him—God, how Elise loved him—and Martha could no longer doubt the young farmhand loved her daughter as well.

Elise had been in a near-panic by the time they had reached Mattie Ruth's house, and Stan's description of Janson's condition had served only to frighten her all the more—Martha had tried to talk her out of going to him, thinking of the lateness of the hour, the dampness after the heavy rain, of her daughter's condition; but Elise would not be stayed. She was going to Janson's side, and there was no force in heaven or on earth that could stop her. None.

Martha had come with her, as had Stan, trudging through the woods along a path Stan knew. They had all been damp, chilled-through, by the time they had reached the small, three-room house—but Martha had been glad she had come once she had seen Janson Sanders's condition. William had lied to her. He had fully intended to kill the boy, and had almost done so—one look at the young man's battered and bruised body, one look at the torn, muddy, and blood-covered clothes that had been removed from him, and she had known the truth. William had beaten the boy to within an inch of his life, beaten him and left him for dead. If it had not been for Stan using that road as a shortcut home tonight—but, no, the Lord moved in mysterious ways, and Martha could little doubt He had guided Stan's movements on this night.

Janson Sanders had been badly beaten, then exposed to the chill rain and cold November air for hours before he had been found. Martha had realized it was little less than a miracle that the man was still alive when she had entered the house behind Elise and her youngest son to see him feverish and twisting on the straw-stuffed mattress; he was obviously in a great deal of pain, only semi-conscious, delirious, but calling for Elise with almost every breath—he had quietened the moment Elise had touched him, the girl going to his side, taking his hand, kissing the bruised lips, crying quietly as she touched the battered face, saying she would never let anyone hurt him again. He had stilled, his voice quietening to soft mumblings from which Martha could still discern her daughter's name, then his breathing had become deep and regular, and he had at last seemed to move into a natural sleep.

Martha stared at them, somehow wishing that she could reverse time, that she could make it be as if the past year had never taken place for them all. She wanted to go back to the months before this harmless-looking young man had ever come to the County, to a time when her daughter would be forever hers, when there had been nothing within William she had not known and loved, and when it had seemed as if the world would never change—but she knew she could not. She looked at Janson Sanders, wishing for a moment that she had never once set eyes on him, that he and Elise had never met or fallen in love, but knowing that in him lay Elise's future. He was badly hurt, but he would live, or at least recover from his injuries—whether or not he lived depended on how well they could all keep a secret, and on how well they could manage the next weeks while he mended enough to do the right thing by Elise. Martha had to get her daughter married to this young man, and the two of them away to someplace safe—and she had to do it before William could find out that the boy still lived and was on Whitley property, much less that he had gotten his daughter with child. If either of those two things happened—but, no, it would not help to worry about that now.

Mattie Ruth came to the side of the bed to lay a gentle hand on Janson's forehead, then smiled up at Elise. Elise lifted his hand and pressed it to her lips briefly, then held it to her cheek, her eyes settling back to his face—they would never have an easy life, Martha well knew, Elise and this farmhand. But it was a life Elise had chosen for herself, a life that she had determined to have, and it was that determination that had brought them all to this day.

The back door to the small house opened and Titus came in, followed by Stan—poor little Stan, tonight had perhaps been hardest on him of all. It had been difficult, learning hard truths about his father. William Whitley was not the saint his youngest son had always thought him to be, and there was now a grim acceptance in the boy's eyes of the reality he had discovered this night. He had spoken hardly a word since Elise had confirmed everything Mattie Ruth had told him, but he had accompanied them back to the Coates' house to see about his friend—he had gone back out with Titus to pull William's car from the ditch where he had left it earlier. In the morning everything must appear normal, the events of the night completely hidden, locked away until Janson could recover and he and Elise could be far away from here, safe from William's reach.

"We got th' car pulled out 'a th' mud," Titus said. "It's outside now."

Martha nodded, not speaking. She knew Titus and Mattie Ruth were risking everything in caring for Janson. If William should ever find out, they would be immediately thrown off the place, left with nothing, and there was little Martha could do to help them if that should happen. They would be left with no home, no money, no livelihood; even the farm tools Titus used in the garden belonged to William. They were risking everything they had for the young farmhand they had grown to love, and for the girl they had known all her life—they were good people, good in a way Martha had never taken the time before to see, and she realized suddenly that each moment that she, Elise, and Stan stayed here not only increased the danger to Janson, but also to Mattie Ruth and Titus as well—and they had already been here too long.

"Elise, we've got to go now," she said softly.

Elise looked up, clinging even more desperately to Janson's hand, her eyes pleading. "Please, not yet. Can't we stay just a little—"

"It's not safe. If your father wakes—" She left the sentence unfinished.

Elise understood. She nodded her head reluctantly and looked back down to the young man sleeping quietly now on the straw mattress. She lifted his hand to her lips again and kissed it briefly, then gently untangled her fingers from his. Martha moved toward the door to give her a moment's privacy, glancing back to see her rise from the bed, then bend over the sleeping young man to kiss his bruised lips gently and brush her fingers against the smooth black hair at his temples, her eyes never once leaving his face.

After a moment she joined her mother at the door, turning her eyes to Mattie Ruth who stood nearby. "You'll take care of him for me, won't you?"

Mattie Ruth smiled and took her hand for a moment. "You know I will, honey."

Elise looked back to Janson, then reluctantly followed her mother through the door and out onto the narrow porch.

"I'm prayin' hard fer you, Miss Elise, an' fer Janson, too," Mattie Ruth said from the open doorway behind them.

Elise stopped for a moment and turned back to hug the older woman. "We'll need your prayers," she said quietly, smiling though she looked as if she wanted to cry.

We may all need them before this is over—Martha thought as she walked down off the porch and into the dark yard. We may all need them.

THE DAYS passed in misery for Janson, not from the pain, or even from the soreness that now seemed to inhabit his body, but from worry over Elise. He was of little use to her now, laid up in bed from the injuries he had suffered during the beating her father had given him. He had no hope of looking after her or protecting her; he had to depend on Mattie Ruth and Titus, her mother, and Stan to do that.

He hated being confined to the bed, but it hurt too much to move around, so he just lay there, feeling of little use or good to anyone, watching as everyone else went about their chores, and wishing there was something he could do to help, something that would help to pass the time, something that would just occupy his hands and his mind for even a few moments. Elise came whenever she, her mother, or Stan could manufacture some reason for her to be away from the house, but still long stretches of time passed when he could do nothing but lie there and think, and worry about her. It was easier for her to see him now, now that her mother and Stan knew and were helping—and now, Janson well knew, that William Whitley thought he was dead.

It had been hard on Elise when he had told her of coming to consciousness in the well, hard on her, and on her mother and her brother as well, but he had realized the necessity of telling them, for their own sake and safety, as well as his own. William Whitley thought he was dead, thought he had killed him—and any man capable of doing what Whitley had done, capable of throwing a living human being down a well to drown, or to die slowly of starvation, could be capable of doing anything, and no one, not daughter or wife or son, could be safe in dealing with him. Janson knew how lucky he had been that there had been little water in the old well, just that terrible muck he had come to consciousness in, and he still did not know how it was that he had been able to climb out and to drag himself into the road where Stan had found him—the memories of that place stayed with him still, haunting him as nightmares from which he would waken bathed in a cold sweat, his hands clawing at the quilts that covered him, his mind terrified once again that he would never be able to climb out, never be able to see Elise again.

But, as horrible as the nightmares were, the look on Elise's face when he told her of waking in that place had been so much worse. She had clung to him and cried, and he had held her, propped up against the headboard of the bed, in spite of the soreness in his body and the pain her arms had caused him. Mrs. Whitley had left the room without a word, her eyes filling with tears, and Stan had just sat in silence, staring straight ahead, as if seeing things for the first time in his young life. It was not easy on any of them now, but at least knowing made them safer—please, God, it made them all safer.

It had surprised Janson to find out that not only did Mrs. Whitley and Stan know about him and Elise and their plans, but that they somehow seemed to approve of them as well. The first few times Mrs. Whitley had come with Elise to visit him, she had seemed cool, reserved and distant, speaking to him only when she had been forced to, but now even that had passed—he and Elise belonged together, she had told him, and she would do whatever she had to do to see to it that they could leave, be married, and have the life they had both dreamed of.

But now Janson wondered if that life would ever be.

He stood at the side window in the Coates' small kitchen that morning, looking out, waiting for Elise. He was dressed in freshly ironed overalls and a clean, though worn, workshirt—it was the first time he had worn anything other than a nightshirt since the day of the beating, though it had taken more than an hour to dress himself that morning amidst the pain and soreness in his body. He had been determined not to face Elise in night clothes on this of all days, for this would be the first time they would have alone together since the beating her father had given him—and it would probably be the last time he would see her for perhaps a very long while.

The money was gone—no matter how many times he told himself that, he could still hardly believe it. The money he had worked so hard for and saved, all the plans and dreams they had made—gone. Titus had found his things lying at the edge of the road near where he had been found, and had brought them to him. The old Bible and book of poetry Elise had once given him were both water-marked, but not ruined, the photograph of his parents left somehow undamaged among the yellowing pages of the Bible; his few clothes had been rain-soaked and mud-spattered, but had been set right with the washing Mattie Ruth had given them—if anything could ever seem right again after finding that empty sock, the one he had the money knotted into, among his other things. It had felt as if the world were coming to an end—all the plans they had made, all the dreams of the life he would give Elise; that little, white house on those red acres, the best cotton land in all of Alabama, all stolen from them now—and so much more.

No matter what Whitley had done to them, no matter the lies he had told or had forced them to tell, no matter the beatings he had given or the threats he had made, he had been unable to take Elise from Janson or to keep them apart—until now. When Whitley had thrown him in the well to die, he had done more than just try to take his life; he had stolen the only way Janson had of making all the dreams come true. He had stolen the money Janson had worked so hard for, dreamed so long over—and he had at last stolen Elise from him.

Janson had known he could never have hoped to give Elise the kind of life she deserved, the kind of life she had always known—but, with the money, he could have given her a good life, a happy one, back on his parents' place in Alabama. They would have had a home, land to farm, and each other—but now that would never be, at least not for a very long time to come.

He stared out the window at the barren yard, watching for the first sight of Elise, knowing this would have to be the last day he would see her for a very long time. He would be leaving tonight, leaving though his body still hurt almost too much to stand or to walk—he could not stay here any longer on Mattie Ruth and Titus's charity, knowing the danger he was putting them in by even being here, and the danger his nearness also created for Elise, her mother, and Stan. She did not know yet that the money was gone, did not know that they could not be married in a few days or weeks as she planned, did not know that he would have to leave tonight—he would leave a message for her with Mattie Ruth once it was too late for anyone to stop him. She would know that he loved her, that he was leaving only to earn the money it would take to make their dreams a reality, and that he would be back, if she would only be waiting for him.

He knew he was somehow lying to her with his very silence, but he also knew he could not face her now, could not tell her that the money was gone and that he would have to leave alone, at least for the time being. He could not see her tears, could not let her talk him into taking her along to whatever kind of life he could provide for her now, for he well knew she could, and he knew somehow that he wanted her to. He did not want to spend years alone without her, perhaps lose her forever for the decision he had been forced to make. He knew that a man could not ask a woman to wait forever for a dream; she had a right to a husband, a home and family—but he could not take her to the only kind of life he could give her now, as the wife of a sharecropper or farmhand, living hand-to-mouth for years, perhaps even for the remainder of her days. Elise Whitley was a lady, and he could offer her nothing less than the best he could give her, not even if that meant years alone and the risk of losing her—please, God, don't let me lose her, he prayed silently, staring out the window.

He knew there would be a danger in leaving her here with her father, knowing now what Whitley could be capable of doing, but he hoped the danger to her would be gone once he was, and he also knew that her mother and Stan, Mattie Ruth and Titus, and J.C. Cooper as well, would be there to look after her. He did not know yet where he would go or what he would do once he left here, and it really did not matter. He would hop a freight and go wherever it took him, find work, and save every cent he could—it did not matter what he had to do, whether it be run moonshine, cheat or steal, he would get the money it would take to give Elise the kind of life he had promised her; and then he would come back for her, if only she would be waiting. She had to be waiting.

He stared through the window, watching as she came to the edge of the woods along the rarely used path she had followed from the big house. She stopped for a moment to look around, making sure she was unobserved, and then crossed toward the small, unpainted house where he waited. A lump caught in his throat as he stared at her, his eyes trying to memorize every movement, every line of her body—how could he leave her behind, not touch her, not see her again, for years. He watched as she crossed through the fall garden, the sun catching in her red-gold hair and turning it to fire—God, how he loved her. He knew this would be the hardest day he had ever lived through, leaving her behind without even letting her know, with only the message he would give Mattie Ruth to say goodbye, when he wanted to say so much more. But those would be words he would not be able to give her for a very long time, not until the day he came back—if she would only be waiting. Please, God, if she would only be waiting.

JANSON WANTED to see her—that was the message Mattie Ruth had brought Elise that morning. In the days, weeks now, since the beating, there had been so little time they could spend together, even with her mother, Stan, Mattie Ruth, and Titus all now helping with excuses and reasons that would allow her to be away from the house—Janson would be alone today, and he would like to see her, to be alone with her, if she could manage to get away.

Elise made her way down the long rows of turnip and mustard greens there in the Coates' fall garden, going toward the front of the small house where Janson would be waiting for her—it had been easy enough to slip away that morning, easier than she had ever thought it might be. Her father and Bill had gone all the way to Columbus on business for the day, and she had simply lied to her mother to keep from having to go to school—Martha Whitley had come into the dining room only moments after Mattie Ruth had given Elise the message from Janson, and Elise had simply told her that she was feeling nauseated, too nauseated to sit through classes for the day, and her mother had believed the lie easily enough. No sooner had Martha turned her back, however, than Elise had been out the back door of the house, headed here—Janson wanted to see her, to be alone with her, and that was all that could matter.

She slipped through the garden, and then cut across the narrow yard, going toward the rear porch of the house, her eyes searching the area to make sure she was not being followed. She knew her father and older brother were both far from here today, but still she could not abandon caution altogether, especially since she knew that Janson's life could be the price exacted for that kind of carelessness. Knowing she had been the cause of the beating he had suffered would already haunt her through the remainder of her days—and what had happened afterwards had been even so much worse. She could not allow herself to think of Janson having come to consciousness in the old well, hurt, so badly beaten; she could not allow herself to think of how he had been forced to drag himself up the side of the well in order to save his life—and she could not allow herself to think of the horror of that place as it must have been to him in those moments. He had believed he would die there, alone in the darkness.

Elise could not now look at her father without thinking of that place as it must have seemed to Janson, of the fear he must have felt, the horror—her father no longer forced his presence on her, no longer saw her except at the supper table each night. He thought he had killed the man she loved; she knew that, though he had told her he had only had Janson taken out of the County and left, alive, at the side of some road. He planned to send her away to school again in only a matter of weeks—how surprised he would be when she was long gone from here by then, run away with the man he thought he had killed. How surprised, and how furious—but he could burn in hell with his fury for all she cared; she and Janson would be far away, in Alabama, living on that land he had told her of so often.

She stopped at the foot of the few board steps that led up to the porch of the little house, turning back toward the woods one last time to make sure she was not being followed. Then she walked up the steps and crossed the narrow porch.

Janson must have been watching for her, for the door swung inward as she touched the knob, and she was suddenly in his arms even before she had a chance to enter the house. He drew her in and closed the door behind them, and she pressed her face to the sun-dried freshness of his shirtfront for a moment, enjoying the feel of his arms before lifting her eyes to his, expecting to be kissed—but he did not kiss her, staring at her instead as if he had not seen her for a very long time, making her somehow uneasy with the very intensity behind his green eyes. She noticed that he was in his best overalls and workshirt, his black hair neatly trimmed and combed back with something that made it shine—she knew he was trying to appear as if nothing had happened, though the bruises were only now beginning to fade from his face, and the soreness in the side he still favored clearly attested to the beating he had suffered at her father's hands.

"I was hopin' you'd be able t' come," he said, wincing slightly at the pressure of her arms around him. She slid her hands down to his waist, not wanting to hurt him, but he held her only more tightly against him in spite of the pain she knew it made him feel. After a moment, he looked down at her again, taking her face in his hands and staring at her as if he were trying to memorize her every feature. At last he kissed her, his lips moving over hers slowly, lingering with hers for a long moment before he looked down at her again. Then he released her and moved away.

She stood staring at him as he crossed the room, wanting only to still be in his arms as he walked to the mantle to lean against it and stare down into the fire burning there in the fireplace.

"How'd you manage t' get away without your ma comin' with you?" he asked, not turning to look at her.

"I just slipped out. I told Mama that I was sick once Mattie Ruth told me you wanted to see me; that way I wouldn't have to go to school today."

"Oh." That was all he said. He stood staring down into the fire, seeming so very distant from her in that moment, though he stood only the space of a few feet away. She watched him, telling herself that it was only the pain in his body that made him seem so strange, though she could feel something different, almost a physical presence standing between them, such as she had not felt in a very long time.

She wandered about the kitchen, his silence seeming almost loud in her ears. She wanted to touch him, to hold him, to talk about their dreams and plans for the future, but somehow she could not. She saw his old Bible lying nearby on the worn kitchen table, the Bible she had seen in his room so many times, the aged leather binding cracked and worn from the many years of use both his parents had given it. She walked toward it, wondering briefly why he would have left it lying out here in Mattie Ruth's kitchen, for she knew he could not read it, at least not well enough to understand the words he saw, though he could quote much of it from memory due to his mother's and his grandmother's teaching. Then she understood. The edge of an old photograph was visible from between its yellowed pages, a photograph she knew, for he had shown it to her once months before. She gently opened the pages, then stood looking down at the picture, at Janson's parents from years past when he had been little more than a boy. She traced a finger over the proud faces, the tall man with the thick, wavy hair and eyes so like Janson's, and the beautiful, dark woman. How she wished she could have known them, this man and this woman who had given Janson life, just as she and Janson had given life to the child who grew within her now, the child she had not even told him of yet.

She felt his eyes on her even before she turned, staring at her, touching her somehow from across the room. He did not turn away as she looked at him, but only continued to stare, looking at her in a way he had never looked at her before; and, suddenly, for some reason she could not understand, she felt lonely. So very lonely.

Finally he turned away, and she felt almost as if he had touched her, almost as if he had taken her, so intimate had the look been that he had held on her for such a time. She wanted to go to him, to put her arms around him and hold him, to tell him how much she loved him, how much she would always love him—but, for some reason, she could not. She could only stand and stare at him, and wonder what was wrong.

"You think your ma'll come lookin' for you when she realizes you're gone?" he asked, as if the moment had never taken place between them.

"No, she'll know where I am. I think she'll let us have some time together." Or, at least, so she hoped, she thought, still staring at him.

"Titus said your pa an' Bill were gone."

"They had to go to Columbus on business. They'll be gone all day; we won't have to worry about them—"

"Your pa, he's leavin' you alone?" he asked, turning to look at her again.

"He hardly speaks to me anymore. After what he thinks he did—" She did not finish the sentence, and did not have to. They both knew what her father thought he had done to Janson; she did not have to say the words.

She did not want to talk about her father, to waste this time they had. She wanted to talk about the future, and their plans, and all the years they would have together.

"I've been thinking; in another couple of weeks we'll be married and living in Alabama—I can hardly wait to meet your grandparents. I feel like I know them already from everything you've told me—" What a wonderful life they would have, back on his parents' land in Alabama: Janson, her, and their child. She already knew exactly how she would tell him about the baby; she would wait until they were married and in Alabama, and she would ask him to take her to that land that was such a part of him, the land they were going to buy, and she would tell him once they were there that he was going to be a father—oh, it would all be so perfect. So very perfect. They had been through so much to be together—but it would all be over so soon, just as soon as they could leave here together.

She realized how terribly silent he was being as he turned to look back down into the fire again, but she continued to talk, feeling inside that there was something wrong, but not knowing what it might be. He continued to stare at the flames, and she could feel him thinking, feel his thoughts touching hers—she could not understand the loneliness she felt, the sadness. She wandered about the room, unable to go to him, to touch him as she wanted to. She felt his eyes on her again, but she didn't turn to look at him. She stopped by the kitchen window instead, staring out, folding her arms before her chest, feeling suddenly chilled. She knew she was talking about their life in Alabama, but was suddenly unsure as to what she was saying. Her words fell silent, and she just stared out. She felt his eyes leave her, and she knew he was once again staring down into the flames—she did not have to turn to see; she could feel it, know it, just as surely as her eyes could ever tell her.

For a moment, silence stood between them. Then he spoke. "The money's gone, Elise," he said quietly.

She turned to look at him, his eyes rising to meet hers from across the room. She could only stare at him, not believing—

"It's gone, every cent," he said again, his eyes not leaving hers.

"Gone—but, it can't be—" It couldn't be true, not the money he had worked so hard for, not the money he had saved, their entire future.

"It is. When Titus found my things, th' sock I had it tied int' was there, but the money was gone—"

"Daddy." The word came as a statement, and the anger within Elise increased.

He nodded his head, not speaking, and she turned away—all that work, all those months of waiting, and her father had—

"I'm gonna have t' leave t'night, Elise, by myself."

She turned to stare at him again, not believing he had said—but he was suddenly there, crossing the room to her in a few broad strides in spite of the soreness in his body, holding her in his arms, saying it again, though she did not want to hear—

"I got t' go on by myself for right now, but I'll be back in a couple 'a years, maybe even less, as soon as I can get th' money again t'—"

She pulled out of his arms and took a step back to stare up at him. "You're going to leave without me?"

"It ain't like that. It'll only be 'til I can get th' money again t' give you th' kind'a life I promised I'd give you—" His eyes were pleading, begging for her to understand, but she could not. "I knew I shouldn't 'a told you, but I couldn't just stand there an' listen t' you talkin' about—"

"You weren't even going to tell me? You were going to leave and not even—"

"I was gonna give Mattie Ruth a message for her t' give t' you. I—"

"I thought you loved me." She could hear the tears in her voice, feel them choking the back of her throat, but she refused to allow herself to cry—he was going to leave her. He was going to—

Suddenly his arms were around her, holding her close, and she could not resist, could not pull away. "I do love you; you know I love you. That's why I got t' leave for now. I got t' be able t' make some money an' save it, so I can give you th' kind of life I promised I'd—"

"But, you weren't even going to tell—"

"I knowed what'd happen if I told you. I knowed you wouldn't want me t' go—but I'll be back soon as I can. An' then we'll leave an' be married an'—"

"Why can't we leave now? We still have the money you gave me, and some I've been saving; it's enough to get started somewhere on. I don't care if we can't have the house and land. All I want is to be with you—"

"We cain't do that."

"But, why not? Why—"

"No." He released her and moved a step away, turning his back to her, clenching both hands into fists before him as if he wanted to strike out at something that neither of them could see. "Don't you understan'; I ain't got nothin' t' offer you now. Nothin'—no home, no wage t' put food on th' table; I couldn't even put a roof over your head—"

"None of that matters, just so long as—"

His eyes came back to her again, eyes that were filled with anger. "It does matter—do you think I could take you t' th' kind 'a life I'm gonna have t' go t' from here? I couldn't ask you t' live in a tenant shack or in some room off a barn. I couldn't ask you t' eat just whatever it was I could provide for us t' eat. I couldn't stand t' see you bein' cold in th' winter, or havin' t' work in th' fields—an' I couldn't stand t' see you start hatin' me for th' life I'd be givin' you. If I go on by myself, it won't take much for me t' get by on my own. I can sleep wherever I find myself, an' I'll be savin' every cent I make—in a couple 'a years, maybe even less, I can come back for you, an' I'll be able t' give you th' land an' th' home I promised I'd give you. There ain't no way we can get married now an' leave t'gether; I don't have nothin' at all I can give you now, nothin'. It's got t' be like this, Elise; there ain't no other way—"

She opened her mouth to tell him that he had to marry her, that she was going to have his baby, and that he had to make her his wife and take her with him no matter what else he had to say—but somehow she could not. She could only stare up at him, knowing, realizing that he would marry her if she told him, realizing that he would take her with him and provide her and their child with the best life he could provide for them—and realizing that he would grow to hate himself for the very life he provided. She could not tell him—she could not. Not like this. Not like—

She turned away, hugging her arms for warmth, and, after a moment, heard his voice again, from very close behind her. "You don't know how bad I want t' take you with me," he said, quietly. "You don't know how it feels, knowin' I won't be able t' see you for years, knowin' I won't be able t' touch you or hold you—but there's nothin' else I can do, Elise—"

But she could not speak. She could only bow her head and shake it slowly back and forth, feeling tears begin to slowly move down her cheeks, knowing she could make him take her with him, knowing she could make him marry her—but not like this. Not like—

"Please don't hate me—" The words were spoken so softly she could barely hear them, and she turned back to see the look of pain in his green eyes, pain greater than any she had ever seen there before. "Please—I couldn't stand it if you hated me—"

"I just want to be your wife—don't you understand that? It doesn't matter to me where or how—"

"Elise, I cain't give you anythin' now. Nothin'. I cain't do that t' you—"

"Don't I have a right to decide for myself? Don't I—"

"You cain't even understan' th' kind 'a life I'd be takin' you to if you left with me now, even with th' little bit 'a money we'd have—Elise, you ain't never lived that way. You shouldn't have t' live that way, in a tenant shack or in some rented room—"

"Couldn't your grandparents take us in until you could find a—"

"They'd take us in. My gran'pa might even could use somebody for a while, but that wouldn't be fair—"

"Fair on who?" she said, seizing upon the idea, wiping at a wet cheek with the back of one hand as she stared up at him. "You said he could probably use somebody, and if—"

"It wouldn't be fair on you. You cain't know th' kind 'a life—"

"That wouldn't matter, not so long as we could be together—"

"Elise, you don't even know what you're sayin'; you cain't even understan' th' life you'd be choosin'. They'd take us in; I know they would, but we'd be livin' in a place not much bigger than this, sharin' it with both my gran'parents, an' my cousin, Sissy, an' two 'a my aunts, an' just whoever else might be visitin' at th' time. It wouldn't be anythin' but a roof over our heads an' a bed t' sleep in—we wouldn't have but just that little bit 'a money t' get started on, Elise, nothin' 'a our own. I could find work as a hand for wages once he couldn't use me no more, an' find us a place t' rent—but there's no tellin' how long we might have t' live like that, just gettin' by from one day t' th' next, with us tryin' t' save every cent we could so we'd be able t' have that place 'a our own someday."

"That wouldn't matter, not so long as we'd be together. I know it would make it harder on you, with two of us to support—" Three—she told herself, once the baby arrived; but she pushed that thought out of her mind.

"Two of us wouldn't matter—but, Elise, you cain't even understan' th' kind 'a life it'd be. You've never knowed anythin' like it. It wouldn't be fair on you; I cain't—"

"Do you think I'd rather live here in that big house with all Daddy's money than be with you? Do you think that could make me any happier than living with you in your grandparents' house, or in a rented place, or even a sharecropped house—"

"You wouldn't never have t' live in no sharecropped place, not so long as I'm able t'—"

"Don't you understand, it wouldn't matter to me. Not so long as we're together."

For a long moment he stared at her, then he moved to take her hands in his and draw her over to one of the benches by the kitchen table, making her sit down, and then kneeling at her feet, his face grimacing in pain with the soreness in his body. He looked up at her, holding both her hands tightly in his own. "You got t' listen t' me, Elise," he said quietly, his eyes never leaving hers. "I don't want us t' have t' be apart for years any more 'n you do, but I cain't ask you t' live th' way you'd have t' live if my gran'parents took us in—so many people in that little house; you cain't know what it'd be like. An', once he couldn't use me no more, we'd have t' find us a place 'a our own—you ain't never lived in a house where th' roof leaks an' th' wind whistles in aroun' th' door, but that might be th' kind 'a place we'd have t' live in if we left t'gether now. We'd never have t' sharecrop an' lose half a crop every year, not so long as I'm able t' do anythin' else; I'd be workin' as a hand for a wage—but it'd never be much. We'd have t' scrimp an' save an' just squeak by lots 'a times. You wouldn't have nice things, an' a lot 'a times you might even have t' do without things you really needed. When I had th' money, goin' back t' Eason County didn't seem s' hard, but now—now we'd be goin' back with nothin', Elise; you cain't imagine what livin' with nothin' is like—"

"It doesn't matter—"

"Yes, it does matter. If we leave t'gether now, we'll be fightin' it for years, maybe even for th' rest 'a our lives, t' ever have anythin' that'd be our own. There'd be a lot 'a years 'a hard work, a lot 'a doin' without—I cain't ask you t' live like that. You cain't even imagine—"

"I know it would make it harder on you. I know it would take years longer for you to have your dream if you had a wife and family to support and worry about while you were trying to save the money to—"

"It wouldn't matter if it took longer—don't you know by now that you're more important t' me than th' land is? I want it back, just as bad as I ever wanted it back, but I want it for you, for us. You're th' most important thing in th' world t' me, us bein' t'gether—"

"Then why can't you understand that I feel the same—" Suddenly she was crying in earnest, and she could not stop herself, no matter how hard she tried—she did not want him to see her like this, but the tears would not stop. "Why can't you understand that being with you is all that matters to me as well. I don't care if we have to live with your grandparents; I don't care if we have to sharecrop for someone; I don't care if we have to live in a rented house with a leaky roof and the wind coming in around the door—I just want to be with you. I don't want to spend years without you, to have to worry if you're safe and dry, to have to worry if you're even alive or dead. I just want to be your wife and live with you and have your children. I just want—" Suddenly she was crying too hard to even speak. She was on her knees with him and in his arms, and she did not even know how she had gotten there. He held her, gently soothing her, letting her cry, his hands gently touching her hair, her face—

"I won't leave you, not if you really don't want me to. I won't leave you—" He was saying the words, over and over again, as he held her. "We'll get married an' go t' Eason County if that's what you want. I'll give you th' best life I can, I promise—Elise, please don't cry. Please—"

She looked up at him, the tears streaming down her cheeks. "You really want that; it's not just—"

"You know I want it." He kissed her and held her close against him, his arms tight around her in spite of the pain in his body. "All I ever wanted was you—an' I'll give you th' rest, no matter how long it takes me, no matter how long—"

"You won't hate me if it takes longer? You won't—"

"I could never hate you," he said, cupping her face in his hands and looking down at her. "Never—"

She buried her face against his shoulder, unable to turn him loose, to let him go. "Just hold me—"

For a moment his arms tightened around her, then he released her and pushed himself to his feet, drawing her up to stand beside him. He put an arm around her waist and led her to the old iron bedstead he had there in the kitchen from Mattie Ruth and Titus's charity, then lay down with her and held her, slowly beginning to touch and love her in spite of the pain and soreness that filled his body. She held him, gently touching the bruises, seeing what her father had done to him, knowing what he could do again—she began to cry anew as he drew her close and entered her, unable to let go of him, unable to quit touching him, to quit loving him, even as the pleasure came and she lay crying in his arms afterward, hearing him say the same words, over and over again:

"I won't never leave you. We'll be together always. I won't never—" And she could only pray in that moment that he would not grow to hate himself, and her as well, for the words he said.

# 23

THE NIGHT WAS COLD AND clear, with a bitter chill in the air that told of a hard winter that would be soon settling in over the Georgia countryside—but they would be far away from here by then. It was still hours before daylight, but the minutes seemed to be slipping by quickly, and Janson found himself looking again and again toward the east to assure himself that dawn was not yet ready to come—there was no lightening of the horizon yet, no growing hues of pink and yellow to show that day was about to begin, but still he was worried. They would have to be away soon or they would lose the cover of night and sleep that lay across the countryside, and each moment that passed now only increased that danger, only increased the chance they might be found out and stopped, and he knew he would not live to see another day if that should happened.

He stood to himself beside the old truck Titus would be using to take them out of the County—his grandparents would be expecting them as soon as they could arrive in Eason County. Elise had written to them from Janson's instructions, explaining they would soon be married, and asking if they might be put up for a while in exchange for work Janson could do on the place. They had received a letter back by return mail, a letter addressed to Mattie Ruth Coates, a letter never once asking why it should be posted to a stranger—Janson had been told to come home and to bring his bride, that they were welcome, that they would always be welcome, and that Tom and Deborah Sanders's home would be their home as well for as long as they needed it to be. Elise had cried as she had read him the letter, cried and told him it was a decision they would never regret making.

He watched her now as she stood in the yard near the far edge of the porch, her mother and Stan beside her. She was saying goodbye, goodbye to her family and to this place that had been her home all her life. Janson knew she might never see these people, this place, ever again after they left here today, and he was determined not to rob her of even one of her goodbyes, though he knew that each moment that now passed only increased the danger they might both be in.

He knew there were tears on her cheeks now, though he could not see them in the dim light that fell through the narrow front windows behind her, and he wondered again how he could be doing this to her, taking her from so much, to offer her so little. They were leaving here with nothing, with only each other, and with the money Elise had in her purse, money he had given her that day in the graveyard, as well as what she had been saving for months now without telling him, and money her mother had given her from the household allowance—it was not much, but at least it was something to start their life on. He could give her nothing else now, nothing except himself, and yet he was taking so much away from her that she deserved to have—but it was what she wanted. She had told him that time and again in the past weeks. He had done everything he could to make her understand, to make her see the kind of life he would be taking her to, the hardships they might have, the years of work and doing without—but none of that had seemed to matter to her. She wanted to be his wife, to live with him, no matter the life he might be taking her to—he would do whatever he had to do now, struggle for as many years as he had to struggle, to give her all she deserved to have, and to make sure she would never regret the choice she was making in him today.

Mattie Ruth and Titus came out of the house and down off the narrow porch to him. He watched them, knowing how very much he and Elise owed them already—if it had not been for their kindness and help, this day might never have been; he might have lost Elise forever, or died in trying to make her his, and that was a debt he knew he could never repay.

Mattie Ruth smiled as she reached his side, and then stretched up to hug him one last time. "I feel like I'm sendin' my own off," she said, holding him at arm's length away to stare up at him. "You jus' be careful an' keep a eye out for Mist' Whitley 'til you're good away from here."

"I will," he said. He kept telling himself that he and Elise would be safe once they were gone from here, that not even William Whitley could touch them once they were out of Georgia and in Eason County—but he knew how wrong he might be. He knew Whitley could still reach them, in Buntain before they could be married today, on the train to Alabama, even once they were in Eason County. He knew his very life, and Elise's future, could very well rest now in the hands of Mattie Ruth and Titus Coates, as well as in the hands of Stan and her mother, in how well they could all keep a secret in the following days, and in the years to come.

"You take good care 'a yourself, an' Miss Elise, too. You remember th' kind a' man I think you was raised t' be, an' you'll be a good husban' an' a good provider."

"I will—" Suddenly she seemed to remind him so very much of his mother and his gran'ma, though she looked little like Nell or Deborah Sanders either one. She was the same kind of woman, however, good and strong and caring. He bent and kissed her cheek. "You take care 'a yourself, too, Mattie Ruth. I won't never forget all you an' Titus 'a done for us. I cain't never tell you how grateful we are, how much we owe you—"

"You don't owe us nothin'. We ain't done nothin' more for you than we'd 'a hoped somebody'd 'a done for ours if he'd been away from home an' needin' help."

"You did a lot. If it wasn't for you, me an' Elise wouldn't be leavin' t'day, an' we might never been able t' leave. I might not even be alive right now—"

"You an' Miss Elise would 'a worked it out," she said with assurance, reaching up to pat his arm. "You'd 'a been t'gether, an' you'd 'a got married, jus' th' same—God made you an' her t' be t'gether. No matter what anybody else ever says, you two was born fer each other, an' you've lived fer each other; nobody here on this earth could 'a stopped that, not nobody."

Janson nodded his head, then lifted his eyes to watch Elise and her mother walking toward them from the far side of the porch, arm-in-arm, looking more as if they were sisters than mother and daughter in the dim light. "She's been through s' much in th' past months. I just wish I could be takin' her t' somethin' more now."

"There ain't too much in life that's important but what you got," Mattie Ruth said from beside him. "You got each other, an' that's somethin' cain't never be took away from neither one 'a you, not ever," she said as Elise reached his side and put her arms around him, Elise pressing her wet cheek to his shoulder for a moment to hold him.

She was trembling slightly against him, and it struck him again that this had to be the hardest thing she had ever done in her life, to leave behind everything she had ever known in the world and go into a complete unknown with him. He squeezed her tightly to him and pressed his cheek to her hair, then lifted his eyes to the woman beside her, the woman who would today become his mother-in-law, a woman who would not even see her daughter wed this day. She had done so much to help them in the past weeks, even knowing that in that helping she would take her daughter from herself forever, and possibly damage her own marriage beyond repair.

Martha Whitley looked at him for a long moment without speaking. When her words finally came, her voice showed the strain within her, but also the resolve. "You've gone through so much to be with Elise. I know you'll take care of her and be good to her. Please—" She visibly struggled for a moment against the tears, turning wet eyes back to her daughter as Elise released him to move into her arms, her voice a bare, choked whisper as she continued. "Just make her happy—"

Mother and daughter held each other for a moment, both crying, and again Janson wondered if he was doing the right thing, taking Elise from her family, taking her from all she had ever known—then she left her mother and came to him, putting her arms around him to press close, her wet cheek against the front of his shirt, and he knew there could be nothing wrong in loving her so, or in wanting a life with her.

Stan stepped up from behind his mother and held out a hand, a hand which Janson shook solemnly. "I'm sorry for all Daddy's done to you. I know we can never make up for—"

"You ain't got nothin' t' make up for," Janson said.

Stan nodded and looked at his sister, fighting back the tears Janson knew a boy of fifteen could not cry and still maintain his dignity. Stan moved to kiss his sister's cheek and hug her for a moment. "Goodbye, Elise—I love you—" Janson heard him say quietly, the tears that threatened his masculine pride even more evident in his voice.

"Goodbye, Stan," she said, wiping at a wet cheek with the back of one hand. "I love you too, and I'll miss you—"

"I know," he nodded. "And I'm going to always miss you—" He kissed her cheek again, then turned away—but not before they had all seen the tears that had come at last.

Titus was in the truck waiting, and Mattie Ruth had returned to the porch, standing in the dim light as she dried her eyes on one corner of her apron. Janson nodded a last farewell to her, and she smiled through her tears and nodded in return—there were no words left to say; it was time that he and Elise leave.

He hugged her to him for a moment, and then kissed her when she looked up at him, her eyes bright and her cheeks wet from crying. He smiled and squeezed her once more, then released her and moved to get into the truck, wanting to give her one last moment alone with her mother and Stan before she would have to leave them forever. She hugged and kissed them both one last time, all three crying openly now, then slid into the truck beside him, Stan closing the door after her. Janson saw her look back to her mother and brother one last time as Titus backed the truck up to begin the long journey that would forever take her from her home. Martha Whitley and Stan stood before the old house now in the darkness, one arm around each other, their faces lost in absolute shadow as they waved one last goodbye.

Elise was crying as she lifted her hand to return the farewell, her heart breaking on her face as Janson watched her. She was leaving behind the only home she had ever known, the family that had loved and nurtured her all her life—and for what? To live with so much less than she deserved to have; to go to a strange place, and strange people, and ways such as she had never known; to leave behind forever a world of comfort and luxury, and see instead a life that Elise Whitley was never born to see.

As the old truck made its way down the winding red clay road, its headlamps barely picking out the way ahead, reflecting off the dark pines and the wide expanses of cotton fields in between, Elise's home and the world she had always known disappeared behind them forever. Janson held her hand and let her cry, her face turned away from him to stare out the dark window at memories he could never see. There was nothing he could think of to say.

WILLIAM SHATTERED Martha's favorite vase in his rage when she told him, picking it up from the table in the front parlor where it had rested for more than twenty years, and hurling it across the room to shatter into bits of nothing against the stone hearth of the fireplace. He turned on her, his hands clenched into fists before him, his face red with rage—Martha had never before believed he would strike her, but now she shrank away, putting the distance of a chair between them, feeling as if there were nothing left within him in that moment of the man she had married those many years ago.

"You goddamn stupid—how could you help your own daughter run off with that red-Indian trash! Don't you have any—"

"I did what I had to do!"

"Had to—you had to help her run off with that half-Indian dirt farmer! You know he's only after my—"

"He's not like that! He's a good boy, and he loves Elise. He—"

"Goddamn it—don't you even know what you've done, you stupid bitch!"

For a moment, Martha could only stare at him in shocked silence. No one had ever called her anything such as that before in all her life, and now here stood her own husband, speaking to her as she had never believed anyone would speak to her. She looked toward Bill where he sat in silence on the parlor sofa, believing somehow that her first-born would speak up to defend her, that he would somehow stop this nightmare from going any further—but her heart went cold as she saw the look on his face. There was a fury in his expression that went even beyond that of the man who stood yelling at her, a cold, hate-filled fury that frightened her even more than anything William could ever have done. She might fear that William would strike her—but the look on Bill's face said he could easily do murder. It said—

"Where are they?" William demanded, dragging her attention away from their son. "Where in hell did that trash take her?"

"I don't know."

"You're lying!" he yelled, taking a step toward her, one fist raised as if to frighten the words from her.

Martha lifted her chin defiantly, clinging to the back of the chair before her for the support her legs so badly needed. "Even if I was, do you think I'd tell you?" she asked, meeting her husband's eyes evenly, refusing to show anything of the fear she felt. "You've already tried to kill that boy once; I won't let you do it again. Elise loves him—"

"God damn love!" he shouted. "Love doesn't mean anything!"

Martha stared at him, knowing beyond doubt in that moment that there was nothing left within him of the William she had married, the William she had defied her own parents to love all those years before. She had hoped to reach something within him, something that might still—

"You just better goddamn well hope I find them before it's too late—" he said, his voice quiet, deadly, sending a chill through her such as she had never felt before. She stared at him, feeling as if her knees would give way beneath her.

"You won't ever find them. Ever—"

"I'll find them, and, when I do, that red-trash is dead. Your daughter is going to wish she was dead as well before I'm through with her—"

Elise—dear God, he wouldn't—

But he had already tried to kill Janson Sanders once, had beaten the boy near to death, and then had thrown him unconscious into a well to die. A man who could do that could do anything. Elise might be his daughter, but—

William stood staring at her for a long moment, then turned and left the room without another word, going down the hallway, then out through one of the front doors, slamming it so hard behind him that the sound echoed and re-echoed through the house time and again. She turned and looked at Bill, and somehow her chest constricted so tightly that she could hardly breathe—there was no humanity left on that face, nothing decent or good there. There was—

Bill stood and walked out of the room, following his father through the parlor doorway, and Martha stood in shocked, impotent fear for a moment, staring at the doorway through which they had both disappeared—but they could not find Elise and Janson now, she told herself, trying hard to fight back the fear that was rising within her. They could not—

But she knew they could, they might. William knew everyone in the County, and everyone knew him. All he would have to do would be to put out word, let it be known that—

Someone could have seen Elise and Janson. Someone could know. Someone could tell. Someone could—

She released the chair and moved slowly toward the parlor sofa to sit down on it heavily, praying more fervently in that moment than she had ever before prayed in all her life.

TODAY WAS Elise's wedding day—and, yet, behind all the feelings of joy and happiness, there lay a sense of fear, a feeling of being lost and adrift somehow in the world on this day. She stood on the sidewalk before the small, white-painted Baptist church where in such a short while she would become Janson's wife, trying to memorize the image of this place where her world and her name would be changed forever. She clung tightly to Janson's hand, unable to let go of him, frightened still that her father would somehow find them, that he could still reach out and put an end to their marriage even before it could begin—and frightened for other reasons as well, for reasons she could not explain or even understand. She did not know who she was anymore, who Elise Whitley was, or who Elise Sanders was expected to be—and that frightened her more than anything else could on this day.

Titus had driven them into Buntain even before daybreak that morning, and had treated them both to breakfast at the small dining room of the old hotel where they would spend their wedding night before leaving for Alabama on the early train the next morning. Elise had eaten very little, simply picking at the food on her plate, her nervousness increasing the nausea that the baby already created within her—she had wanted so badly just to be alone with Janson, to just sit and hold his hand and look at him, and, yet, she had somehow also not wanted Titus to leave, for with him would go the last ties with her home and with the girl she had always been.

But Titus had left, leaving her alone in the hotel dining room with the man who would today be her husband, and she had realized suddenly how very alone they were in the world now, with no home, nothing that was their own; only each other—and that could be taken from them so very easily if her father found them out.

She had clung desperately to Janson's hand as they walked the few streets away to the church where her mother had made arrangements for them to be married, knowing all the while that this wedding would be nothing as she had always imagined her wedding would be—there would be no white satin dress, no pink roses for her to carry, no father to give the bride away. She would not even have a wedding ring, for Janson was Holiness, and the Holiness did not believe in jewelry—but she and Janson did not need any of that, she kept telling herself. They had each other, and that was all they needed. That was all they would ever need.

Janson squeezed her hand gently as they stood before the church, looking so handsome in his good shirt and Sunday trousers—but for the first time she noticed that the shirt sleeves were frayed at the cuffs, and the trousers faded from repeated washings, and wrinkled now from the long trip into town in the old truck. She watched as his eyes moved over her face, a worry behind them now as he looked at her. "Are you sure you want t' do this, Elise?" he asked quietly. "It ain't too late even now; I can still take you back if you've changed your mind."

"You're not having second thoughts, are you?" she asked, searching his eyes, a new worry filling her.

"I'd never have second thoughts about marryin' you; you know that. It's all I've wanted for s' long—"

"You know I wouldn't change my mind either," she said. "You know I want to be your wife."

"It's just that—I want you t' be sure. You're givin' up s' much; I don't want you t' be sorry later that you married me—"

"I'd never be sorry," she said, and she knew she meant it. She would never be sorry, no matter what came later.

He smiled for a moment, then drew her close into his arms there on the sidewalk and kissed her, letting his mouth linger with hers for a moment. Then he smiled down at her, resting his forehead against hers. "I guess we ought t' go on in an' get married then," he said quietly, and she smiled.

He took her hand and led her up the wooden steps and through the front door of the small church, but drew her back as she started to push open a second set of doors to go from the narrow vestibule into the church auditorium. He pulled her into his arms again and kissed her briefly, then smiled down at her, brushing his fingers against her cheek. "I got somethin' t' show you before we go in," he said, his green eyes happy as he looked at her.

"Something to show me?"

"Yeah, I've had it for a while now. I wanted it t' be a surprise for t'day—"

"Oh?" She smiled, watching him as he pulled an old handkerchief from his pocket and began to unfold it, expecting a ribbon or a small bit of lace, some present he had bought her weeks ago before her father had found them out—but she stared in surprise as the folds of the handkerchief fell away to reveal what lay within. A small, gold wedding ring lay in the middle of the worn old handkerchief, shining and perfect in the light that filtered in through the glass panels set into the wall on either side of the front doors behind them. She looked up at him, seeing his smile at her surprise.

"I hope it fits. I had t' guess at it—"

"But, how—I mean, when—?"

"I bought it th' day after you said you'd marry me." He smiled, watching her face. "I had it folded up in th' handkerchief ever since, an' every once in a while I'd take it out an' look at it, knowin' what it meant. Even after I lost everythin' else, I didn't lose it—an' now it's goin' where it b'longs—" He took the ring from the center of the handkerchief, lifted her hand, and slid it onto her finger. "It even fits—" he said, smiling at her.

She stared at it for a long moment, watching it shine on her left hand through the tears now filling her eyes. She gently touched the index finger of her right hand to it, amazed to see it there, then she looked up at him. "But, I thought—you're Holiness; I didn't think the Holiness believed in jewelry, not even in wedding rings."

"They don't, but you're not Holiness. Besides, this is somethin' just between you an' me."

"But, if you don't believe—"

"I was raised t' be Holiness, an', even if I don't go t' church every Sunday like I ought t', I still believe th' way I was raised—but this is somethin' just between you an' me. I think God knows that sometimes there's things between a man an' a woman' that ain't strictly by th' church—"

She understood. They had been intimate for months now, lying together, loving each other, and were only now about to be married. Religion condemned physical love outside of marriage, and yet neither she nor Janson had seen anything wrong with the love they shared—God could not condemn them for loving, Janson had told her so many times, when He had caused them to love in the first place.

"Your grandparents and the rest of your family, they won't say anything?"

"You're my family now—an' it ain't nobody's place t' say anythin'. That ring says you b'long t' me—ain't nobody got a right t' say nothin' about that—"

"I love you so much," she said, realizing she was crying no matter how hard she tried not to.

"An' I love you." He drew her close against him to kiss her. "I always will."

"Always—" she said as he pressed his lips to one damp cheek, and then the other, then dried her tears with the edge of the handkerchief.

"I guess we better get married," he said after a moment, smiling down at her, then lifting her hand to gently remove the wedding ring from her finger. "It'll go back on in a minute," he said, smiling in response to the disappointed look that came to her face, "an' it won't come off again after that."

"Never," she said, watching his eyes, knowing in that moment it was a vow she would never break, not so long as she lived.

THE MINISTER stood before them, tall and sparse, with eyes that were kind, eyes Elise knew she would never forget. "Dearly beloved—"

She tried to pay attention as the ceremony was read, wanting to remember this moment forever, but somehow she could only look at Janson, his eyes touching her face as he smiled and held both her hands in his. Beloved—yes, he was beloved. He was everything, and she loved him more in that moment than she had ever loved him before, more than she had ever thought it possible to love anyone. She heard the minister's words, but somehow they did not seem to matter, not as much as did the love and promise she could see in Janson's eyes.

Janson stood looking at her for a long moment after the ceremony was finished, a light smile touching his lips. "You're Elise Sanders now—" he said, so softly that only she could hear. She was Elise Sanders.

PHYLLIS ANN buttoned her blouse as she descended the wide staircase to the first floor of Hiram Cooper's home that morning. J.C.'s father was out of town for the day, and she and J.C. had been getting cozy in his bedroom upstairs when the telephone had rung—he had left her in order to go downstairs to answer it, telling her to stay where she was and wait for him; but she was tired of waiting, tired of all the many things that demanded his time away from her.

She could hear the low sound of his voice coming from the small office to the left of the staircase as she reached the bottom floor. The door was closed, the conversation obviously intended to be private—but

Phyllis Ann did not like closed doors, or private conversations; anything that concerned J.C. was her business. If he was talking to some other girl—

She leaned against the door for a moment, straining to hear, then opened it a crack to better make out the words. She peered into the room cautiously, finding his back to her as he sat before the rolltop desk set against the far wall, the telephone held close to his mouth in one hand, the receiver to his ear in the other—he would never know, she told herself. She opened the door wider, and stood listening.

"Yes, I was worried about her," he said. "I knew they'd have to do something soon—"

Her—he was worried about some other girl, Phyllis Ann thought, staring at his back through the open doorway, the jealousy filling her. Who was he worried about, when he should be thinking only of—

"I knew Mr. Whitley had hit her. I saw the bruise on her face a few days later—"

Elise—it was Elise, always Elise. Phyllis Ann's right hand tightened into a fist, which she pounded noiselessly against her upper thigh—always Elise. Always—

"I knew they'd have to leave sooner or later; I just didn't think it would be this soon—" Then he listened for a moment, straightening in his chair suddenly as if shocked by what he was hearing. "Good God, I didn't know about that! Is Janson all right?" Again he listened, and Phyllis Ann leaned forward, knowing she would gladly give ten years from J.C.'s life in that moment to hear the other end of that conversation—could it really be? Mr. Whitley had hit Elise, had bruised her up a bit, and she had finally run off with that—oh, but that would be too good to be true!

J.C. sighed, the sound seeming to come from deep within him. "Well, at least they're away from it now; and you don't have to worry, Janson loves Elise, and he'll take care of her. Yes—yes, I understand completely; I won't tell anyone they're in Buntain. Yes—let me know if there's anything I can do, Mrs. Whitley. Goodbye—"

He placed the receiver back in the cradle and sat the telephone down on the desk before him, staring at it for a long moment. Phyllis Ann quietly closed the door, then turned to lean back against it, a smile slowly coming to her face—oh, what interesting things one could learn while listening at doors. So Elise had finally run away with her farmhand, and William Whitley was not supposed to find them out—oh, what a delightful bit of information she now held in her hands. Mr. Whitley had hurt Elise, had hit her, and had apparently done something far worse to Janson Sanders—he would be in a killing mood now; his only, precious daughter run off with nothing more than a red-Indian dirt farmer. If he were to find her and her farmhand now—oh, what interesting ideas that brought to mind. If William Whitley found them, he would be certain to beat his daughter to within an inch of her life—and there was no telling what he might do to Janson Sanders. That red trash had threatened her once, had kept her from giving Elise what she so richly deserved—but he would get what he deserved now; oh, he would get that, and so much more. Phyllis Ann had once asked Elise for her help—now there would be no help for Elise, or for her dirt farmer. William Whitley would see to it that she finally learned what Phyllis Ann had lived with all her life—and he would see to so much more. So very much more.

Phyllis Ann stood in the hallway for a long moment, smiling to herself. Buntain—yes, so many interesting things could be learned while listening at doorways. So many interesting things.

Elise Whitley might lie with her farmhand tonight, Phyllis Ann told herself, smiling with the thought—but she would surely wake in hell tomorrow.

# 24

ELISE SANDERS WOKE ON the first morning of her married life to feel the warmth of her husband sleeping beside her. She smiled to herself and brushed her hair back from her eyes, then propped up on an elbow to look down at Janson's sleeping face. She lightly traced the line of his lips with a finger, smiling softly at the look and feel of this man who belonged so completely to her.

She rested back against him, careful not to wake him, and closed her eyes, replaying her wedding day, and her wedding night, in her mind. Janson had touched her, had loved her, had been part of her body so many times—but none had ever been so special as the night she had just spent in his arms. Her wedding had been nothing as she had ever imagined it would be, but there was not one moment of it she would now change—and, certainly, no one could ever have loved so beautifully as they had loved as man and wife.

Nothing had ever felt so right in all her life as it felt to be Janson's wife. She opened her eyes and looked at her wedding ring in the early morning light, moving her hand so that the light caught the small band of gold and made it shine—nothing else could ever have been so right. Nothing. God had made them for each other, and, as the minister had said, what God had joined together, no man could put asunder—no one could separate them now; no one could take them from each other again, not once they were out of Georgia, not once they were far away from her father. They could be together and live in peace for the remainder of their lives, for the remainder of forever. Janson would at last be safe, and she would never have to worry again. Never—

She looked at her new husband as he lay quiet and asleep at her side, a surge of protectiveness coming over her. Her father had hurt him so badly; she had been a witness to the beating, and had seen and tended the bruises in the weeks while he mended—she knew she could never bear to see him hurt that way again; never. He was so strong and so brave, but there was also a part of him so gentle and so loving. He had fought and struggled through much of the twenty years of his life, and had almost lost that life because of her. He deserved at last to find a little peace, to be free from danger—but he was not safe even now, and would not be, not until they were out of the state and on their way to Eason County. And perhaps not even then.

A sudden feeling gripped her. They had to be away from here. They had to leave this place. They had to be on their way to Eason County before her father could find them—they were still too close to home, still too close to too many people her father knew. It might be all too easy for him to find them even now. All he would have to do would be to put out word—

Why had she not realized sooner. Janson was no safer here than he had been in Endicott County—and he would not be safe, not until they were where her father could not find them, and where Janson's people could protect him if he ever did. They no longer had any home to go to, no place that was their own, just that one, badly misspelled letter from his grandmother, a letter promising them shelter in a place she did not know, but a place she now longed so desperately for. Oh, how she wished they were there already, where Janson would be safe—

She gently shook him awake, watching the black lashes flutter and open, the green eyes crinkle at the corners as he smiled at her and reached up to touch her face. "Good mornin', Mrs. Sanders," he said, his voice lazy with sleep. "Did you have a good rest?"

"Yes, fine—Janson, we've got to get dressed and get to the train station. We need to be on the first train west—"

"We got time," he said, still smiling. He did not even glance at the clock that stood on the table beneath the nearby windows. "Th' first train don't leave out 'til 9:15." His hands began to touch her, to explore.

"But, we need to be there, ready. Daddy could still find us—" She tried to ignore the things his hands were making her feel, the familiar need they awoke in her, but she knew that she was losing.

"I ain't worried about your pa right now," he said, easing her back and propping over her, then brushing his fingers along her cheek. "I ain't worried about nothin' but us, an' how much I want you right now—you're my wife now; that's all that matters."

"But, he could still find—"

"Don't even worry about that. Worryin' ain't gonna help nothin' now, an' it ain't got no place keepin' us from touchin' and lovin' each other now that we're married."

"But—"

"No—" he said firmly, stopping her words with a gentle finger to her lips. "There ain't nobody in th' world right now but you an' me," he told her. "There ain't nothin' but what we feel an' what we need from each other—I love you so much, Elise. I love you—" His mouth came to hers in a kiss that took the breath from her body and drove the worry to some far part of her mind. His hands touched her, and she began to touch as well, re-learning parts of his body she now knew so well—he was right; he needed her, and she needed him. Nothing else of the world could exist beyond that. Nothing.

But he was not safe—some part of her mind still warned. Her father could still find them, could still hurt Janson as she had sworn she would never see him hurt again, could still—then his penetration eased all thought from her mind. There was only love, only pleasure, only Janson, and the minutes slipped by unnoticed, for somehow time could no longer exist in their world.

THE SUN was high, but the morning chill as Janson and Elise left the hotel on their way to the train station. The streets were busy, the rush of Sunday morning traffic to church services just beginning, the sound of car horns and automobile engines seeming loud to Janson's ears. He held tightly to Elise's hand, forcing himself to walk more slowly so she would not have to run to keep up—she was talking nervously, talking about the day, about the weather, about their destination; he did not know. He could not make himself pay attention to what she was saying, could not even really listen to her words—a knot of nervous tension was growing in the pit of his stomach, had been growing there over the past minutes now. He just wished they were on the train already, waiting for it to pull out of the station. Once they were on the train, no one would ever be able to take Elise from him again; once they were on the train and on their way to Eason County—but they where not on the train yet, and time was growing short before it would pull out of the station. If they missed the—

He knew that perhaps they should have left the hotel earlier, as Elise had wanted to; but that hour spent in her arms was one he would never regret, no more than he would ever regret any time they had been together, that he had loved her, that he had been part of her body. No matter what it might cost him—women were always having premonitions anyway, he kept telling himself, but premonitions did not mean William Whitley was any closer to finding them. Premonitions did not mean—

But somehow he could not make himself believe that. The knot of tension tightened inside of him—women's premonitions did not mean anything. But now the hairs along the back of his neck were rising as well.

He had never wanted anything so badly in his life as he wanted to be on that train with Elise, to be away from here and on their way to Eason County together. Somehow the life he was taking her to no longer seemed to matter, somehow the fact that he would not be giving her the house and land and something of their own—he just wanted to be on that train with her, to know they were safe, that no one could ever take her from him again, that—

The area before the train station seemed crowded with people; cars moved by along the street, headed toward the large, brick Methodist church two streets away. Janson held tightly to Elise's hand, realizing she was again having to almost run to keep up with him—but she had not once complained. Her words continued, words he could not hear for the sounds of the cars and the church bells and his own tension—if only they were on the train. If only they were—

Suddenly she stopped short with a small cry, her hand tightening almost convulsively over his. Janson turned back—but he already knew. He already—

Franklin Bates stood staring at him from just behind Elise, his eyes cold, unfeeling, one of his massive hands closed firmly around her upper arm. Janson stared at him, realizing suddenly the lesson experience had been trying to teach him all his life, that once a man awoke, the dreams were supposed to end.

He could only hope Elise would not see him die.

ELISE LAY against him for a long time after the Ford had come to a stop in the curve of the drive before the Whitleys' great house, her face pressed to his shoulder, her eyes closed, her tears wetting the front of his shirt. Janson held her, unwilling to let her go, unwilling to give up even one moment when there could be so little time left to—

He knew when Bates got out of the car, knew when Whitley came out onto the veranda and then down into the yard, for he could hear Mrs. Whitley's pleading voice as she followed after him, and Stan's words, though he could not tell what the boy was saying—Janson knew he was about to die for what they had done, what they had chosen to do in running away together, but he could not think of dying now, could not think of leaving the earth and the sky and the land he loved. All he could think about was Elise; all he could remember was the way she felt against him, the way she had felt against him so many times in the past. He had wanted nothing more than to love her, nothing more than to live out his life with her at his side—but now he would not live that life out at all. He would not live his life out—and that thought made him angry, angry beyond anything he had known in his life, angrier still than the night a fire had burned in a cotton field, a fire that had ended a part of his life forever.

"Get out of the car, Elise." It was her father's voice, from just beside the car, his words tense, but still showing little emotion. She did not move, but only tightened her arms about Janson instead, something beyond fear tensing her body as she pressed her face to his chest and cried all the harder. Janson touched his lips to her hair one last time, then lifted his eyes to meet the eyes of the man who was now his father-in-law, the man who he knew intended to kill him before this day was over.

"Get out of the car!" Whitley's voice rose, his thin veneer of control threatening to break about him. When still she did not move, he yanked the car door open and reached in to drag her out, tearing her from Janson's arms, causing her to cry out with pain as much as from the fear Janson knew she felt. Whitley shook her soundly as they stood by the car, causing her hair to go wildly into her eyes as she tried to pull free, and then he drew his hand back, preparing to slap her—but Janson was already out of the car, his hand closing over Whitley's arm instead, stopping the blow before it could come, and bringing the man's eyes back to his in a murderous rage. "Get your hands off me, boy—" The words came as a hiss, spoken through barely parted teeth, as though the muscles in his jaws were clenched so tightly the words could hardly escape them. "Get your goddamn hands off me or I'll—"

"Let her go," Janson said, his eyes never leaving Whitley's gaze. When Whitley did not respond, Janson stood his ground, refusing to die as less than a man so long as there was life left in his body. "I said, let her go!"

Whitley stared at him for a long moment, a muscle working in his jaw, then he released her with a slight shove that sent her into Franklin Bates's arms. She stumbled, almost fell, but Bates caught her and held her up, pinning her arms against her sides as she tried to struggle away again. Janson looked toward her for a moment, assuring himself that she was unhurt, then he brought his gaze back to her father, releasing the man's arm at last, and seeing nothing within him now but hatred and rage, and a thirst for blood that would assure Janson's own death at his hands.

William Whitley met his stare, his eyes never once leaving Janson's face, a muscle clenched tightly in his jaw. "You goddamn son-of-a-bitch, you're going to beg to die before I'm through with you today. You're going to—"

"Please, God, no—" Elise's voice begged from where Franklin Bates held her. Janson wanted to turn to look at her, but somehow he could not. He could only stare at Whitley, and then beyond him to the eyes of Bill Whitley as he moved up behind his father.

"Let me and Franklin handle it, Daddy," Bill said, staring at Janson. There was a nervousness about him, and also something more, something Janson could not put a name to. "There's no need for—"

"William, please—" Martha Whitley dragged at her husband's arm, but he only shoved her away, staring at her as she fell against Stan, the boy catching her to keep her from striking the ground.

"I'll deal with you later, you—all three of you." His eyes moved from his wife, to Elise, and then to Stan. "You're going to learn never to go against me again. You're going to—"

"This ain't got nothin' t' do with them," Janson said, bringing Whitley's gaze back to him. "It was me that talked Elise int' runnin' off with me. It ain't gonna make you no more a man t' hurt two women an' a boy—"

"Shut your goddamn mouth!" Whitley shouted, tightening one hand into a fist to drive it hard into Janson's stomach, doubling him over and making him gasp for air. Janson staggered backwards, but remained on his feet, lifting his eyes only a moment later to meet Whitley's gaze, his look seeming to make the man only angrier.

"William, stop this! It's—"

Whitley turned on his wife again, raising a fist as if he would strike her as well, and she shrank away, her words silenced before she could even utter them. Stan seemed to stare at his father for a moment, then he turned and ran toward the house, stumbling, almost falling as he reached the front steps and started up them toward the open double doors. Janson stared after him, praying he would call the sheriff, praying that he would call J.C. Cooper, or anyone else who would help—it would probably be too late for him by then, but there was still Elise, her mother, and Stan. There was still—

"Daddy, stop it!" Elise screamed, sagging against Bates, all the strength seeming to leave her. "He hasn't done anything to you! He hasn't—"

"He took something that belonged to me!" her father shouted at her in return. "I raised you for better than—"

"But he's my husband! We were married yesterday—and I love him! He's my—"

Her father stared at her for a long moment, then his eyes returned to Janson. "You put your goddamn hands on my daughter and you ruined her last night, didn't you, boy. You son-of-a-bitch—I'm going to kill you with my bare hands. I'm going to kill you, and she's going to watch—"

"Do you think it'll make you more of a man t' kill me in front of a girl?"

"Let us handle it, Daddy," Bill said, his words cutting into Janson's, his voice sounding almost agitated now as he stood close beside his father. "There's no need to do it here; somebody could drive up. We'll make him pay for running off with Elise and rutting with her like some animal. Let us handle—"

But it was too late. Bill's words had torn away the last shreds of control, of humanity, left within William Whitley. Whitley lunged at Janson, screaming with rage, his hands closing around Janson's throat, squeezing, cutting off the supply of oxygen even as Janson tried to pry his fingers away—Janson began to choke, to gag, fighting for air. He heard Elise scream, and saw the horror on her face—then his knees went weak beneath him, the edges of his vision becoming blurry, darkening. He struggled for breath, his face feeling hot and numbing, his senses beginning to spin, his eyes unable to leave Elise's face as the world grew dark around him, unable to—

A shot rang out, loud, undeniable—the pressure at his throat was suddenly gone, his lungs greedily taking in deep drafts of air, his chest hurting, feeling as if it were on fire. He sank to the ground, confused, his senses addled, the sound of blood pounding in his temples so loud that he could hear little else. His eyes sought Elise, his vision still unclear—she was all right, staring toward the house. They were all staring toward the—

He turned his eyes in the same direction, coughing, forcing himself to breathe, feeling a sense of shock move through him as his eyes came to rest on Stan Whitley where he stood on the veranda steps, the boy lowering a rifle from the shot he had just fired into the air. Stan pointed the gun at Franklin Bates, it shaking badly in his hands as he walked down off the steps and into the yard.

"Let my sister go!" he demanded, his voice loud but unsteady. Bates stared at him for a moment, as if assessing what he might be capable of doing, then he took a step back, releasing Elise and holding his hands out to his sides as she moved to drop to her knees beside Janson. Her face was frightened, concerned, and Janson tried to speak, to reassure her, but was overtaken by a fit of coughing instead as she touched his face, his lungs still hurting for air.

"Give me that gun—" he heard Whitley say as the coughing subsided. Janson lifted his eyes to see Whitley slowly walking toward his son, one hand out. "Give me that—"

"You leave Elise and Janson alone," the boy said, shaking so badly Janson thought he would drop the rifle.

"This isn't any of your concern—now, give me that—"

"I won't let you hurt Janson. I won't let you—"

"It's for Elise's own good. You're just too young to understand—"

"I'm not too young!" Stan shouted. "You just let them go!"

"Elise is nothing but a child, and neither are you. I won't let her ruin her life by letting her run off with some red-Indian—"

"What right do you have to tell me what's good for me!" Elise demanded, rising to her feet beside Janson. She stared at her father, rage tensing her body. "You never cared about me or what I wanted! All you ever cared about is yourself and your stupid dreams of owning part of that damned cotton mill. I was never anything more than a property to be bargained off in the process!"

"Is that what he's told you? That's what he said that made you run off with him?"

"Quit lying!" she shouted at him, more rage in her in that moment than Janson had ever thought possible to see within her. Her face was flushed, both her hands tightened into fists against her sides. "You tried to kill Janson to keep us apart—you told me you had him left beside some road, but you lied. You took the money he had worked so long for, and then you threw him in that well to die, you son-of-a-bitch! You threw him in that well to—"

"What the hell are you talking about?" her father demanded, staring at her.

Janson pushed himself to his feet, a wave of nausea and dizziness hitting him and making him cling to Elise for support. Whitley stared at him, accusation in his eyes.

"You goddamn—that's how you did it. I never had you thrown in no well. I ought to break your goddamn neck for—"

"Stop lying!" Stan screamed from behind him, tears streaming down his cheeks now. "I found him myself!"

Bill seemed to shift from one foot to the other, his eyes moving from Whitley, to Franklin Bates, then to the gun in his younger brother's hands—and suddenly Janson understood. His eyes went to Bates, and he found the man staring at Bill as well.

Bill moved toward Stan, and Janson opened his mouth to warn the boy—but another fit of coughing overtook him, almost doubling him over, making his tortured chest and bruised throat ache. It had been Bill and Franklin who had—

"You goddamn lying son-of-a-bitch, I'm going to—" Whitley moved toward Janson again, shoving Elise aside, his hands closing around Janson's throat to—

"He's not lying," Bates voice rose above the pounding of blood in Janson's ears, and Whitley froze, his fingers pressing into Janson's neck. For a moment he only stared at Bates.

"You know I never—"

"But he was thrown in a well," Bates said, his eyes never leaving Whitley's face. There was nothing to show in the man's expression.

Whitley stared at him for a long moment, then his eyes moved to his eldest son, his hands dropping from Janson's throat.

"Are you going to believe the word of that half-breed trash and Bates over me? I never—"

"Shut up," Whitley said quietly, staring at him—he knew; Janson could read it in his expression. He knew.

"Bill—" Elise's voice was quiet where she stood now beside Janson.

"I didn't have him thrown in no well!" Bill's eyes darted quickly from Franklin Bates to Janson. "Why would I—"

"I don't know why he wanted him dead, but he did," Bates said coldly, his voice still emotionless as Bill's eyes came back to rest on him.

"He had me stop the truck at some burned-out old sharecropper shack—Bill kicked him down into the well himself—"

"You lying—"

"Shut up!" his father yelled, and Bill fell silent, staring at him. For a long moment there were no words, only silence as the two men stared at each other, tension filling the air around them. Whitley's eyes came back to Janson and Elise, and the silence became almost a physical presence—the man's eyes were cold, knowing, filled with realization, and with hate.

"Get the hell off my property, both of you," he said quietly, his eyes moving from Elise, to Janson, and then back again. "Get the hell out of my County, and don't ever come back again—"

"No!" The word was filled with fury, with more hate than Janson had ever before heard in his life. Bill Whitley quickly crossed the distance to Janson and Elise, grabbing Janson by the shirt collar to slam him backwards against the side of the Model T, driving the breath from his already tortured lungs with the impact. "I'm not going to let—"

"Let him go!" Whitley yelled.

"You goddamn stupid old fool, we can't let—"

Whitley stepped up and wrenched the rifle from his youngest son's hands, the boy giving a small cry as it was torn from his grasp. Whitley turned and leveled it at his elder son, and at Janson. "I said—let him go!"

Bill stared back over his shoulder at his father for a long moment, his breath coming in hoarse, angered sounds from somewhere deep within his chest. He turned his eyes back to Janson for a moment, his body shaking with rage, then he released him with a push and turned again to look at his father, his eyes filled with nothing but hatred.

Elise moved into Janson's arms, and Janson held her, meeting Whitley's gaze over the top of her head as the man lowered the rifle and stared at them. After a moment, Whitley's eyes settled on his daughter. There was absolutely no feeling on his face. "I want you out of my sight, both of you—and don't ever come back again, or I will kill him—" he said, staring at her as she finally lifted her eyes to meet his. "You wanted your dirt farmer—well now you have him, and you'll hate him for it. Just try to live for a while with what he can give you, and what he can't give you. You should have thought about what it was you were wanting so badly, because now you have it, and you'll never live another happy day because of it. You'll hate him, and everything there is about him—and don't think you can come running back home when you realize what you've done. You'll never be welcome in this house, or in this County, ever again—"

He stared at her for a long moment, and then his eyes moved to Janson, eyes that were cold, unfeeling. "You slipped up, boy. She'll take no money with her, and she's used to the finer things in life, things you'll never understand—but she's your problem now, and you'll learn to hate her for it. Now take her and get the hell off my land," he said, turning to start toward the front steps of the big house behind them. As he reached the veranda, he stopped for a moment, speaking back over his shoulder, not bothering to turn to look at either of them. "You're both dead to me now," he said. "I no longer have a daughter."

THERE WERE hurried goodbyes, a train leaving from Goodwin they would have to catch or the next to Alabama would not be until morning—and they could never spend the night in Endicott County. Her father could still change his mind, and there was Bill—but Elise refused to think about that now. They were leaving; her father had written her off for good, and Janson had to be safe—it was over. It was finally over.

She sat beside Janson on the rear seat of the Model T, holding tightly to his hand as Stan started the car down the long drive toward the road that would take them into town. She kept telling herself that she should be happy, that there was nothing more she could want in her life than what she had now—but there was another feeling as well as the car pulled away, a sadness and a longing she could not understand. She put her arms around Janson and held tightly to him, pressing her face to the roughness of his workshirt where it covered his shoulder. Then she lifted her eyes to stare past him and through the rear window-glass of the car, toward the house where she had spent all her life; toward her mother where she stood on the wide front steps, one hand raised in parting, the tears streaming down her cheeks; toward this place and these people she knew she would never see again, the only home she had ever known—

Elise Whitley Sanders stared out through the rear window of the Model T Ford long after the house had disappeared from sight behind them, somehow both child and woman, and somehow having gotten at last what she had wanted most in the world.

All she wanted to do now was cry.

WILLIAM WHITLEY stood staring out the front parlor windows of his home, an unlit cigar clamped between his teeth. His eyes were on the red-clay road that wound from before his house, past the cotton fields, through the woods, and toward the main road to Goodwin—the road his daughter had just gone away from him on. He heard someone enter the room behind him, and he knew without having to turn to look that it was Martha, marveling again for a moment that, even after all these years, she still moved like a young girl. So much like—

She stood silent in the doorway, and he could feel her eyes on him. He wished she would speak, or just go away, anything but just stand there in silence and stare her accusations at him. "You got something to say?" he asked her at last, not turning from the view beyond the window.

"Damn you, William," she said, her words quiet, but as hard as any words he had ever heard. He turned to stare at her, seeing hatred in her eyes, hatred, where only a few short months before there had never been anything for him but love. "Damn your soul straight to hell—"

He turned his back on her, turned once again to stare out the window, and after a moment he heard her leave the room—hell gets every man sooner or later, he told himself as he stared toward the long clay road that led from before his home. He did not need her hatred. He had enough of his own.

He continued to stare toward the road for a long time, the silence of the house close about him—one day soon, he told himself; one day soon, and they would all realize he had been right. Elise would come home—young people never knew their minds, anyway, he told himself. She would realize what a fool she had been; she would tire of her farmhand

and the life he could give her, and she would come home begging to be taken in—he had done nothing more than put a scare into her today, telling her she could never come home. But she would plead, and he would give in—of course. After all, she was his daughter. After all, she was a Whitley.

Once she was home, that insane marriage could be forgotten; once she was home, where she belonged, everyone's lives would get back to normal. Martha would realize he had been right all along, and Stan would no longer look at him as he did now, and Bill—but, no, things would never be the same with Bill. William now knew there was something within his eldest son that he had never known had existed there before, something capable of attempting a cold-blooded murder. When William had almost killed Janson Sanders, he had done it out of rage and anger and concern for his daughter, but what Bill had done had been out of hatred, and something far worse. William did not like knowing there was a part of himself capable of so easily trying to kill a man, but he could not condemn himself for that part. If any man had ever deserved to die, Janson Sanders did—but not as Bill had tried to kill him. What William had done had been only for the sake of his family—Martha would see that, as would Stan, as would Elise; and there would still be plenty of time for Janson Sanders to pay for what he had done to this family. There would still be time.

William knew his daughter. Elise was nothing more than a spoiled child, a child playing at being a woman, a girl accustomed to being petted and pampered and forever getting her way. She had been reared to a nice home and lovely things, and a husband far different from the one she had taken—only a few months, maybe less, of the life she had chosen, and she would come running home, begging to be taken in. Only a few months—

He turned from the window and crossed the wide rug to the mantlepiece, taking out a match from the crystal box there, and bending to strike it on the hearth and light his cigar. He drew in on it heavily, and then watched as the smoke drifted upwards, toward the ceiling—only a few months, he told himself. Only a few months, and Elise would be home. Only a few months, and she would learn the lesson that most spoiled children had to learn in the end, that they should always be careful of what they wished for, for fear they just might get it.

*For fear they just might get it.*

J.C. COOPER sat staring into the fire that burned in the Bennett's parlor fireplace. The flames were uncomfortably warm on his face and hands, but he could not make himself move away. If he got up, if he crossed to the door to leave the room, he would have to go past Phyllis Ann—and he did not trust himself not to strike her if she were that close.

She sat on the upholstered sofa behind him, her voice a dull, continuous monotone as she talked to herself—but he could not even turn to look at her. He wished there were some way he could stop himself from thinking, stop himself from feeling, from realizing what it was she had done, but thought and feeling would not stop, nor would the realization. Phyllis Ann had told William Whitley where Elise and Janson had gone. She could have cost them everything—but Phyllis Ann did not even care. She had only laughed when he had confronted her, had laughed and said she would do it all again.

"Yes, I did it! And I'd do it again—she deserves whatever happens to her. She deserves—"

"You idiot! You could have gotten them both killed! You almost did get Janson killed!"

"I don't care—I hope he does kill her! I hope he does—"

He grabbed her, filled with a rage he had never before known in his life, and shook her as hard as he could, shook her until the short, dark hair fell into her face and her eyes were wild with insanity.

"Go on, hit me! Go on—I know you love me! I know you do! I know—"

J.C. had stared at her for a long moment, and then had shoved her away, shocked that he had almost struck her, that he had almost struck a woman—what in the name of heaven had she made of him? What had she made of what had once been a decent, caring human being—

He sat staring into the fire, wishing it were possible to somehow reverse time. He had wanted her so badly, for so many years, thinking he could never have her—and then she had become his. The beautiful girl he had dreamed of for so long had loved him, had cared for him—but fantasy could so quickly turn to nightmare. He wondered now at how blind and stupid people could be, to want something so badly, and then finally to have it, only to discover that dream becomes nightmare in their hands.

He could hear her talking quietly to herself from the sofa behind him, her words continuous, repetitive, sounding again and again in his ears. "I only wanted somebody to love me—" she said. "That's all I ever wanted, somebody to love me—"

J.C. turned to stare at her, his heart breaking inside of him—God help me, but I still do, he thought. God help me, I still do.

JANSON WAS going home—not to that white house and those red acres he had thought to return to, but to the sharecropped land his grandfather worked, to a small room in a tenanted house shared with so many other people, and to a way of life he had sworn he would never have. He was going home.

He sat within the train that afternoon as it pulled out of the station in Goodwin, little changed from the man who had come here to Georgia those months ago—just a year older, perhaps a year wiser. The worn portmanteau at his feet was the same, the faded clothes he wore much the same—but there was a difference. Today he was not leaving Endicott County in a stinking freight car as he had come here, but as a paying passenger of the train, having spent a little of their precious money in order to pay for the fare—and he was leaving with Elise Whitley at his side.

Sanders—he reminded himself. She was Elise Sanders now, his wife. And he thought she was crying.

She sat with her face turned from him, her eyes staring out the window at the passing cotton fields and pine woods as the train swayed over the tracks, each moment taking her farther and farther from the home she had always known. He could feel her tears in her silence, in the tenseness of her body as she sat beside him, in the sadness of the spirit that touched his own—but he did not turn to look at her. She deserved her privacy. He would allow her the right to cry for herself in peace.

He stared straight ahead as the long trip passed slowly, wondering how he could be taking her from her family and home, from all the nice, beautiful things in the world, taking her to a life such as the one that waited for them in Eason County. She clung to his hand almost desperately now, and somehow that made the worry within him all the worse—he was all she had left now. He had taken everything else from her today in asking her to leave with him, and she had come, knowing how little he had to offer. She loved him, and he knew she loved him; she loved him enough to be willing to give up everything else in her world. She loved him.

He closed his eyes for a moment, thinking of that white house on those red acres he would give her one day. He could see it so clearly in his memory, the house as it had been in years past, the rows of cotton starred over with white, that red land his parents had worked so long to have, had worked so long to give him—it would be theirs one day. No one would stop him from touching that dream again, no one would stop him from giving that home to Elise, and to the children they would have, no matter the fight he might have to go through to have it, no matter the struggle—he was long accustomed to struggle anyway, and it did not frighten him. There were few things in life that could frighten him anymore.

The train clacked and swayed over the tracks, the conductor announcing when they crossed the state line into Alabama, and Janson felt Elise's hand tighten over his, though she did not turn her face to him—they were almost home now, almost home. He stared past her and out the window, seeing the red land grow more familiar by the minute, the rolling hills more known, and his soul ached for sight of the land that would be his again one day—theirs, when he could at last make the dream a reality again, the dream that had burned inside of him for the past year, the dream that had burned inside his father all his life. He would not be taking Elise to a life like the one she had always known, but he would make her happy. They had each other, and they would be together. There would be children, many years ahead to spend with her and to make a family—and that land and home when the time came, the home he would give her, the home he would give their children, the land that would be his again one day. He had not been defeated, no more than had any of the people whose blood flowed in his veins. No man could be defeated if he held to a dream.

An obscure Bible verse rose in his memory, something he had heard his mother say, or his grandmother, and he tried for a moment to remember the remainder of the passage . . .

> And, when they saw him afar off, even before he came near unto them, they conspired against him to slay him.
>
> And they said one to another, Behold, this dreamer cometh. . . .

Janson Sanders stared out the window of the train at land growing only more familiar by the moment.

The dreamer was coming home.